Praise for *Fierce People*

'A sweet coming-of-age book that mutates midway through into an over-heated summer beach read, complete with sex, money, death, and incest – Wittenborn is clearly having fun.' – *The Village Voice*

'A riveting page-turner that offers a haunting and fascinating glimpse into the lives of the super-rich – truly the fiercest class of all.' – **Candace Bushnell**

'Wittenborn offers plenty of unusual spins on the usual coming-of-age formula, and his eclectic, idiosyncratic characters provide plenty of enter-tainment . . . this peek behind the scenes of a wealthy family remains novel and fascinating from start to finish.' – *Publishers Weekly* **(starred review)**

'[Wittenborn] wields his moments of hilarity, but *Fierce People* is serious stuff, Earl an engaging protagonist, and this tale of irony and disillusion-ment sharp and commanding.' – *Baltimore Sun*

'Fierce satire.' – *San Diego Union-Tribune*

'A brilliant coming of age story.' – *Denver Post*

'Lurid and tremendously entertaining. Skewering the lifestyles of the wealthy is not a new sport, but Wittenborn brings a witty, decadent energy to it.' – *Miami Herald*

'For lack of a fussier phrase, this is a great f*@#ing story, and Wittenborn's book is no doubt the read of the summer.' – *Black Book*

'Sharp and savvy, *Fierce People* is both a souped-up coming-of-age novel and a satire on class and the American aristocracy – a species which is commonly held not to exist, but which Wittenborn anatomises with a wit and insight born of personal experience.' – *Telegraph* (UK)

FIERCE PEOPLE

Dirk Wittenborn

BLOOMSBURY

Published by Bloomsbury, New York and London
Distributed to the trade by Holtzbrinck Publishers

The Library of Congress has cataloged the hardcover edition as follows:

Wittenborn, Dirk,
Fierce people / Dirk Wittenborn.
p. cm.
ISBN 1-58234-242-3
1. Teenage boys–Fiction. 2. Social classes–Fiction. 3. Single mothers–Fiction. 4. Mothers
and sons–Fiction. 5. Women physical therapists–Fiction. 6. New Jersey–Fiction. I. Title.

PS3573.I924 F54 2002
813'.54–dc21
2001056595

Paperback ISBN 1-58234-292-X

First published in the United States by Bloomsbury in 2002

This paperback edition published in 2003

1 3 5 7 9 10 8 6 4 2

www.fiercepeople.com

Typeset by Hewer Text Ltd, Edinburgh
Printed in the United States of America by
R.R. Donnelley & Sons Company, Harrisonburg, Virginia

To Kirsten
for being the best thing that ever happened to me

I would like to thank the following people:

My mother, Sarah Wittenborn, for reading
me to sleep as a child.
Gretchen and Jim Johnson, for saving my
life.
Ephraim Rosenbaum, Eric Konigsberg, and
Andy Gershon, for reading endless drafts of
this novel and pretending they were
interested, even when they weren't.
Melissa Chassay, for all that she has taught
me about the value of loyalty, and for
wanting to know more.
Griffin Dunne, for his contagious enthusiasm,
and pestering me to finish this novel.
Alexander Waugh, for reading over my
shoulder in Malta.
The divine Caroline Dawnay, friend and
agent, for coming to my rescue before she
even met me.
Liz Calder, for making an American feel
more at home than he ever did at home and
my editor, Rosemary Davidson, for her
thoughtful pruning, sage advice, and calm
voice over the telephone. The support and
camaraderie you and everyone else at
Bloomsbury have shown me has made me
feel lucky to be a writer.

1

'Oh, my God!'

When we lived in New York City, those three words out of my mother's mouth at 6.30 on a Saturday morning could only mean one of two things: either something had caught fire in the toaster oven again, or Mom had a new boyfriend.

'Oh, my God. Yesss!' I knew it wasn't the toaster oven.

We lived on Great Jones Street, between Lafayette and the Bowery, just across from the firehouse. It was June 1978. The block was a decade away from being trendy then. I was fifteen; my mother was thirty-three. I'll save you the math. Elizabeth Anne Earl, a.k.a. my mom, got pregnant two weeks into her first semester at the State College she attended after humiliating herself and her parents by not getting into Wellesley. My mother liked to say I was an accident. Don't worry: whenever she said it she would always give me a hug – a kiss if she'd had a couple glasses of white wine – and add: 'Best accident that ever happened to me.'

I stopped buying that when I was twelve. That's when my mother's father gave us twenty sessions of family therapy for Christmas instead of the trip to Kathmandu my mother had asked for. Grandpa was a semi-famous shrink. We'll get into that later. The point is, I was convinced then and am still now that my mother got pregnant on purpose. Why was I so certain she wanted me? She needed me. She wanted to run away, and was too scared to do it by herself. But such precocious insights into my mother's rebellion did not make my own any easier.

*　　*　　*

My mother's bedroom was right next to mine. She slept on a second-hand foldout in a high-ceilinged space that tripled as our living room, kitchen, and her bedroom. An uninsulated wall was all that separated us.

The foldout squeaked three more times, then she gave a long, brittle groan that sounded like a board getting ready to break. I could tell she and whoever she was with were trying to be quiet. I tried to go back to sleep, but closing my eyes just made it easier for me to see what I was hearing.

I looked at the black-and-white photograph of her holding me when I was only a couple of weeks old. She was trying to be a beatnik, but she looked more like an immigrant from Ellis Island. Her boobs take up practically half the picture. She was big on breast-feeding.

The day that picture had been taken, my grandparents had driven to the city and begged her to move us back to the suburbs with them. They had already fixed up an apartment over their garage. They said it wasn't fair to me. She could go back to school. They gave her a thousand-dollar check just to think about it. My mother retells this story like it's a Norse saga, and always ends it the same way: 'I thought about it just long enough for the check to clear, then called the Fun Killers up collect and told them, "Sorry to disappoint you, but I'm going to make it in New York."' If she'd ever actually made it in New York, I wouldn't have minded hearing her retelling stories like that to every new guy who came in the house. But then again if she'd made it, she wouldn't have had to tell them.

Mom had tried making it as a folk singer (she'd actually sung back-up for Phil Ochs at the Village Vanguard one night), a sandal-maker, and a painter – that was the year we moved in with a fairly famous abstract expressionist; when he threw a lit cigarette at me for walking on one of his wet canvases she moved out. If you look carefully you can see my footprints on a triptych that hangs on the second floor of the Museum of Modern Art. After that she had a go at being a real-estate agent, then a brief fling as a hat-maker before she found her true calling.

For the last two years my mother had been making it as a

masseuse. I was embarrassed to walk with her when she pushed her big black folding massage table on rollers around the city. Her clients said she had healing hands. Who knows? I stopped letting her give me foot rubs when she turned pro. The therapist told her it was a healthy way for an adolescent boy to establish boundaries. Oh yeah, and right now she was making it with . . . The first time the toilet flushed, I knew it was her: no footsteps. Besides knowing which floorboards squeaked, Mom always walked on tiptoes when she was in her underwear – or was she naked? It made me nervous thinking about my mother that way.

I rolled over on my stomach with a flop. A copy of *Club International* slipped out from its hiding place between the boxspring and the mattress of my single bed. The centerfold sprawled open eighteen inches from my nose. May's Club Girl lay stretched out in all her pink glory, reaching up to me. The toilet flushed again. This time it was him. The floorboards squeaked so loud as he made his way back to my mother's bed you would have thought he was walking on an accordion.

Actually, he played the guitar – at least there was a guitar case and a pair of red, hightop sneakers inside the front door. It was my turn to tiptoe to the bathroom. My mother's overnight guests had gotten younger, and been musically inclined of late. I heard an English accent as I flushed the toilet and snuck back to bed.

I don't want to give the wrong impression. It wasn't like my mother had a new guy over every other night. Actually, it had been almost two months – a relatively long season without rain for her. And she never dated anybody she massaged professionally. Except for the Scientologist; even she admitted he was a mistake.

I wasn't crazy about hearing some English guy asking my mother in the first light of day. 'Hey, luv, got any Vaseline about for Mr Johnson?' But everybody who was my age and lived in a loft in the late seventies knew their mom did it. (They were doing it again now.) Especially if they didn't have dads.

My father was a photo of a blond man with deep-set eyes and a broken nose that sat in a chipped dime-store frame on a bookshelf next to my little-league trophy. He looks uncomfortable in the rumpled seersucker suit he's wearing. His name was Fox Blanchard. He's actually kind of a famous anthropologist. There's an article he wrote in a copy of *Natural History* I keep hidden under my mattress with my beat-off magazines.

He was guest-lecturer to my mother's freshman Intro to Anthro 101 course. I was conceived a few hours after he gave a lecture on the Yanomamö – the Fierce People. They're this really weird tribe of South American Indians that live in the most remote corner of Amazonia, along the border of Venezuela and Brazil, that had never seen a white person who owned a TV and all until my dad showed up.

'First contact' is what the anthropologists call it. And besides being cool, it's really scary on account of they shoot poisoned arrows tipped with curare and snort hallucinogenic drugs every morning of their lives. And instead of shaking hands to say 'Hello', they hit each other with clubs and give each other rabbit punches to the kidneys. And when you have something they want they don't beat around the bush. They come right out and tell you: 'If you don't give me your peanut butter, your wife or your machete, I'll chop your thumbs off and shit in your hammock.' They call the Yanomamö 'the Fierce People' because basically, they're the meanest people on the planet. Or, at least, that's what I thought then.

Anyway, the point is, Dad was back in South America when he found out my mother was pregnant. It wasn't a one-night stand. They dated a bunch and talked all the time on the telephone while he was on lecture tour that fall. He came to see us once after I was born but I was too little to remember. My mother said they talked about him leaving his wife, but she said it was 'complicated'.

My grandfather, being a psychologist, tried to put a more under-standing spin on it: 'Your father's field work is expensive . . .'

A point which my grandmother further clarified: 'His wife has the money, dear.'

When I was little, I used to think my father loved the Yanomamö more than Mom and me. Once I started reading about the Fierce People, I knew that was bullshit. I mean, he had to like us more than them: after a big meal, the women hide the leftovers in their vaginas;

4

and everybody has green mucus running out of their noses from snorting *enebbe* all day. If you think I'm exaggerating, look it up. No, in my view of things it wasn't the Yanomamö's or my father's fault. It was money.

Though I had never met my father, I had read every article he'd ever written on the Yanomamö, and every book in the public library that referred to the tribe. I was prepared to answer any question he might ask me. I was ready to impress the absolute stranger I called Dad. You see, after much pleading I had persuaded my mother to write Mr Fox Blanchard about his progeny's budding interest in anthropology. And to our surprise and his credit, Dad had called immediately upon receiving the letter, and invited me to spend this July and August with him and the Yanomamö on the banks of the Orinoco River. He had made a point of saying his rich-bitch wife was looking forward to getting to know me. And he even offered to send the ticket. My mother had insisted money wasn't the issue; which, of course, we both knew was bullshit, because my grand-parents were coming over for lunch to talk about whether they'd spring for the ticket.

If it weren't for the Yanomamö I would have gotten out of bed and barged in on my mother and the Englishman. Driven him and his fucking Johnson from her bed with embarrassment and reduced her to tears with guilt. I was good at stuff like that. Once I ambushed one of my mother's barefoot suitors with thumbtacks on the way back to the foldout, but that's another story.

The point is, I needed Mom to come through for me that day. Besides, even though I've made her out to be a total fuck-up, she could be great. I mean, when I was little, she'd laugh at cartoons with me for hours. Come on, how many kids can honestly say their moms were happy debating whether Space Ghost could beat up Speed Racer? Of course, it helped that she was high.

But the drugs were like the sex back then – everybody's mom was doing it in '78. I don't know when cocaine became an ingredient in our lives. A year, year and a half ago, about the same time she started bringing home wads of cash from the McBurn Institute. That was this ritzy private hospital on the Upper East Side. There was this old jillionaire who had cancer who handed her three hundred bucks

5

every time she gave him a backrub. He's the one that told her she had healing hands. Whatever. She never snorted it in front of me. I pretended not to notice she was always sniffling when she came out of the bathroom. It was all pretty obvious. I mean, last Thanksgiving a white rock the size of a lentil fell out of her nose and landed in the gravy lake right in the middle of her mashed potatoes. I guess no one was watching but me.

It wasn't like cocaine was a constant problem. In fact, to be perfectly honest, sometimes blow had a downright positive effect on my mother. I'd come home from school and suddenly find her baking Christmas cookies, or dyeing Easter eggs, or making a yuletide wreath with dried roses and a glue gun. Doing what one of those projects moms who read *Family Circle* do. OK, sometimes it was weird, her getting all Christmassy in the middle of July, but the point is, she made an effort. And she definitely was better at Parent-Teacher night when her nose was running. If she hadn't talked to Mr Kraus, my wedge-headed gym teacher, for forty-five minutes about winning second place in the Mr Staten Island beauty contest, no way that muscle-bound steroid freak would have passed me in PE.

'Oh, my God!' My mother's toaster oven was on fire again. She groaned, 'Fuck me,' as the foldout slammed against the wall. I tried to distract myself by thinking about the Yanomamö. I tried to blot out what passed for passion next door out of my mind by re-reading the *Natural History* article the father I'd never met had written about people I'd never seen. But a photo he'd taken of a topless, fourteen-year-old rain-forest chick with torpedo tits, naked save for her tattoos and the quills that pierced her cheeks – looking oh-so Stone Age punk – just made me horny for the pierced runaways of St Mark's I was too shy to talk to, much less hit on. I grabbed the hairless Club Girl from my bedroom floor and tried to imagine what it would be like to have her touch my nakedness, but ended up remembering a winter's evening when my mother was hurrying to get ready for the Parent–Teacher night where she talked Mr Kraus out of flunking me. Mom called to me from the bathroom to bring her the bottle of shampoo she had left in a grocery bag on the kitchen table. I closed my eyes when I passed it into her in the shower, but taking it from my hand, she snagged the shower curtain. The curtain and the rod holding it fell like a sail lowered in a gale. The shower sprayed in my face. My mother jumped back with a start and slipped. Grabbing hold of the hot-water faucet to keep from falling on her ass scalded her butt so badly that she leapt from the shower and into my arms with a yelp . . . Believe me, the first time you hold a naked woman in your arms, you don't want it to be your mom.

It all happened so fast. I kept my eyes shut and, as God is my witness, I wouldn't even have been tempted to look if she hadn't started to laugh. (I have always been a sucker for laughter.) She giggled like a girl, not a mom. Doubled over in mirth, her breasts pushed together in a cleavage worthy of *Penthouse*, a dollop of soapsuds in her pubic hair, I guess it was funny. I was too startled by my mom's nakedness to see the humor in the situation.

Uncertain whether it was my mom, the centerfold, or the Yanomamö maiden with the d-cup giving me a hard-on, I felt worse than guilty.

My mom and the Englishman were giggling now. I knew they weren't laughing at me, but that didn't make me feel any better. I felt like I was the butt of a colossal, cross-cultural inside joke. The Yanomamö; the Fierce People chick with her coy smile and sharpened stick; the glossy Club foldout grinning like a village idiot as she sucked a Sugar Daddy and spread her legs for a gynecological exam; my mother, lubed up for the guitar-playing Englishman; they all seemed to be in on the same gag, everyone got it but me. You see, to add to all of my other problems that morning, I was the only virgin in my class I knew besides Slurpee – and he had an excuse: one of his legs was eight inches shorter than the other. And he slurped.

I felt better when I heard the Englishman pick up his guitar and clomp down the stairs. I went to the window and watched him go out the front door. He wore leather pants and his hair was cut in a shag. As he hailed a cab, he turned, looked up at our floor and waved. Christ, what a moron. Couldn't he see I was giving him the finger?

In a few minutes, there was a knock on my door.

'You want to come out and have some breakfast with me, lambie?' My mother only called me 'lambie' when I was sick or she was happy.

'No!' I knew she was trying to be nice, I just didn't feel nice.

'Come on, Finn.' That was my name.

'No!' I threw one of my skin mags at the door to let her know that I meant it. Or, was I hoping that she would take the challenge, throw the door open, and see the other women in my life?

'I'll make you pancakes . . .'

'Screw your pancakes.' I knew we didn't have any milk, anyway.

'Finn?' She opened the door. She didn't even see the open skin mag at her feet. Her cheeks were flushed with beard-burn. She looked more like a mom and less like a pet in her old terrycloth bathrobe. Her hands shook ever so slightly as she lit her first cigarette.

'I thought you quit smoking.' I didn't want to fight, but I couldn't resist.

'And I have.' She opened my window and threw the cigarette out. 'Are you mad at me?'

'No.' Like I said, I didn't want to fight.

'Do you love me?'

'Yes.' It was sweet and spooky how a lie my mother wanted to hear could light her up inside. Like a candle in a jack-o'-lantern, it made her seem hollow.

I figured everything was going to be OK then. It was eight-thirty, my grandparents weren't coming until two. My mother had plenty of time to get the apartment and herself together. After my mother pulled an all-nighter with a new guy, she always had a strange surge of domestic energy. She'd put on a Bob Marley tape, rearrange the furniture, scrub the bathroom floor, change the shelf-paper – like I said, a gram of coke turned my mom into a downtown Betty Crocker. I was confident she'd be able to con my grandparents into paying for the ticket to South America over a Gruyère omelette and small talk about cousins who were doing better than she. They'd leave thinking she was OK. Then she'd crash, and everything would be OK, at least until I could get myself up the Amazon to my father and the Fierce People. I don't know what I expected to happen in South America. Lose my virginity to a teenaged Yanomamö woman of the third world at spear-point? Save my father from being stripped to the bone by a school of piranha? Render him so grateful he'd rescue my mom in turn? Somehow I was convinced if I just made it up the river to my father everything was going to be OK. I guess I inherited my mother's love of a pretty lie.

If I were a fifteen-year-old Yanomamö, I would have had a shaman come over ASAP and cast a spell to drive the *Amahiri-teri* from my bedroom after my mother left. They're these sort of degenerate third world leprechauns the Yanomamö have who dwell in a parallel universe that lacks a jungle, so they come up to our world to chow down on the souls of children. But instead I masturbated quickly and fell into a dreamless sleep.

I would have dozed the whole morning away, but an hour later I was jarred back to reality by a bed-shaking, window-rattling crash. I ran, sticky-crotched, out into the loft. My mother was pinned to the floor beneath a wall-wide, floor-to-ceiling bookcase. She'd pulled it down on herself.

'Oh, my God.' It was an unfortunate choice of words on my part. She thought I was mimicking and mocking her. Perhaps I was. She cursed and kicked at the books that half-buried her.

'Is this your idea of getting the house ready for Grandma and Grandpa?' *Little House on the Prairie* this wasn't. The toppled bookcase was just part of the mess. Cushions were scattered across the room. Sheets torn from the foldout. She had upended all three of her purses on the floor, and knocked over an ashtray full of butts and condom wrappers. She was the only person left in the seventies who still used rubbers. She said she didn't think birth-control pills were healthy for a woman. Like cocaine was.

'What are you doing?'

'I was looking for something. Get this fucking thing off me.' I lifted the bookcase up enough for her to wiggle out from underneath it, but instead of helping me tilt it back to the wall, she began to rummage through the mound of books. Grabbing one after another, she'd hold them upside down, shake them, then throw them over her shoulder. The dictionary, the atlas, *Anna Karenina*.

'What are you looking for?' I knew she had forgotten where she had hidden her cocaine, but I had to ask.

'Something . . . I've misplaced.' She was on her knees. With a crazed methodicalness, she pawed through one volume after another. She was on to the *Encyclopedia Britannica* now.

'What sort of something?'

'Something that's important to me,' she answered tartly. She was oblivious to the fact that she'd just kicked over a half-empty bottle of red wine. It pooled on the carpet like blood at the scene of an accident.

'Tell me what it is and maybe I can help you find it.' I was calm, she was frantic; we were equally out of control.

'I can find it myself.' She lit the wrong end of her cigarette, cursed, and told me, 'It's none of your business.' She was so out of it she mistook the opened jar of Vaseline for an ashtray. Next to it was the crumpled-up square of paper that had held her last gram.

I picked up the thesaurus she'd won at a public-speaking contest in high school and held it upside down and gave it a shake. Mom's eyes brightened when she saw something small and white fall from between its pages. When she realized it was just an old gum wrapper a tear ran down her cheek.

'What are you looking for?' I demanded.

'It's something personal,' she told me hoarsely.

'Such as?' I always hated kids that pulled wings off flies, or burned ants with a magnifying glass, and here I was doing worse to my mother.

'Such as . . .' She looked at me with half-open eyes. I knew she was going to make up a lie. But the one she chose was so double-edged we both winced. 'A letter from your father.'

Five minutes later I was dressed and running down the stairs. I wasn't racing out in search of a maid. I could have gotten the house together in time for my grandparents, but my mom was the sort of mess I couldn't clean up on my own.

I couldn't let them see her like this. No way they'd give her the money to buy a ticket to South America. They'd be at our door in less than three hours. They had spent the night with friends in the city. If I'd known the names of the people they were staying with I would have called and told them Mom had food poisoning. I had to hurry. If she crashed before they arrived, I'd never wake her up. If she was still awake when they got there, it would be even worse.

Out the front door – I took the five-step stoop in a single bound – I started to run and immediately fell flat on my face. I had forgotten to tie my shoelaces. The firemen were backing the hook-and-ladder truck into the station.

'Hey, Finnski!' The fireman, who was stopping traffic so they could back in, called out. 'What's the rush?'

'Gotta get something for my mom.' I had sixty dollars in my pocket. It was going to go towards a pair of snake-proof boots I had seen advertised in the back of *Field and Stream*. The highly poisonous Fer-de-lance being but one of the many venomous drawbacks of hanging out with the Yanomamö. But if I didn't get my mother through that day, I wasn't ever going to have a chance to get snakebit.

'Hey, Finn, it's Meatloaf Night.' The firemen had me over for dinner a couple of times a month. They felt sorry for me. I was trying to worry and tie my shoes at the same time.

'Hey, Finnski, bring over that good-looking mother of yours.' She was pretty, and I knew they were trying to be friendly, but all I could think to say was, 'Fuck you.'

'Hey, kid, we didn't mean it like that,' I heard him shout as I ran away.

I was heading to a bodega on the corner of Avenue A and Second Street. A kid I let cheat off me in geometry class told me you could buy anything there. He stayed back three times and had been shot twice. He let me feel the .32 caliber slug that lay just under the skin between his third and fourth ribs. He wasn't the kind of kid who'd bullshit about stuff like that. Or at least, that's what I hoped.

That part of the East Village wasn't cutting-edge back then, it was downright dangerous. Third was safe, especially on the Hell's Angels' block, but I had to zigzag down to Houston to avoid a gang that called themselves Los Locos. They were crazy and they had pit bulls.

I had it all figured out. I wasn't just going to buy a gram and hand it to her. I'd slip it into her purse while she wasn't looking, then casually suggest she check her purse again for that 'letter from my father'. I told myself I'd yell at her about the cocaine after my grandparents left. But I knew that was bullshit.

The bodega was called Sammy's. It was sort of like a deli, except there were bars on the window and not much stuff on the shelves. A Rottweiler and its owner sat next to the cash register wearing the same expression. The latter sipped Colt 45 through a straw. I was sweating and breathing hard when I came through the door.

'What you running from?'

'Nothing.'

'What you want?'

'I want to buy some . . .' I heard someone snorting in the back aisle of the bodega. A guy in a business suit that looked like he worked on Wall Street before he got bitten by a vampire sniffled towards me. He sneezed twice, each time with an expletive.

'Ah-shit. Ahhhhh . . . shit!' The first sneeze he caught in his bare hand. The second one sent a long dollop of mucus catapulting out of his nostrils. It landed on the Rottweiler's snout. The dog growled. He reminded me of a photo I'd seen of a Yanomamö just after he'd had *ennebe* blown up his nose. They saw their gods when they got high. I wondered what he and my mother saw. The thought of the Fierce People made the place seem less scary.

'I want to buy some . . .' I didn't need to repeat myself. Even the dog knew what I was there for.

'*Está detrás de los* Lucky Charms.'

'Lucky Charms?' I pretended like that made perfect sense, and walked in the direction he was pointing, like I knew what I was doing.

I stood in the back of the bodega staring at the cereal on the shelf for a full five minutes wondering what would happen next. Was someone going to meet me? Was there a door I didn't see? I jumped when a voice from nowhere hissed, 'Behind the Charms, asshole.' When I took the lone and much-handled box of Lucky Charms from the shelf, I was surprised to see a face smile at me through a hole that had been cut in the wall. The man had a black hairnet on that capped his skull like a giant spider.

'How many?' he asked. I held up one finger. He told me fifty dollars. I gave him a twenty and three tens and he handed me a neatly folded packet. I gave the box of cereal to the customer who was now standing behind me, put the packet in my pocket and was on my way out of there thinking, 'What more could a mother ask,' when I bumped into a big guy in a hooded sweatshirt.

I said, 'Excuse me,' and tried to get by. When he grabbed hold of my wrist I got scared. When I saw the police badge that dangled from a chain around his neck, I was terrified.

In a heartbeat, the bodega was swarming with plainclothes cops. And the Rottweiler was barking, berserk.

'Hold the dog, motherfucker, or I'll shoot him!' one cop snarled.

'Put your hands up!' another plainclothesman shouted.

The guy at the cash register was cursing in Spanish, saying, 'How can I hold up my hands and hold onto the dog at the same time.' Two cops were in the back of the bodega attacking the cereal aisle with a chainsaw and a sledgehammer. They shot the dog with a taser and hit its owner with a nightstick.

'What do you got in your pocket, pal?' As the cop asked me the question, he stuck his hands into my jeans and pulled out the coke and my library card. It had my address on it.

'This where you live?'

I didn't want to cry, so I smiled and whispered, 'Yes.'

'You think this is a fucking joke?' When I started to tear up, he could tell I didn't think it was funny. 'If you're lucky, it'll turn out to be powdered sugar.' He opened the envelope and stuck the tip of his tongue into it. 'Looks like you're not lucky.'

The cop looked at me and smiled. Suddenly I was sure that he was going to let me go. Then he handcuffed me and put me in the back of the patrol car. We drove west on Third Street. He was taking me to Juvenile. I had that sick falling sensation, even though I was sitting down. Trying to find something to hold onto, I thought about what I would say to my grandfather when I called him to bail me out. He'd be at our house by now. He would have seen how fucked up she was. I was wondering how many hours of family therapy he'd punish us with. I thought the worst had happened when the cop suddenly stopped in front of our building.

'Get out.' He held the door open for me.

'What are we doing here?'

'Your parents home?'

'No.' He knew I was lying.

'Come on, get out of the car.' There was no resisting. 'They're going to find out sooner or later. Your mother can ride down to Juvenile with us.'

'I'd rather do it by myself.'

'No, you wouldn't.' The fireman who I'd told to fuck off watched as the cop led me up the steps in handcuffs. He pushed the buzzer and unlocked the cuffs.

We didn't have an intercom. There was no way I could warn her. He'd know she was fucked up as soon as she opened the door. He'd see the mess. He'd see her. He's a cop, he'd see the crumpled-up coke paper in the ashtray by her bed.

My mother stood in the open doorway. She looked like . . . a different person. Her hair was washed, her face scrubbed, the beard burn had been rouged into a healthy glow. Christ, she was even wearing a kilt.

'Is your mother home?' The cop thought she was my big sister.

'I'm his mother.' She could tell something was wrong.

I could see inside the loft. The bookcase was back against the wall, the books were in place, there were flowers and a wedge of Brie semi-circled with crackers on the coffee table. She had found her stash and pulled it together. If I hadn't been busted it would have been a miracle. He showed her his badge and got to the point.

'At twelve-forty-five we arrested your son buying this.' The sight of the cocaine blew out the candle that illuminated her hollow smile. My mother's tears kept the cop and me from seeing her pupils were contracted down to pinheads. My mother wasn't just desperate for coke this morning. She was fermenting her high with smack.

The cop was just trying to fill an awkward silence when he said, 'Your son says he was buying it for someone else.'

'If he said it, it's true.' My mother's eyes and mine were locked. Though we were four feet apart, I don't think we'd ever been closer than we were at that moment. Intimate doesn't do justice to the bond that now held us. You wouldn't think it could get any worse. I didn't realize my grandparents were standing behind her.

14

'Tell us who you were buying that . . . that stuff for,' my grandmother demanded.

'Tell them, Finn.' My mother wanted to be punished.

I shook my head no, I couldn't. That would have been letting her off too easy.

2

My mother didn't want her parents to come, but they insisted on driving her down to the Juvenile Corrections Building on Center Street. They followed the cop and me in their green Volvo station wagon. Its bumpers were stickered with their sensibilities. 'McCarthy '72', 'Ban the Bomb', 'Save the Whales', 'A Mind is a Terrible Thing to Waste'. I could see them giving my mother shit in the rear-view mirror. Every time the cop went through a yellow light, he had to pull over and wait for them. My grandfather prided himself on never having had an accident. He was on the lookout for the other guy.

'Juvenile'. The place conjured up visions of mugshots, fingerprinting, sadistic guards giving you a wake-up call by raking their billy clubs against the bars of your cell; strip-searches for contraband hidden in body cavities; and, of course, your gratuitous holding-cell gang rape. The way fate was treating me this morning I figured it would be just my luck to lose my virginity to some two-hundred-and-fifty-pound juvenile offender named Rashid with 'Fuck Whitey' tattooed across his chest. My grandparents would have said that was a bigoted thing to think. But that's what happened to Matt Dillon's kid brother in a TV movie of the week that was popular that year. 'Give it up, chump' was the line that kept playing in my head.

But like most psyche-scarring, life-ruining experiences I have embarked on, Juvenile proved to be worse than the nightmare I had imagined for the simple reason that it wasn't the nightmare I had prepared myself for. There were no mugshots, fingerprints or strip-searches. The closest thing to a sadistic guard I encountered was my grandmother. Nana, as she liked to be called, insisted on 'keeping me company' when they locked me in a windowless room while my grandfather 'helped' my mother, the cop, and a social worker named Miss Pyle go through the paperwork necessary to get me released to my mother's custody.

In retrospect, I can see my grandmother was a no-nonsense sixty-eight-year-old woman who believed with all her heart that having a Negro bridesmaid, voting for Adlai Stevenson, getting a Masters in social work, not having her hair done at the beauty parlor, insisting on playing golf only at public courses, skinny-dipping in front of her grandchildren at the lake, and wearing blue jeans added up to something: they made her a better person. Specifically, a better person than you. Of course, being a better person, Nana never said that out loud. As long as you recognized her as a superior moral force, she could be quite compassionate.

When I walked into that windowless room with her in Juvenile, she was just a white-haired old woman with capped teeth who gave me better presents than my grandfather. After sharing a Snickers and some small talk, my grandmother pulled her chair close to me. 'We're friends, aren't we, Finn?'

'Sure . . . I mean, we're related.'

'Exactly. And since I'm your friend and your grandmother, I would hope that you would feel that you could tell me anything.' She thought she was making progress when I looked at my feet. She had no idea I was wondering if they would have taken my shoelaces away if I had been alone in the room. (In that TV movie I saw, the kid hung himself with his shoelaces.) 'What I mean is, you can trust me not to repeat to anyone anything you tell me in confidence.' Now that I knew she was lying, I felt free to bullshit her.

'I know that, Nana.'

'Good!' She hugged me and kissed my cheek. She smelled of cheese and crackers and Chanel No. 5.

'So tell me, Finn, truly, who were you really buying that . . . that stuff for?' Nana didn't want to say the word 'cocaine'.

'Me.' In a way it was true.

'But you told the policeman . . .'

'Grandma, I was lying . . . He's a cop. I was just trying to talk my way out of it.'

'You think you're doing this person a favor by taking the blame?' I didn't like the way she said *this person*.

'I'm not taking the blame for anyone.' Nana took my face between her thumb and forefinger and forced me to look her in the eye.

'Do you think your grandfather and I are stupid?' I knew then she knew.

'I never said that . . .' I was sick and tired and scared by all the lies I was telling. I was just digging myself a deeper ditch to climb out of. It was my mother's problem, not mine. I thought of my mother's squeaking bed, and the fucking Englishman, and the Vaseline, and when Nana took my hand in hers, I was ready to tell her anything.

'I'll give you one last chance, Finn. Tell me the truth now, and I'll still give you the plane ticket to see your father.' If she hadn't said it like she'd won, if she hadn't been so sure she had my number – in fact, if she hadn't had my number – I would have told her what she so obviously wanted to hear.

'Did you know the Yanomamö believe witches hide their magic wands in their vaginas?'

'You're as crazy as she is.' I watched my grandmother's gray eyes turn milky with tears. She looked at me the same way I had seen her look at my mother.

'You're not helping your mother or yourself.' That's when the social worker opened the door. My mother, my grandfather and the cop were standing behind her. My mother was clutching my release papers with both hands. I could tell she needed a fix. The caseworker reminded my mother we had to appear in juvenile court in three weeks. The cop warned me that if I got caught buying drugs again he'd make sure I got sent to a juvenile home. I shook his hand and said 'Thank you' like he'd done me a favor busting me.

Wanting to get out of there before it got any worse, I took my mother's hand and started pulling her towards the door. The social worker was telling my grandfather that she had read some book he'd written when she was in graduate school. She shook his hand. 'Really, it's an honor to meet you, Dr Earl.'

My grandfather fingered his bow tie. 'I'm sorry it's not under pleasanter circumstances, Miss Pyle.' As he told her to call him and gave her his card, Nana whispered something into my grandfather's ear. The cop was feeding quarters into the Coke machine by the exit sign, when my grandfather cleared his throat and announced, 'Officer, I'd just like to say in Miss Pyle's presence that I think you have arrested the wrong person.'

'Look, I was there and . . .' The cop had tried to be nice, now he was getting pissed off.

'What I mean is, the boy was buying drugs for his mother . . . it's not a pleasant thing to have to say about one's own daughter, but . . .'

'How could you . . .' My mother was trembling.

'Why'd you wait until now to tell me?' The cop was being a cop.

'I'd hoped seeing this happen to her own child would shock Elizabeth into realizing she needs help and accept responsibility.' My grandfather did a lot of learning experiments with rats and electricity.

The cop stepped closer to my mother and gave her a sideways look. He wasn't fooled by her tears this time. He could see her pupils were pinned. Her sniffle was suddenly very suspicious. He looked at her like she belonged under a rock.

'What do you want me to do?' the cop asked my grandfather.

'If my daughter won't turn the child over to us and enter a rehab program today, I would like you to search her apartment. I'm sure you'd find enough narcotics to . . .'

'I'd need a warrant.'

I yanked on my mother's arm to go. The cop blocked our path. They weren't going to let us get away.

'I suggest you search her purse.' When Nana reached for the bag, my mother jumped back and knocked over a chair.

'Liz, why are you making this so hard on us?'

My mother, clutching her purse to her chest, wasn't just trembling now, she was shaking. She opened her mouth. When nothing came out, I screamed for her and lunged at them.

'Stopppittt!' The Yanomamö believe when a child cries its soul can fly from the body and be eaten by its enemies. I don't know if I believed it, but I was definitely losing it.

My mother pulled me back. 'It's OK, Finn.' I knew it wasn't, but there was a calm to my mother's voice I hadn't heard before.

My grandfather stepped forward. He parked his nose an inch from my mother's forehead and looked down on her. 'Elizabeth, you don't know how much this hurts me.' She hated it when anybody got in her face like that. I could see he was goading her with his calm. He wanted her to lash out at him, to lose it in front of the social worker who'd read his fucking book. He was counting on her pushing him or, better yet, hitting him in front of the cop. Then he could have her arrested for assault. The social worker/fan made the perfect witness. They'd hold my mother and take me. Suddenly it was clear these Volvo-driving *Amahiri-teri* were going to kidnap me and take me back to their jungle-less suburb.

My mother handed the cop her purse. She had given up. I could see it in her face. The cop turned her handbag upside down on the social worker's desk. Seven one-dollar bills, thirty-seven cents, a hairbrush, and a condom were all they had on her. Everybody but my mother was speechless. As we walked out the door she paused just long enough to say, 'Disappointed?' It seemed like we won. It didn't feel that way. As we walked home, I knew everything in my life had changed.

'Things are going to be different now.' My mother gripped my hand like she thought one of us was going to get lost. 'We're going to make it.' She'd been saying that for years.

'I know.' I hadn't held her hand like that since I wore mittens.

When we got back to the loft, my mother looked in the bathroom mirror, took her hairbrush out of her purse, and carefully popped out the rubber pad that held the bristles. There were two small white packets of coke folded like little envelopes, and a yellowish glassine bag of heroin hidden inside. (That's when I found out she was doing speedballs.) I was surprised she didn't bother to close the bathroom door. I guessed we were beyond hiding things. Or at least the drug thing.

I was thinking: So this is how things are going to be different. I was getting ready to start screaming about what would have happened if the cop had checked out her hairbrush when he'd searched her purse. To say the least, I was surprised when my mother flushed her shit down the toilet.

Then she took the phone into the bathroom and closed the door. That's where all private telephone conversations were held in our household. Still stunned she'd flushed away her stash, I was slower than usual to put my ear to the door. Like most teenagers, I felt all secrets should be shared but my own.

I didn't start eavesdropping in time to hear who she'd called. All I caught was her saying tersely, 'I can't reach my cartridges now.' *Cartridges?* Thinking paranoid, I wondered if she'd had second thoughts about flushing her shit and was talking code to a drug dealer. *Cartridges?* Thinking really paranoid, it occurred to me she could be talking to somebody about shooting herself. It didn't matter that we didn't have a gun. Or that she had such an aversion to weapons of any kind that she wouldn't let me keep the BB pistol one of her ex-boyfriends had given me in what would have been a thoroughly successful attempt to buy my friendship. Trusting neither my mother nor my imagination, and being naturally nosy, I looked through the keyhole.

She was sitting on the toilet seat, lighting the last cigarette of her pack from the Marlboro she'd just dragged down to the filter. She knew I was spying on her. She told whoever she was talking to, 'Don't go away . . . promise?' She leaned forward to open the door, then fell back onto the toilet seat. 'Finn, I'm not hiding . . .' I could see she was having trouble staying awake '. . . anything from you.' She hadn't slept in over forty hours. Her tongue was having trouble talking. 'I'm just trying to . . .' Her eyes rolled back in their sockets. Her neck turned to rubber. The side of her head hit the wall, bringing her back to her stream of consciousness with a thud. 'I'm just trying to work something out for us.'

'Who are you talking to?'

'I'll tell you later. Be an angel and get me a cup of coffee and some cigarettes down at the corner.'

As I walked to Joe's Diner on the corner of Lafayette, I played with the fantasy that she was talking to my father in South America. Maybe I misheard her through the door. Maybe she said, 'You can't reach your cartridges?' Like he was in trouble. Like maybe the Yanomamö had turned on him; like, I knew it was babyish to play those kind of games in my head, but those kinds of thoughts are as irresistible as a really cheesy episode of *The Waltons*. You're embarrassed to be wasting your time that way, but you just can't turn it off until you feel like a jerk for starting to cry.

By the time I had gotten the cigs and the coffee for my mother, and a dinner of well-done French fries for myself, I decided that even though I knew she wasn't talking to my dad on the phone, maybe the fantasy wasn't such a dopey idea. Maybe this was the moment for her to call my father. In his letter he said he had a radiophone at the base-camp in Venezuela. I calculated the time zones involved. He'd be awake. She could surprise him and say we were both coming to visit.

When I got back home it was too late for the coffee or the call. My mother had passed out on the bathroom floor with the phone cradled to her chest like a baby.

3

When I woke up the next morning, I had a piss-boner – perfectly normal. But my mother was in my bedroom packing my suitcase – highly suspicious. She looked like someone who had tried to get rid of the flu by falling down a flight of stairs.

'Are you sick?' She was sniffling and doubled over with cramps.

'It's called withdrawal.' I tried to appreciate her honesty as I pulled on my jeans. 'It's going to get worse before it gets better. I'll be OK in a couple of days.'

I pointed to my suitcase with my bare foot. 'Where am I going?'

'With me, of course.'

'Where are we going, then?' I knew it wasn't South America, because she was packing my sweaters. I figured she must have given in to my grandparents when she put my one-and-only gravy-spotted necktie into the bag.

'We talked about this last night, Finn.'

'No, we didn't.' It pissed me off she'd forgotten about passing out on the bathroom floor. 'Where are we going?' I was impatient for answers.

'Vlyvalle.' She said it rather proudly.

'Where the hell is that?'

'Somewhere . . .' The monkey on her back was squeezing her bowels. Cramps and diarrhea sent her hobbling to the bathroom. After she flushed the toilet, she gave me the bad news. 'It's somewhere in New Jersey.'

'New Jersey?' I said it like I'd been sentenced to Devil's Island. In my imagination, there was no place on the planet further from South America. 'For how long?'

'A while.'

'Why? Why New Jersey?'

'Because I got a job there.'

'When?'

'Last night.'

'New Jersey's the asshole of the world. It's like one big truck stop.'

'Vlyvalle's different.'

'What sort of job?'

'Doing physical therapy . . .' She was cramping again.

'For who?'

'. . . for a . . . man. He's giving us a house and . . .' She sat down on my bed quickly. She was about to fall down.

'You call up some guy in the middle of the night and he gives you a job and a house?'

'I'm not going to be cross-questioned by a fifteen-year-old . . . who do you think you are?'

'I'm the kid who got busted buying . . .' She held up her hand for me to stop. I knew other ways of hurting her. 'Is this guy a personal friend?'

'Yes.'

'Like your Englishman.' She shook her head no. 'I'm going to have to go to school in New Jersey?'

'I don't know, Finn. We'll figure it out in the fall.'

'I have to know . . .' I hated the feeling that I was dependent on parents, grandparents – an extended adult world that could only be relied upon to ambush me with disappointment. I preferred the Fierce People of the Amazon I was never going to see, who you could rely on to greet you with, 'Hello, I want your flashlight, and if you don't give it to me, I'll cut off your ears with my axe.' Who singed each other with burning sticks when they didn't get the answer they wanted. I was also a teenage virgin. 'In New Jersey all the girls have big hair and pink lipstick.'

'Not all of them, Finn.' My mom laughed and I scowled – we could have been playing parts in a sitcom if she weren't kicking smack and I hadn't felt like slapping the smile off her face.

'What about my friends!' I shouted.

'What friends?' It sounds mean, but actually she was just being honest. 'You mean like Hector?' He was the one who'd been shot.

'Slurpee? You're honestly trying to tell me you're going to miss Slurpee?' My mom felt sorry for him, but she took personal offense at the slurping sound he made whenever he ate. She had good manners for a junkie. 'You'll make better friends where we're going.'

When the doorbell rang my mother jumped. 'See if that's the driver.' My mother said it like drivers rang our bell every day.

'What driver?' She was ambushing me again.

'The man I'm going to work for is sending a car to pick us up.'

'Does he have a name?'

'It's Mr Osborne.' That was the jillionaire who paid her so much for backrubs she was able to afford a drug habit. Seeing how Osborne was older than my grandfather and just got out of the hospital, I felt a little guilty for suggesting he was in the same category of male friend as the Englishman. But there was definitely something suspicious about him suddenly offering her a job.

'Finn, open the window and tell them we'll be down in ten minutes.'

'Do Grandpa and Nana know about this?'

'No . . .' Just mentioning their names scared her. 'We'll tell them where we are after I'm . . . clean.'

I figured my grandparents must have found out because when I looked down, there was an out-of-state cop car parked in front of our house. A black cop, wearing a wide-brimmed Smokey-the-Bear hat had his thumb to our buzzer. When I told her what was waiting downstairs, my mother let out a wail like someone had just closed a car door on her hand and was about to drive off. 'They're going to do it again,' she sobbed.

'Who?'

'My parents.' Suddenly, there were two frightened teenagers in the room.

' "Again" . . . they had you arrested?'

'They had me . . . committed to Oak Knoll.' That was the name of this ritzy mental hospital we passed whenever we took the bus up to my grandparents' house in Connecticut.

'Why'd they send you there?'

'Because I wouldn't . . . get rid of you.' The buzzer was ringing.

'They wanted you to put me up for adoption?'

'They wanted me to have an abortion. They said you'd ruin my life. Now they're saying I'm ruining yours.' As I tried to take in what she said, my mind drifted to the Yanomamö. They didn't have abortion. Unwanted children were left out to die. Then they burned them and ate their ashes. I couldn't think of the word for it.

'But if you were committed and everything, how'd you stop them from . . .'

'I made a bargain with your father's wife.' She was crying for both of us now.

'The rich-bitch?'

'Rich people can fix things.'

'Endo-cannibalism.'

'What?'

'The Yanomamö eat the ashes of their dead children.' The buzzer had stopped ringing. I'd heard enough. I didn't want to ask her any more questions. The only person in the world I felt sorrier for than myself was her. 'We gotta get out of here.'

My mother wasn't listening. All she could do was sob, 'I didn't want to lose you.'

Suddenly, it was us against the world. It was that way from the beginning, I guess. I knew more than I ever thought there was to know. I thought I had heard the worst. I was glad because I thought that meant there were no more surprises. This was the last ambush.

'We can go up to the roof, climb over to the next building, sneak down and . . .' Talking about running away made me believe there was a way to escape. I was pulling on her arm, but she just sat there staring straight ahead; paralyzed.

The black cop was now squatting on the fire escape, looking in on us. He was so clean and pressed you would have thought he was on parade. He peered through my bedroom window like he was looking into a dirty terrarium. He tapped the glass with a ring on his finger to get our attention. Then he took a small notebook out of the breast pocket of his khaki, epauletted shirt.

'Elizabeth Earl?' My mother looked around like he was talking to someone else. He was opening the window now.

'You Finn Earl?' The cop put one leg through the window. When I

26

blurted out: 'Do you have a warrant?' He looked like he had just stepped in dog shit.

'No. No warrant.' My challenge didn't even slow him down. 'Mr Osborne led me to understand one wouldn't be required.'

My mother stood up and wiped away her tears like they belonged to someone else and smiled.

'Mr Osborne didn't tell us he was sending a policeman to pick us up. I'm sorry we acted so . . .'

Instead of accepting her apology, he handed her a card. It read: 'REGINALD T GATES, Chief of Police, Vlyvalle, New Jersey.' Beneath his name there was a motto: 'To Protect and Serve.'

In my closet-sized bedroom he looked bigger than life. Built like a Port-O-San, he had a shaved head, dark and smooth as an eight ball. He reminded me of something. A seal? Idi Amin?

'Mr Osborne thought you might need some help.' Chief Gates' voice was slow and flat. He gave you time to think about what he was saying. And worry about how much he was keeping to himself.

'Mr Osborne also instructed me to tell you you're under no obligation to accept his offer. If you've changed your mind, he'll understand.'

I answered for both of us. 'I'll get our stuff.'

4

We said goodbye to New York in the back of a police car via the Holland Tunnel. There was a wire grille between us and Osborne's police chief. It was like we were in protective custody. The monkey on my mother's back was still tying her bowels in knots. Every time she tried to make small talk to him she ended up apologizing, and asking Gates to stop at the next restroom. We pulled in to two diners and one turnpike HoJo's before we'd gone twenty miles. While we were waiting for my mom to come out of the first of those bathrooms, I asked Gates, 'Does Mr Osborne do this sort of thing . . . often?'

'To answer that truthfully,' Gates was eating sunflower seeds, 'I'd have to say,' one by one he split them with his gold front tooth and spit the shells into a Dixie cup, 'I'd have to say "yes" and "no".'

The second time we pulled over for mother, I enquired with the bold bluntness of the resentful teenager I was, 'What does this Osborne guy . . .' Gates spit a sunflower seed in my direction as a reprimand for my familiarity. We were leaning against the hood of the cop car. 'I mean, Mr Osborne, what does he do besides being rich?'

'If you've got enough money, being rich is a full-time job.' It was a better answer than I realized.

By the third bathroom stop for Mom, I was working up the impertinence to ask the sunflower-noshing cop just how exactly Mr Osborne got so rich, but the chief had a question for me.

'What's wrong with your mother?' Gates didn't look at me when he asked the question. He just stared out at the traffic and the strip-malls and the muffler shops that forested the horizon.

'Food poisoning,' I blurted out. Thinking details would make the

28

lie more convincing, I babbled on, 'I think it was bad shrimp. We had Chinese take-out last night. And the egg rolls seemed a little funky.' In the distance I could see a bulldozer burying New York's garbage.

'Your mother's lucky.'

'How's that?'

'Food poisoning like she's got sends some people to the hospital.'

'It looks more serious than it is.'

'That's what Mr Osborne thinks. No Chinese in Vlyvalle,' he warned me.

'I'm the one who likes Chinese.'

'Is that a fact?' My mother came out of the bathroom with a piece of toilet paper stuck to her shoe. That wasn't half as embarrassing as watching Gates pretend not to see her wash down the last of her Valium with a Yoo-Hoo.

I thought Gates was a bigger prick than the cop who had busted me until he said, 'You sit up front with me. Let your mother lie down in back and rest herself.' It wasn't the words, it was the way he folded up his cop jacket to make a pillow for her head.

Driving west, the landfills and the strip-malls and the big hair gave way to suburbs where girls I wasn't above lusting after, wearing their boyfriends' high-school varsity jackets, loitered in front of head-shops and soda fountains. Gates knew every short cut. We zigzagged first through tract-house suburbs with postage-stamp lawns, then cruised into tonier communities, distinguished by maple-lined avenues and six-bedroom houses. The further we traveled, the blonder the girls seemed.

Soon, we started passing through towns without sidewalks where everybody seemed to drive BMWs and Mercedes Benzes, and even the guys who drove the delivery trucks looked like they shopped at LL Bean. And nobody walked. I missed New York even more than I did when we were in Newark. It was the kind of homesickness that made me want to kick over some garbage cans and scatter trash across these vast and tidy lawns. I felt a whole lot more comfortable in New Jersey when I thought it was one big dump.

My mother was out cold in the back. I guess I would have been more embarrassed if she was snoring. I only hoped she'd be awake when we got to wherever we were going. I didn't want to have to ask Chief Gates to help me carry her. We were on a three-lane highway now. There were lots of signs telling me how far we were from towns I had never heard of, but I was totally lost. The green of golf courses gave way to the patchwork of farms. Roadside stands selling Jersey tomatoes and Jersey corn were minded by pale-skinned Jersey girls that wore polyester shorts and tank-tops with bra straps showing – hillbilly first-cousins to the big-haired girls of the landfill. I was missing the girls in the varsity jackets that I knew I'd never meet.

A sign punctuated with double-nought buckshot, telling me Vlyvalle was still seventeen miles away gave me the illusion I knew where I was going and prompted me to break the silence. 'Why has a town in Jersey got a German name?'

'Vlyvalle's Dutch, not German. It means "Fly Valley".' Gates offered me some of his sunflower seeds. I took a handful, but passed on sharing his Dixie cup full of gobbed husks, and spit mine out the window.

'They got a lot of bugs there?'

'When my father was a kid the flies were so thick you'd leave your screen door open at night, you'd wake up and a dozen of them would be drinking the tears from your eyes.' Gates offered me some more sunflower seeds and fed me some more down-home bullshit. 'I'm telling you, we used to have a serious fly problem before Mr Osborne's time.'

'Mr Osborne get rid of the flies?'

'Not personally.' I was imagining some rich old fuck hiring a bunch of Jersey hillbillies to douse his valley with DDT, Agent Orange and every other manner of carcinogenic pesticide. I appreciated having another reason not to like Mr Osborne.

'He brought in some bugs from South America. Ate the fly larvae before they had a chance to hatch. One year they was there, and the next they was gone.'

'Assassin Beetles?'

'How'd you know that?' Gates was impressed.

'I'm a really good student.' It was a total lie, but I thought it might come in handy. There was an article about Assassin Beetles in the same issue of *National Geographic* my father was in. 'It's pretty cool Osborne using bugs to get rid of bugs.'

'Not if you like ladybugs.'

'What do you mean?'

'When Mr Osborne's bugs finished off all the flies, they started on the ladybugs.'

'So?'

Gates looked at me like I was a fool. 'Ladybugs eat spiders.'

'You got a lot of spiders?' Spiders were the only other thing besides snakes I didn't like about South America.

'We used to. You'd go to sleep and wake up with webs between your fingers and toes.' Suddenly I wasn't sure if he was bullshitting me.

'So what'd Mr Osborne do about that?'

'He imported some sort of tufted African something or other,'

'What are they?'

'Birds. Kind of like swallows, but bigger beaks.'

'What do they do?'

'Besides eat the spiders? Nothing so far, 'cept shit on my car.' I wondered what problem Mr Osborne imported us to take care of. Who were we to feed on, and who in turn would feed on us? Gates forgot I was there for a second. 'Mr Osborne always likes to mess with the food chain.'

'Is Mr Osborne a nice guy?'

'Your mother can answer that better than me.' I was starting to like Gates until he said that.

'How much further?'

'We've been in Vlyvalle for the past three miles.'

At first glance, it was no different than the farmland we had been driving through before we turned off onto the gravel road. Except that every twenty feet there was a sign that told you in block letters:

NO TRESPASSING. VLYVALLE HUNT CLUB.
VIOLATORS WILL BE PROSECUTED.

'Who belongs to the Vlyvalle Hunt Club?'

'Everybody who lives in Vlyvalle.'

31

'Must be a big club.'

'Twenty-eight families.'

'There're only twenty-eight families in Vlyvalle?' There was more than a touch of panic in my voice.

'Well, there are guest members.'

'How many?'

He looked at me and smiled. 'Two.'

You couldn't see the houses where the people of Vlyvalle lived from the road. Every quarter of a mile or so, there was a driveway that would disappear into some woods, or vanish around a cleverly landscaped rise. The places with big, wrought-iron gates hinged on columns, crowned with the heads of cement horses, dogs, unicorns, lions, and in one case, a pair of pineapples, had names like Bellevue, Sans Souci, Drumthwacket. The more understated spreads, the ones whose entrances were just a pair of Volkswagen-sized boulders that distracted you from the surveillance cameras, or a rustic, white-washed, remote-controlled wooden gate in the midst of a half-mile stretch of white picket fence barbed with roses, had neatly painted signs identifying them as farms – Treetops Farm, Cold Brook Farm, Windhill Farm. At that point, all I knew of country life was what I'd learned from Eva Gabor and Eddie Arnold on re-runs of *Green Acres*. Something told me that the people in Vlyvalle were a whole different kind of rich than anything you could see on TV.

Town was a steepled church, a graveyard with fresh flowers and little American flags in front of old tombstones. A post office, a volunteer fire department and a general store called the 'Butler's Pantry'. Even though it was summer, the place looked as stiff and cold as a Currier and Ives Christmas card from Nana. Sitting in Chief Gates' green and white cruiser, my mother passed out in the back, I felt like I was in a WASP witness-protection program.

About a mile past town we turned into a driveway of a Victorian house with gingerbread trim and a big porch. There was a jungle gym and a set of swings in the front yard. I asked Gates, 'Whose house is this?'

'Mr Osborne's.' I couldn't believe it. It wasn't just that there wasn't a gate.

'Mr Osborne has an above-ground swimming pool!' It was just like the ones they advertised on TV during Yankee games.

'No . . . I do.' The big, black, bald-headed cop seemed to enjoy making me realize I was already a snob. Gates slowed down and called out the car window to a tall, thin, copper-skinned woman who had a profile that looked like it belonged on a wooden nickel. 'Your husband around?'

She answered, 'No.' It was his wife.

In the backyard, his teenaged son was rifling footballs through an old tire that hung from a tree-limb. A year older and forty pounds heavier than me, he was the kind of kid that made me embarrassed to take my shirt off. Grunting as he gunned the ball, he would have looked scary, if it weren't for the Coke-bottle glasses perched on his nose. Gates slowed the car and rolled down the window. I thought he was going to introduce us. 'Anybody can do it that way,' he called out.

'I couldn't.' I didn't mean to say it out loud. Gates gave me a look that told me to shut up. We watched as his son dutifully gave the tire a swing, then quickly ran back to a wheelbarrow full of footballs, and grunting 'Hut one . . . hut two . . . hut three . . .' put three clothesline spirals through the swinging whitewall, pigskin never touching rubber. I was impressed. Gates spit a mouthful of sunflower husks in his son's general direction, and announced, to no one in particular, 'Life isn't going to stand still for you,' and drove on.

Gates' driveway didn't stop at his garage. It hooked up to one of the seven and a half miles of private roads that criss-crossed Mr Osborne's estate. Facts and figures about the size and geography of the estate rolled off Gates' tongue as we splashed down a puddle-rutted lane that bisected a wood of long-needled pines. Now that we were in Mr Osborne's domain, Gates sounded more like a tour guide than a cop.

'Nine thousand three hundred and fifty-six acres, that's over ten square miles. Miss Duke's place is bigger, but size isn't everything.' I didn't know he was talking about Doris Duke, but I was impressed. In fact, I was so overwhelmed I felt trapped.

When we crossed a metal bridge that spanned a fast-moving stream, Gates told me above the echoey thump of tires on plank trestles, 'Haverkill's best trout brook east of the Mississippi.' And now, as we passed through an orchard with pears growing inside glass bottles, Gates did not decrease my awe by saying, 'Mr Osborne makes his own pear brandy. Just like they do it in France.'

Gates finally stopped the car in front of a yellow cottage, umbrellaed by sugar maples, guarded by a privet hedge. It sat oddly askew in the middle of a perfectly flat, fifty-acre rectangle of thighhigh corn; like it just had fallen out of the sky. *The Wizard of Oz* always gave me nightmares as a kid.

My mother did not stir when Gates announced, 'This is it.' Pearls of milky sweat beaded her lip and neck. Her skirt had ridden up, and beneath blue tights, stretched to transparency by the unexpectedly voluptuous curve of her hips, Gates and I could both see the white of her panties. I was glad she had remembered to wear underwear. I was even more relieved when the chief got out of the car and told me, 'You'd better take her feet.' I knew from experience in New York I couldn't carry her alone.

Gates looked away as I reached into the back seat and pulled down my mother's skirt. When she'd passed out before, lots of times on the couch, once in the tub, as soon as she felt my touch she'd moan, shift her position, and at least snap out of it long enough to slur, 'What's wrong, lambie?' Or 'pumpkin'. Or 'baby'. That's the one . . . I liked least. This time she didn't move a muscle; not a twitch. When the back of my arm brushed against her face, it was cold and damp and lifeless as a formaldehyde frog's stomach. And suddenly I'm thinking: She couldn't have ODed. She didn't take enough Valiums with that Yoo-Hoo. Was she still breathing? I looked at her chest. I couldn't see anything but her bra strap. I started to reach out and feel for her heartbeat. But my hand stopped just short of her breast. Gates was watching. I didn't want him to think my mother and me were any weirder than we were. I jumped back from her body when she suddenly opened one eye, hitting my head on the top of the car door.

'Shit!'

'What's wrong?' The expression on Gates' face told me he, too, was thinking the worst.

34

'Not a thing in the world,' my mother announced calmly. Gates was as startled as I was to see her step out of the back of the police car with a smile on her face and not a trace of toilet paper on her shoe. 'The house is perfect,' she purred.

Before our eyes my mother morphed into June Allyson. The clammy sweat had vanished from her face without the help of powder or pads. She held her arms out to the butter-yellow clapboard colonial with green shutters like she was going to give it a hug. 'It's a dream, isn't it, Finn?'

Looking back on the moment, I can see my mother was actually doing Audrey Hepburn doing June Allyson. I had seen her pull her act together, but never like this. Was it the sudden burst of fresh air in her lungs? The prospect of living in a house she knew Nana would envy?

Gates looked at her witchcraft in disbelief. 'You feeling better?'

'Much better!' My mother rolled her shoulders and stretched like a cat. 'Sorry I dozed off on the ride. We had some *Chinoise* last night that didn't agree with me.' My mother said saying anything in French made it taste better.

'Your boy told me about the egg roll.'

'Must have been a bad shrimp,' my mother added. The way she smiled at me and tousled my hair, I almost believed that was the extent of our problems.

Gates and I took the suitcases and her black, folding/rolling massage table out of the trunk. As I pushed it towards the front door, one of its wheels got stuck in the soft grass between the flagstones of the path. When I tried to lift it up, it came unfolded on top of me. It smelled of sweat and a body oil called 'Orangegasma'. My mother laughed. It's one of those things that's funnier when it happens to someone else. Cursing as I struggled to fold it, and the things its odor made me imagine, back up, my mother suddenly shouted, 'Impatiens!' I was about to tell her to do it herself. When she announced, 'I love impatiens.' Realizing she was talking about the white flowers that bordered the path, I wondered: Who is this person impersonating my mother?

There was a scurrying sound inside as Gates unlocked the front door. He cocked his head to listen. But when he turned on the lights, it was gone. 'Probably a bird in the chimney.' The house was cool and dark and smelled like those balsam pine-needle pillows they sell in roadside gift shops in Maine.

'Adorable . . . fantastic . . . fabulous . . . too perfect for words.' Every room elicited a new phony set of adjectives. I mean, the place was nice and all. *Ye Olde*, without being too Betsy Ross. It was my mother, not the decor, that offended my sensibilities.

The ceilings were low and beamed, and the walls were two feet thick and painted with a sponge. The wide board floors were aubergine. And sprinkled with tiny dots of color. It was just like walking on a bad Jackson Pollock. If I'd read *Architectural Digest*, I would have recognized it as the signature of an interior decorator by the name of Sister Parish.

Each room had a fireplace and in each hearth, logs, kindling and freshly crumpled newspaper waited only for the touch of one of the foot-long matches they had in tubes painted to look like marble. There were towels and toothbrushes in the bathrooms, and every kind of over-the-counter elixir from Poli-Grip to Preparation H in the medicine cabinet.

A full refrigerator, with a glass door just like they have in restaurants. Cabinets full of gourmet canned goods and crackers from France. Fresh flowers in every room. Cool stuff on the mantel that I knew I'd break even before my mother told me not to touch it. An Indian tomahawk. A bronze dagger. A crystal ball on a brass octopus. And the wing of a red-tailed hawk. Full bookcases, empty waste-paper baskets. Last week's magazines. Today's papers. Bowls of cashews. Boxes of candy and two types of cigarettes. All casually placed on coffee tables and sideboards, like whoever lived here had just walked out the door.

'Why didn't the people who lived here take their stuff?' I asked. I mean, there were framed photographs and baby pictures and stuff like that. Gates looked at me.

'No one lives here. Mr Osborne keeps it for his . . .' Gates hesitated ever so slightly before he added the word 'guests'. I was under the impression that my mother was an employee. I wondered if 'guest' was a promotion or a polite way of saying something else. Was there more to my mother's massages than I wanted to think about? The way Gates told my mother that someone named Herbert would come by tomorrow and go over the schedule made it clear that being Mr Osborne's guest, while nice work if you could get it, was also a full-time job.

My mother stood in the doorway and waved as the police car disappeared down the road in a cloud of dust. As soon as Gates was out of sight, she groaned, 'Jesus Christ, I thought he'd never leave,' and hit the floor like a sack of dead batteries.

Once I checked to make sure she was breathing and all, it was kind of nice to have her back to her old self again. For sure, it wasn't half as scary as having a voice behind me whisper, 'Does she do that often?'

A face peered out at me from the hall closet. Big forehead, lidded eyes, lantern jaw, and a nose that looked like it had had an unfortunate encounter with a baseball bat; the nicest way to say it was she bore a striking resemblance to one of those statues on Easter Island.

Tired of telling the Chinese-food lie, I answered like it was my house. 'Who are you?'

'Jilly . . . Jilly Lumkin.' Her voice didn't go with her face. It was deep and funny, with just enough of a speech impediment to make her sound exactly like George Jetson's talking dog, Astro. Me being a huge *Jetsons* fan, that observation should be taken as a compliment.

'What are you doing in the closet?' I asked.

'I'm the maid,' she answered with a laugh, as she pulled herself and a vacuum cleaner out of the closet, crowded with raincoats and parkas for guests of assorted sizes.

Jilly wore an old-fashioned, button-up-the-front, gray domestic's uniform, with a starched white collar over a pair of labia-splitting jeans and a tube-top. All the buttons on the uniform were unbuttoned. Her body was as perfect as her face was unfortunate.

'You're a maid?' My voice cracked with excitement. Her tank-top had ridden up, exposing the gravity-defying upward curve of the underside of her right breast.

'Three days a week I help out on the farm. You know, summer job until I figure out what I want to do with life after high school. I graduated and all, they just didn't give me a diploma. I flunked Home Ec. Pretty pathetic, huh?' She told me all this without taking a breath. I was fascinated.

'That's great.'

'You think so?' She didn't sound convinced. She was buttoning up the front of her uniform now. I guess she thought I was staring at her chest, which I had been, but I wasn't at that particular moment. 'I keep it unbuttoned because I'm allergic to wool.'

'I'm allergic to peanuts.'

'Watch out for Burger King.' She could tell she'd lost me. She stopped buttoning and explained. 'The secret sauce has peanut butter in it.'

'I didn't know that.'

'Me neither, until I saw on the news how this woman's daughter who was super-allergic to peanuts throat closed and died before she even finished her Whopper.'

'Wow.'

'She's suing Burger King for ten million dollars.'

'Peanuts just give me a spastic colon.' I regretted it even before she said,

'Gross.'

'Think I could sue them for gas?'

'Gross me out.' The way she said it this time, I could tell she gave me points for a quick recovery. It wasn't exactly Algonquin wit, but I felt quite proud of myself until she suddenly stopped laughing and said, 'Are you just gonna leave your mom there on the floor?'

We each took one of her arms over our shoulders. It was surprisingly unembarrassing having Jilly help me carry her up the stairs. Partly because she didn't make a big deal about it, but mostly because I was distracted by the pressure of her half-tubed right breast against the back of the arm I had wrapped around my mother's ribcage. I guess you could call it a cheap feel, but it didn't feel that way to me. Maybe having my mother between us made it different.

We laid her out in the bedroom at the top of the stairs. We each took off one of her shoes, and tiptoed back down to the kitchen. I opened the refrigerator like I was Lord of the Manor.

'Want something to eat or drink?'

'Sure.' Jilly reached for a beer, then hesitated. 'Is it cool?'

'Hey, I'm having one.' I nonchalantly exchanged the bottle of Mountain Dew I was holding for a Heineken. Savoring a beer with tube-topped Jill Lumkin was a decidedly more satisfying enterprise than chug-a-lugging a purloined Budweiser with Slurpee. In fact, it was so heady I became lost in the wonderment of how fate had delivered me to such a delightful place and time that I just sat there staring at her.

How quickly the contentment of blissful silence turned to panic. Suddenly, I had no idea what I could possibly say to her next. Was it the beer I was now nervously gulping? The anxiety of the last twenty-four hours? The thought of what she'd look like without that tube-top? I desperately tried to think of something clever to say about the Yanomamö. Telling her that the women in the tribe hide meat in their vaginas seemed too forward.

'You're waiting for me to tell you what I was doing in the closet, aren't you?'

'Exactly.' All I cared about was that the silence had been cracked.

'When you and Gates pulled up . . .' I nodded, so it seemed less obvious I was staring at her tits again. '. . . I was smoking a joint. He's already busted me once and . . .'

'You were the bird in the chimney.'

'I like that.'

I'm not being overconfident when I say she thought me rather poetic for putting it that way.

'How old are you?'

'Fifteen and a half. Actually, I'll be sixteen in a month.' I cursed myself for not telling her I was seventeen.

'You want to get high?'

'Sure.' She pulled a joint from her tube-top, and moistened it between pursed lips. Needless to say, when Slurpee did that with the pot I stole from my mother's purse, I didn't get a chubby. Half a joint later, I decided that those statues on Easter Island were really rather beautiful. In an exotic way, of course.

'What's that thing?' She pointed to my mother's black massage table.

'It's my mother's . . . treatment table.' I'd told so many lies for my mother in the last forty-eight hours, why not one for me?

'What sort of treatment?'

'Homeopathic.'

'She's like a doctor?'

'Sort of. She's not a medical doctor. But in France they'd call her a doctor.' My mother had talked about studying homeopathic medicine at this hippie institute in Paris, so it wasn't a complete lie.

'And she's here to treat Mr Osborne?'

'Yeah.' That much was true.

'Does she think she can cure him?'

'I don't know.'

'My mom's such a jerk.' Jill exhaled a cloud of cannabis into my face. 'She told me your mother was a . . .' Suddenly, a car honked outside.

'A what?'

'Nothing. I'll set her straight.' Jill was running towards the front door.

I looked out the window. There was a guy in a convertible GTO revving the engine with the top down. 'Who's that?'

'My boyfriend, Dwayne.' She handed me the joint. 'Don't ever tell him we got high.'

'Why?'

'He'll kick the shit out of you, silly.' The boyfriend was old. To me that was anyone over eighteen. He was kind of handsome, except he had these big Dumbo ears. And there was so much beef to him, I wanted to stick a meat thermometer in his back. As I stood in the door and watched them drive off, he gave me the finger.

By the time I finished the joint, I had stopped worrying about telling Jilly my mother was a French doctor, and started getting paranoid about what her mom had told her about my mom.

40

5

I was on the Uraricoera River in a dugout canoe with my father. He looked just like his picture in *Natural History*. The river was high from the rains. In the distance, I saw a sloth swimming against the current. There were a dozen Yanomamö women collecting wood by the shore. Naked, except for red vegetable-dye circles on their backs and parrot feathers. I knew it was a dream because when I got out of the canoe, I was wearing those snake-proof boots I was going to buy with the money I spent on cocaine at the bodega. Still, it was very cool and very real. I could hear the birds squawking in the trees overhead . . . even after I opened my eyes and realized I was in the smaller of the two bedrooms that took up the second floor of Mr Osborne's guesthouse. The tree outside my window was thick with a flock of whatever was the name of those birds Osborne brought in to eat the beetles that ate the bugs that used to eat the spiders when they got finished eating the flies. I saw what Gates meant. Every time they squawked, they shit.

Anyway, the point is, they pissed me off on two counts: they made it impossible for me to go back to sleep, and they reminded me I wasn't going to get to go to South America. Thinking about Jilly gave me an erection, which always improved my mood, and did so that morning, until I was horrified to realize I had left my beat-off magazines back in New York. Horny and homesick, I headed for the bathroom.

It was all wood-paneled and had a Jacuzzi bath. Something I'd been too stoned to notice when I went to bed. There was a basket full of little bars of soap wrapped in tissue paper and miniature shampoo bottles just like in a hotel.

Five minutes later I was up to my neck in suds pretending Jilly was in there with me getting up close and personal. I don't know if it was what she said about her boyfriend kicking the shit out of me, or the excitement of the last forty-eight hours, but the harder I worked at it the less hard I was. I even tried it with my left hand, which always seemed to have a more feminine touch than my right. A fifteen-and-a-half-year-old doesn't know the meaning of the word impotence. Refusing to take no for an answer from my body, I ran back into the bedroom and grabbed the issue of *Natural History* with all the Yanomamö titties in it. It did the trick. But after I had spent my seed in the jungle of my mind, I felt worse than when I started. Somehow, in the course of all the excitement, I let the magazine slip into the bath. When I tried to rub the pages dry with a towel, my father's face disappeared.

When I went downstairs for breakfast, I wasn't just pissed off. I felt raw and unsatisfied. My mother was sitting at the kitchen table reading a paperback titled *How to Kick Cocaine in 14 Days*.

'Does it have a happy ending?' My mother answered me with a look. And she didn't look good. Her eyes were darkly circled like a raccoon who'd lost a fistfight.

'When did you get up?' I asked belligerently.

'A little after four.'

'You found that book *here*?'

'For your information, I bought it several months ago.' She was waiting for me to make eye contact. There were so many types of cereal in the cupboard to choose from, it was easy to avoid her glare.

'You know, Finn, I've known I've had a problem for some time.'

'Me too.' I couldn't decide between granola with freeze-dried raspberries or Frosted Flakes.

'Does being a shit make all this easier for you?'

'Sort of.' I bumped into her as I juggled milk, bowl, banana and Frosted Flakes (I decided to go with an old standby – at heart I'm a traditionalist) on my way to the kitchen table. It was an accident . . . sort of.

'Jesus Christ!' she shouted. 'Will you watch where you're going?'

'I barely touched you.' I was about to say something really shitty, but from the grimace on her face, the way she clutched her side, I knew she was really hurting.

'Sorry.' I actually meant it.

'Every part of me hurts.' There were tears in her eyes. 'The book says the physical part of withdrawal will get easier in a couple of days.' I wanted to ask her how long the mental part would last, but I knew she'd think I was being a wiseass if I asked it like that.

'What are those?' She had several mounds of capsules and pills in front of her. Tablets of every color and size imaginable. It looked like she was playing pharmacist.

'Sudafed, vitamin E, B-complex, St John's Wort, and these are ginseng.'

'Are you sick?' She gave me a look. 'I mean, like the flu?'

Deciding to give me the benefit of the doubt, my mother used the chart in Chapter Three of *How to Kick Cocaine in 14 Days*, to explain, ' "The antihistamines, coupled with the vitamins, reduce the body's craving for $C_{12}H_2NO_4$ . . . the addictive alkaloid in coke." ' Suddenly, she was a chemist.

'Do you snort them?' For a second, I thought she was going to slap me. When she laughed and hugged me, it was almost as cozy as when she used to get high in the bathroom and come out and watch *Speed Racer* with me on Saturday mornings.

'No, lambie, you don't snort them.' She was dividing them up, putting groups of seven in a plastic, two-week pillbox that looked like it was made to hold fishing lures.

'Where'd you get all this stuff?' I was helping her divide up the pills now.

'I drove to a pharmacy on Route 22.' She pointed out the window. 'Mr Osborne's butler, Herbert, brought over a car for us to use, and went over my schedule while you were sleeping.' A pale blue Peugeot station wagon was parked in the drive.

'Can I drive it?'

'No.'

'You let me drive in Maine when we visited Nana.'

'That was different.'

'All the roads here are private property. Gates told me so himself.'

'You don't have a driver's license, Finn.'

'Neither do you.'

'That's beside the point.'

'Really?'

'Finn, we're going to do things the right way now.'

'You have a book that tells you how to give up smack?'

'As a matter of fact, I do.' She pulled a bible-sized volume out of her purse and handed it to me. *The Complete Book of Chinese Healing.* She had dog-eared a chapter titled 'Opiates – recreational'. I read aloud the list of things she wasn't supposed to eat to wash the poppy from her system. ' "Cruciferous vegetables (that's stuff like broccoli, in case you've got a problem), garlic, raw fish, seaweed, almonds, bee pollen . . ." Wow. Where's the rhino horn and tiger gallbladder?'

'I know you're angry with me.'

'I'm not angry. I just want to drive the damn car.' I wasn't expecting her to throw the car keys in my face. They bounced off my forehead and landed in my cereal bowl with a splash.

'You win,' she said softly. It didn't feel that way. 'If you get arrested, I'll say you stole it.'

'You're not going to come with me?' She shook her head no and walked slowly to the liquor cabinet, took out a quart of gin and a fifth of vermouth. I thought she was going to resort to a martini.

'It's no fun if you're not there to freak out.' Slowly, she began to pour the liquor down the drain. Tossing the keys back into her purse, I helped her dump the contents of the liquor cabinet. While her back was turned, I hid a six-pack of Heineken in the crisper for Jilly.

I wasn't a total jerk. An hour later, I was sitting at the desk in my bedroom, making up a list of all the things I was never going to say or do again to hurt my mother's feelings. The trouble was, the list got so long so fast, I started to get depressed – if I stopped picking my mother's scabs, I'd have to start picking mine.

Thinking if I poured salt in my own wounds for a change, I might feel better, or at least have some sense of atonement, I decided to write my father a letter instead. He was waiting to hear if I was coming; why not tell him the truth? Get it off my chest. Reality was so unkind to all concerned, I balled it up when I found myself writing about the English musician asking my mother for some Vaseline.

Deciding to really punish myself, I tried to write a letter to my father as if nothing bad had happened, just to see how it would have felt.

Dear Dad,
   I will be arriving on the afternoon of the 24th. Being able to spend the summer with you and the Yanomamö is the most exciting thing that has ever happened to me. I read the book on kinship and primitive societies that you recommended . . .

After a few more false starts, I finally decided on the following distortion of the facts:

Dear Dad,
   I am sad to say I don't think it will be possible for me to spend the summer with you. Mom and I discussed it, and decided both you and I would get more out of the trip if I waited until next year (that way I would be old enough to drive the Land Rover for you). I apologize for the last-minute change in plans, and hope it did not cause you any inconvenience. You will be glad to know I will be putting my time to good use this summer preparing for my SATs and working on my Spanish. Two areas that will need some improvement if I want to get accepted at Harvard . . .

Considering that I'd flunked Spanish and my combined Math and Verbal PSAT score was under 800, I had a better chance at playing shortstop for the New York Yankees than I did of getting into Harvard. But it was where my father went to college, and I thought it was the sort of letter he would have liked his son to write. The fact that I wasn't that person was beside the point. Why should both of us be disappointed in me?
   Knowing my mother would have wanted to know what I had written, I didn't tell her about the letter. When she loaded her rolling massage table into the back of the Peugeot, and drove off to her first session with Mr Osborne, I set out for the Vlyvalle Post Office on foot.
   I retraced the route Gates had taken when he drove us onto the estate. Kicking a stone down the dirt road that edged the cornfield,

my shoes caked in dust, seeing a white-tailed buck in the piney woods rubbing the bloody velvet off his antlers on a tree trunk, stopping in the middle of the bridge and spitting into a trout pool, the smell of honeysuckle and horse manure in the air, all with a letter to my father in my pocket that spoke of my intention to attend Harvard University . . . I felt like JohnBoy-fucking-Walton.

In fact, by the time I had walked a country mile, I was thinking to myself, 'Why *not* Harvard?' Every single one of the teachers who had flunked me made a point of telling my mother I was an incorrigible under-achiever. What if I did spend the summer studying the SAT book my mother bought me and listening to my Spanish ALM records? So what if I left them in New York City with my beat-off magazines? Mom would buy me new ALM records. '*Hola, Isabella,*' I repeated to myself, '*Como está usted?*' '*Está Bien?*' '*Sí, gracias.*' This was going to be the first day of the rest of my life. I had made up my mind. I was going to make everything I'd written to my father come true. In my mind, I hadn't just gotten into Harvard, I was graduating – with honors in Anthropology. I'd written an article about my experiences with my father and the Yanomamö. It had been published in *The New Yorker*. My father had ditched his wife and was sitting holding my mother's hand, and I had an old MG, just like the one Ryan O'Neal drove in *Love Story*. And a girlfriend who looked just like Julie Christie. She wasn't in *Love Story*, but she was more my type than Ali McGraw.

Who knows what I would have gone on to accomplish if Jilly's boyfriend hadn't fishtailed around the corner in his jacked-up GTO. He didn't look happy to see me. Especially when Jilly started shouting, 'Stop the car – it's Finn!' He slowed just long enough to throw an empty beer can at me.

'Yo, pothead, stay away from my girlfriend or you're dead meat.' I wondered why she had told him about smoking pot, and ducked. When he missed, he slammed on the brakes, backed up, and took aim with a full one, which would have hit me for sure if she hadn't grabbed his arm. As they sped off she called him an asshole, then looked back at me and mouthed the word, 'Sorry,' with a big smile on her Easter Island face.

After I hid in the bushes for ten minutes, I felt brave enough to step out into the middle of the road and shout, 'Fuck you!' I picked up the beer cans. It was what my father would have expected. It was also something to throw in case Jilly's boyfriend decided to come back for another try at roadkill.

I hadn't walked very far when I heard a conversation coming at me down the road. A girl with a bored voice was in the middle of telling a story about somebody named Bryce, who'd dyed his hair white and taken somebody named Coco to Bryce's cousin's débutante party. From the way they were laughing, you would have thought it was funny. A boy with a shrill voice was incredulous.

'He took Coco who went to Concord to Piping Rock?'

'Did they let her in?' another guy asked, who had kind of a fake English accent that sounded like a female impersonator doing Katherine Hepburn.

'They had to. Bryce said she was his fiancée,' the bored girl answered.

'What did his mother say?' the shrill one wanted to know.

'Congratulations,' a second girl deadpanned. Everyone thought this was a scream.

'I do not understand the joke,' an Italian accent protested.

'Coco's a Negro,' the bored girl whispered, like it was a dirty word. The Italian still didn't seem to see the humor. He wasn't the only one.

'She's black,' someone said. 'And really rich. Her father's, like, King of Nigeria.'

'Black and Negro, they are the same, no?' the Italian asked.

'Sometimes.' A couple of them thought this was a scream, too. The voices were heads now, bobbing on the other side of a hedgerow. Three boys, and two girls. They sounded older than they were. When they came into full view, I stepped back behind a tree so they couldn't see me. They were on horseback. Even if they hadn't been in costume, it would have been clear that these were members of a different local tribe than the one Jilly and her boyfriend belonged to. They were all wearing jodhpurs and riding boots, and velvet hard hats – the whole tally-ho bit.

'Bryce thinks he's so sophisticated it makes me want to puke.' A big fleshy boy with two chins, a spare tire, and a set of titties that could have filled a B-cup was talking. 'His whole liberal act . . . he just does it to get attention. Christ, the guy's always dragging some Hawaiian out to play golf at Maidstone.'

'Ian, I don't mean to be rude, but isn't your grandmother a Hawaiian?' A blonde girl with breasts just like Ian's interrupted. She was the bored voice. Ian didn't look Hawaiian to me. Red-headed and sunburned, he had the face of a baby that had been parboiled.

'My grandmother's Catholic.' Ian had the la-di-da accent.

I was baffled. A Catholic Hawaiian is more socially acceptable than a Protestant Hawaiian? This was definitely a different tribe. They were speaking English but I didn't understand what they were saying. Their horses had stopped to drink from a brook. The quiet girl threw one leg over her saddle and blew smoke rings sidesaddle, as casual as if she was sitting on a barstool. Her hair was pulled back in one long braid. Her face was tan, except for the whiteness of a scar that ran from the corner of her lip to just below her ear.

'Bryce is an idiot.' Ian wanted to get off the subject of Hawaiians.

'He got into Harvard, Mr Rollins.' The blonde smiled sweetly.

'Low blow,' a skinny boy with hair down to his shoulders said it like he was a referee.

When they stopped laughing at him, Ian turned to the blonde. 'Blow me, Paige.'

'In your dreams.' She turned to the skinny boy. 'What did your 'rents say when you totaled your Porsche?'

'Actually, they were kind of proud of me that I passed the breathalyzer test.'

'I guess it's a good thing you stopped drinking and started taking 'ludes.'

'Rollins is the best college in Florida.' I thought Rollins was Ian's last name.

'Wow, I'm impressed.'

'My point is, Bryce's act isn't as irresistible as he thinks.' Ian wouldn't let it go.

'Then why are you always talking about him?' It was the first thing the girl with the scar had said.

'Because it just pisses me off he thinks he's soooo cool.' Harvard? Nigerian princess? Bryce sounded pretty cool to me.

'Ian, you just haven't forgiven my brother for beating you up after you got caught copping a feel off Amanda's retarded sister.'

'Hey, Maya, I didn't know she was retarded.'

'She's hydrocephalic, for God's sake. She has a forehead you could land a plane on.' The other three shrieked with laughter. It was actually pretty funny how Bryce's sister nailed him. Somebody said, 'Ouch,' and Ian's horse reared up. Ian cursed and yanked the horse's head around, then walked the animal in my direction. That's when he saw me.

When he got up close enough for the animal to bite me, Ian talked down to me.

'You new here?'

'Yeah.' I was still holding the beer cans.

'Well, if you want to keep your job you better pick up the cans you missed down the road.'

Unbelievable but true: in the wilds of New Jersey I had found a tribe as strange, cruel and unlovable as the Yanomamö. I was grotesquely fascinated.

6

We'd been in Vlyvalle two weeks. In the morning, my mother worked on Mr Osborne. In the afternoons, she went to AA meetings. The rest of the time, we tried not to argue. Except for two trips to a supermarket the size of an airplane hangar over on Route 22, and my schlep to the village post office, I hadn't set foot beyond the yellow guesthouse and its rectangle of yard. My mother was feeling better. The antihistamines? The bee pollen? To this day, I think the key to her cure was the constant stream of Diet Cokes and Marlboro Lights she inhaled throughout the day. Caffeine, saccharin, and nicotine. She called it her poor-man's speedball. She wasn't as much fun as she used to be, but she could still be funny.

I really began to worry about who my mother was becoming when she started to jog. Wearing Nikes and sweatpants, her sports bra silhouetted beneath the damp cling of a T-shirt with a smiley face on it; she'd come panting into the house. Wanting me to feel better so she'd feel better about feeling better, my mother would pop open a can of Diet Coke, light up a Marlboro Light and wheeze, 'Why don't you go outside and explore . . . enjoy nature. Get some fresh air . . . Maybe you'll meet some kids your own age.'

I hadn't told her about my encounter with the natives on horse-back. I don't know whether it was boredom or loneliness or the fact that the TV was broken that prompted the budding young anthro-pologist in me to make notes on them as if they were a lost tribe in the Amazon Basin, rather than five spoiled rich kids who snubbed me on a country road.

Ian   Mean fat kid on white horse, felt up retard. Hawaiian, but doesn't look it.

Maya	Scar on face. Sister of Bryce. Blows smoke rings.
Skinny kid	Has own Porsche. Gave up liquor for ludes.
Italian	Can't tell if stupid, or just Italian.
Paige	Blonde, big boobs. Always sounds bored.
Bryce	?

Next to my father, my all-time favorite anthropologist was Napoleon A Chagnon, author of *Yanomamö: The Fierce People*. (A classic, native tittie-filled text I am embarrassed to say I was presently using as a replacement for my waterlogged copy of *Natural History*.) But my point is, when I wasn't jacking off to the pictures, I noticed that some of the stuff Chagnon said about his experiences in Amazonia seemed to apply to my situation in Vlyvalle. What's an anthropologist but the new kid in town? Like Chagnon said when he moved in next door to the Yanomamö, 'I was determined to work my way into their moral system of kinship and become a member of their society – to be "accepted" by them.'

Admittedly, I had gotten off to a bad beginning. I let that fat asshole Ian dismiss me as one of the hired help, and had been too chicken to set the record straight. But I took some comfort in the knowledge that even the great Chagnon was so depressed after his first meeting with the locals, he wrote, 'I am not ashamed to admit that had there been a diplomatic way out I would have ended my field work then and there.'

I found a pair of binoculars hanging from a hook in a back porch that Jilly called the mudroom. Several times a day I scanned the horizon, hoping to catch sight of the five exotic teenagers on horseback who had captured my imagination. Lots of people rode within sight of our yellow house. One morning I was awakened by a pack of fifty brown-and-white foxhounds, closely followed by as many men and women on horseback, some but not all wearing red tail coats and top hats, all galloping at full throttle after an unseen fox. But by the time I got my binoculars to my sleepy eyes, they were too far away for me to make out the faces of the riders. I don't know what I thought I would have said to make them stop and take notice of me.

Why was I not equally intrigued with Jilly and her people? I knew now that her father was Mr Osborne's head dairyman and her mother one of Mr Osborne's maids. What if Jilly had a Porsche? And blew smoke rings on horseback? Having only recently accepted the fact that I was a pathological liar, I was reluctant to admit to being a natural-born snob. I told myself my interest in Jilly wouldn't have waned (though I still wasn't above watching her clean with her uniform unbuttoned) if her boyfriend hadn't threatened to kill me.

I looked for those five rich kids every day. Each night I went to bed without seeing them, I became more and more certain that contact was an impossibility; acceptance, a pipe dream. The idea that I would never find out how Maya got her scar, or ride in the skinny kid's Porsche, or see just how big Amanda's hydrocephalic sister's head was, or meet Bryce, who dated a Nigerian princess named Coco, made me feel like a total loser. I wasn't sure which was more depressing, the awareness that I wanted to be accepted by them, or the realization that I never would be.

7

The fifty acres of corn that surrounded the guesthouse that imprisoned me seemed to have shot up a full foot since we arrived. I felt like a big green wall was growing between me and a life I could not define but knew I was missing.

'Why do you go all the way to Morristown for your AA meetings?' It was a forty-minute drive each way. My mother only had her learner's permit, and was terrified of getting busted.

She had changed out of her jogging outfit, and was standing in front of the mirror, checking out a lime-green sweater set she wouldn't have been caught dead in back in the city. Not even when she was dressing to hit up Nana and Grandpa for money.

'Because I feel more comfortable sharing in front of people who don't know me.' The weird thing was, I could see my mother liked the look. She gave herself a conspiratorial smile in the mirror. I wasn't trying to be mean . . . yet. But I could tell she didn't like hearing me say, 'No one knows you in Vlyvalle.'

'Well, when they get to know me, I'd rather they hear about my problems from me rather than . . .'

'I thought the whole idea of AA was it's anonymous.'

'You know how people are.' The only person I thought I really knew was her. And I was starting to have my doubts.

'So, we're going to tell everyone the truth?' I was surprised how much I liked the idea. Like most habitual liars, dishonesty wasn't something I prided myself on.

'Eventually.' My mother stopped looking at herself and turned toward me. 'I'm trying to make a good life for us.'

'When are you going to introduce me to Mr Osborne?' It wasn't as much of a *non sequitur* as it seemed.

'I work for Mr Osborne . . .' She was looking for the keys to the Peugeot she still wouldn't let me drive. 'Staying in his guesthouse doesn't mean we're friends . . . I'm an employee.' She was talking to herself as much as to me.

'Is that his helicopter?' A blue and white Bell Jet helicopter flew low over the tree tops like a big bug.

'Looks like it.'

'Think he'd give me a ride?'

'He didn't bring us here to socialize.'

'Why'd he give us a guest membership to the Hunt Club?'

'What are you talking about?'

'Gates told me we were guest members.'

'When?'

'When you were passed out in the back of his car.'

'Why didn't you mention it?' I'd heard that same urgent edge to her voice when she'd misplaced her blow.

'It didn't seem like a big deal.' I could tell it was to her. She would have made a super-big deal out of me not mentioning it if Jilly hadn't walked in. She cleaned two half-days a week for us.

Jilly punched me in the arm as she said, 'How's it hanging, Finn?' If she didn't do it so hard, I would have thought she was flirting.

'Hi, Mrs Earl.' My unwed mother had become a 'Mrs' since she'd arrived in Vlyvalle.

'Hi, Jilly.' There was a dismissive tone in my mother's voice; she wanted Jilly out of earshot so she could talk to me about the Hunt Club.

'Mrs Earl?'

'What?'

'I was just wondering, do you prefer to be called "Mrs Earl" or "Dr Earl"?'

'What?' If Jilly hadn't been assembling the vacuum cleaner she would have known something was up from the expression on my mother's face.

'Finn told me how you went to homeopathic medical school in France and my mother said I should ask you whether you like to be called "Mrs" or "Dr", because Mr Slossen, the dentist, always gets his nose out of joint if you forget to call him "Dr".' I could see my mother's jaw muscles tighten. The veins in her neck pulsed.

'I'd like you to call me . . .' My mother had to think about it for a moment. '. . . Liz.'

'I wish my mom was like you.' We all smiled stupidly at each other.

'Finn, I have something for you in the car.' I followed my mother out of the house, like a dog that knows it's going to get beaten for leaving a mess. As soon as we were out of sight she whipped around and grabbed my wrist so hard her fingernails gave me a blood blister.

'What are you trying to do? Telling her I'm a doctor? Are you crazy?' Once she realized I was ashamed of her, my mother's rage rose to the second power.

'Want me to go in and tell her I lied?' My mother tightened her grip on my arm. 'You want to tell her the truth?' When I threatened her, she let go of me.

Jilly was around the side of the house, emptying the vacuum bag into the garbage. She called out my mother's name, awkward with the familiarity. 'Doctor . . . I mean, Liz . . .'

'Yes, Jilly?' My mother sounded like she was on staff at General Hospital.

'Is it easier to get into medical school in France than in the States?'

'Much easier,' my mother told her between clenched teeth.

'Mom's just being modest – it's really hard.'

'You think I'd have a shot at it? I got twelve hundred on my college-board SATs combined.'

'France is pretty far away. Why don't you go to college in the States and then decide?' My mother got in the car. She started out the driveway, then stopped, backed up and rolled down the window. She was about to say something, but I beat her to the punch.

'Forget something, Doc?' What bothered me most was, I wasn't sure whether I was trying to make things harder or easier for us.

Back inside, I flopped on the living-room couch and watched Jilly vacuum a threadbare carpet my mom told me was a prayer rug that belonged in a museum. Actually, I mostly watched the way her breasts jiggled inside her tube-top each time she pushed the vacuum head out across the carpet, and then pulled it back again. She kept her maid's uniform buttoned up when my mother was around, but when we were alone in the house, her wool allergy always seemed to act up, and she'd unbutton it.

'Jilly?' I asked.

'What?' She couldn't hear me over the vacuum.

'The other day . . .' I was working up to asking her if she knew the kids on horseback.

'What'd you say?' She silenced the vacuum cleaner with her toe.

'You know the road where you and Dwayne threw the beer cans at me? Did you happen to notice . . .'

'I figured that's why you've been ignoring me.'

'I haven't been ignoring you.'

'You haven't offered me a beer.'

'You want a beer?'

'Yes please.' I got two from the six-pack I had hidden in the crisper. 'Why's your mom keep 'em in there?' She'd followed me into the kitchen.

'They stay fresher.'

Jilly laughed and told me, 'You're funny.' She finished half her Heineken in one gulp, belched loud and long, and we both laughed. 'You want some Vlyvalle red?'

'What?'

'Homegrown.' She pulled a damp, folded newspaper out of her purse. Inside, was a two-foot-long marijuana plant. It didn't look at all like the shit Slurpee and I bought in Washington Square Park. There was still dirt on its roots.

'We'll dry it out in the oven. Got some aluminum foil?'

An hour later, we were so baked my lips were numb, and my mouth was so dry I felt like someone had stolen my saliva. After considerable effort, I was finally able to articulate, 'This is good shit.'

'Yeah,' Jilly held in her toke until she gagged. 'The insecticide gives the buzz a kick.'

'The what?' For some reason I thought this was very funny.

'DDT, Bug-B-Gone, they're always spraying it with something.'

'Who?' I was so high, I didn't even notice her tube-top had shifted around, exposing the top half of her right breast and the bottom half of her left one. Except for nipple, I was seeing total tittie.

'Maya and Bryce.' I had forgotten that they were part of the reason I had started this conversation two hours ago.

'You know them?'

'Well enough to steal their pot. They've got this whole big, huge plot of it over by the gorge.'

'What are they like?'

'Weird . . . but good weird.'

'What's good weird?' The homegrown that had me talking like Lenny in *Of Mice and Men* suddenly made Jilly loquacious.

'Like on Christmas Eve when they were little kids, they'd have this huge tree and get all these presents, I mean like two of everything from Schwartz's toy store. But come Christmas Day, they'd only get to keep one present.'

'What'd they do with all the other presents?'

'They'd have to re-wrap them, then their father would dress up as Santa Claus, and put Maya and Bryce in these elf costumes, and he'd drive them around the county, and they'd have to give away all the rest of their presents to farmers' kids.'

'I would have hated that.'

'I don't think Bryce liked it too much either. I remember one year he had these two remote-controlled toy cars, I mean, this was like ten years before you could buy them at regular stores, one was red and the other was white. He knew his parents would only let him keep one, and he couldn't decide which one he wanted to keep. When he started to cry over it, his father made him give them both away.'

'What a bummer.'

'Not for me. That year I got a stuffed bear that talked to you. I remember they said it cost over seven hundred bucks.'

'How'd it talk?'

'It had a tape recorder inside.'

'What'd it say?'

' "I'm stoned." ' Jilly was funnier than the story.

'That's fucked up.'

'They're not as fucked up as the rest of the rich people out here. Of course, maybe that's just because they're richer than everybody else. Except for old man Osborne. He's Mrs Langley's father.'

'Really?' The homegrown and Jilly's anecdote had me thinking about our last Xmas in NYC. My mother was so high when she wrapped the presents she got my gift mixed up with the one she bought for the Scientologist she dated to get through the holiday blues. It was sort of funny, unwrapping a present from your mother and discovering *The Joys of Tantric Sex*.

'My dad says it's genetic.'

'What?'

'Weirdness.'

I hoped her dad was wrong.

'He breeds cows. And he says with animals and people all you gotta do is look at the bloodline. Course, he doesn't know shit about people, but he knows all about animals. And like, if you dated Dwayne as long as I have, you know that's all guys are, so, who knows, maybe they do get it from their grandfather.'

'Get what?' I looked at the joint in my hand, and wondered what I had caught from my mother.

Jilly suddenly decided to cut the small talk short. 'Open your mouth.' I watched in amazement as she abruptly put the joint, burning end first, into her mouth, locked her lips on mine, then exhaled. I felt like I had the tailpipe of a car that was burning oil shoved down my throat.

As I gagged for air I could taste her Chapstick on my lips. Laughing, she draped her arms over my shoulders. 'You never had a shotgun?'

'Total virgin.' I blushed at my choice of words. I was too stoned to realize she thought I was egging her on.

'Want to fool around?' She propositioned me with a giggle. At that moment there was nothing I wanted more in the world. She pulled her tube-top down, closed her eyes, parted her lips, and waited for my kiss. There was no time to check my breath. I bent my face towards hers. Then, not wanting her large, but now adorable, Aku-Aku schnoz to get in the way of the most romantic moment I had so far experienced in my life, I tilted my head and readjusted my approach angle.

If I had not hesitated, I would never have been distracted from Jilly and her now naked, gravity-defying breasts. But out my kitchen window, I suddenly saw a blur of black and chrome veer off the dirt road and plow into the cornfield. It was a convertible Bentley. When it came to a stop, a small man with a silver goatee wearing nothing but a paisley bathrobe and unlaced hiking boots stepped out. He pulled an ear of corn from a stalk and husked it with a sure hand, wafting it under his nose, like he was savoring the cork of a bottle of Chateau Rothschild '37. Then he bit into it and chewed thoughtfully.

When I reached for my binoculars, Jilly realized my mind was elsewhere. Seeing what I was distracted by, she pulled up her tube-top and told me, 'You're weird,' and went back to vacuuming. I knew she didn't mean 'good weird'. When I looked back, Osborne was gone.

8

I woke up at 3.23 a.m. and vomited. I was so upset about the opportunity I had missed with Jilly that I made myself sick. I had waited over fifteen years – eighteen thousand, one hundred and fifty-nine days for a girl to ask me to fool around and when it finally happens, I get distracted by an old man in a bathrobe.

How could I have blown it so completely? She had pulled down her frigging tube-top for me. Why hadn't I kissed her? I should have at least given myself the satisfaction of touching at least one of her titties before I reached for the fucking binoculars. As I flopped back in bed, my mouth sour with puke, her breasts glowed perfect, white, round and delicious as vanilla wafers in the darkness of my imagination. What was wrong with me? I was so angry, disappointed and disgusted with myself that I didn't even attempt to beat my meat to the memory of her offering. It was the least I could do to show her I cared.

The next day, when my mother answered the phone in the kitchen, a frown crossed her face. She told whoever she was talking to, 'I'm going to switch phones,' and asked me to hang up when she was on. Naturally, I listened in. It was my grandfather. He was shouting, but he sounded like he was going to cry.

'I can't believe you'd resort to something like this.'

'I don't know what you're talking about.' From the way she said it, I knew she knew.

'Mr Osborne's lawyer came to see me at the university. My graduate students were there, for chrissake.'

Nana chimed in, 'Hurting us doesn't change the fact that you still need help.'

'I've got help.' I could hear my mother inhaling with a smile. 'What'd the lawyer have to say?'

'You know goddamn well what he said. He's trumped up a restraining order signed by the Chief of Police to have us arrested if we – I believe the expression he used was "continued to harass and menace" you and Finn.'

Nana was talking at the same time. 'He implied your friend, Mr Osborne, is in a position to cost your father his grant.'

'Well, maybe you two should stop harassing and menacing us and fuck off.'

It was definitely cool to hear my mother tell her parents to fuck off. But I wished I'd hung up before I heard Grandpa say, 'Elizabeth, you've always had a problem with low self-esteem and promiscuity but, for Finn's sake, you ought to remember you'll need us when he finds a new sexual outlet.'

When my mother came downstairs, she asked me if I wanted pancakes. It was three in the afternoon.

Two days later, when Jilly came to clean the house, she didn't even say hello. I had this whole apology worked up. I was going to blame my seeming lack of interest on the insecticide-dusted pot. But as soon as I started to grovel, she turned on the vacuum. Jilly acted as if I wasn't even in the room. Sadder still, in spite of her wool allergy, she kept her maid's uniform buttoned up to her neck.

Oddly enough, what really hurt my feelings was that she didn't even bother to say something insulting. I was desperate enough to tell her the real reason Osborne had the power to blind me to her charms, but I knew if I blurted out what was short-circuiting my libido, 'I think my mom's rubbing more than Mr Osborne's back,' I would have had to tell Jilly my mother was a masseuse – which would have meant admitting I was lying when I led her to believe my mother was a homeopathic doctor who studied in France. Which, in turn, would have implied I was embarrassed by my mother. Which, of course, would have made me seem as appealing as something dirty stuck to the bottom of her shoe. Unless, of course, I confessed why I had good reason to be embarrassed of my mother, which would have in turn opened up a still nastier can of worms which . . . Anyway, you get the general idea why I decided it was probably best for all parties concerned for me to let Jilly go on thinking I was a simple, straightforward jerk.

It wasn't like I didn't try to make it up to her. I even helped her carry out the garbage. She didn't actually say 'Thank you'. But a curt 'Screw you' was better than nothing. At least we were communicating. While she loaded the dishwasher, I pretended I had stuff to do in the kitchen. When I saw her unbutton the top two buttons of her maid's uniform, I thought she might be warming up to me. She let me know this was no thaw in her icy reserve when she called her mother up on the phone.

'God, this job sucks.' I could hear her mother tell her not to say 'sucks'. 'OK, it eats shit. It's boilin' in here. You know how to turn up the air-conditioner?' Jilly held the receiver away from her head. Her mother's voice was loud and metallic. I could hear her cluck:

'Jeez-Louise, Jilly, of course it's hot. It's the first frigging day of summer.'

The magnetized calendar on the refrigerator door hadn't been changed since the day we arrived. I reset the date so Jilly wouldn't think I was eavesdropping. She was on the phone to Dwayne now.

'Yes, he's in the room, unfortunately . . . No! I don't want you to come over and beat him like a red-haired stepchild . . . Why? Because if you left work in the middle of the day you'd lose your job, silly.' I let the magnetized two and one click into place on the refrigerator door. June 21. Suddenly it hit me. I'd been in Vlyvalle nearly three weeks. June 21 – 4.30 p.m. My mother and I were supposed to be in Juvenile Court. It was three-thirty.

'Fucking shit!' I shouted.

I didn't even hear Jilly tell Dwayne, 'No, he's not talking to me . . . he's yellin' at the refrigerator door . . . I don't know why – I told you, he's a weird kid.'

I ran up the stairs to my mother's bedroom. The social worker had given her some papers. There had to be a number to call.

'Fucking bitch.' I screamed, as I slammed her door behind me. The irony that my mother was unreachable at an AA meeting was not lost on me. The cop said if I fucked up again I would be sent to a juvenile home.

Thinking up and discarding excuses, I upended my mother's

purses and rummaged through her drawers, searching for the court papers. I could say I was sick . . . they'd want a doctor's note. And even if I got away with faking it, they'd wonder why my mother wasn't calling to reschedule. But if I just broke my leg . . . just like ten minutes ago? Good concept, tough to fake. I looked out the window and down at the ground and calculated. If I jumped, I could break my neck. (As panicky as I was, I still had the presence of mind to realize I would rather be in a juvenile home than be wheeled around in a wheelchair by my mother for the rest of my life.) But if I hung from the windowsill and shortened my fall, I could be reasonably certain of walking away with a doctor-certified broken leg. Or if I was lucky, maybe just a broken ankle.

I still needed the number of the social worker. (Better to make the call before I jumped out the window.) I would have called New York Information, but I couldn't remember her name. Jilly was knocking on the door now. I guess she heard me shriek, 'What the fuck is she thinking about?'

'Hey, Finn, what's wrong?'

'Everything.'

'Can I help?'

'Not right now.' For a millisecond, I considered asking her to come in, unbutton her uniform, pull down her tube-top, and help me search the room for the court papers. But I knew I didn't have time to explain or enjoy the experience. 'Maybe later.' Once I found the number and called the social worker and jumped out the window, I'd need someone to drive me to the hospital.

'OK, but I'm still mad at you.' Nothing in her drawers or her purses. I pulled a suitcase out from under her bed. It was locked. The court papers had to be inside. I looked at the alarm clock on the bedside table. We were supposed to be in court in thirty-five minutes.

'Why is she doing this to me?' I wailed to myself, and then it hit me. My mother wanted me to miss the court date. She wants me to go to a juvenile home. Now that she's sober, she's talked it over with her pals at AA, and decided her new life in Vlyvalle would be a whole lot easier without a little shit like me complicating everything by telling people she was a French doctor and . . . I popped the lock of the suitcase with a nail file.

The court papers were there in a folder. Pyle was the name of the social worker. I called her number. It was busy. I tried it again and I got through. Miss Pyle asked me to hold before I even got my name out. I was halfway there. Now for the big lie.

I stopped scanning the part of the document that outlined what would happen if I missed the court appearance when I read 'Miss Elizabeth Earl and/or her legal representative is ordered to appear in Juvenile Court, Room 203, 17 Chambers Street, New York, New York at 4.30 p.m. June 23.' That was the day after tomorrow. I'd panicked forty-eight hours early. Miss Pyle was on the line now.

'How can I help you?' I was so fucked up on so many different levels, I didn't know where to begin.

'Sorry, wrong number.'

The fact that I was a panic-artist was no news to me. But when I returned my court papers to the suitcase and looked inside a large manila envelope that was wrapped up in an old nightgown, I did get a surprise. Inside, were all these neatly clipped magazine and newspaper articles about Mr Osborne: *Time Magazine*, the *Herald Tribune*, the *Tatler, Town & Country*, the *New York Sun, Forbes*, the *Wall Street Journal, Yachting, Hollywood Confidential* – some of them were fifty years old. She had a file on Osborne as thick as a ham sandwich.

Why was my mother hiding this man's life in a locked suitcase under her bed? Why had she gone through all of this effort? Had she done it since we moved to Vlyvalle? When she said she was going to AA, was she really at some library? Or had she checked him out when he was in that hospital in New York and she first started putting her healing hands on him. The fact that my mother was studying the old man was almost as disconcerting as the idea that she was climbing onto the massage table with him.

Hearing the Peugeot pull up in front of the house, I quickly stuffed the articles back into the suitcase and shoved it under the bed. As my mother walked towards the front door, I hurriedly refilled the upended purses and quietly closed the dresser drawers I had rifled. I was standing at the top of the stairs when she stepped into the house. I could tell she was in an extra-good mood because she was singing 'The Way We Were' to herself: ' "Memories light the corners of my mind . . ." '

'What were you shouting about?' Jilly asked as she put the vacuum cleaner away, and got ready to leave.

My mother answered for me. 'He hates Barbra Streisand.' At that moment, I hated her more than Babs. My mother sang another verse just to show me nothing, not even a belligerent teenager, was going to spoil her natural high.

'How was your meeting?' I asked innocently. Jilly didn't act like she knew I was referring to AA. My mother shot me a look for threatening her anonymity.

'Fine.' She had a large white box under her arm. 'How was your day?'

'Interesting.'

'You sound serious.'

'I think I'll go now.' Sensing a storm was coming, Jilly slipped out the door.

'What's wrong?'

I waited until she was out of earshot before I answered.

'You know, we have to be at court the day after tomorrow.'

'You don't have to go.'

'What?'

'Finn, I know I was the reason you got in trouble. That doesn't excuse what you did. You did something foolish that was also illegal, and I hope the whole experience makes you realize how dangerous drugs are. But . . . part of AA is accepting responsibility for one's actions so it's my responsibility to keep you from having a criminal record.' She took a deep breath and closed her eyes, like a kid saying her prayers. 'Let's make this a fresh start. For both of us.'

I would have preferred a simple 'I got you into this mess, I'll get you out of it'.

'Why don't I have to go to court?'

'Mr Osborne fixed things.'

'How?'

'He knows everybody. It wasn't official until this morning.'

'What's in the box?'

65

'Mr Osborne bought me a dress.' I didn't know the interlocking Cs on the box stood for Chanel, but I could tell it was expensive.

'He fixes my court and he buys you a dress? What's going on?'

'He invited me to the Hunt Club. We're going there tonight.' She looked at her watch. She ran up the stairs two at a time. 'He said he'd been meaning to take us up there and show us around. I've got to wash my hair and be out of here in an hour.'

The prospect of going to the Hunt Club improved my mood considerably. I ran up after her. 'Do I have to wear a tie?' I followed her into her bedroom.

'I thought it'd be better if the first time I went by myself.' I watched her pull a sleeveless pink T-shirt with a circle pinned on it over her head. 'You understand, don't you, lambie?'

'Hope you wear a bra tonight.' I understood.

Drugs used to be the secret passion my mother did not know we shared, now we had Mr Osborne. As soon as she left for the dinner I had convincingly pretended I didn't mind not being invited to, I ran up to her bedroom, pulled out her stash of clippings and began to read.

Two hours of skimming told me the following: everything about Ogden C Osborne except what the C stood for. He was born in 1903 in Hoboken, New Jersey. His father, Jake, was an unsuccessful hardware salesman but a gifted amateur photographer. When Osborne was fourteen, his father transformed himself into a man of substance overnight by obtaining a contract to supply wire to a telephone company that was stringing a wire from St Louis to San Francisco. The contract was for all the wire. Ogden was packed off to someplace called St Mark's. After that, he went to Harvard but dropped out in the fall of his freshman year – that's easy to do when your father drops dead in the ninth inning of the third game of the 1923 World Series and you inherit just under two million dollars. A sum which, according to the March 1975 issue of *Forbes*, Osborne managed to husband into a little over three billion dollars – not so easy to do.

A lot of the business stuff was lost on me. The gist of it was he invested early in crackpot ideas everybody who finished Harvard

66

said people would never pay for. All of it seemed pretty obvious to me. I mean, you'd have to be a dope not to realize people would rather listen to cheap radios in cars as opposed to having no radios at all. And staying home and watching black-and-white TV instead of just staying home? Or flying tourist instead of not flying at all? Talk about no-brainers. I have to admit, though, his latest scheme seemed pretty hare-brained to me. It was something called cellular phones. I just couldn't see people carrying around telephones the size of a suitcase. Especially when talking on them cost like a hundred bucks a minute.

Even though I didn't read every word of every article, it was obvious Osborne's life wasn't all about making money. He married a governor's daughter, and took her on a six-month honeymoon in Italy. Two weeks after they got home, she died of influenza. After that, he dated Merle Oberon and *Leave it to Beaver*'s mom, and was engaged to the daughter of this South American dictator, who I never heard of but who was a total babe. He ended up married to a Standard Oil heiress and had a daughter he named after a sailboat – Pilar.

There were a lot of pictures of the Standard Oil wife jumping over fences on horses named after inclement weather. I kept expecting to come across an article about her divorcing him because even though he was married, all these magazines kept printing pictures of him out on dates with movie stars. One was this Swedish bombshell with mega-boobs who I'd never heard of named Anita Ekberg. An English magazine called *Tatler* had this great picture of her on Osborne's yacht holding a towel up to her chest. You could tell she was naked. The article said it was 'rumored' Osborne nailed Grace Kelly on the same boat. I believed it.

In 1958, he ran for Senate as an independent and lost. After that, people said he was kind of a rat for giving megabucks to both parties so it didn't matter who won. None of the articles said he was retired, but it seemed to me that for the last ten years or so he devoted himself to hobbies like saving endangered species, buying art at rip-off prices that turned out to be bargains, and donating large sums of money to causes he knew would piss off his rich friends.

When I finished the last of the articles, it was both easier and harder to imagine my mother doing it with Ogden C Osborne at age seventy-three (if he had been fifty, there would have been no question about it). I was jealous, I was envious, and most disturbing of all, I became aware of a cold reptilian lobe in my brain tempting me to consider the possibility that my mother screwing this billionaire fossil wouldn't be the worst thing that could happen to me.

As I put the articles back in the envelope, I felt so low I would have needed a stool to touch bottom. When I was checking the room to make sure everything was where my mother had left it, I found a clipping had fallen behind the headboard. It was a faded page from the financial section of a paper that had long since gone out of business. I didn't bother to read the whole thing, but Osborne gave some advice on page fourteen to the readers of the November 5, 1961 issue of the *Herald Tribune* that I've always remembered but never followed:

In business and in love, there's only one way to avoid disappointment. Never ask a question you don't already know the answer to.

9

My mother left the house every day at nine, and didn't come home until after six. She had a whole life I didn't know about. It wasn't a secret; I just couldn't imagine it. She made a list before she went to bed each night of all the things she had to do the next day. She did Osborne between nine-thirty and eleven-thirty. They had lunch every day at twelve. On Mondays, Wednesdays, and Fridays, she drove to the Summerville Y for an aerobics class. On Tuesdays, Thursdays and Saturdays, she went to yoga lessons this lady with thirteen cats gave in her living room in Bernardsville. Seven days a week, rain or shine, five o'clock sharp, she was in the front row of the AA meeting in the basement of the Presbyterian church in Morristown. On Sundays, we argued about why I wouldn't go jogging with her in the morning. In the afternoon, I watched her read self-help books. It was like living with Rocky Balboa. She was in training for being a grown-up, full time. Sometimes, just to piss her off while she was making her lists at night or stretching for a three-mile run or grossing me out by putting orange juice instead of milk on her granola because it was healthier, I'd sing the theme song to *Rocky*. 'Getting strong now . . .'

I didn't mind the stuff she did in Bernardsville and Morristown and Summerville. It's what went on in the heart of that Bermuda Triangle of health, wealth, and happiness between nine-thirty and eleven-thirty with Osborne that bothered me.

The morning after I found the clippings, I set off on foot thirty minutes before my mother left to give Mr Osborne his daily massage.

She had told me when the weather was good they 'did it' (her expression, not mine) outside on a terrace beneath his screened-in sleeping-porch. The sky was screaming, seamless blue. Not a cloud in sight. I was determined to be there when she arrived. I was going to watch the whole thing, see just how she applied the oil and her healing hands to his flesh. I had even brought my binoculars.

Would she warm her hands by rubbing them together before she laid them on him? Or use the heat of her breath? Maybe they no longer bothered with the pretense of massage. If they went up to the sleeping-porch, I would follow. My mother said they locked up the Alsatians when she came over. She was scared of big dogs, Mr Osborne excepted, of course. I wasn't going to make a scene or burst in on them. I hoped if I saw it I would no longer secretly want it to happen.

The only problem with my plan was I didn't know exactly where Osborne's house was on the estate. When I asked my mother where he lived, she had gestured in a vaguely south, southwesterly direction. There were pictures of Osborne's mansion in the stuff I'd read. It was built out of limestone and marble. The limestone came from New Hampshire. He shipped the marble over from Italy. It was four stories high, and fifty-nine rooms big. I figured if I kept walking, I wouldn't miss it.

It was hot out. I walked in the cool fringe of the forest that bordered the dirt road my mother headed down when she went to work. Not wanting to be seen by her or anyone else, nervously looking over my shoulder every other minute for a car, I tripped over a stump and landed face first, mouth open, in a sea of toadstools. Spitting and wiping my tongue on my shirt-tail, I was waiting to be poisoned when my mother drove by. Windows down, she was singing along to an eight-track of Sly and the Family Stone. 'It's a family affair . . .'

As my mother turned right and disappeared into the woods I began to run. Binoculars bouncing off of my sternum and into my chin, bumping into pine trees, slapped by branches, I cursed myself for not leaving earlier as I cut across the forest. I caught sight of the road she was on just as her car disappeared round a bend.

I was chasing a cloud of dust now. Sweat dripped from the tip of my nose, and blisters reminded me I should have worn socks. My chest heaved, my lungs burned; I was losing her.

The road snaked back and forth through the forest. It was uphill now. I was sure when I got to the top of the rise I would be able to see

Osborne's house. But when I topped the hill, the king's palace was nowhere to be seen. Worse, there was a fork in the road. My mother was so far ahead of me that the dust that I'd been tracking had already settled.

Mouth open, tongue out, panting, I circled the V in the road, whimpering like a dog who'd lost the scent. Do I go left or right? If I didn't get there soon, I'd never know for sure whether my mother was really doing him, or just doing him. If I got there too late, even if she was just massaging the old goat, there would still be the possibility that they'd already done it. And she was just now giving him his post-coital rubdown. The old fuck was seventy-three: he'd been in the hospital for chrissake. Once would probably be enough. They'd be done quicker than a three-minute egg. Slurpee's joke, not mine.

I started running down the road to the left, then changed my mind, ran back and took off down the road that veered in the other direction, up into the woods.

Twenty minutes later I knew I'd made the wrong decision. A steel chain was strung across the road and padlocked to the trunk of an oak tree. My mother didn't have anything but car and house keys on her key chain. Black squirrels romped above me in the tree tops. Their chatter mocked me. One of them dropped an acorn, another took a shit that just missed my foot.

I threw a rock at one of the bastards, and missed. When it landed there was a whoosh of feathers on air as a covey of doves took flight down the steep incline to my left. It sounded like a huge deck of cards was being shuffled.

The quail disappeared into a pocket of dogwood petaled pink and cream, and there, parked discreetly behind a threesome of Atlas cedars, was a blue Peugeot station wagon. Silently, I moved closer. I did not feel the thorns of the wild raspberries, or brush away the gnats that lighted on my lashes. Unblinking, I crept forward to see what I would see.

On the other side of the Peugeot was a clump of rhododendrons and, on the other side of that, there was a playhouse that was equal parts Adirondack camp and Russian Dacha. I knew all about it from a 1953 issue of *Town & Country* magazine. Osborne had built it as

71

a surprise for his first wife. But she died before they could party in it. 'Playbarn' would have been a more accurate name for it. It was made from sixty-foot links of Engelman spruce, unstripped of their bark, and stacked like Lincoln Logs. Its shutters and gingerbread trim were painted like a Ukrainian Easter egg.

I knew from the article that it overlooked a gorge where the Haverkill fell forty feet into a pool surrounded by a patio made of huge slabs of pink granite, brought down from New Hampshire by railroad. There had been a photograph of Osborne, mid-thirties, casting a fly from a lounge chair. I didn't think Osborne and my mother were fishing.

The windows on my side of the playhouse were narrow and curtained. There was no way to get around to the gorge side. It was cleverly positioned for privacy. As I walked towards the door, I was greeted by a moan and a grunt. I could hear the faint squeak of a . . . boxspring mattress? The wheels of the massage table? Sound effects wouldn't satisfy me; I wanted to see them doing it. The front door was locked. But through its windowpanes I could see a sports bra and a pair of woman's underpants. The old-fashioned high-rise kind that my mother wore when she was having her period, balled up and discarded, near the mouth of a polar bear that had ended up as a rug. I darted to another window, closer to the animal noises. Its sill was six feet off the ground. Standing on tiptoe, my nose pressed to the glass, I struggled to get a glimpse of what I knew was going on inside.

The playhouse was one ballroom-sized room. But at the far end, a staircase banistered with antlers spiraled up to a loft and there, on a bed, I saw them. It was some massage. I couldn't see their faces, just her legs, and the top of a white-haired head buried in her crotch. I jumped up, I had to see her face. There was one more thing I needed to know – was she enjoying it? I jumped again but all I saw was the fleshy blur of figures rolling off a mattress. I ran from window to window. I heard footsteps inside, but saw nothing.

I stepped back against the trunk of an elm and slowly slipped down. Crouched on my haunches, I waited for them to come out. I'd changed my mind about not wanting to make a scene.

Tense; anxious; when a twig snapped behind me I jumped to my feet and spun around in terror. I don't know what I thought was sneaking up on me – Osborne's Alsatians? A bear that had escaped into the afterlife as a rug? Certainly something other than Mr Osborne's middle-aged daughter, Mrs Langley. I had read an article about her wedding – Ray Charles had played. She was about forty, tan, and dressed for tennis, she was the kind of flat-chested woman that looks a lot younger until she comes close enough to see her wrinkles. All she was armed with was a tennis racket and a can of Tab.

'Sorry, I didn't mean to sneak up on you,' she said.

'That's OK.'

'I'd be furious.' She didn't look much like her daughter Maya until she lit a cigarette and blew smoke rings.

'You would?'

'I hate surprises.'

'Me too.'

'You're Lizzy Earl's son.' I'd never heard my mother called 'Lizzy'. 'I'm Mrs Langley.' She held out a child's hand, and gave me a lopsided grin. 'And your name is . . . ?' Before I could answer she squinted her eyes and made a thoughtful face. 'Don't tell me . . . I know . . . because when your mother mentioned it I thought "what a delightful name" . . . Finn. Am I right?'

'That's me.' I was so flattered she knew who I was I almost forgot about my mother and Mr Osborne.

She turned her back to me, and gazed into the forest. 'I think Bryce stood me up for tennis.' Looking nervously at the playhouse door, I hoped my mother and Osborne stayed inside. All I needed was Mrs Langley finding out. Was I protecting them, or saving them for myself? Her back was still to me. 'You haven't seen my firstborn, have you?' I glanced back at the playhouse, and there was Bryce, sweaty and naked except for an erection, standing just inside the glass of the locked door. I'd never seen Bryce before, but I knew it had to be him – his hair was dyed white. It was his head, not Osborne's, I'd seen between those thighs.

Bryce put his fingers to his lips in a request for silence, then stepped back out of sight. If that wasn't my mother inside, who was it? My mind was full of questions. And why was her car parked there?

73

'There's nobody here but me.'

'Do you play tennis?' She put her hand on my shoulder as she took a pebble out of her shoe.

'No.' I held up my binoculars. 'I'm a bird-watcher.' I thought it was a convincing touch.

'Good for you.' I could tell she was pissed off about her son pulling a no-show from the way she flicked her cigarette onto the ground. But mostly, I was still wondering why my mother's car was there if she wasn't in the playhouse. For a nanosecond my paranoia licked at an even more grotesque possibility: my mother and Bryce?

When Mrs Langley got into the driver's seat of the Peugeot I announced moronically, 'You drive a blue Peugeot.'

Bryce's mother laughed at me in the nicest possible way. 'Does that mean something I should know?'

'No . . . they're just great cars.'

'Well, if you hit the tennis ball with me sometime, I'll let you drive it.'

'Really?'

'Sure.' She started the engine, and was backing out.

'I'd better practice first.'

'Your driving or your tennis?'

'Both.' She laughed and waved as she drove away. Relief was not the word for what I felt.

The squirrels chattered, but they were no longer laughing at me. My mother wasn't inside. She was at Osborne's house, doing her job; whatever that was. But to be honest, at that moment, massaging the old man suddenly seemed as innocent as . . . My reverie was interrupted by a short, sharp whistle. Bryce Langley was leaning out a second-story window. He was twenty? Twenty-one? His platinum dye-job glowed in the forest sunlight round his head like a halo. He looked like a pop star posing as a saint for an album cover.

'Sir!' he proclaimed grandly. 'You are a gentleman and a scholar and a gifted bullshitter.'

'It was nothing.'

'I'm in your debt, Finn.' He knew my name, too! It almost seemed like I was popular. I felt all was right with the world until he turned back to his unseen guest and said, 'I'll be with you in a second, Jilly.'

Bryce didn't seem to notice the way her name melted my smile. Osborne's grandson flourished a bow worthy of Robin Hood, closed the leaded window, and was gone.

Better Jilly than my mother . . . but still, it hurt. Why hadn't she told me? At least hinted there was something going on between herself and Bryce? All she said was she knew him well enough to steal his pot. I wondered, did Dwayne know? Did Bryce care? Not likely.

As I walked away from the playhouse, for the thousandth time I thought of Jilly as she was the week before in our kitchen. Tipsy on the vapors of DDT and Vlyvalle Red, tube-top down, eyes closed, waiting for a kiss – a kiss that in my mind would have changed everything if Osborne hadn't driven into that cornfield in his Bentley. The way I was now figuring it, if I had kissed Jilly, my hand might have had the pleasure of slipping into the panties that now lay by the mouth of the polar bear Osborne should never have turned into a rug if he was so worried about endangered species. And if I had made it to third base with her then, what would I be up to now? In the logic of my unreasonable brain, my face, not Bryce's, would have been buried in the luxury of Jilly's thighs. Everything would have been different if it wasn't for Osborne.

I felt strangely grown-up for not blaming Bryce, or even Jilly. (Well, maybe Jilly just a little.) Of course, it helped that my innate narcissism had quickly and conveniently led me to the rationalization that she had turned to Bryce because I had rejected her. I also possessed enough common sense to realize that even if I hadn't blown it with Jilly, I was no competition for Bryce. Rich, handsome, protector of retards, and possessor of infinite cool. At least I had made a good impression on Bryce. I knew the morning could have turned out far worse. This way, maybe I could be friends with both him and Jilly. Trying to look on the bright side, I reminded myself that at least Mrs Langley had halfway promised to let me drive her car. It's sad, when a fifteen-and-a-half-year-old is lonelier than he is horny.

As I walked back to the chain that blocked the road, I saw that there were tennis and paddle courts hidden behind a windbreak of poplars. It was afternoon now. My mother would be finished with whatever she did to/with Osborne. I would have to wait for my questions to be answered.

Having run this far, I decided to walk a little further, and see if I could figure out where Osborne lived. I had not given up my quest, I would be there waiting tomorrow morning. I made a resolution to get up earlier, and reminded myself to wear socks.

I left the road and followed a bridle path carpeted in woodchips that meandered down to the Haverkill. A six-foot-high chain-link fence, toped with three strands of barbed wire ran along the opposite bank. Clearly designed to keep people out, I figured Osborne's place must be somewhere on the other side. A couple of hundred yards downstream a fallen maple spanned the river. Two and a half feet across at the base of its uprooted trunk, it seemed like an easy and dry way to get to the other side. It wasn't.

As soon as I climbed on the trunk, I knew I was going to fall in. It was covered with green slime, slicker than owl shit. I decided to get it over with. Not bothering to watch my feet or hold out my arms, I fucked the balancing act. Pretending I was being chased by canni-bals, I let out a whoop and ran. I still fell. I just did it on my own terms.

I fared better with the fence. The barbed wire ripped the seat of my pants, but spared the backside of my balls. Things were looking up. The woods on the other side of the river were so thick with deadfall, overgrown with honeysuckle and prickers, I couldn't take three steps without shouting an expletive 'Ouch!' I gave up trying to walk in a straight line and followed a deer trail up the hillside. When the hill crested and the forest flattened out, walking became easier. I saw a gray fox, a porcupine, and a herd of red deer. The deer were different from the whitetails that grazed on the impatiens that lined the walk. When Nana went to Scotland for a psychology convention, she sent me a postcard of one of them. Antlers worthy of an Elks' lodge, and strawberry-blond coats, they didn't belong in Jersey any more than I did. I figured I was getting close when I came upon a clearing in the woods. It was a perfect circle, and in the center, on a block of stone, was a life-sized marble statue of a naked woman. Arms outstretched to-wards the sky, she made me think of a gigantic bowling trophy, until I realized it was a grave: 'LOUISA 1906–1927.' That was the name of Osborne's first wife.

Three hours later I saw Louisa again and knew I was lost. The sun low in the sky, standing in the shadow of a grave, it would have been spooky, even if I hadn't spotted the carcass of a dead red deer, lying in the ferns at the edge of the clearing. All the hunter had taken were its head and its liver. At least, I hoped it was a hunter.

I told myself not to panic. Mostly because the rational part of my brain knew that if I didn't calm down and find my way home on my own, I'd have to wait for my mother to get freaked out and call Gates, who'd call Mr Osborne, who'd tell Mrs Langley, who'd tell Bryce, and Jilly, and everybody else how I got lost. Which would have been worse than embarrassing – even I knew if I got lost in the wilds of the Garden State, how was I ever going to find my way in Yanomamö country. Clearly, this was a test.

I vaguely remembered, from my two weeks as a boy scout, Slurpee saying if you're lost in the woods, climb a tree. The trouble was, the lowest limbs were out of my reach, and the trunks were too thick for me to grip. I tried to pull myself up a vine as thick as my wrist, but it snapped just about the same time I realized it was poison ivy. My head hit the ground with a whiplashed thump . . . and then I saw it. Twenty feet up, in the crook of one of the trees, there was a plywood platform. I'd walked right under it and never seen it. Lengths of two-by-four were nailed to its trunk to form a ladder. I began to climb.

Fifteen feet up, I had a clear view of the river. It was less than a quarter-mile away. I wasn't lost. Two more steps, I could see the dome on the roof of Osborne's mansion. It had a weather vane in the shape of a golden bull. I threw my leg up onto the platform and started to pull myself up when something buried in a mound of dead leaves tore into my right foot. I had been bitten by something. My head swiveled. The steel teeth of an animal trap had ripped open my sneaker and cut me to the bone. It was the blood, more than the pain, that made me lose my grip. Falling, clawing at the makeshift ladder, I heard someone shout, 'I got ya.'

I hit the ground with the bloodied flop of one of the pigeons Slurpee shot with his BB gun from our rooftop. If the dead leaves hadn't been there to cushion my fall, I would have broken my legs, if not my back. The wind wasn't just knocked out of me, I felt like my organs had been rearranged without my permission. My foot was still in the jaws of the trap. A figure stood over me. Boots, tucked army-surplus pants, olive-green pullover, stocking cap, and a face striped and menacing with green and black camouflage greasepaint, the right hand held a crossbow.

'Where's your gun?' The voice barked.

'My foooot.' I lacked the breath to scream. All I could do was groan.

'Tell me where it is and I'll take the trap off.'

'What are you talking about . . . Jesus Christ, get it off, it's killing me.'

'What did you do to that deer?'

The stocking cap was pulled off in disgust. It was Maya, Bryce's sister.

'I didn't do anything to your fucking deer.' I was screaming now.

'Don't you remember me? I was on the road.'

'That doesn't mean you're not a poacher.'

'Poacher?' I screamed. 'This isn't fucking Sherwood Forest.'

'That's right. It's my forest.' I was trying to pull the trap off. Just touching it made it bite deeper into my foot. I pulled the jaws apart with my fingers. It opened an inch. Before I could pull my foot free, it slammed shut.

'That's not how you open it.'

'I was fucking bird-watching, you sadist.' All that pain and still able to lie. I held up the binoculars I'd brought to spy on my mother and Osborne. 'You can ask Bryce.'

'Oh, my God, shit, I'm sorry.' Dropping her crossbow, she knelt down and released the spring of the trap with the heel of her hand. 'Oh my God, I'm so sorry. Are you all right?'

'I don't know.' I gasped and bit my lip as she pulled off my sneaker.

'Jesus Christ.' She didn't sound encouraging.

'What's it look like?' Her body blocked my view.

'Like, uh . . .' She was pouring water on it from a canteen. 'Like ceviche.'

'What's that?'

'Raw appetizer.' It was weird but, when she said that, I stopped being mad at her. I pushed her aside so I could see for myself. My foot was already starting to swell. It was purple and red where the trap's teeth had torn open the flesh. It looked like a sea animal. Pouring more water on it compounded the pain. My leg trembled, I could see a bluish bit . . . tendon? She wrapped her pullover around my foot before I could get a closer look.

I was trembling all over now. Her fingers had my blood on them. She helped me to my feet.

'Where are we going?'

'My house. It's not that far.'

'I can't walk.'

'You won't have to.' She propped me against a tree, and disappeared into the darkening undergrowth. In a few minutes she returned, leading a gray horse.

'You've got to be kidding.'

'Are you scared of horses?'

I was, but I said 'No.'

'I didn't think so.'

'Why's that?'

'I don't like people who don't like horses.' I wished I had more time to savor the possibility that that was a backwards way of saying she liked me. She offered her arm. I grabbed hold and sprung off my good foot. I was surprised she was strong enough to pull me up behind her.

'Put your arms around my waist.' My foot throbbed as we trotted through the forest. My face pressed against the nape of her neck, my chest to her back, I could feel her breathing, and felt a dizziness that could only be partially attributed to loss of blood.

'Have you done this before?'

'What do you mean?'

'Caught people.'

'No. You're my first.' That's when I started to get a hard-on.

We rode out of the woods, shortcut through twenty acres of alfalfa, then galloped across a corralled field with a half-dozen turned-out horses running alongside us. The pull of a chain opened a counter-balanced gate that swung closed with a clang. Kicking into the sides of her horse, she guided us through a rose garden that gave me a glimpse of her home. It was a house that had started out the last century as a cottage, and had been added on to so many times it was now the most unpretentious of mansions. It had green houses and wings and porches and pillars. But just to show you the people who lived there didn't take it too seriously, they had painted it pale pink. At sunset, which was now, it didn't just glow, it blushed.

A pair of Jack Russells and a three-legged Lab greeted us as Maya reined in her horse in front of a green barn. The exhausted animal was drenched with sweat, and tendrils of foam and drool hung from its mouth. What I thought was a Latin boy with a limp, but turned out to be a Venezuelan jockey who'd had a bad fall, grabbed hold of the reins.

'Where's my mother and Bryce?'

'They went to visit your papa.'

'Enrique, call and tell them I've taken him to the hospital in the Dooley.'

The Dooley was a huge white four-wheel-drive pickup, with two sets of rear tires. She had to sit on a feed catalogue to see over the steering wheel. Gripping the Brody knob that was attached to the steering wheel with one hand, lighting a menthol cigarette with the other, she muscled the behemoth pickup out onto the main road like a long-haul trucker.

While the pain in my foot had leveled off to a dull throb, the rest of my body was just beginning to let me know how much it hurt. My back ached, my neck was stiff and my ribs were bruised. I lit up one of her menthol cigs even though I knew there was a good chance I might get carsick. I was beyond being embarrassed, but still wanted to be cool.

It was fifteen miles to Griggstown hospital. The first half of the trip was mostly her apologizing and me saying stuff like, 'Don't worry about it,' 'It's OK,' and 'I'm not mad at you.' But when she announced, 'I just can't stand cruelty to animals,' I surprised myself by pointing out the obvious. 'What about cruelty to poachers?'

'Poachers are assholes.'

'Because they kill deer?'

'First, they're our deer, and second, there's a difference between shooting anything that moves and culling the herd.'

'What's culling?'

'Killing the immature males . . . so the herd doesn't get too big.'

'So that's what you were trying to do to me.'

'My mother takes care of that. She doesn't seem it, but she's a real prude.'

'So you shoot the deer anyway?'

'Once a year.'

'Why not invite the poachers?'

'The poachers are locals.'

'So are you.'

'I mean, like, townies.' I wondered what word she used for people like me.

'So?'

'So, even if we invited them and they came, which most of them wouldn't, they'd still sneak in at night and slaughter deer.'

'Why?' She looked at me as if I was stupid.

'They don't like us.' She could tell I still didn't get it. 'They work and we don't. It's not fair; it's just the way it is with money. Bryce says it's ritualized class warfare. We let them kill our deer so they don't kill us. Bryce likes to be dramatic.'

'Maybe Bryce is right.' She didn't like that idea.

'Look, I'm not a snob.'

'I never said you were.'

'I wouldn't have set the trap if it wasn't for Jonah.'

'Who's Jonah?'

'My dog. The poachers shot him, that's why he only has three legs.'

We were at the hospital now. It was bigger than I expected. She left the Dooley in an ambulance zone. My arm over her shoulder, she helped me hop through the automatic doors. A nurse with mega-hair and a lot of attitude gave us a dirty look. Maya's face was still striped with camouflage paint. We were filthy, smelled of horse sweat, and blood was dripping out of the pullover that bandaged my foot onto a freshly mopped floor; we looked like refugees from an action movie.

'Move the truck, wipe up the floor, and fill one of these out.' The nurse handed me a clipboard with a form on it. As she turned her back on us, she added, 'It's going to be at least an hour and a half. Lot of people ahead of you.' The waiting room was crowded with bicycle accidents, dog bites, sick babies, whiplash victims, and a fat woman who wasn't sure whether she was having a heart attack or indigestion. Everybody was complaining.

Maya took the clipboard from my hands before I had even started to fill out the forms and held it out to the nurse.

'I'm Maya Langley.'

The nurse turned round to face us. Clearly, this changed things. 'I'm sorry, I didn't recognize you.' The waiting room looked up. Talk turned to whispers. Even the babies stopped crying. There was no longer an hour wait. A wheelchair was produced.

'Go into the first examination room on the right. I'll put a note so they don't tow your truck. Dr Leffler will be with you in a minute.'

I was embarrassed. And yet, with the guilt of association came empowerment. It was easy to see what they thought of her: rich bitch. There was nothing else to think until Maya said, 'We can wait.'

It was what they wanted to hear. People stopped whispering, the baby began to cry, the fat woman agreed it might be indigestion after all when her husband reminded her she had stopped off at Dunkin' Donuts after having a whole bucket of Extra Crispy for lunch. The nurse helped me into the wheelchair.

'I don't know. That foot looks like something Dr Leffler will want to see right away.' She didn't know what was wrong with my foot. It was still wrapped up in Maya's pullover. It was an exchange designed to make it easier for everybody to keep kidding themselves that we live in a democracy.

As Maya wheeled me down the hall, she told me, 'I hate pulling that shit. But you'd be stuck out there for ages if I didn't.' The idea that she was doing it for me made it admirable. Also, my foot was killing me. We passed a plaque: GRIGGSTOWN MEMORIAL HOSPITAL. BUILT IN LOVING MEMORY OF LOUISA OSBORNE.

Dr Leffler looked like one of the guys that advertised men's hair dye on TV. When he walked into the room, he went to kiss Maya on the cheek, but stopped short when he saw the camouflage paint.

'Maya, when did you enlist?' He thought it was funny. As he unwrapped my foot, he introduced himself and told me 'Mr Osborne tells me your mother's, ah . . . treatments have been working wonders. I've been meaning to call her.' As he poured disinfectant on my foot I wondered what he knew that I didn't. 'So, what happened?' he asked me. Maya looked at the floor.

'I fell out of a tree.'

'How'd you cut your foot?' On the top and bottom of my foot, I had two perfect semicircle gashes. Maya started to say something – I cut her off.

'I landed on a tin can.'

Maya's head rose slowly. She was trying not to smile. As Dr Leffler bent over to examine the bottom of my foot, Maya rolled her eyes and mouthed the words 'tin can?'

'You're lucky it missed the tendon. How did a tin can cut you on the top and bottom of your foot?' I had to think about this for a minute.

'It was jagged, like somebody opened it with a knife instead of a can opener – you know?'

'I'm listening.' I winced and closed my eyes as he poured iodine straight into the gash.

'And when I landed on it, it crumpled around my foot.'

'Almost like a trap.'

'Almost.' When I opened my eyes, Bryce and Mrs Langley were standing in the doorway of the examining room. They were all dressed up like they were going to church.

'What has my daughter done to you?'

'Nothing.'

Bryce peered at my foot and pretended to be horrified. 'If I were you, Finn, I'd sue us. I have a really good lawyer.'

'Bryce, this isn't funny.' I could tell Maya didn't like him putting on a show.

'People sue us all the time. They come for miles around to have accidents at our house. Why shouldn't someone I like sue us?'

Bryce's mother held up her hand. 'Be quiet, I want to find out what happened.'

'Finn, I'll pay for the lawyer and we'll split fifty–fifty? Hey, if

you've got a limp, there could be a hundred grand in this for us.'
Even I was laughing.

Mrs Langley put her hand on my shoulder. 'What really happened?'

'I fell on a tin can.' It sounded even less believable the second time out of my mouth. Bryce bent over my foot and looked at it closely.

'Jesus, it looks like he stepped into one of those muskrat traps a friend of mine put out for the poachers.' Maya didn't like Bryce teasing her.

'It was a tin can.' No one believed me.

'Like I just said, it looks exactly like the tin can I stepped on last year. It left the same marks on my foot. Wanna see?' Bryce kicked off a Gucci loafer and started to take off a sock. The doctor laughed as he gave me a tetanus shot.

'I hate to break up the party, but that foot might be broken. I'm going to need some x-rays.'

As the nurse wheeled me down the hall, Mrs Langley called out: 'I called your mother as soon as I got off the phone with Enrique. She's on her way here as we speak.' Until I heard that, I was in a pretty good mood.

My foot was x-rayed – no broken bones. Dr Leffler bandaged it, gave me some painkillers, antibiotics, and a pair of crutches, and told me not to walk on it for a week. Maya was waiting outside the examination room next to the elevator. She'd washed the war paint off her face and put on pink lipstick. I could hear my mother and Mrs Langley laughing in Dr Leffler's office. Bryce was telling a funny story when Maya blurted out, 'Wanna meet my dad?'

'Sure.' We took the elevator to the third floor. The way everyone treated her made sense now. Her father was a doctor. I paused to tuck my shirt in and make myself more presentable. She opened a door halfway down the hall. 'Hi, Daddy,' I heard her say. Putting both my crutches under my left armpit, I hobbled into the room after her and reached out to shake his hand. I felt sort of stupid. Her dad wasn't a doctor, he was a patient. Except for the machine he was hooked up to, and the nurse who was reading *People* magazine, you would have thought you were in a suite in a really expensive hotel, not a hospital.

Her father looked like he was sleeping. But from the way she kissed him, you knew he wasn't going to wake up. Handsome, almost pretty, he looked just like Bryce, only his hair was prematurely grey, not dyed platinum. His fingers were curled up, like the feet of a sparrow that had fallen out of its nest.

'Dad, this is Finn.' She sat on the edge of his bed.

'Hi, Mr Langley.' I decided it would have been weird to say, 'Pleasure to meet you.' The nurse put down her magazine.

'Your mother and Bryce had a nice long visit. I'll be just down the hall if you need me.'

'What's wrong with him?'

'He's been in a coma for almost three years.'

'How'd it happen?'

'He fell . . . sit down . . . he won't mind.' She made room for me on her father's hospital bed. It felt creepy, but I did as she asked. 'I come to talk to him a couple of times a week.'

'You think he hears you?'

'The doctors say he can't. But I like the idea he knows what I'm doing.'

I was about ready to say I think I better go down and see my mom now when she leaned forward and kissed me with an open mouth on the lips. It wasn't like with Jilly. Nothing could distract me, not even the living corpse of her father. She took my hand in hers and slipped it inside her shirt. It was more romantic than it sounds.

10

What is the chivalrous thing to do after you feel up a girl with her comatose father lying next to you like a big root vegetable? I didn't know the etiquette, and had no one to ask. The magic of the moment could not be easily recapped, but it was felt: the hospital room that wasn't, the brain-dead dad who witnessed it but could not see, listened but did not hear.

The oddness of the set-up gave a strange potency to what followed. The surprising weight of her breast in my hand. Her nipple teasing my palm. Lifting her shirt. Kissing it once . . . twice, with just enough time to see it stiffen and blush from shell pink to coral red in my lips before the nurse knocked and re-entered. It was fleeting, but complete. Satisfying in its promise. Surreal, and then some. It was as if it had happened to someone else like me, but more deserving. Perhaps that's what I liked most.

The next day, I tried to call Maya as soon as my mother left for Osborne's. (Maya, and a foot with toes swollen and discolored as plums, forced me to put my investigation into that mystery onto the back burner of my brain.) I had more immediate problems. The Langleys' phone number was unlisted. I immediately thought of taking the Peugeot, driving over to their house and leaving a note when my mother came home and went for her jog. But what if someone else read it and laughed? Worse, what if she read it and laughed? After a moment's consideration, it was clear: if I snuck over there in the car, I'd have to knock on the door. But what if Maya's mother or Bryce answered? Just thinking of having to say 'Is your sister home?' to Bryce made me cringe. And even if I was lucky enough to have Maya appear when I knocked, then what would I say?

'Hi, I liked kissing you . . . thanks for letting me touch your boobs, can I do it again . . . I think I've fallen in love with you . . . it was a pleasure talking to your dad . . .' It was all too easy to see myself chickening out halfway to the door. I imagined Maya, Bryce, and the mother looking out the window as I scurried back to the purloined Peugeot on crutches that had already rubbed my armpits raw.

I called Information again just to see if the first operator was lying. She wasn't. I asked to speak to a supervisor and introduced myself as irate customer Mr Finn Earl, and told the old bitch it was a medical emergency. But still, no number.

Maya had made first contact – it was up to me to show an eagerness for more. The problem was, how do you let someone know you're dying to see them without seeming desperate? I wanted her to know I liked her, but not to think I was a stalker. I knew people who I could get the number from. I could call Dr Leffler at the hospital. But he would be sure to tell Mrs Langley I had the hots for her daughter. Jilly? After what I saw in the playhouse, it was a safe bet Jilly had Bryce's number. It was also a sure thing she'd tell him. I could just hear Bryce cracking wise about my ardor. If the jokes weren't at my expense, they'd be at Maya's. Gates? It wasn't really a police matter – yet. But his job was to tell Osborne everything, who'd then tell my mother, who'd then make a big deal about it. The point is, I didn't want anyone else to know how important this was to me, especially not Maya.

A fat black tome with *Social Register* written in scarlet lettering caught my eye on the bookshelf to the right of the mantle. I don't know why I even opened it. Fate? The hand of God? The satisfaction that comes from seeing your name not listed? The snob's bible was an answered prayer. It had a half a page on the Langleys, and about a million other people I couldn't give a shit about. It listed their nicknames (believe it or not, Mr Langley's was 'Dozer'), their ages (Maya was just a few weeks older than I was), clubs (Racquet, Union, Jupiter Island, Maidstone, Bath and Tennis, Vlyvalle Hunt), where they went to school (St Mark's and Yale for Dad, Miss Porter's and Vassar for Mom, likewise Miss Porter's for Maya, and Hotchkiss and Harvard for Bryce – he was a Junior). Most importantly the *Social Register* contained the telephone numbers of their residences – an apartment in New York's Riverhouse; Blue Arches in East Hampton; the Big Pine Ranch in Jackson Hole, Wyoming; Petit Cul de Sac in St Barthélémy, FWI; and best of all, Coldbrook Farm, Vlyvalle, New Jersey. I was golden.

I thought about rehearsing what I would say, but was too eager and nervous to hear what I dreaded and longed for: the sound of her voice. I dialed cold. It rang. A maid answered. It could have been worse.

'Langley residence.'

'Is Maya there?'

'Who may I ask is speaking?'

'This is, uh, Finn Earl. You don't know me, but . . .' I sounded like I was selling insurance. 'I'm the guy that fell out of the tree.' I winced when I added the last part.

'Oh.' In my brain that registered as, 'Oh, no.' Then the maid added, 'She's not home right now, can I take a message?'

'No . . . I mean yes.'

What to say? I opened my mouth, but could not speak. I should have thought of this. My breathing grew heavier.

'I'm sorry, I didn't hear you. You'll have to speak up. What was the message?'

'Just tell her Finn called.' I started to put down the phone, then remembered I had left out the most important thing. 'Waitmyphonenumber's . . .' I had to look on the telephone, '472–8998.' The line went dead. Had the maid heard me? I said it so fast I couldn't understand what I was saying. Could she? The only thing that was clear was that I had blown it. And if I had blown it with the maid, I'd blown it with Maya. Should I call back and give her the number again? It's what any sane person would have done. But I was rabid.

Pacing, waiting for the phone to ring is exhausting, especially if you're on crutches. I logged a good quarter-mile in that living room. When the phone finally rang, I was so excited I forgot there was a coffee table between me and the couch. Crawling on all fours, grabbing at the phone, dropping it to the floor, I tried to sound cool, calm and collected. 'Finn here.'

'What's wrong?' It was my mother calling to tell me she was having lunch at Osborne's.

I waited for a call that never came all that day. When I went to bed, I left the door open so I could listen for its ring in my dreams. My mother thought I was upset about my foot. I complained a lot to keep her from guessing. She was smart about stuff like that. The only thing that made my romantic predicament bearable was my mother not knowing anything about it. I could just hear her, 'Oh, lambie, is that all you're worried about? She's probably shy, and waiting for you to call back. Why don't you invite her over for . . .' What with the AA, and the sweater sets, she was dying to do her sitcom-mom act sober.

The next day, a FedEx package arrived from my father containing a 16 mm film he'd made of a Yanomamö feast. He was working on a documentary for Channel 13. There was a note with it.

Dear Finn:
    Sorry we won't be seeing you this summer. Let's try for next year. The Land Rover is waiting, but with the mud there's not many places to drive.
    This footage will give you a good idea of what's in store for you. I want you to see it all before it's ruined, i.e., civilization is more of a curse than a blessing for these people – maybe for most people? Write and tell me what you think of the film.
    Know that I love you and miss you even though I haven't seen you since you were the size of a turkey.
    Love Always,
    Dad

ps Glad to hear about Harvard.
pps Tell your mother I think of her more than she would imagine.

It was the first time my father had ever said he missed me. I'd waited a long time for that. But now it depressed me on two counts. I felt a little guilty for bullshitting him about Harvard. But what bothered me most was the realization that even as I read this longed-for letter, I was still listening, waiting, hoping the fucking phone would ring and it would be Maya. I was so preoccupied with Maya, I didn't even stop my mother from reading it.

'I didn't know you wrote your father.' She took a deep breath, and looked out the window when she read the pps about her.

'Somebody had to tell him I wasn't coming.'

'What reason did you give?'

'Don't worry, I didn't tell him what happened.'

'That's not what I asked. And what's this about Harvard?'

'I told him I thought it would be best if I spent the summer studying the SATs so I could get into Harvard.'

'Why did you say that?'

'I didn't want him to think I was a loser.'

'You're not a loser.' If she knew how many long-distance calls to Langley residences I had made in the last forty-eight hours she would have thought differently.

'You have to say that.'

'Why's that?'

'If a parent has a kid that's a loser, then the parent's a loser too.' I gave in to the urge to make her feel as miserable as I was. As usual, getting my mother all teary-eyed only made me feel worse. I wondered when I would learn.

'Do you want me to look at the movie with you?' She was trying to make the best of a bad situation, i.e., having a son like me.

'We don't have a projector.' I took the film out of the can, unraveled a few feet of it, and held it up to the daylight. I could barely make out two white men, surrounded by a crowd of Yanomamö. My father looked so tiny and far away I wasn't even sure if he was in the picture.

11

The next day, this guy who worked for Mr Osborne brought over a 16 mm projector and a screen. He set the whole thing up, fed the film through the sprockets, all I had to do was dim the lights and flick a switch. Instead of doing either, I spent the whole morning staring at the empty screen. Still no word from Maya.

Jilly showed up a little after one. 'How's it hanging?' she called from the front hall. When she didn't get an answer, she shouted, 'What are you doing?'

'Watching a movie.'

She stuck her head in the living room and caught me staring at the blank screen. 'Did you take all your painkillers at once?' I hadn't, although now that she mentioned it, it wasn't a bad idea.

Jilly unbuttoned the top half of her uniform like nothing had happened between her and Bryce. She was wearing a pink tube-top. I looked, but the thrill was gone. I had Maya on the brain. To show you how naïve I was, after what I saw go down, so to speak, in the playhouse I expected Jilly to come in and tell me she was in love. 'Are you high?' she asked innocently.

'Just bored. Are you going to see Bryce today?' I was working up to asking her to relay a message to Maya.

'I see him almost every day. When he's around the farm.'

'Doesn't Dwayne ever get jealous?'

'You're the only one Dwayne's got to be jealous of.' She kissed me on the cheek.

'Confidentially, Dwayne think's he's a fag.'

'I guess we both know Dwayne's got that wrong.'

'I don't know, Bryce dyeing his hair blond and all, he could be AC/ DC.' Jilly stopped dusting and lit a cigarette. 'Personally, I don't care about stuff like that. Whatever floats Bryce's boat.' It's weird – she really acted like Bryce was no big deal to her. 'I heard about you and Maya Langley.'

'What did you hear?'

'That you stepped in one of the traps she put out for Dwayne and his dad and the rest of them.'

'Dwayne's a poacher?'

'Shit, yeah. He's semipro.'

'What's he got against deer?'

'He sells the antlers and gallbladders to this Chinese guy in Plainfield who makes hard-on medicines out of them.' I didn't really feel like talking, but she caught my attention.

'Do they work?'

'Osborne takes them.' It was a piece of information I could have done without.

'Why'd he shoot the dog?'

'You don't know he did that. People are always blaming Dwayne for everything.' I was surprised she was still sticking up for him after Bryce. I would have admired her loyalty if it had been anybody but Dwayne.

'What? He thought the dog was a deer? It's a fucking black Lab, for God's sake. Thing's only got three legs now.' I was never that crazy about dogs. I guess it bothered me, because when my grandfather sent us to the family therapist, the shrink showed me a picture of this storybook family in a storybook house in this storybook village. And when she asked, who did I identify with, I pointed to the dog.

'If I were you, I'd be pissed off with Maya for putting out the trap.' As far as I was concerned, it was the best thing that had ever happened to me in my life.

'I didn't step in a trap.'

'I heard all about the tin can. Dwayne almost stepped in one himself. He's not through fucking with them yet.'

'What gives Dwayne the right to fuck with everybody?'

'Mostly he just fucks with rich people.'

'What's he going to do next, shoot one of their horses?'

'I'm not Dwayne.'

'Dwayne's an asshole.' I thought I was safe in saying this, what with all I knew about her and Bryce in the playhouse.

'You don't know Dwayne.'

'Anybody who shoots a dog is an asshole.'

'I'll tell him you said that.'

'Good. And while you're at it, tell him if he ever throws another beer can at me, or tries to fuck with me, I'll have him arrested.'

'Gates isn't going to arrest Dwayne for fucking with you or your new rich friends.'

'Why's that?'

'Dwayne could cause a lot of people a lot of problems.'

'How?'

'Check out Mr McCallum's ears.'

'What does that mean?' I could tell she'd said something she wasn't supposed to.

'Let's forget it and have a beer.'

'We don't have any.' I'd found a case in an old refrigerator in the basement that my mother hadn't known about when she purged the household of alcohol. She could get her beers from Dwayne or Bryce.

Poachers, muskrat traps in trees, Mr McCallum's ears, Dwayne's diplomatic immunity, Osborne taking hard-on medicine made of stolen gallbladders: the food chain did not compute. Unable to connect the dots of my world, I turned off the lights, flicked on the projector, and retreated into the world of the Yanomamö and my father's voice.

My father was the narrator. It was strange and soothing to hear his voice for the first time that way. I pretended he was just talking to me. As the camera panned the naked Indians that swarmed around him when he first arrived, he cautioned me, like Polonius to Laertes, 'It is both a privilege and a responsibility to live among a tribe that has had no contact with, or knowledge of, the outside world. The very presence of an observer changes them in ways that cannot be measured . . .' His voice was younger and more enthusiastic than I expected. He sounded like me when I have a cold, only smarter.

A lot of the stuff in the film I already knew about. I had read and daydreamed so much about the Yanomamö, it was like watching home movies of distant relatives I had not yet met. It was cool to see the men snort *enebbe* and work full time at being fierce, and I saw the shamans casting and uncasting spells to protect themselves and steal the souls of their neighbors' children. And I enjoyed sharing a joke with my dad as he dryly observed that when couples who are unmarried, or married to someone else, want to have illicit *koi-koi* (sex) they always use the same lame excuse to sneak off into the bushes: 'I have to go to the bathroom.' (My father subtitled everything, so you could understand exactly what the natives were saying.)

The documentary focused on a feast the tribe my father was studying had decided to throw for a neighboring village a day's walk away. Two weeks of shooting Basha monkeys with poisoned arrows, digging armadillos out of their holes, and picking plantains is intercut with shots of the Yanomamö getting dressed for the party they are clearly having second thoughts about. The subtitles made me laugh out loud. 'Why are we going through all this work for these anteater sperm-eaters?' and 'Maybe we should just steal the women now, kill one or two of the gluttons, and eat all of the food by ourselves quickly.' My dad could have put it more eloquently, but the point of social intercourse amongst the Yanomamö was basically, 'Let's have the neighbors over and really scare the shit out of them so they don't come back and fuck with us.'

'Finn!' The feast was just getting started and Jilly was shouting over the vacuum. I hoped if I didn't answer she'd leave me alone.

'Finn!' The Yanomamö of the neighboring village were dancing into the clearing with bows drawn, arrows tethered, and grimaces in place, as ready to fight as they were to party. The Waiyamu chanting had begun.

'Finnnn!'

I stopped the film and left the projection light on. A Yanomamö with his foreskin tied up to his waist by a string was frozen mid-leap on the screen. A naked girl wearing stripes of red dye squatted on her haunches. I was trying to figure out if she was looking up at him or his dick with such indifference. Crutches to sore armpits, I hobbled across the room and threw open the door and shouted: 'Look, I'm trying to concentrate. Can't you . . .'

Jilly didn't look up from her vacuuming. 'Your friends are out front.'

'What friends?' I looked out the window. Maya and Bryce were tying up their horses to a wrought-iron bench that encircled one of the sugar maples in front of the house. Maya's horse was wet and without a saddle. Knee-high cowboy boots and a T-shirt that said 'Life Isn't A Rehearsal' over a wet bikini. I guessed she had been swimming. Bryce was as formal as she was casual. White jodhpurs, black boots and a polo shirt that actually was a polo shirt.

Jilly unplugged the vacuum and retracted the cord with her flip-flopped heel.

'I gotta vacuum upstairs.' I figured she was embarrassed to be seen cleaning. I had my own mortification to deal with. I'd slept in the shirt I was wearing, and the front of it bore traces of the last three meals I had eaten, one of which had been chocolate ice cream. It had been two days since I'd washed my hair, and I'd been too depressed to get around to popping the zit I'd woken up with on my chin.

As Maya walked towards the house, I pulled off my shirt and smelled my armpits. Jilly watched in amazement.

'What, are you going to get naked for them?' Figuring I'd be OK if I kept my elbows down, I popped the zit into the gilt mirror in the front hall.

'I just Windexed that!' There was a spot of pus where my reflection had been. Maya was almost to the front of the house. There was no time to run upstairs for a clean shirt. I wiped the pus from the mirror with my smelly shirt, threw it in a closet, turned and opened the door just as Maya lifted her hand to knock.

'I got something for you.' Maya laughed and kissed me right above my zit, like it wasn't even there, and handed me a sealed envelope. 'It's an invitation. To our birthday – mine and my grand-father's. It's Saturday night, six-thirty sharp at the Hunt Club.' Bryce lingered on the lawn and looked at his horse's hoof. When he gave

95

me a thumbs-up sign, and mouthed the words, 'She's crazy about you,' I knew there was nothing wrong with his horse. Did he know I needed all the help I could get?

'You can come, can't you?'

'Yeah, sure . . . I mean, yes – absolutely.' She leaned forward, so close I could feel her breath; the brush of her lips against my ear gave me goose bumps as she whispered, slow and deliberate, 'I missed you.'

'Me too.' I said it quickly, so Jilly, who was lugging the vacuum up the stairs behind me, wouldn't hear.

'Hi, Jilly,' Maya waved nervously. 'I didn't see you.'

'Oh, I'm here.'

Bryce was walking towards us. Riding-crop in hand, he bowed. 'Sir, could I impose upon your hospitality for some liquid refreshment?'

'You want a beer?'

Jilly stopped halfway up the stairs. 'A beer?'

'Yeah, I just remembered there's some in an old refrigerator in the basement.'

'I'll go get them,' Maya volunteered. 'You want one, Jilly?'

'I've got to work.'

'Come on.' I played the part of the man of the people with conviction. 'Have one with us, Jilly.' I would have felt more like a rat if I hadn't been so happy to see Maya, her lips were again whispering in my ear.

'I wanted to come by myself, but Bryce followed me.'

'I heard that,' Bryce announced as he reached out to shake my hand. Maya ran to get the beers. 'The fact is, I came to see Jilly.'

'Right.' Jilly looked at him suspiciously. There was either more or less to this relationship than I realized.

'Jilly.' He clutched his heart and made a face like she'd hurt his feelings.

'Bryce, if it's about the pot . . .'

'Jilly, our shit is your shit, so to speak. It's pretty good if you don't wash off the insecticide.' Bryce reached over the banister and kissed her hand, like he was Rex Harrison in *My Fair Lady*. Jilly was so taken aback by this public display of affection, she dropped the vacuum. Bryce picked it up for her like a knight errant. It was funny: everybody felt cooler around Bryce – he had a gift. It wasn't that heat-lamp kind of charm that a phony can turn off and on, his warmth was real. He made you feel like you were sitting in the sun. You didn't think it was weird a guy his age hanging around kids four years younger. You just thought it was nice, like being fifteen wouldn't suck half as much if everyone who was twenty treated you that way.

Maya came back with four Heinekens, and we all lit up cigarettes. After a swallow or two standing around on my crutches, my armpits began to hurt, and I remembered I was the host, and asked everyone to sit down in the living room. I wasn't used to entertaining. Compared to having Slurpee over to shoot pigeons with his BB gun, it was all extremely grown-up for me. Bryce went into the living room, plopped on the couch and put his feet up on the chair that was so fancy and rickety, my mom wouldn't even let me sit in it. The way he made himself at home made me feel like it was my home.

'I'm not sure I should let my sister see this.' I had completely forgotten about my father's documentary. The room was dark. The projector's light was still on. Smoke whirled up from it. The Yanomamö were still frozen, mid-leap. Bryce pointed to the string that held the foreskin of the Indian's penis to his belly. 'Now this is a happening look.'

Maya turned to me and grimaced. 'Doesn't that hurt?' I shrugged, not sure whether or not I should be embarrassed.

'That's disgusting.' I was surprised how prudish Jilly was, given what I had seen in the playhouse. I turned off the projector and switched on the lights.

'It's a film my dad made about these South American Indians. He's an anthropologist. It's gonna be on Channel 13.' Maya put her hand on my shoulder with a familiarity that continued to amaze.

'Can you and I watch it sometime?'

'That's my sister's subtle way of telling us to get lost, Jilly.'

'Bryce . . . shut up.' Bryce was looking at the film canister.

'Fox Blanchard is your father?'

'Yeah.' Hoping no one would notice I didn't have his last name, I tried to change the subject. 'Anybody want another beer?'

'We read you father's book in my anthropology class at Harvard. He's fantastic. I knew you were a gentleman and a scholar! Finally, someone intelligent moves to Vlyvalle.' Like I said, he made you feel like you were sitting in the sun. 'Finn's father and Chagnon are the two most famous living anthropologists.'

'Thanks for telling me.' Jilly looked at me like I'd betrayed her.

Maya smiled. I could tell she liked the fact that her brother was impressed.

'What's he famous for?' Jilly asked.

'The Yanomamö.' Bryce and I said the word at the same time. Then Bryce told a whole string of funny stories about the Fierce People and my dad. I would have liked to have had the chance to impress Maya with a couple of them myself. But still, Bryce being so impressed with my dad made me feel pretty good about myself. Even I was sophisticated enough to know it was always better to have somebody brag for you.

Maya finally interrupted. 'Bryce, can somebody else say something?'

When Jilly finished the last of her beer she asked, 'Why's your father's last name Blanchard and yours is Earl?'

My silence made it more awkward. I could tell Jilly wished she hadn't asked the question. In 1978, it wasn't cool to be an unmarried mom. Unable to think of a clever way to segue out of Jilly's *faux pas*, Bryce announced, 'Time to watch the movie.'

'My father and my mother never got married.' I was surprised I didn't make up a lie. 'He was married to someone else when they met.'

'My mother had a bun in the oven when she married my father . . . Richard Pryor's my real dad, but don't tell anybody.' Bryce was trying to help me out.

'Bryce, you'll say anything to get attention.' Maya placed her hand on mine.

'Zoroastrians believe that being boring is a mortal sin. It's one of their Ten Commandments: Thou Shalt Not Be Boring.'

'What's a Zoroastrian?' Maya asked.

'Pre-Christian fire-worshippers,' I answered numbly.

'Sorry, Finn.' Jilly picked at the label of her beer. I could tell she wished she was upstairs vacuuming.

'No big deal.' It was, but saying more would only make it worse. 'I was going to spend the summer doing field work with him in Venezuela.'

'I'd kill to do that with your old man. Why didn't you go?' Bryce asked.

'I got busted.' I wasn't sure if it was the painkillers chased with beer, or if I was getting into the dangerous habit of telling the truth.

'What'd you get busted for?' Maya looked at me with new-found respect.

'Coke.' I left out the fact that I was buying it for my mother.

'Cool,' was Jilly's take on it.

'I'm impressed.' Bryce was, I could tell.

'My mother thought living in Vlyvalle would be a wholesome influence on me . . . anybody got a joint?' Everybody laughed. Even I was impressed with myself. It was even funnier when Jilly pulled a joint from her tube-top and lit up.

'I'm surprised your mother lets you hang out with my sister.'

'Bryce.'

'Maya got busted for pyromania at boarding school. Set her dorm on fire.'

'Why'd you do that?' Jilly wasn't the only one that was curious.

'I didn't do it on purpose, right? My hot-plate caught on fire . . .'

'You're leaving out part of the story,' Bryce kibitzed as he passed the joint to his sister.

'All right, I admit it: I hid it under my pillow and forgot to unplug it.'

'You're still leaving something out . . .'

'OK.' Maya exhaled a blue ring of pot smoke and deadpanned, 'I was stoned.' We all thought that was hysterical.

'What'd the school do to you?' It was my turn on the joint.

'Kicked me out. That's why I didn't get your message until last night. My mother was dragging me around New England, trying to find a boarding school that would take me that doesn't have bars on the windows.' We were laughing so hard our stomachs hurt.

Jilly gave Bryce a shotgun. After he returned the favor she announced proudly, 'I set the front seat of Dwayne's car on fire once.'

'On purpose?' Maya asked hopefully.

'I pretended it was an accident.'

'What'd he do that could piss you off?' I wondered aloud.

'Gave me crabs. In my eyelashes.'

When everybody stopped laughing, I turned out the lights and started the film. Sitting in the dark, on a hot summer afternoon, we passed joints and drank beers and watched the Yanomamö's feast begin.

If I hadn't been high, I would have been nervous about them watching the film. Bryce made the same wisecrack about the *enebbe* as he did about the ten-year-old bride: 'Where can I get some of that?' Maya said the shaman that started giving smoked monkey meat to the guests to get them to leave the party early reminded her of Mrs Nichols and the fruitcake, which Bryce and Jilly thought was hysterical. I laughed, too, even though I had no idea who Mrs Nichols was. Too stoned to think of anything funny to say, I began to chant along with the Yanomamö, as I beat my crutches on the coffee table, everyone joined in. When the neighboring tribe still wouldn't leave after the monkey-meat party favors, everything got fierce. Insults turned to chest-pounding duels, which started a club fight, that ended with the shaman getting his eye knocked out of its socket, and all the while we cheered and hooted like we were watching professional wrestling.

I wasn't sure this was exactly the response my father was hoping for, but everyone really liked it. In fact, they liked it so much we watched it twice. The second time was even better, because the projector was on rewind and everything happened in reverse. It was neat to see the eyeball fly back into the guy's eye, and watch the green *enebbe* snot slime back up their noses as they got un-high.

Bryce didn't just like the movie – he loved it. When I finally turned the lights back on, the joint was parked in the corner of his mouth, and he was tugging on his hair.

'Man, that is it. The Yanomamö have it figured out.'

'Bryce, be quiet, you're stoned.'

'What do you mean?' Jilly was interested.

'What I mean is, unlike us domesticated creatures, they're still human beings. It's the fuck/kill thing. If they like something, they fuck it. If they don't like it, they kill it.'

'That's romantic.' Maya made a face.

'You and Dwayne ought to get together, Bryce,' Jilly suggested.

'That's what I like about Dwayne, he's not watered-down.' Bryce said it again: 'Fuck/kill.'

'Stop saying "fuck".' Maya was getting bored with Bryce's act.

'Virgins fall into two categories: they either love the F-word, and don't wanna do it, or hate it, and do wanna do it. My sister falls into the latter.'

'Bryce!' She was embarrassed. I appreciated the information.

'Finn knows I'm right.'

'About virgins, fucking or killing?' All I knew was I'd kill myself if anyone found out I was a virgin.

'The three are connected.' Bryce was stoned.

'When I kill somebody, I'll let you know.' Maya liked my answer. Jilly looked at her watch.

'Well, I'm fucked and your mother's gonna kill me.' My mother was due home in a half an hour. The house was messier than when Jilly got there. Bryce didn't say anything – he just started to vacuum. He was the first person I'd ever met who made being nice seem cool.

While Bryce Hoovered and Jilly spick-and-spanned the kitchen, Maya and I cleaned the bathrooms and made out with an intensity that left me with a hard-on that lingered even after we stole our last kiss over the toilet bowl and they rode home.

Dwayne showed up just as they disappeared down the lane. When Jilly hugged me goodbye he gave me the finger and shouted, 'You're asking for it, faggot!'

But I just smiled and waved.

When my mother got home, I was looking at the invitation Maya

101

had handed me for their birthday party. She was turning sixteen, Osborne was going to be seventy-four. The invite was engraved on double-weight paper with a gilt edge:

You are cordially invited
to a dinner–dance in honor of . . .

It was only then I noticed how a calligraphed hand had addressed the envelope:

Mr Finn Earl and Dr Elizabeth Earl.

I knew my mother would be pissed off if she saw the doctor myth was spreading. More to the point, I wasn't at all sure I wanted her to come.

'How was your day?' My mother inquired with a sigh of resignation that told me she had over-shared at AA.

'Pretty good.'

'Well, that's a positive mood-swing.'

'Maya and Bryce Langley came by.'

'What did they want?'

'Just to hang out.'

'I'm glad one of us is popular.'

'They invited me to Maya and Mr Osborne's birthday party at the Hunt Club. It's a dinner–dance.' I followed her on crutches as she walked to the kitchen.

'You're kidding.' She was stunned.

'You mean, like, "Why would they want me?"'

'No. I'm just surprised . . . and happy for you.' She gave me a hug. She was happy for me, but I could tell she felt left out.

'They invited you, too.' I showed her the envelope. You would have thought she'd won the lottery. She didn't even get pissed off about the doctor thing.

'Oh God, it's formal.'

'What's that mean?'

'We've got to get you a tux.'

'Is that a problem?'

'No. No, but . . .' She suddenly looked at me and stepped back. 'Be honest – would you rather go by yourself?'

'It'll be more fun if we go together.' It wasn't exactly true, but she liked hearing it.

'I wonder if Mr Osborne knows.' All of the sudden, I didn't want her to come.

12

I knew the birthday party was a mega-big deal to my mother when she skipped the AA meeting where she was supposed to get her thirty-day chip to go into New York to shop: a dress for her, a tux for me. She wasn't backsliding, she just had her priorities. She took the train from Morristown instead of driving, because she only had a learner's permit, and what with the bad karma from blowing off the meeting she was sure it would be just her luck to get pulled over on the New Jersey Turnpike.

She'd wanted me to go with her, but I said my foot hurt too much. It hurt, but I wanted to get her out of the house. Maya had called the night before and asked to come over and watch TV. It was a more exciting prospect than it might sound – when I told her our set was broken, she breathed into the receiver: 'We'll find something to do.' But at the last minute, she phoned back, and said her mother was making her go down to Maryland to see this girl's school that was willing to take her if her grandfather gave them a new indoor riding rink. Maya didn't want to go there because the uniforms were dorky, and the teachers were all dykes and/or nuns. I was impressed, not because of the dykes, or the indoor riding rink bribe, but by the way she said goodbye. 'Big kiss, gotta run, King Air's waiting.' When I asked who King Air was, she laughed. I never expected Finn Earl to have an almost-girlfriend, much less one with a private plane.

My mother returned from her shopping expedition triumphantly laden with boxes and bags. 'You are going to look so handsome.'

The stuff was all from Bergdorf–Goodman and Saks. My wardrobe had previously been purchased on Canal Street, with a yearly back-to-school outing to Macy's, if Nana was feeling generous. I was pretty excited, until my mother pulled my formal attire out of a brown paper bag from the St Anne's thrift shop.

'You bought me a used tux?' I was furious.

'It'll look fantastic after I press it.'

'I don't believe you.' My mother held it up for me to try on. I refused.

'Old is better than new.'

'I didn't know they sold second-hand dresses at Bergdorf–Goodman.'

'I could have bought you a new one.'

'Why didn't you?'

'Because then everybody would have known you didn't have a tuxedo, and you had to run out and buy one. And if you didn't have one, then they'd know you'd never been to a fancy party.'

'Why don't we want to them to know?' I hadn't been nervous about the party until now.

'It's just better if they think you're used to all this.' I couldn't figure out how an ex-hippie like my mom knew so much about being a snob. She hadn't learned it from Nana. Had she somehow absorbed it just being in Vlyvalle? Was it something in the water, or the air? Either way, I was beginning to get the picture. I tried on the dinner jacket. It looked good, in a kind of corny way.

'It smells like mothballs.'

'It won't by Saturday.' She opened a Brooks Brothers box and took out a pair of patent-leather loafers with bows in the toes.

'You couldn't find any second-hand ones?'

'Old money isn't suspicious of new shoes.'

13

People started pouring into Vlyvalle for the party on Friday afternoon. The dirt roads were thick with lost limo drivers bringing people out from the city. Lear jets and G2s and Citations circled our house with dizzying regularity, waiting to land at Osborne's private airstrip.

My mother called Gates when she saw guys with guns in the woods. After what happened to my foot, she was on the lookout for poachers. The chief stopped by to apologize for not letting her know that Secret Service would be on the farm until Sunday. The Vice-President was spending the weekend at the playhouse. It was funny to think of the VP and his wife in the same bed Jilly and Bryce used. It would have been funnier if I'd known the Vice-President was bringing his mistress.

The incoming traffic continued into the next day. Every spare bedroom and guesthouse in Vlyvalle was filled with the chosen people. Jilly told me the pilots got put up at the hotel in Morristown; the drivers had to make do with a Motel 6 on Route 22.

It was so hot and humid that by Saturday noon, even the walls were sweating. My mother was in a panic, she didn't have a sleeveless dress to wear. Certain she was going to pit out in front of everyone, as soon as she finished massaging Osborne, she drove all the way to the Short Hills Mall to buy some shields. She laughed and threw one at me when I called them armpit diapers. I was thinking about wearing them myself. If I started to sweat in my new old tux, I'd have mothball BO. But at five o'clock, as if on command, a cold front from Canada rolled in a thunderstorm. Quick, but torrential, it washed the dust from the day, and air-conditioned the night.

My mother prepared herself for the evening with the same somber deliberateness of the gladiators in *Spartacus*. I listened to her bathe, and smelled a powder with a different fragrance than the one she normally used. Her clothes were laid out on her bed like armor. A black silk dress, a lace jacket with tissue paper stuffed in its sleeves, stockings sheer as a veil, and a purse too small to conceal any weapon other than her lipstick.

She was in the bathroom a good forty-five minutes when she called out to me, 'Finn, bring me the bag in my purse.' Remembering the naked eyeful I didn't want to get last fall when I brought her her shampoo and the shower curtain fell, I was careful to knock.

'*Entrez*.' I opened the door. 'We're getting awfully formal.' I didn't mention the shower incident. She had on a black slip and the kind of high heels she always made fun of on other women.

'Wow.' Her eyelids were dusted blue-black, and her cheeks were rouged to look like she'd just been slapped. It was a look in the seventies, just not one I expected to see on her.

'You don't think it's too much?' A hairbrush clenched between her teeth like a dagger, she wielded a hair-dryer in one hand and a can of hairspray in the other. Every day was a difficult hair day for my mother. Nana always used to delight in telling her, 'It's a shame you got your father's hair instead of mine.' My grandfather was bald.

'No, it looks very grown-up. What's in the bag?'

'Take it out.' It was a foam tube about three inches long.

'What the hell is this?'

'My secret weapon.' I watched her with amazement as she brushed her hair forward over her face like *Cousin It*, then I helped her pin the foam tube to her scalp an inch or two behind her hairline, then she tossed her head back.

'What do you think?' It looked like she'd been to Mrs Langley's hairdresser. 'Good big hair? Or bad?'

'Nana would be jealous.' It was just what my mother wanted to hear.

'You got that one right.'

I thought about Maya as I put on my tux. I'd been thinking about her while I'd been doing everything that week – so why stop? I was off crutches, and onto a cane now. Osborne had offered to loan me one via my mother, and I accepted via the same way. It was made of narwhal tusk, and had a silver handle. Narwhals were one of the endangered species he was big on saving. I guessed he'd had a change of heart. So had I. Ogden C Osborne had gone from rival to ally without me ever meeting him. The more time my mother spent with him doing whatever it was they did, the more time I'd have alone with Maya.

I still wanted to know the sordid details I was sure were at the heart of his kindness, but my curiosity was no longer tempered with jealousy and outrage. I wanted to know the secret that linked my mother and the old man so I could safeguard it, so I could make sure nothing happened that would separate me from Maya. What was it that so attracted me to her? Sure, teen lust and the promise of escaping the bondage of virginity were part of it, but there was more. The fact that Maya had chosen me made me think more of myself.

Maya had called me several times each day since our aborted TV rendezvous: twice from the plane, once from a car phone. They had flown on from that girls' school in Maryland, which even Mrs Langley had dubbed too dykey, to someplace called Ethel Walkers, who were willing to give her a second chance in exchange for a new chemistry lab. Which, according to Maya, seemed to her grandfather more like philanthropy than extortion when compared to an indoor riding rink. Our phone calls had escalated from, 'I keep thinking about you,' to 'I can't stop thinking about you,' to 'I'm crazy about you,' and finally a deliriously husky, whispered confession, 'I'm seriously in like with you.' I convincingly echoed each of her sentiments, knowing I didn't mean it. I wasn't just seriously in like with this girl, I was in love. I know, it's a ridiculous idea to think someone my age knows what that means, especially since I'd spent all of eight hours with her. Naïve, foolish, impossible? No question. But when you're fifteen and a half, you think you're different, and you are . . . sort of.

The only thing she said that gave me any cause to think anything could go wrong was, 'I hope you like to dance.' Naturally, I lied and said 'I love to dance.' The truth was, I'd only danced with two women in my whole life, and they didn't count – i.e., Nana and my mother. That alone wouldn't have bothered me; I was prepared to love anything she loved. Even the cane wouldn't have gotten in my way – it was kind of cool, actually. But the new patent-leather Brooks Brothers pumps were a test I didn't know if I was up to. My good foot felt pinched, and the other was still so swollen, tears came to my eyes as I jammed my foot into the patent-leather vise. One hand on my cane, I turned on my radio, and attempted a lame shuffle. The bump and the hustle were painfully out of question, but when I looked in the mirror, I was surprised to see a smile that hid any trace of my discomfort. Knowing that Maya was out there, waiting for me, gave me such a belief in the future that I was numb to all that was lacking in the present.

'Are you ready, Finn?'

'Almost.'

My mother tied my bow tie for me. I zipped up the back of her dress. I told her she looked beautiful. She said I looked handsome. Like an old married couple who have recently become swingers, we each wanted the other to be happy, so we could be happy with someone else.

The party started in fifteen minutes. It was at least that long a drive to the Hunt Club. Impatient, I wanted to get in the car and go. But my mother told me, 'We don't want to be the first ones.'

'Why?'

'We don't want to seem to eager.' When I still didn't get it, she told me, 'Have a cigarette and relax.'

'You're kidding.' I was kind of surprised. Smoking, along with drinking and drugs were the only things I wasn't allowed to do.

'I know you smoke when I'm not here.' I was relieved she wasn't wise to my two other new-found vices. I lit up and blew a smoke ring, just the way Maya had taught me.

'I thought you quit.'

'Understand, I'm just giving us permission to smoke this one night, and this one night only.'

'Why's that?'

'We're nervous.'

Gates' car was parked at the turn-in to the Hunt Club. Clipboard in hand, he checked the names to the faces of the people in the Mercedes stretch that was ahead of us in line. When it was our turn, he just smiled and waved us on like we were regulars.

The drive was lined with potted gardenia trees in full-scented bloom that Osborne had flown up from Florida to perfume the evening's already rarefied air. A faint mist, flickered with fireflies, played its way through the golf course. The sun set, torching the horizon pink and mauve. As I watched a family of deer dine solemnly on the putting green of the eleventh hole, rabbits nibbled between the lines of a deserted grass tennis court. All was right in this world that I had never seen before. And when the guy parking cars at the entrance to the long, wide-porched clubhouse I didn't know was designed by Stanford White, opened our car door and said, 'Nice to see you again,' I actually felt that we were regulars.

Cocktails were being served in the dining room. There was a circus-sized tent adjoining, being set up for dinner. When we stepped into the party, we were suddenly assaulted by the white noise of two hundred people talking at once. It was like that pre-cable feeling of waking up in the middle of the night with the TV on, after they stopped broadcasting, when static's on maximum volume, and you suddenly don't know where you are.

'Night and day . . . You are the one.' A dance band playing this corny love song, me standing on tiptoes scanning the room for Maya: it was corniness squared. My mother put on her glasses, hoping to catch sight of Osborne. When we didn't see them, we took each other by the hand, and 'excuse-me'd' through the crowd looking for them. We criss-crossed back and forth across the room so many times one of the guys passing champagne asked if we'd lost something. It wasn't like I expected Maya to be waiting at the door for me, to see me the moment I walked in and shout 'Finn!' and run across the room and throw her arms around me like she hadn't seen me after a two-year hitch in Vietnam. Not that I wouldn't have liked it. But I was realistic. Sort of.

No Maya, no Bryce, no Mr Osborne, no Mrs Langley. We stood in the center of the crowd and pretended like we were having a good time. Everybody seemed to know everybody, or at least somebody, except for us. I was so desperate for recognition, that when I saw the snob that needed a bra, Ian, and the blonde that were riding with Maya the first time I saw her, I actually waved. I was genuinely happy when they waved back, until I figured out they were

110

acknowledging the presence of someone behind me. Even my humiliation was corny. They looked right past me. I didn't exist. I was invisible, and didn't like the feeling. My mother was so anxious, she was actually relieved when somebody called her: 'Dr Earl?'

When she saw it was Jilly, all she said was, 'Could we have two Diet Cokes, please?' Jilly was a waitress.

'Hi, Finn.'

'Hey, Jilly, how's it hangin'?' Talking always made me feel less invisible.

'Another day, another dollar,' Jilly answered. My mother gave me a look that made it clear: talking to the help was worse than talking to nobody. But I didn't care. At least Jilly was glad to see me.

'Have you seen Bryce?'

As she walked away to get our Cokes, she told me with a smile, 'No, and I haven't seen Maya either.'

Once Jilly identified us, the people standing around us gave us a quick, sideways up-and-down look. The polite ones stepped back out of earshot to gossip. I'm not being paranoid when I say I knew what they were whispering, because this one old guy in a midnight-blue tux with a silk scarf draped over his shoulders, who thought he looked like Errol Flynn, even though his ears stuck out from the side of his head like signal flags, didn't even have the courtesy to lower his voice.

'So that's Osborne's new Wonder Drug.' I looked right at him, but he didn't stop. 'What do you think? Prescription, or over-the-counter?'

Another jerk said, 'Think she charges by the orgasm, or the hour?'

After they all got through laughing, somebody else added, 'At least they don't look Hawaiian.'

I stopped listening when a woman with skinny legs and a belly that was all liver joined the conversation. 'Are you boys telling dirty stories without me again?'

I knew we didn't belong there, but I didn't want to go home. 'What do we do now?'

'Smile.' My mother's happy face was so fake you would have thought she had a coat hanger in her mouth. 'Do you have a cigarette, dear?'

'You know I do, dear – you gave them to me.' I watched her light the wrong end. I was careful not to make the same mistake. Before I could light up she hissed, 'Please don't smoke.'

'But you said . . .'

'It sends the wrong message.'

'They've got the message.'

'If you want to go home, say so.' When I didn't answer, she told me, 'I have to go to the ladies' room.'

My mother ditched me, and my feet were killing me. As I gingerly worked my way across the dance floor, the guy who'd made the crack about my mother being Osborne's new wonder drug was foxtrotting with the liver woman. When he stepped on my bad foot, I screamed out loud.

'Walking wounded off the dance floor!' was his idea of a funny apology.

When I said, 'Excuse me,' to the asshole, I felt even lamer than I was.

There were a couple of empty stools at the kitchen end of the bar. I sat down, looked at the silver clock behind the bar, and considered what would have been unthinkable thirty minutes earlier: *If she's not here in ten minutes, I'm going home.* I considered it; I knew I didn't mean it.

I could feel my foot bleeding inside its patent-leather prison. I knew if I took it off I'd never get it back on. When the bartender asked me what I wanted, I said, 'I'll have a vodka martini: shaken, not stirred.' I was trying to make a joke. No one laughed but a black kid in a brand-new tux with a butterfly bow tie so big it looked like he had a pigeon tied around his neck snickered like it wasn't funny.

'Would you like that with an olive, or with a twist?' The bartender took me seriously. I wondered if the tux made me look older, or was I invisible to the bartender, too?

'I'll go for the olive.' I had never had a martini, but I liked olives. The black kid looked familiar.

'That's a serious drink.' Downing half the martini in a single gulp, to show I was serious, I finally recognized him.

'You're . . .' was all I got out before the delayed reaction of the alcohol torched my esophagus. 'Chief Gates' son,' I gasped. He'd looked bigger throwing the football.

'Is that brilliant deduction based on the fact that he's black and I'm black?' Clearly, he was looking for a fight. I was already beaten.

'It's based on I saw you throwing the goddamn football when your father brought us to this hellhole.' I lit a cigarette, and took another swallow of martini. It made me feel dizzy. I hoped I looked more relaxed than my mother, who was now chain-smoking by herself on the terrace.

'So you're the anthropologist?'

'What?'

'That's what Mr Osborne calls you. What's that about?'

'I'm interested in primitive peoples.'

'Well, you came to the right place.'

'You friends with these people?'

'I'm the token Negro's token son.' He was working hard at sounding mad. He took a hard rubber ball out of his pocket and began to squeeze it. 'Strengthens my fingers.'

'For football.'

'For the cello.'

'You don't look like a cello kind of guy.'

'Seeing how you're more comfortable with stereotypes, I also play a soulful bass guitar. That's Slim's and my band.' He pointed to four kids who were setting up microphones and a drum kit under a smaller, open-sided tent pitched at the far end of an Olympian cabana-lined pool. Slim was the kid with the Veronica Lake hairdo on the horse who took Quaaludes and wrecked his Porsche. Gates' son introduced himself with a soul-shake as Marcus.

'What's your band called?'

'Eat The Rich.'

'Good name. Why aren't you playing with them?'

'Mr Osborne wanted me to come to his party so I could meet some fat cat he thinks can fix me up with a football scholarship to Stanford.'

'Osborne say you couldn't play with them?'

'Osborne loves that shit. My father thinks if the man sees me playing with Slim, he'll peg me for a faggot.' Gates' son asked for a Coke. The bartender didn't mind jiggering out liquor to underage kids, but he had a problem waiting on Marcus. He made the only black person at the party ask for the damn Coke three times, and the one he finally poured him was in a dirty glass.

'Well, *thank* you.' Marcus said it like 'fuck you' and asked me in a pissed-off voice, 'Any other anthropological questions I can answer?'

'Actually, there are a couple.'

'Shoot. No one else is going to talk to me but you.'

'What's a Hawaiian?'

'A Hawaiian . . . where do you get off with that Hawaiian shit?' The question pissed him off.

'I heard somebody say that fat kid's grandmother was a Hawaiian.' I pointed to Ian, who was talking with his mouth full to the Italian kid. They both wore Madras pants with their dinner jackets.

'Ian's a dipshit.'

'And tonight, somebody said about my mother and me, at least we weren't Hawaiian.'

'It's asshole code for ham-dodgers.'

'What?' The expression was new to me. He could tell I still didn't get it.

'People of the Jewish persuasion.'

'I'm part ham-dodger.' My shrink grandfather changed his name from Earlenberger to Earl when he went to Yale.

'I'm not putting you down. It's just a fact. They don't want anybody from the outside to know they're anti-Semitic, so they call 'em Hawaiians.' He wasn't pissed off at me anymore. 'Fuck, you are an anthropologist. What else you want to know?'

'What's with Mr McCallum's ears and Dwayne?'

'Man, you know all the dipshits . . . you mean *that* Mr McCallum?' He pointed to the man who'd stepped on my toes and talked about my mother.

'Yeah, that's him.' I should have recognized the ears.

'That's ancient history.'

'I'm an anthropologist.'

'Who told you about that shit?'

'I heard it from somebody.' I pretended I knew what I was talking about.

'Well, it's true. He's Dwayne's daddy. And Katie's.' He nodded towards a waitress who would have been pretty, if it weren't for the McCallum ears. 'And he's Pete the bartender's daddy, too.' He gestured towards the jug-eared bartender that didn't like serving him the Coke. 'Their mothers were all maids. They used to call him "Maid to Order McCallum".'

'Why'd they all want to do it with him?'

'Not all of 'em did.'

'You mean he raped them?'

'He raped Dwayne's momma, that's for sure. Doped her up and dead-horsed her.' Another new expression.

'How'd he get away with it?'

'Money. Everybody in Vlyvalle's his cousin. The only person richer than him is Osborne.'

'Jesus Christ. Does he still do it?' I watched the old fuck pat Jilly on the ass as she moved by him with a tray of *hors d'oeuvres*.

'Dwayne's momma was the last. Osborne saw to that.'

'What happened?'

Marcus hunched his shoulders, leaned close, and whispered in my ear like he was trying to sell me drugs. 'Some big bald-headed black guy pulled him out of his Mercedes Benz in Newark, beat the shit out of him. But the Twilight Zone part of the story is, when McCallum got out of the hospital, that black guy was Vlyvalle's Chief of Police.' Marcus looked me square in the eye for a long beat, then burst out laughing. 'I got you good. You believed that bullshit, didn't you?' If he hadn't laughed so hard, it would have been easier for me to be sure he was just fucking with me.

I looked back out on the terrace. My mother was still standing there, shivering, a small pile of half-smoked Marlboro Lights in the ashtray on the railing by her elbow. She looked at me and gave a half-hearted smile. Then her expression changed. Suddenly, my mother and everyone were applauding. I turned round, and there was Ogden C Osborne, bigger than life.

I and everyone else moved closer. He seemed smaller, jollier, better groomed and older than he did in the cornfield. Decked out in white tie and tails, a cigarette smoldering in an ivory holder clenched in his yellow teeth, swollen belly, red nose, pink cheeks, and pointy white beard – from where I stood, he looked like Santa Claus out for a night on the town in the off-season.

The way they applauded, you'd have thought he just won an election. The way he smiled, you knew that was the only thing he hadn't won. Even the Vice-President was clapping. Hoots, whistles, tears, what was Ogden C to these strange people? As I crowded closer, I heard a woman with blue hair and yellow diamonds sigh, 'They don't make them like him anymore.' It seemed sad. The last of a kind always is.

Maya was standing next to him. Across the room, she looked different. Her hair was braided with pearls, and coiled up on top of her head like a crown. Between the do and her high heels, she towered over Osborne. She wore a cream silk, double-breasted tuxedo without anything on under the jacket, except a pearl choker. When she bowed at her grandfather's urging to the crowd, me and everybody else could see her breasts. I wouldn't have minded if Ian and the Italian kid weren't front and center.

Marcus was right behind me. 'Rich girls don't look sixteen when they're dressed up, do they?' He was right. Someone else said a makeup artist named Way Bandy had been brought out from New York to do her up. The scar was gone. I missed it. She looked too perfect to be real.

Bryce had his arm around his mother's shoulder, and was holding up one of his legs, showing off the fact that he was wearing a sarong instead of trousers with his tuxedo. On him, it was a happening look. Osborne's wife was there, too. Maya warned me she'd had a few too many face-lifts from a Brazilian plastic surgeon. Thin and pale as a dried rose, she looked elegantly scary, like a really, really good-looking mummy. She spent most of the year in Palm Beach. The way Osborne kissed her, you would have thought she was his mother.

I figured I'd wait until the family finished their act before I went over and said hello to the girl I now knew it was moronic of me to think of as my date, much less my . . . well, we've already been through that. The martini on an empty stomach wasn't the only thing that left me queasy.

I turned my back to it all, and took one of the champagne glasses that was being filled at the bar, hoping I would feel less invisible if I were fucked up. It is a memorable moment in a certain kind of boy's life, when he decides to reach for a drink or a joint (I'd already counted on Jilly to get me off) in pursuit of a feeling he has misplaced and wants to find. Most people get so loaded they vomit and forget the first time they deliberately crossed that line. I remembered the exact instant I started thinking that way, only because as the first gulp of bubbly failed to quench my thirst, I heard a sharp whistle, followed by 'Finn!'

It was her, standing on a chair at the other end of the room, hands cupped to her mouth, shouting my name over the dance band. It was better than my fantasy because it was hers.

Couples stopped dancing and looked as she leapt off the chair and ran, delightfully spastic in her high heels, across the room. Smiles and laughter applauded her impulsiveness. You could see them saying to one another as they got out of her way, 'So cute . . . Isn't she adorable? Who's the lucky boy?' When they saw it was me, their looks became slightly circumspect. Women with daughters added under their breath, 'I wonder what Mother thinks of that? An unusual choice.' And the ones that had teenage sons made a mental note to remind their boys not to wait too long to invite little Maya out to East Hampton, or up to the vineyard . . . but I didn't know that was how Vlyvalle thought then. I wouldn't have thought it mattered, even if someone had warned me.

Maya threw her arms around me. She nearly knocked me over with the certainty of her embrace. My feet no longer hurt. The champagne was superfluous. But it was her whisper that knocked me over most of all. It was hoarse, nervous, and slow. 'I – love – you!' The exclamation point was her biting my ear. When she pulled her face away from one, most of her makeup was on my cheek. I could see the scar. She was real again. And even though Bryce was standing right there, I said it out loud. 'I love you more.' I was sure it was true, but it didn't matter.

'Impossible.' She took my cigarette from the ashtray, blew a smoke ring and put her finger through it.

'More than more.'

'It's great, isn't it?' She kissed me right on the mouth. She didn't care who saw.

'You two make me sick.' Bryce made a face like he was gagging and reached for some champagne.

'Bryce hates PDAS.'

'What are those?'

'Public Displays of Affection, my dear Finn.' Bryce translated as he shook my hand. 'They're so un-Yanomamö of you.'

'Bryce has gone native.' Maya tugged at his sarong. Bryce made a big show of re-tying it, exposing himself to half the room in the process.

'Maya, please, I don't have any underwear on tonight, and I don't want any of the other men to feel short-changed.'

'Bryce you always have to take it one step too far.'

'Someone has to do it.' He was wearing velvet slippers with gold fox heads on the toe. Maya was sitting on my lap now. Her hands patted out the rhythm of the band on the inside of my thighs. I switched to Coca-Cola. I wanted to be as wide awake as possible.

'I'm sorry we're so late.'

'That's OK. It's been fun.'

'They were horrible to you.' She knew how to translate my lies.

'No, it was interesting . . . in a horrible sort of way.'

'Polite, yet honest. A rare and dangerous combination.' Bryce, unsatisfied with the knot, untied and re-tied his sarong yet again.

'Jilly, can you help me with this thing?' You had to hand it to him – he knew how to get mileage out of his thing.

'Not tonight, Bryce.' Jilly liked the attention.

'Bryce, next time I have a birthday, why don't you just not wear anything at all?'

'Why wait?'

Maya ignored him. 'We would have been on time, I mean, I wanted to be here when you got here, but when we went to the hospital, so Daddy could give me my present, the most amazing thing happened . . .'

I smiled and nodded, like it was perfectly normal for a guy who was brain-dead to give his daughter a present.

'I picked out your birthday present.' You could tell it bothered Bryce his sister acted like their father wasn't in a coma.

'Bryce, don't spoil it.' He watched my face as she explained. 'When I kissed Daddy, his eyes opened for a second.'

'That's unbelievable.'

'That's one word for it.'

'Shut up, Bryce. I was the only one who saw it, but the doctor said it could be a major positive sign, and I just know he's gonna get better.'

'That's great.' I didn't know what else to say.

'"Hope is the thing with feathers that perches in the soul, and sings the tune without the words, and never stops at all."' Bryce smiled and took a rose from one of the floral decorations and put it in the buttonhole of his sister's jacket.

'Did you make that up?' I was impressed.

'I write poetry under a pseudonym – my pen name's Emily Dickinson.' I was even more impressed.

Maya jumped off my lap. 'Don't let Bryce move you from this spot; I'll be right back.' I watched her sashay to the bar on the opposite side of the room, where Ian and the Italian and a dozen other teenagers, wearing the costumes and expressions of middle-age, worked at looking bored.

When she was out of earshot, Bryce bummed a cigarette, and confided. 'I just don't want her to be disappointed.' I felt special Bryce was confiding in me.

'Maybe she won't be.' I tried to sound middle-aged, too.

'That's a nice idea.' It was the first time I ever saw Bryce look anything but happy. The *joie de vivre* drained from his face, and left him a sad and angry child. I recognized the look. I saw it in the mirror every day.

Maya returned with the blonde girl that had been out riding with them that day. Thin lips and big boobs, she was a seventeen-year-old doing a good job of impersonating a thirty-seven-year-old divorcee.

'Finn, this is Paige and yes, that is a diamond in her front tooth.' Paige lifted her lip to show off the accessory she had embedded in her left, front incisor.

'Mick has one just like it, except his is only a ruby.'

'OK, Paige, I'll brag for you. Finn, please act like you're impressed to hear that Paige met Mick Jagger at Studio 54.'

Paige smiled sweetly and said, 'Bitch.'

As we shook hands, Maya added, 'Paige is my cousin and oldest friend.'

'I thought I was your oldest friend.' Bryce tongue-kissed Paige. She was surprised, but she liked it.

Maya was getting impatient. 'Bryce, what is your problem?'

'I'm lonely, and I'm glad to see Paige.'

'Where's Coco, Bryce?' She had trouble sounding bored with Bryce pressing up against her.

'She had to fly home for her brother's coronation.' Paige waited for him to light the cigarette she put in a holder.

I thought he was kidding until Maya interjected, 'Bryce, I told you you should have gone.'

'I thought about it. But, I mean, coronation in a small African country? Just a few thousand naked people, the Prince of Wales . . . What's that compared to this?'

'Why didn't you go?' Paige asked.

'I'm worried about my mother.' He scanned the dance floor. McCallum had Mrs Langley cornered in a conversation. 'I think I better save her.'

'Jesus, I wonder how my mother's doing?'

'Relax, she's with Grandpa.' It wasn't such a relaxing thought. Maya pointed her out. She was talking to Osborne and the Vice-President. She said something that made them and the Secret Service man laugh. Like I said, she could be funny, when she was feeling good. Then the creep who we'd overheard say, 'Looks expensive,' came over and asked to be introduced. It was almost funny the way she smiled when the asshole kissed her hand and bowed. I felt guilty for wondering what they would have thought if they'd seen my mother trapped under the bookcase, cursing because she couldn't find her blow.

'Finn, are you listening?' I hadn't been. 'Paige asked you a question.'

'What? I'm sorry.'

'It doesn't matter. I already know you got arrested for dealing coke. Got any?'

'No.'

Maya gave her a look that let her know she was no longer her oldest friend.

'He wasn't dealing. Who told you that, anyway?'

'Everybody knows the story.' She sounded extra bored.

'No they don't.'

I wasn't about to tell it to them, but I had to say something. Maya looked at me, and her eyes widened like she'd seen something she'd missed. Then she touched my cheek to let me know it was safe.

'It's no biggie. Look at my brother.' Paige was trying to be friendly.

'Her brother got kicked out of Princeton for making Quaaludes,' Maya explained, adding, 'He's the smart one in the family.'

'So what brings you to our neck of the woods?' Paige asked.

Maya answered for me: 'His mother and my grandfather are old, old friends.' It was news to me. Truth, rumor, kind lie on Maya's part? I didn't say anything, but it made me wonder.

A gong rang. Mrs Langley announced casually as one can when you're serving two hundred plus, 'I think dinner's ready.'

Maya grabbed my hand. 'You're sitting next to me.' My mother was seated on Osborne's right, his wife was at the opposite end of the tent. And I couldn't stop thinking '*old, old friends*'.

It would explain why he was so nice to us. But just exactly how old friends were they, and what kind of old friends? She told me she met him in the hospital. My mother was four tables away, but she was right next to me in my head. I didn't want to worry about what I did and didn't know about her. I didn't want her past to eclipse my present. I was wishing I'd never shown her the goddamn invitation, when Maya whispered in my ear, 'It isn't as bad as you think.'

'What do you mean?' I whispered back.

'Whatever really happened to you in New York.' She knew I lied.

Ian shouted, 'It's not polite to whisper.'

Maya threw a roll at him. 'That depends what you're whispering.' Then, turning back to my ear, she told me, 'Don't worry, your secret's safe with me.'

'What secret's that?' I felt found out.

Her voice was more of a hiss than a whisper. Like a snake, she told me, 'You're good.'

She certainly made me feel that way as we held hands under the table and dipped our spoons into lobster bisque. Hidden by the tablecloth, her fingers teased the inside of my thigh. My hard-on stiffened down my pant leg, towards her touch. The tip of my penis was a half-inch from her hand, and creeping closer. Did she know? If she touched it by accident, would she jump up and shout 'Gross!' I was short of breath and close to lift-off. I was about to excuse myself when she put her other hand under the table and whispered, 'It's OK.' The way she whispered killed me.

They were passing the entrée now. You had a choice: rack of lamb or Chilean sea bass. I took the lamb, asked Maya where the men's room was, and left the table with my hands in my pockets, trying to keep my jizzed-up jockey shorts from leaking through the front of my tuxedo pants.

I chose the bathroom in the deserted men's locker room. There were freshly polished golf cleats laid out on benches and old photographs of guys playing tennis in long white pants. I ducked into one of the old-fashioned marble-walled stalls, took off my trousers and pulled off my underwear. I used the dry part to wipe myself off with. I wasn't being anal, just optimistic. I was hoping she'd put her hand down there again, and I didn't want her to get a sticky surprise. I wondered – did she know I came? I didn't know enough to be embarrassed. It had never happened to me before . . . with another person, that is. And I wasn't sure if I was supposed to say anything or not.

Tux trousers back on, jockey shorts in hand, I was going to throw them in the garbage can by the sink, but just as I was about to open the stall door, somebody else came in whistling 'Night and Day' which I was just starting to think wasn't such a bad song. I'm standing there, waiting for him to leave, and just when he gets to the 'You are the one,' part he cuts this really loud fart, and then laughs like he's really proud of himself. It smells like a dead animal that's been left in an unplugged refrigerator. Olfactory instinct takes over. Putting my hands to my face, I suddenly find myself sniffing my own soiled underwear. Repulsed, I drop them. When they land in the toilet, I've got another problem. Fish them up and wring them out, or leave them for someone else? I decide to flush. As the water rises ominously towards the top of the bowl, I know I've made a serious mistake.

When I hear the whistler flush and leave, I'm ready to bolt, but two more sets of footsteps enter. Stuck with the water just starting to slowly cascade over the top of the toilet bowl, I silently put down the toilet seat and step up out of harm's way. The footsteps turn into people, when I hear Marcus and Slim's voices.

'Relax. No one's here.' Slim's tongue was chemically drunk on Quaaludes.

'Shut up.' Marcus checks all the stalls to make sure. He thinks my stall is locked because the toilet's broken. He's not wrong. Then he pulls Slim into the stall next to me. He slams Slim against the divider. I know they're not getting high when Marcus says, soft and urgent, 'You're fucked up.' His voice sounded more hurt than angry. It was a different kind of pissed off than I had heard.

'I just did a couple of chips.' Still standing on the john's seat, I peered over the top of the stall. Marcus gripped the lapels of Slim's velvet jacket in his fists. He was shaking him.

'Do you do this fucking shit because you're ashamed of me, or what we do?' I thought he was going to start hitting him. When Marcus kissed him, and they began to make out, I stepped down into the toilet water that was flooding my stall, silently lifted the latch, and tiptoed back to the party.

I didn't know what to think, except that I was surprised I wasn't more shocked. When I passed the Vice-President's table and heard him whistling, I laughed out loud. The joke was on everybody, there were no rules. When I sat back down next to Maya, she asked, 'What took you so long?'

'I had a religious experience in the men's locker room.'

'You're starting to sound like Bryce.' She made it clear that wasn't a compliment. When I whispered in her ear about the Vice-President farting and me flushing my underpants down the toilet, she laughed so hard she knocked over her wine glass and kissed me. 'I take it back – you're not at all like my brother.'

Leaving out the part about Marcus and Slim, I was like her brother. We both liked our secrets. He knew how to tell people everything, and nothing. I was learning.

As we ate our lamb chops, the old lady with blue hair and yellow diamonds told us how she got kicked out of boarding school. 'The headmistress called my mother in, and said, [it was funny to hear an old lady imitate an old lady] "Abigail's a bright girl, delightful girl, an attractive girl, but I'm afraid to say I'm going to have to let her go." And when my mother asked why, Miss Hewitt – that was the name of the headmistress – said, "Well, to be perfectly frank, with that big diamond rattling around in her school bag, she's a distraction to herself and the other girls."'

'Where did you get the ring?' Maya leaned forward, her hand was in my lap again.

'I was engaged to a banker from Virginia.'

'How old were you?' Someone else asked.

'Fifteen.' When she smiled, you could see she must have been a total babe a hundred years ago.

'What happened then?' Maya liked this story.

'All my girlfriends got excused for a long weekend, so they could be bridesmaids, and we were married.' I thought the punchline was the six carat headlight on her third finger.

'God, that's romantic.'

'Not really. He beat me.'

As the plates were cleared, I watched Osborne introduce Marcus to the football connection. I could tell that's who he was because he was gesturing like he was throwing a ball, and squeezing Marcus's muscles. Marcus smiled slyly, as he allowed the aging jock to feel him up.

When the birthday cake was rolled out, my mother was showing Dr Leffler a yoga position, and the old lady with the diamonds was telling us why her third husband was her favorite out of the five she'd outlived. 'He knew how to make a woman feel very, very good. Now I have to make do with chocolates.' She had already eaten all the candy from the triple-decker silver thing that was in the middle of the table by herself.

There was something about that night, the bottomless glasses of Chateau Haut-Brion, the humidity, the gardenia-scented dark – it was as if everybody had decided to go for it. Whatever it was.

The toasts were a blur of good cheer and amusing anecdotes.

124

Maya filled me in on who everyone was and what they were talking about, and I laughed along like I'd known them my whole life. My face hurt from smiling, I was having so much fun. And the best part was, I wasn't faking it.

When Slim's band started to play, we ran down to the tent by the pool. Maya saw me limping, and told me to take off my shoes. Realizing I was embarrassed, she kicked hers off, and we left our shoes in the damp grass. Better than that, when we reached the dance floor . . . I suddenly thought I knew how to dance. 'Satisfaction', 'Respect', 'Chain of Fools', Slim's band sounded better than they were. Marcus sulked on the edge of the dance floor, and shouted to me, 'So many white people, so little rhythm.'

Hot and sweaty, we stopped dancing in the middle of a slow song, and ran off into the shadows and made out, then ran back before we were finished, buttoning and zipping ourselves back together, because Bryce had taken over the microphone. Cocktail glass in hand, dyed white hair, he looked like an albino Dean Martin, as he crooned 'Everybody Loves Somebody Sometime', which anybody could have told you was a totally uncool song in 1978. Except when Bryce did it it somehow became cool. He even got Maya and Mrs Langley and Osborne onstage to sing the chorus. When the song was over, Osborne bowed, palms folded together, like an Oriental potentate, and waved goodnight. My mother was standing next to me. I saw him whisper something to Maya as he left the stage.

To her credit, my mother started to walk away when Maya approached us. She was doing a good job of giving me space. 'Dr Earl . . . I'm Maya Langley.'

'I'm not a doctor, Maya.' My mother was trying to set the record straight.

'My grandfather told me you didn't finish medical school, but he says you're the doctor that saved his life. So you're doctor here whether you like it or not.' When Mr Osborne was doing the talking, say it three times and it was true. 'Anyway, I just wanted to introduce myself.'

'Well, it's a pleasure meeting you, Maya, and thank you so much for including us in your party. I've had a wonderful time.' My mother was on her third cup of coffee. I could tell she was ready to go.

'Can I drive Finn home?'

'You're only sixteen. You have to be seventeen to have a driver's license.' My mother was memorizing the motor-vehicles regulations of the State of New Jersey for her driver's test next week.

'I have a farmer's license. You can drive at sixteen, as long as it's farm business. Which this is, indirectly.' I knew my mother was going to say no.

'Go slowly.' My mother kissed me on the cheek. 'Don't be too late, lambie.' I didn't even mind her calling me 'lambie'.

The band played until almost four. Then the waiters rolled out carts laden with eggs, sausages, and bacon. By that time, I'd been introduced to a couple of dozen kids whose names I couldn't remember, but seemed like old friends. We played Quarters with shots of Tequila at the table, and shotgunned pot into each other's brains in the bushes. Everyone was really nice to me, partly because of Maya, but mostly because Paige had exaggerated me from just getting busted for coke into being some kind of preppie Superfly. I just smiled and nodded and acted like I'd been there and done that when they tried to impress me with all the nightclubs and bars they went to in the city that I'd never heard of. It's easy to make a good impression when you're stoned.

I knew I was out there when I agreed to play golf with Ian and the Italian kid, whose name was Giacomo, but I kept calling Pinocchio, which Maya said was a scream, because he always lied.

We drove home in Maya's birthday present – a Land Rover, painted in zebra stripes, just like the one on *Daktari*. Bryce did it because that was her favorite TV show. At this point my expectations were so gilded I would have thought it was shabby if it hadn't had a custom paint job. We took the back roads, cutting across farms, and four-wheeling through the estates of Vlyvalle.

The night sky turned indigo for dawn as we bounced down dirt roads pocketed with fog. Missing the turn we veered off-road, laughing and not bothering to stop. Maya downshifted through saplings and bounced us over fallen logs. The headlights danced through the woods as we looked for the lane. When our headlights flashed across Dwayne's GTO, a fleshy glimpse of Jilly doing it with him in the back seat made me horny and prompted Maya to shout out the window, 'Go for it!'

When we stopped in front of my house, Maya forgot to put the stick in neutral before she took her foot off the clutch to kiss me. The Land Rover jumped forward into a bed of impatiens. Maya kissed me quickly.

'I have a surprise for you.'

'What is it?'

'You'll know day after tomorrow.'

'Why do I have to wait?' She started the Land Rover up. I didn't want the night to be over.

'You're having lunch with Grandpa tomorrow. He wants to meet you.'

14

When I opened my eyes, my mother was sitting on the edge of my bed, staring at me. I'd only managed to get my jacket and one shoe off before I passed out on top of my covers five hours earlier. It was eleven o'clock, and my head felt like it had spent the night in a paint-shaker.

'You were drinking last night.'

'No I wasn't.' When she lit a cigarette and exhaled in my face, I thought I was going to puke.

'I saw you having wine at the table.'

'Why didn't you say anything then?'

'I didn't want to make a scene. I thought it'd be better if we talked about it in the clear light of day.'

'Mine was ginger ale – honest.' My mother handed me a Coca-Cola.

'I was told you were drinking.'

'Thanks for the Coke.' I tried to change the subject. I didn't want to fight.

'Look, I know it wasn't just you. Dr Leffler's daughter, Boopie, came home last night and vomited all over her bed.'

'Gross.' I vaguely remembered doing shots with her. She had black hair and big eyes, and they called her 'Boopie' because her father thought she looked like Betty Boop, which shows what an old fart he was. 'Did Dr Leffler call you to tell you I was drunk, or to say Boopie blew lunch?'

'Actually, he called to invite me to the theater.'

'With his wife?'

'He's separated.'

'Aren't we supposed to have lunch with Mr Osborne?'

'He asked to have lunch with you by himself.' I could tell that made my mother nervous.

'Just him and me?' My mother nodded. Now I was getting nervous. I thought Maya and the rest of her family would be there.

'Why?'

'I don't know that, but I will not tolerate your drinking.'

'You want to punish me?' I thought of the million and one liquor bottles I carried out to the trash for her.

'I don't want to, but I will.'

'OK, you tell Mr Osborne I'm grounded and can't come to lunch because the waiters at his party kept filling my glass up with booze.'

'Promise me you won't drink again. You're not even sixteen.'

'I had a good role model.'

'Are you trying to hurt me?'

'Just being honest.' That got her.

'All right, after lunch at Mr Osborne's, you are grounded for two weeks.' I knew she wanted me to go. She had a freshly ironed shirt hanging on my doorknob.

'Then I'm not going to lunch.'

'You think this is a game?'

'Yeah.' Knowing I'd won that round, I hit the shower, and thought of Maya as I washed myself with a fresh rosebud of scented soap. My mother came in to my bathroom.

'Alcohol destroys brain cells, Finn.'

I thought about saying, 'Then why should I listen to you?' but opted for 'Remember that conversation the family therapist had with us about boundaries? I'm trying to take a shower, could I have some privacy?'

My mother drove me to Osborne's. She gave me the worst kind of silent treatment – she sang. She thought she was making a point when she put one of her favorite oldies on the tape deck. 'Help! I need somebody . . .'

My mother had this thing about the Beatles. Very queer. She always made a big deal out of the fact that when she was in high school, she snuck into the city to hear the Fab Four play. She didn't seem to get the fact that the Beatles broke up. I decided not to raise the question, 'Why don't you play one of the songs those has-beens wrote about LSD or heroin?' My mother started singing again, 'Help!'

Osborne certainly had a lot of it. On the way over I counted eight farmers, six guys mowing lawns, three Japanese gardeners (Jilly told me Dwayne said they were gay and married in some kind of Oriental 'Until death do us part' threesome, which I was actually curious about), and two security men who hung out in this little gatehouse that was part of the six-foot brick wall that guarded Osborne's house and the formal gardens that surrounded it. And this was on a Sunday.

My mother pulled into a cobbled courtyard in front of a house that was bigger than a mansion and smaller than a monument. There was a uniformed chauffeur loading luggage into a maroon stretch Mercedes. My mother still hadn't said anything. She was waiting for me to make a move. I felt like telling her off right then and there so Osborne could come to the window and hear it all. Then I thought of the surprise Maya promised to give me tomorrow, took a deep breath and threw my arms around my mother's neck. 'Mom, I'm sorry. You're right about the drinking. I made a mistake. I swear to God, may I go to hell if I ever do it again.' My mother started to cry before I even got to the hell part.

'Oh, lambie, that's all I wanted to hear you say.' Which of course is the reason I told her such a bald-faced lie. 'I just worry about you and us, and I want you to be happy . . . in the long run, and the short run.'

'I know that.' It was funny, her hugging me and crying felt so good, it didn't feel as though I'd not only lied, but doomed myself to eternal damnation.

'You're going to be fine, Finn.' I wasn't sure of that. 'Call me when you want me to pick you up.' She handed me the cane to give back to Mr Osborne.

'Mom . . .' She looked up at me as I got out of the car. 'Am I still grounded?'

'No, Finn, you're not grounded.' I didn't feel the least bit guilty until she drove off and I heard her start to sing another goddamned Beatles song. 'When I find myself in times of trouble'

Osborne's home was about a half a city block long. Six columns, a roof like a Greek temple, and a fountain out front as big as a swimming pool with bronze nymphs and a guy holding a trident. To me it looked like a set from a gladiator movie. All I could think of as I walked towards the door was that line in *Spartacus*, 'We who are about to die salute you.' It was spooky, before I even touched the bell, the massive bronze double-doors opened with a creak. It was Osborne's wife. Black pant suit with big white buttons, and a blood-red lipstick smile. She looked less like a mummy in the daylight and more like Cruella de Vil's meaner, older sister.

'I'm Finn . . .' I held out my hand, but instead of shaking it, she gently took hold of my chin, turned my profile to the light, and peered at me through red-framed reading glasses that hung from her neck on a jeweled gold chain.

'Not much of a resemblance, but from what I saw last night, you certainly inherited his hormones.' Her fingers were cold and damp.

'You know my father?'

She laughed at me and let go of my face. 'Intimately.'

Intimately? I found it hard to imagine the father I knew from the Yanomamö film getting it on with a white raisin like Mrs Osborne. But I'd learned enough to know in Vlyvalle anything was possible. One thing was definite: she was telling me something, something I didn't know, something I wasn't sure I wanted to hear. Herbert the butler hurried down a curved staircase, and handed her a Hermès case. I'd never seen a butler before. Except for the uniform, he looked like a diplomat.

Mrs Osborne rolled a combination built into the clasp and checked the contents. It was stuffed with enough jewelry to fill a window at Tiffany's. Satisfied, she snapped it shut and called out over her shoulder, 'I'm leaving now, so you two can get acquainted without me eavesdropping.'

As soon as the butler closed the door behind her, the door to the library opened, and Osborne appeared. 'Now that my wife is safely on her broom, come on in and chew the fat.' His voice was deep, and slightly comic, like Foghorn Leghorn without the drawl. He wore a Hawaiian shirt with *Aloha* written all over it, a New York Yacht Club blazer, freshly pressed but heavily mended khakis and gold sealskin slippers.

I followed him into a library that was practically the size of our house. Shelves up to the ceiling, full of books and a ladder to get to them, that you knew he hadn't climbed in a long time. There was a big painting of a naked woman with blue skin – that I knew was a Picasso, because the signature was about a foot long, – and tons of black-and-white photographs I wanted to look at, but I had too many questions rattling around my head to enjoy the scenery.

'Mrs Osborne knows my dad?' It was about ninety degrees outside, the air-conditioning was blasting, and he had a fire in the fireplace.

'She thinks she does.' Osborne threw another log on the fire. Sparks jumped out onto the Persian carpet. He carelessly kicked them back into the hearth, leaving burn marks on the rug.

'What does that mean?'

'My wife is convinced you're my son.'

I felt like I'd been kicked in the stomach.

'Don't worry, I'm not your father.'

'Then why does she think it?' I was angry – with them for fucking with me, and with myself, because I knew for a nanosecond, that that greedy valve in my heart of hearts opened wide to the idea I was heir to part of this.

'She thinks it for two reasons, and neither one is any of your goddamn business.' He clipped the end of a Cohiba, and smoked it without ever lighting it. He wasn't used to explaining himself to anyone, much less to a teenage boy. 'But, since you never know if someone's worth trusting until you trust them with something that can hurt you, I'll tell you. Reason one: though I'm not particularly proud of it, I've got a number of bastard children running around this world. Some of their mothers I was in love with, others . . . well, good bad or indifferent, I set up trust funds for each and every one of my progeny. So while they may be complete bastards . . . I'm not. Reason number two . . .' Unsatisfied with inhaling an unlit cigar, he struck a match. 'Me smoking this cigar, along with all the rest, stays in this room, right?'

'Right . . . what's the second reason?'

'Your mother.' I knew it, but still, it shocked me.

'So you and my mom are . . .' He knew what I was saying. It made him smile, his eyes narrowed like he was looking at the horizon, not a four-million-dollar blue nude's ass.

'Unfortunately, we're just friends.'

'You're trying to tell me your wife thinks I'm your kid, but there's nothing between you and my mother?' He was surprised by my tone of voice. So was I. He liked it . . . sort of.

'I didn't say "nothing", and it's a whole hell of a lot easier for a rich man to find lovers than it is friends.' I was so tightly wound, a knock on the door made me flinch. The butler wheeled in a table with lunch laid out under silver chafing dishes. When he left, Osborne admitted, 'My wife doesn't think I'm capable of being friends with a woman I haven't slept with . . . perhaps "friend" isn't the right word.'

I had a choice – get mad or cry.

'Look, I know you're fucking my mother.' I thought he was going to throw me out, and at that moment that was what I wanted. I did not understand these people. The pull they exerted on me and my mother scared me. At that moment I sensed with a strange certainty, that even if they meant me no harm, they would do me no good.

'As they say in the Bible: it's easier for a camel to pass through the eye of a needle than for a rich man to get through the gates of heaven . . . If this doesn't satisfy you, get the hell out of my house.'

I freaked when he slowly unbuckled his belt. As he pulled down his trousers and boxer shorts, I looked for something to hit him with. This was scarier than any TV movie. When he pulled up his shirt, it became a little less frightening and a whole lot more horrible. Osborne's skin was the color of an old porcelain urinal – sickly, yellow-white, varicosed, with ruptured veins. His belly was distended, and zippered with scars, testimony to part of what he had to leave behind to live. But that is not what he wanted me to see.

'Take a good hard look, sonny, cause you're only gonna get to see it once.' He lifted up his long, lifeless, uncircumcised dick and grimly showed me an angry red scar where his balls used to hang. 'The surgical procedure is called an orchiectomy. What it comes down to is they cut off your balls to slow down your cancer. Makes it less aggressive, less hungry. My wife ordered the operation while I was unconscious. My kidneys had shut down, my prostate was the size of a baseball. *Tout le monde mange, et je suis le dîner.* When I met your mother in the hospital, my fucking days were over . . . satisfied?'

I felt like I should say sorry, but I just nodded. The old man pulled up his pants and buckled up his belt. 'So, you want to have lunch with me or not?'

I'd lost my appetite, but I said 'Yes.'

'Good, because I have a chef that makes the best goddamned chicken hash in the world.' Before he dug in, he swallowed half a dozen pills that were laid out on a silver dish by his water glass. 'You want some wine?'

'On the way over here I swore to my mother I'd never drink again.'

'Well, there's only one way to find out if you can trust me.' The wine tasted like a dry autumn. I forget the name of the vineyard, but he owned it.

'I'm not trying to be a wiseass, but why are you and my mother such good friends?'

'She saved my life.' He chewed with his mouth open.

'You mean, you really think she has healing hands?'

'No . . . when she came to my hospital room that first time, I was holding this.' He pulled a small, ivory-handled revolver out of his jacket pocket. 'I would have already blown my brains out by the time she got there, but my hands were so shaky, I dropped the bullets trying to load it. Hooked up to all those goddamned tubes, I couldn't get out of bed to pick them up.' He smiled as he told the story. I guessed, because he didn't blow his brains out, it had a happy ending. 'The first thing I said to her was . . .'

'I can't reach my cartridges.' I finished his sentence for him.

'She told you?'

'I heard my mother say it to you on the phone the night before we came here.'

'When I left the hospital in New York, I told her if there was ever anything I could do for her, that that was all she needed to say.' He picked a bit of chicken out of his teeth with a gold toothpick.

'What'd my mother say when you asked for the bullets?'

'She told me if I still wanted to kill myself after she gave me a foot rub she'd load the gun and help me pull the trigger.' We both laughed.

'You ever have the urge again?'

'At first, lots of times. But then your mother would come to the hospital and we'd talk and . . . your mother gives good conversation, especially when she used to get high.' It was reassuring to know I wasn't the only one who thought my mother's personality had suffered from sobriety.

'You know, my mother has all these articles about you.' I wasn't being disloyal; I thought he'd be flattered.

'I know, I gave them to her.'

'Why?'

'I wanted her to know about me so she could help me decide something.' I wasn't sure whether the fact that he needed my mother's help made me think more of her or less of him.

'What were you trying to decide?'

'Whether it's as empty as it feels.'

He didn't sound like Foghorn Leghorn anymore. Before I left, he let me look at the photographs framed and scattered around the room. They were shots of good times in impossible places: a tiger hunt in Nepal, polo on the green at the White Raja's palace in Sarawak; he told me the guy sitting next to him on the speedboat plowing the Aolian waters was a Rockefeller later eaten by cannibals; Georgia O'Keefe killing a rattlesnake in Abiquiu; Billie Holiday, high as a kite, in the back of a DC-3, kitted out with blond maple bed and bar, the sheets rumpled – have they or haven't they? That one was my favorite.

Osborne summed it all up as, 'White people having big fun, circa the twentieth century.'

My mother beeped to let us know she was there to pick me up. As he walked me to the door, I handed him back his narwhal-tusk cane.

'Thanks for loaning me the cane.'

'Keep it. If you're lucky, you'll need it again.'

15

Maya called me on the phone after I got back from Osborne's. As we I-missed-you-I-missed-you-more'd, I felt myself stiffen. By the time we gushed to 'I love you', 'I love you, too', I had a blue-steel hard-on. It jumped when she told me 'I talked to Grandpa about you.'

'What's he say?'

'That you were a keeper.' I was familiar enough with the rules of the wild to know that that was a fish you keep for eating rather than let go to grow up.

'Does that mean he likes me?'

'It's his highest compliment.'

'So what's my surprise?' Thinking about it, I unzipped my jeans. I had never heard of phone sex. It seemed natural.

'You'll find out tomorrow, greedy.'

'I'm not greedy, just curious.'

'All I can tell you is we're going on a night picnic.'

'That sounds exciting.' I was breathing hard.

'Are you being sarcastic?'

'No.'

'Good.'

'Why is that good?'

'Because Bryce is sarcastic, and I'm sick of Bryce.'

'If you're sick of him, I'm sick of him.' I was getting good at telling people what they wanted to hear.

'Pick you up at six-thirty.' When she hung up, I suddenly felt stupid for having my dick in my hand. I remembered something I had seen scratched above a urinal in Grand Central Station: 'Ain't love grand when you hold it in your hand.'

For the next twenty-four hours I was blissed out on the kind of hormonal anticipation young men often mistake for contentment. No longer having to alternately secretly worry/hope that my mother was getting it on with Osborne, I was free to fantasize about the surprise Maya had planned for me.

I was sure it involved sex. After the delights her right hand had introduced me to under the table at her sweet-sixteen party, I was stupefied with triple-x-rated thoughts of all that surely lay in store for me once we were alone on our night picnic. I came, I saw, and now I was going to conquer those vaginal mysteries that had haunted me since I'd first begun to keep my desires hidden between the boxspring and my mattress. No question, we were going to do it.

I was so happy, I felt sorry for my mother as she drove off to rub Osborne's back the next morning. While she was merely liked, I was loved. I ran after her as she drove away and pounded on the fender for her to stop. When she asked me what was wrong, I answered, 'Nothing, I just wanted to kiss you goodbye.' My mother never knew that I went back into the house and made my bed because I pitied her. There was both an innocence and a sweetness to my ruthlessness.

I was waiting on the lawn when Maya drove up. The sun was setting in shades of purple and blue. The evening sky looked like a beautiful bruise. I was so excited when I jumped into the seat next to her, I leaned in for a kiss with such blind passion, our front teeth collided with enough force to make her shout, 'Oh my God, I think you chipped my tooth.' Teenage girls are not always more romantic than boys.

I could tell she sensed my disappointment. When she pulled over a quarter of a mile down the road, I thought she was going to give me another chance at a kiss, not check her smile in the rear-view mirror and say, 'You ever drive a stick?' She had already decided that I had in fact knocked a tiny chip off the corner of her right, front tooth.

Naturally, I lied and said, 'Sure.'

Popping the clutch, stalling, grinding the gears each time I attempted to get out of first, it became readily apparent this was my first time. Maya laughed and I felt stupid as we lurched down a rutted dirt road towards the big surprise I was now convinced I wasn't going to get.

138

We jerked and bounced and stopped and started through fields shoulder-high with corn and fallow with lavender. Deer romped around us, surfacing and disappearing in the sea of green like dolphins. When we got to a gully with a creek at the bottom, Maya told me to gun it. All four wheels spinning, I careened downwards. The front tire hit a rock. The steering wheel jerked out of my grip. The front fender hit a tree stump with a metallic thud, and the tail-light broke against a boulder. Two 360s later, all four wheels were axle-deep in mud. I shook with adrenalin and embarrassment as I turned to Maya and said softly, 'I'm really sorry.'

'What for? That was fantastic.' We stepped out of the Land Rover, knee-deep in mud and inspected the damage.

'I'll pay to have the fender and the light fixed.'

'I'll say I did it.' She was enjoying this a lot more than I was. 'Looks better all banged up anyway.' Things that could be fixed didn't matter to Maya. I probably would have thought she was a spoiled rich girl if she'd made me pay for it. But that wasn't what I was thinking when she leaned back against the freshly dented fender and pulled me to her. I kissed her on the mouth just the way I wanted to when I had chipped her tooth. She tasted of Marlboro Lights and Gummi Bears. I slipped my hand down her pants.

'Hey, you're spoiling the surprise.' She pushed me away and pulled a coil of chain out of the back of the Land Rover. While I watched, she hooked one end of the chain around a tree stump and started up the winch. Arms and legs caked in mud, she steered the Land Rover up the incline with one hand and smoked a cigarette with the other. It was like she was the guy and I was the girl. I never knew being a wimp could ever feel so sexy.

The moon was up by the time we were four-wheeling through the pine woods that abutted the State Park. When the headlights swept across a small lake, Maya turned off the engine. She pulled off her T-shirt as she walked to the water's edge and washed the mud off her arms and legs. She wasn't wearing a bra.

'You know how to paddle a canoe?' She was drying herself with her T-shirt now. I was going crazy. It was better than anything in *Club International*.

'Just like I know how to drive a stick.'

'That's what I figured.' She kissed me, and started to pull a green canvas canoe down towards the water. She still hadn't put on her T-shirt.

'Where are we going?' I was hoping we were going to do it right there.

'My island.' She pointed out to the middle of the lake. It was more of a big rock with a couple of trees in the middle standing up like a topknot. But it was still cool.

'It's yours?' She was deaf to the resentment in my voice.

'Grandpa gave it to me for my twelfth birthday.'

When I was twelve, my grandfather gave me a right-handed first-baseman's mitt. He forgot I was a lefty.

'Does Bryce have an island?'

'It doesn't work that way. My grandfather gives stuff to us each year, to avoid taxes.'

'How does the money get divided?'

'It's not polite to ask people about their money.' She put on her T-shirt and added, 'Especially if they're rich.'

'You mean it's like asking a hunchback about their hump . . . you're supposed to pretend it's not there?'

'Sort of . . .' She handed me a paddle like she was pissed off.

'Don't worry, I know what it's like to have an invisible hump.'

'You sit in the front.'

'I'll show you mine if you show me yours.' I was relieved when she laughed and splashed me with water.

'Is that all you ever think about?'

I turned out to be better at paddling than I was at driving. When we got to the island, we pulled the canoe up to a rocky beach. She led me up to a one-room shack with a tin roof and a wooden porch that used to be a chicken coop before her grandfather fixed it up and floated it out to the island for her. There was a padlock on the front door, and a sign that she had obviously painted when she was a kid that said, 'KEEP OUT. THIS MEANS EVERYBODY.'

When she lit a kerosene lamp inside, I was kind of surprised. There were horse dolls with tiny saddles and little bridles lined up on the mantel. Horseshow ribbons were tacked to the tops of the windows. A camp bed was crowded with stuffed animals, like she still played with them, and on the walls were all these colored-pencil drawings she'd done of herself riding a pony called Geddyup. Under each one, she neatly printed out, 'Canter. Trot. Gallop.' I'd always thought of Maya as being older than me. Suddenly, in the orange light of the lantern, she could have passed for twelve. Except for her boobs, of course.

She looked at me solemnly. 'You're the first boy I ever brought here.' I believed her. She uncorked a bottle of wine that I didn't know would have cost a hundred and fifty bucks at a restaurant, and we each took a swig. It tasted like cork, but I pretended I liked it. Then she put a bootleg tape on the boom box and turned up the volume to max. She told me it was Bryce's favorite band. I'd never heard of them. They were called the Dead Kennedys. The chorus was, 'Kill the poor . . . tonight.'

Wondering what she expected of me, I sat down on the cot and picked up a stuffed bear that had a bow tie around its neck and smelled of mildew. 'Does he have a name?'

'It's a she . . . and it's Growly.' When a mouse fell out of a hole in Growly's bottom, I screamed, and we were both able to relax.

She used a survival sheath knife with a ten-inch blade to spread peanut butter on Ritz crackers. Then we took the wine and went outside to eat on a blanket by a blackened spot on a rock. Striking a kitchen match on the tooth I'd chipped, she improvised a flame-thrower with a can of lighter fluid, and we had a bonfire in about ten seconds. I was impressed.

Maya let me kiss her, but she didn't seem to want to make out. Disappointed, I looked at the knapsack that had produced the crackers and peanut butter and asked, 'What's for dessert?'

I was expecting Ring-Dings or Twinkies, instead she blurted out, 'Take off your clothes.'

I was so startled, I wasn't sure I'd heard her right. When I hesitated, she began to tug on my belt buckle. When I tried to kiss her, she pushed me back on the blanket and whispered, 'Lie back and close your eyes.' It was like one of my wet dreams was talking to me. When I tried to sneak a glimpse at her pulling off my jeans, she put her hands over my eyes. 'Come on, it won't be a surprise if you look.'

She was pulling down my jockey shorts now. She giggled and I blushed as my hard-on snapped free of the elastic and slapped back against my stomach. It sounded like she had dropped a piece of meat on the kitchen floor. 'Don't worry, I'm not going to tie him up.' Then I felt something pointed and wet slide along the length of my body. She was breathing through her mouth. I could hear her concentrating. Her touch tickled, and sort of smelled like glue, but not glue. The odor made me think of school. It took me a couple of minutes for my olfactory sense to pin it down . . . she was writing on me with Magic Markers. I opened my eye, sure I was the brunt of some horrible joke. You can't imagine my surprise when I saw she was covering me with the markings of a Yanomamö. Red circles on one side, black stripes on the other.

When she was finished with me, I did her. The fire burned, the night made noises; in my head we were no longer in New Jersey. Maya kept her eyes shut tight. Her face almost in a grimace, she flinched as I touched my felt tip to her skin. I didn't know if the Magic Markers were indelible, but I knew that moment would be tattooed on my brain for ever.

Stripped down and marked, Yanomamö-naked, we were members of the same tribe now. In her, I saw part of myself that was scary and irresistible and as savage as anything I'd read about in *National Geographic*.

Without saying a word, we began to kiss and touch each other, and for a minute I thought we were going to do it right there, but then she pulled back and whispered, 'Wait, you have to see yourself first.'

Hand in hand, we stood at the water's edge and looked at our reflections. We weren't fierce people, we were fierce children.

'God, all we need now is some *enebbe*.'

'I knew that's what you'd be thinking.' She unhooked a silver vial that hung from a chain around her neck, unscrewed the top and produced a tiny, glistening spoonful of green powder.

'I couldn't get any *enebbe*, so I stole some of Bryce's cocaine.'

'But it's green.'

'I colored it with Easter-egg dye.'

Two snorts later, my erection was gone, and I was very, very nervous. I watched her take her hits. After each one, she shook her head like horse with a fly in its nose.

'Have you ever done this before?' I thought of my mother.

'Just cause I live in the sticks doesn't mean I'm a hick.' We each took a swig of wine. 'I did it once with Bryce, in Aspen.' It was the same vintage her grandfather had given me at lunch. 'You think the Easter-egg dye will give us brain cancer?' When I didn't laugh, she said: 'What's wrong?'

I wanted to tell her the truth, that I didn't know anything about cocaine, that I got busted buying it for my mother. That I didn't know anything about anything. She knew I was holding something back about what happened in New York, why not tell her? I thought of what Osborne said; about you never knowing if someone's worth trusting until you trust them with something that can hurt you. But they could afford risks I couldn't. I told myself the difference was money, but I was overlooking the obvious about myself – I loved people, I just couldn't see any reason they would love me in return.

'Something's wrong.' She said it again.

'Yeah . . . I'm not high enough.' I don't know if that's what she wanted to hear, but she liked the way I said it. Flat, and sure and sharp as the sheath knife she had used to spread the peanut butter on the crackers.

Squatting on our haunches by the fire, smoke in our eyes, we passed the coke and wine back and forth while bats dined on mosquitoes overhead. The coke tightened my nervousness into an intensity that left no room for second guesses or caution. I knew now why my mother had had a love affair with the drug – it made you feel certain, fearless and bold. I asked Maya questions it would have taken me days, if not weeks, to work up the rudeness to segue into. 'How'd you get that scar on your face?'

'It's ugly, isn't it?'

'No, it's what I like most about your face. It makes you more real.'

'I was dragged by a horse. My foot got caught in the stirrup.'

'And you still like horses?'

'Love horses . . . they're scared of everything, and they don't lie.'

'Like me.' I meant it sarcastically. I could tell she thought I was being honest from the way she kissed me. I didn't set her straight.

'What are you scared of?' She snorted and shook her head like a horse again.

'You.' Now that I was finally being honest, she thought I was kidding.

'You don't act scared.'

'Yes I do.' I pushed her back on the blanket and pried her legs apart with my knee. I could tell she was frightened; it made me feel more brave.

'Finn, I've never been with anyone like this, you know.' I was doing a good job of acting like I had.

'Really?' I wanted to hear her say it again.

'Yes, really.' I was smiling in the darkness. Then she went still. 'Well, that's not exactly true. Once I let Bryce's room-mate touch me there, just to see what it'd be like.'

'That's OK.' It was a nice way of saying 'shut up'.

'Why is it OK?'

'He wasn't a Yanomamö.'

'Bryce beat him up when he found out,' she said softly.

'Good for Bryce.' All at once, I felt her relax and she became a mystery I could taste and touch in the safety of the night. If it hadn't been for the coke, I would have come in thirty seconds. It numbed me just enough so I could be overeager for a long, long time. It was like I was watching myself have the night of my life. The pleasure was just second-hand enough for me to enjoy it. The fact that I could make her moan made me feel in control. I thought of what my family therapist told me: 'Life isn't as perfect as you'd like it. But if you take it as it comes, it will turn out to be infinitely more interesting.' I wondered if the shrink had this in mind when she gave me that advice.

Life was turning out to be infinitely more sexy. Maya whispered my name, breathless and urgent. I was having trouble finding the right approach angle. Both our hands were on 'it'. I was almost inside her. Suddenly her body went rigid. 'Did you hear that?'

'What . . .' All I could hear was the pounding of my heart. Maya scrambled to her feet. Sweat and friction had smeared our markings.

'I heard footsteps, Finn.' We stood back to back, peering into the darkness.

She sniffled. A branch cracked. Yankee *enebbe* and paranoia had us seeing our own demons in the shadow.

'Maybe it's just an animal.' She didn't sound convinced.

'What kind of animal?'

'Could be a deer, or a raccoon.'

We knew what kind of animal it was when it started to laugh. Water, darkness and space played with the sound. We heard footsteps in front of us, then behind us, then nothing. When Maya reached for her shorts, the laughter came back – meaner and closer than before. Maya screamed, 'Stop it!' Suddenly, the footsteps were coming at us through the underbrush with a velocity and recklessness that was terrifying. I grabbed her hand and we started to run.

When we reached the water I shouted, 'Get into the canoe.' It was a good idea, until we realized whoever was chasing us had taken the canoe.

Maya pulled me into the water. 'Swim!' It was a half-mile to shore. I forgot the farthest I'd ever dog-paddled was two lengths of the pool at the McBirney Y on Twenty-Third Street. I was gasping for air and gulping water after a hundred yards. The cocaine fuel-injected my panic. I was glad she didn't tell about the snapping turtles and the water moccasins until later.

Once we were in the Land Rover and the doors were locked and the engine was running and we were rolling, we were able to laugh, and act like it was funny. I made her circle back so I could shout out the window, 'Fuck you, Dwayne.'

'You think that's who it was?'

'Who else?'

An hour later I was back home, savoring the night with a hot shower and a cold beer. I didn't hear my mother come in from her NYC theater outing with Dr Leffler. When I came out of the bathroom, my bedroom door was open. She was standing in the upstairs hallway, looking at herself in the mirror. She liked what she saw. I had just enough time to wrap the beer bottle in the towel that had been around my waist.

'Mom, I'm naked.'

'Well, keep your door closed.' She looked away, giving me time to stash the beer bottle in the closet and re-wrap the towel.

145

'Did you have fun with Dr Leffler?'

'Are you implying something?'

'No, I just meant, did you have . . . a good time. You like musicals and all.' My mother relaxed and smiled.

'You know, I haven't had a date like that . . . ever. It was very, very nice.'

'So, it was a date?' The best defense is a good offense.

'For lack of a better word. Why are you taking a shower at one o'clock in the morning?'

'We went swimming in the lake. I was cold.'

'You and Maya went swimming at night alone?'

'No, there were three of us.'

'It's dangerous to swim alone.'

'I know that.'

16

Four days later, I was treading water by myself in the deep end of the Langleys' pool. I was trying to hear what Maya and her mother were saying under the rose arbor at the pool gate. I could tell Maya didn't want to hear what her mother was saying from her body language. Brushing the end of her braid against her scar, she stood on one foot. With the other she kicked at the ground, like a horse that doesn't want to be reined in. Mrs Langley was still talking when Maya abruptly turned and trotted back to the pool.

'I don't care what you say, I am not going to East Hampton,' she called out as she dove into the deep end with me. She touched the bottom by the drain and pushed off. One of the bright red triangles of her bikini top slipped down below her breast as she surfaced next to me. She said 'Oops,' but she didn't bother to fix it. Her mother was watching. It made me so nervous when she wrapped her arms and legs around me, I inhaled a mouthful of water as I struggled to keep my head above the surface. As Mrs Langley walked towards the pool, garden shears in hand, can of Tab in the other, we bobbed to where it was shallow enough for me to stand. I was coughing so hard, I would have let go of Maya, but I was afraid Mrs Langley would see my erection. It seemed I had a full-time hard-on these days.

I discovered new things about Maya every day. Her body was still uncharted territory. Just then, holding her like that, as her mother looked down on us and sipped her Tab, I saw that Maya had a birthmark shaped like the Dominican Republic on her left shoulder blade, and it was only when she asked me, 'Are you hungry?' that I realized all the fillings in the back of her mouth were gold.

'Mummy?' That's what she called her mother when she was sucking up. 'Can Finn stay for dinner?'

'Maybe Finn would like to have dinner with us in East Hampton.'

'Tonight?' I blurted out. In Vlyvalle, anything was possible. Mrs Langley laughed.

'Unlike my father, we're not rich enough to have a helicopter. Actually I was planning on flying out in the King Air tomorrow. Would you like to come out the beach with us for a week or two, Finn? I could call your mother and . . .'

'He wants to stay here with me.' I would have loved to have gone to East Hampton. They had a house right on the beach called Blue Arches. Even though they called it a cottage, it had enough bedrooms to qualify as a hotel. Besides the fact that I'd never been to that monied watering hole, we were three days into a heat wave. The mercury and the humidity flirted with three digits even after the sun set. Maya looked at me and told me what to answer.

'I'm happy here.' But the thought occurred to me, would I be even happier on the beach in East Hampton? All things were relative. A horsefly bit me on the back, as if to punish me for the thought.

'Come on, it'll give us a break from the heat.' Mrs Langley couldn't see my erection, but she knew I was tempted. 'Bryce wants to go, and so does Finn. He's just being polite.'

'Finn never lies. He'd say if he wanted to go. You and Bryce go. Leave me with Birdie.' Birdie was their cook.

'The four of us could have fun: we could play tennis at the club . . .'

'Finn doesn't play tennis.'

'Finn's a quick learner.' I was enjoying being between them, until Maya let go of me.

'Finn's got nothing to do with this. I don't want to go to East Hampton because I don't want to be away from Daddy.' Maya went to the hospital to see him every day now. 'He's getting better. You heard what the doctor said.'

'Maya, your father would want us to enjoy our lives.'

'You act like he was dead.'

Mrs Langley took a long pull on her Tab.

'You don't think I miss your father? He was my life. When he had his accident I missed him so much, I had to pretend . . .' Her lips were shaking. It looked like she was talking to her rose clippers. 'I still pretend he's with me at night.'

Maya hugged a kickboard. Her eyes darted between me and her mother, trying to triangulate her position in the universe. 'Mother, I didn't mean it that way.'

'Neither did I.' Mrs Langley lifted her head up to the sun, as if to roll her tears back into her eyes. 'At least Finn sees it's not true what they say about WASPs being cold and unemotional.'

Her mother walked slowly back up to the house, Tab in hand. I followed Maya behind the poolhouse. She started to cry. When I held her, she began to sob.

'I know he's going to get well. You believe that, don't you?' I nodded yes, even though I didn't. I wanted her to stop crying, and to comfort her. I knew I couldn't do both, so I tried to distract her and took off her bikini top. Her bottoms were around her ankles when I whispered, 'Let's go back to the island.'

'Is that all you ever think of?' At least I'd made her laugh.

'Is that bad?'

'It's good for the complexion.' She wiped her nose on the back of her arm. 'If we didn't have sex, would you like me as much?' It's a tricky question to answer when posed by a naked girl whose face is full of tears.

'I wouldn't know you as well.' I was glad I was able to answer without lying.

'I wish I'd met you when I was older.'

'Why?'

'Then we could get married before things change.'

'What's going to change . . .?' There was a touch of panic in my voice.

'Everybody changes.'

'That's depressing.'

'It'd be more depressing if they didn't.' She could see she was making me sad. 'We have to save something so if we become assholes or get sent to a convent in South America . . .'

'Who's going to a convent in South America?' Now she was scaring me.

'You know what I mean. If we get split up . . . we'll still have something to bring us together when we're old.'

'What kind of something?'

'Something to look forward to . . .'

'Like?'

'Maybe we shouldn't do it.'

'But I thought you wanted to . . . I mean, we practically . . .' I sounded like a disappointed child because I was.

'That doesn't mean there aren't other things we can do instead.' She smiled, like a cat at a saucer of milk, as she pulled down my bathing suit and went down on her knees.

It was a first for me. I think for her, too. She said I tasted like soap, but good soap.

We smoked half a joint, and lay on big green cushions by the pool, and she started to teach me how to play backgammon. I rolled double sixes four times in a row and lost. I was learning, too much luck at once isn't a good thing.

At about four, Birdie came out and asked Maya to pick up Bryce at the club. Maya said I could drive the Land Rover to cheer me up. As we ran up to the house, I swallowed a fly. I made a joke about all the different kinds of shit it had been hanging out on all day. It made us both laugh, but it left a funny taste in my mouth. As she picked up her keys, I took a big swig out of the Tab her mother had left on the kitchen table. It was more vodka than Tab. I wasn't prepared for it. When I spit it out onto the floor, Maya said, 'What's wrong with you?'

'There was something in the Tab.' Mrs Langley took the can from my hand. 'A bug.'

As I wiped it up with a sponge, Mrs Langley told me, 'You have good manners, Finn.'

The club was packed. It was the day of the member–guest golf tournament. Bryce had won it the last two years in a row. The parking lot was crammed with so many shiny new BMWs and Mercedes Benzes, you would have thought you were at an Aryan car dealership. Unable to find a space, we had to park behind the sheds where they kept the lawnmowers and the help parked. Dented and dusty pickups with dangling mufflers hooked up with bailing wire, Plymouths and Subarus with mismatched fenders and rusted-out rocker panels crowded the back parking lot. Part-time help was pulling in to get the tables ready for the golf dinner. I heard wives who had to wash their own hair remind tired husbands to fix broken appliances and put casseroles in the oven. This was the other Vlyvalle, the invisible members of the tribe, that serviced the world and whims of my new best friends.

The hot gravel hurt my bare feet, softened from indolent after-noons in the Langleys' pool. As Maya and I 'ouch-ed' our way across the service parking lot, I looked into back seats littered with cracker crumbs, and baby bottles filled with sour milk. Cans of paint, bags of rollers and brushes from Ace Hardware somebody was too tired from cleaning up after other people to unpack, much less put to work. I had so much more in common with them than with Maya, it made me feel nervous and guilty. All the hours I'd spent with my mother painting and spackling the shithole spaces we had to move into after they raised the rent on the loft we'd just got finished fixing up made me feel like an impostor.

The blare of a car horn, and the crunch of tires breaking on gravel snapped me out of my moment of conscience. It was Dwayne. He flicked a cigarette at me to let me know I should be happy he didn't run me over. Jilly was practically sitting in his lap. From her uniform, I knew she was working the golf party. Maya pulled on my arm with a let's-get-out-of-here look on her face. Considering the fact that the last words we exchanged with him were 'Fuck you' at the lake, it seemed like a good idea. If I'd had shoes on, I would have run. But barefoot on the gravel, I knew he could chase me down before I made it out of the service parking lot.

'Hi, Jilly . . . Hi, Dwayne.' My voice went up an octave as I tried to sound casual.

'What are you talking to me for?' My double-edged paranoia had me wondering about the subtext of his inflection. Was he really saying 'I'm not rich, I can't help you?'

'You're a friend of my friend.'

'You want to be my friend?' All I could see when I looked at him were McCallum's ears.

'Sure.'

'I'm going fishing up by the lake. Wanna come?' He had two spin rods and a cooler in the back seat.

'Maybe another time.'

'What's wrong with now? I got an extra rod.' The fact that he was smiling the whole time he was talking to me made it even scarier.

'I've got something to do with Maya and Bryce.' He looked at Maya.

'Do you wanna be friends, too, Maya?'

'Nope.' The way she said it made Jilly laugh.

'I gotta get to work.' As she climbed out of the GTO, she mouthed a warning to me, 'You're crazy.'

'I hope you're not fishing with worms.' Maya was big on fly-fishing. She was also fearless.

'Just Clorox.'

'You would.'

'Well, since you want to be friends, Finn, I'll stop by some-time, and you and me will get to know each other . . . have some fun.'

'Great . . . look forward to it.'

Maya looked at me.

'It's a date.' Dwayne laughed as his tires spit gravel in my face.

'Why'd you talk to him?'

'Because I thought if I had a conversation with the jerk he might seem less scary.' Walking along the edge of the golf course, hand in hand, I didn't just feel safe, I felt immune.

'Did it work?'

'No.'

Maya laughed. 'Don't worry, I know you're brave.'

'How do you know that?'

'My family's a whole lot scarier than Dwayne.'

We found Bryce at the bar under an awning at the far end of the pool. He was standing with his back to us. Ten or fifteen golfers, and a couple of tennis people stood around while Bryce held court. I recognized most of the faces from Maya's birthday party: Ian, Slim, Paige, Giacomo, Boopie – most of the group were kids, but there were a couple of guys in their late twenties with guts that were a year or two away from turning into beer bellies, who liked to hang out with what Mrs Langley called 'the young'. Some of them were letches, like Tommy Fowler, who always said the same thing to every teenage girl: 'Why are you wearing a bra? Man, in the sixties, we let it all hang out.' He was like a broken record, and when we walked up he was playing it as he looked down the front of Paige's dress. Others, like the bald guy, George, who was a hotshot at Morgan Stanley, mostly just listened and watched, like he was trying to figure out what he had missed. Maya told me everybody put up with them, cause Tommy gave everybody Quaaludes, and George had great pot.

As soon as Maya saw Bryce, she said, 'Bryce must be pissed off.'

I could hear his relaxed tenor above the laughter. 'Now we'll try something different.'

'He doesn't sound pissed.'

'He always does card tricks when he's about to lose it.'

Sure enough, Bryce was holding a deck of cards. As he fanned the deck, and did a show-off one-handed shuffle, Maya asked, 'How come you didn't win the tournament, Bryce?'

'McCallum disqualified us because of my sarong.' It was the same one he wore to the party. It looked better with a tux than with two-tone golf cleats.

'Fucking dress-code bullshit. They just did it to keep Marcus off the course.' Marcus came out of the bathroom and sat in the empty chair next to Slim. Bryce held out the deck of cards for Dr Leffler's daughter, Boopie. 'Pick a card.' Boopie picked a card and giggled. 'Now don't show it to me. And though I know it might strain your mental capabilities, try to remember the card after you put it back in the deck.' Boopie did as she was told.

As Ian picked the last of the cashews out of the mixed nuts in front of him, he announced, 'Marcus had nothing to do with your being disqualified. It says in the Club Handbook . . . Ian read from it, "Appropriate dress required by members and guests for all club functions." Marcus didn't wear a sarong – you did.'

'That's because Marcus's sarong was at the dry cleaner.' Marcus and Slim thought that was really funny.

'They were afraid of us, Bryce.' Marcus called out.

'And you know that, good sir.' I was surprised Bryce let Ian off that easily. After Bryce had Giacomo cut and reshuffle the deck, he laid it out on a table, face down in a full circle with a flourish. Bryce picked out a card. 'Boopie, what was the card you picked?'

'Three of hearts.' Bryce flipped over the card he was holding. Naturally, it was the three of hearts.

While everybody clapped, Tommy leaned over and asked, 'Maya, why does a liberated girl like you wear a bra?'

'I'll tell you if you buy us a beer.' The drinking age was more strictly enforced at the club when Mr Osborne wasn't footing the bill. Tommy signed a chit for the beer and handed it to Maya, who announced, 'Tommy, the only reason I wear a bra is cause I don't like old horndogs like you staring at my tits.'

Everybody thought that was a riot, except for Tommy's velvet-headbanded wife, who'd just showed up looking for the Portuguese nanny, who was telling Giacomo in broken English, 'Wearing a bra weakens the muscles of the bosom.'

Maya walked her fingers across the back of her left hand – Langley code for 'it's time to bolt'. I was finding it all pretty interesting. With Bryce there showing off, I could observe them without the burden of making small talk, of trying to be cool.

Someone in the crowd shouted, 'One more trick, Bryce.' He didn't have to be coaxed.

'OK, for my grand finale I will tell your fortunes.' Bryce began to pass out cards. He was the only one in the crowd who wasn't drinking a beer, or something with alcohol in it. 'Now put the cards I give you over your hearts.'

'Bryce, you are so full of shit.' It was funny how much Ian both loathed and was fascinated by Bryce.

'If you're afraid of your future, Ian, give me back the card.' Unwilling to give Bryce anything, Ian held the card to his chest with the rest of us.

He did Paige first. As he reached for her card, he let his hand linger against her breast just a moment longer than was necessary, then slowly took the card from her and held it to his forehead. Eyes closed, he asked for silence. When everyone quieted down, he began to smile.

'Bryce, it better be good.' Paige loved the attention.

'I can see already it's going to be good for me, I only hope you'll feel the same way.' Everyone laughed when Bryce announced, 'I predict Paige and I will have a night of nocturnal bliss before Labor Day.'

'Promises, promises.' It was obvious it was just a matter of time with Bryce and Paige. Bryce did the same routine with Slim. Card to his forehead, he began, 'I can't be sure here, but it looks to me . . . in twenty years our friend will either be dead or famous. Both, if he's lucky.' Marcus didn't think that one was so funny.

Bryce took Marcus's card next. His face grew serious when he touched Gates' son's card to his forehead and solemnly pronounced, 'Marcus Gates, Senator from the great state of New Jersey.' Everyone howled but Ian. Marcus stood up and took a bow.

Taking advantage of the momentum, Bryce grabbed Ian's card, then Giacomo's, then Tommy Fowler's, then cards of a couple of people in the crowd whose names I couldn't remember. He squared them off with a crack on the tabletop and held them to his forehead.

'I do not understand; we don't each get our own fortune?' Giacomo protested as he shouted 'Ciao,' to the nanny and Mrs Fowler.

Bryce opened one eye. 'You all inherited money from the same trust.' Everyone laughed. I didn't get it. Maya whispered they were all cousins. Bryce closed his eyes and looked solemn. 'The past and the future are connected here . . . yes.' He sniffed the air. 'I smell Episcopalian voodoo at work. Your great-grandfather made a fortune doing things you go to jail for now. He put children to work in mines and when they grew up and went on strike, he shot them. He also slept with his son's wife . . .'

'That's not funny.' Ian was getting pissed off.

'I know, that's the point.' Bryce continued. 'And here's where the curse comes in.'

'What curse?' Giacomo was confused.

'A thief begets three generations of losers, each lamer and more pretentious than the next.'

'Fuck you, Bryce.' Ian was eating the peanuts now.

'What curse is he talking about?'

'You will inherit a mismanaged trust, too small to sustain the delusions of superiority you've maintained despite the dizzying spiral of your downward mobility and low SAT scores.' The crowd was quiet, but he had their attention. 'By the time you are all forty, you will have to suck up to people you wouldn't share a toilet seat with now.'

'You're an asshole.' Ian threw the bowl of nuts at Bryce.

George, the bald-headed stockbroker, flipped his card down. 'I'm getting out of here while I still can.'

Maya took my hand and started walking. 'We'll get the car, Bryce.'

'Wait, I haven't predicted Finn's future.' He took the card out of my hands as I shook my head no. He held my card to his forehead. 'Very different future here, some of you will be unhappy to know. A true self-made man. But one things is certain: long and lasting friendship with myself . . .' Relieved, I laughed when Bryce slapped me on the back and announced, 'Stick with me kid, you'll see a lot of the bottom.'

As the three of us walked back to the Land Rover, Bryce's golf clubs clanged over his shoulder, Maya told him, 'That was rude.'

'It's the truth. They're all losers.'

'That doesn't mean you have to say it Bryce. I mean, Ian deserves it, but not the others.'

'I don't make the future, I just predict it. It's a terrible responsibility, having my gift.'

'You shouldn't have worn the sarong, Bryce.'

'I didn't feel like playing golf, anyway.'

17

'It's all in the wrist.' Maya was teaching me new stuff every day. Today was fly-fishing in the big pool off the Haverkill just below the playhouse. 'Your rod never goes back further than ten o'clock, and never goes forward past twelve.' She was repeating lessons taught to her by her grandfather and father. The three inches of bare thigh that showed between the denim fringe of her shorts and the tops of her gartered green rubber hip boots was a major distraction. 'Come on, watch how I do it.' Maya flicked her wrist. An Elkhair Caddis took flight in a long, graceful cast and landed on a slick, shadowy patch of water just below a boulder, with uncanny, bug-like action. I could tell she knew what she was doing, even before a trout rose to the surface and took it with a bubbling gulp.

Relaxed to the point of nonchalance, she let the trout get a good taste of the hook before she gently set it. Unrushed, but not unexcited, she took cool pleasure in this sport. She held the rod with one hand, as the drag of the reel zinged metallic, and let the fish run with it. 'You wanna bring him in?'

I shook my head no. I wanted to catch my own fish. 'How do you know it's a him?'

'Fish are always hims.'

Thinking, hands of the clock, I tried another cast. My first two attempts had hooked nothing but branches behind me and cost me flies. This one seemed to go better, until I felt the hook set in the back of my right ear. 'Motherfucker.'

'What's wrong?'

'I hooked myself.'

Maya pulled her fish in, gripped it gently, removed the hook from its mouth, and carefully slipped it back into the water before coming to my rescue.

'You're lucky I use barbless hooks.' She kissed me, like that was going to make me stop bleeding. I didn't feel lucky. And even though I knew it was stupid, I suddenly felt mad. 'The first time my father took me fishing, I caught my eyebrow. It's worse with barbed hooks. He had to pull it through with pliers.' She showed me the scar. Like I said, I was finding out new things about her every day. I kissed the old scar only because I knew that was expected of me.

'Yeah, but how old were you?'

'Seven.' Tomorrow, she was going to start teaching me how to ride. Regretting I hadn't told her I was scared of horses, it suddenly seemed colossally unfair that she knew so many ways to enjoy the day that I had yet to learn. As she stood behind me, gripping the cork grip of the handmade bamboo rod, her right hand on top of mine, her fingers showing my left hand how to release the belly of slack line just after the peak of the cast. Her calm confidence annoyed me. Still guiding my hands, teaching me with her touch, I resented her relaxed laughter in my ear. As a trout rose and took our fly, and she showed me how to bring it in, I wondered who I would have been if I had been brought up with all this.

'Don't you ever feel guilty?' I interrupted her as she was telling me how to remove the hook without ripping the fish's mouth.

'Fish don't have feelings.' With the flick of its tail, the rainbow was a shadow in the bottom of the brook.

'I mean guilty about having all this.' I gestured to the playhouse and the woods and everything else around us with my rod tip. 'About having so much more than normal people.'

'You think I should be feeding starving babies in Bangladesh instead of hanging out with you?'

I didn't like that idea either. 'I didn't mean it that way.'

'All I have more of than your normal people is money.'

'Yeah, but that's like saying to a guy in a wheelchair, "All I can do that you can't is walk."'

'I can't give it away until I'm twenty-one, so we might as well enjoy it now.'

'You're going to give it away?' The idea horrified me.

'I can't win with you today. What's bugging you?'

So many things bothered me, I picked one that hadn't occurred to me before. 'Why'd you tell everybody my mother and your grandfather were old, old friends?' I did a pretty good job of mimicking her.

'Well . . . they are friends.'

'My mother's your grandfather's masseuse. I mean, why couldn't you just tell people the truth about me? Are you embarrassed?' I was. 'What are you going to do in the fall when you're back in boarding school with all your friends, and I'm going to Huntington County High School with Dwayne?'

'Dwayne got kicked out of Huntington High two years ago. Besides, you don't necessarily have to go to public school.'

'Don't you get it? We don't have money. My mother's not a doctor. I made it all up.' I couldn't believe I was telling her this.

'Is the fact I'm rich and you're not going to be a big deal between us?' I could tell she'd had this conversation before. I wanted to think I was the first poor boy she had brought to the party. 'Because if this is going to be a problem, I'm going to have to . . .' She caught herself sounding like someone else.

'I just asked if you ever feel guilty.' I felt that way so much of the time I wanted company.

'Everybody, and I mean everybody, unless they're a saint or something, would like to be rich. Trying to get rich is what most everybody in the world spends their time doing, because they think it makes everything easier.'

'Well, it sorta does, doesn't it?'

'It doesn't make my dad well.'

'But it fixes a lot of things.'

'Yeah, it cleans up messes . . . gets you accepted to schools that don't really want to take you, stuff like that. But it makes some things harder.'

'Like what?' We'd stopped fishing and were sitting on a rock, dangling our feet in the cool of the stream.

'My dad once said people who are really rich can't believe in anything they can't buy, and hate everything they can.'

159

'What's that mean, exactly?'

'Rich people seem more fucked up because, not having to work for a living, they have more free time to be like themselves.'

'Was your dad rich?'

'No. My mom had to pay for her own engagement ring. His parents were college professors.'

'How'd they meet?'

'In Africa. He was in the Peace Corps, Mom and Grandpa were on safari. Grandpa made him head of his Foundation.'

'How'd he get hurt?'

'It had snowed the night before. We were all out looking for Bryce's dog. Daddy came down here and . . .' She pointed to the top of the gorge where the water fell forty feet in a glassy wall. 'He must have slipped.'

I looked at the top of the gorge, trying to imagine how that might have happened. I was wondering whether he was trying to climb down, or had just forgotten how close to the edge he was standing, when someone shouted, 'Are you two naked?' It was Osborne, from the balcony of the playhouse.

'Grandpa, why would we be naked?'

'Why wouldn't you be!' He fumbled a bit as he stepped in the little elevator that slowly lowered him down to the stone terrace by the upper pool. 'I left my glasses in the car, can't see a damn thing.' We splashed through the shallows and climbed up onto the bank and joined him. He hadn't walked more than a hundred feet, and was out of breath and sweating. He squinted, more like Mr Magoo than Foghorn Leghorn as he shook my hand. 'If you're not Finn, I'm going to have to punch you in the nose for trying to steal his girl.' He was the kind of old man I could see myself becoming, only I wondered if it would come off as charming if he weren't so rich.

'Catch anything?'

'Maya caught two.'

'You helped me with the last one.'

'Did she tell you we have a diver down there who puts them on a hook for us.' It was sort of a corny joke, but the way he said it was funny. Maya didn't laugh.

'Grandpa, do you ever feel guilty for having so much more than everybody else?' She looked at me as she posed the question.

'You mean having more money than most?' It was understatement at its best.

'For example,' I piped in.

'I don't feel any more guilty for making money than Ted Williams felt for batting over four hundred . . .' He watched his hands shake, and then went on. 'I used to feel guilty for what I thought I could accomplish with money.'

'What'd you think you could do with it?' Maya asked.

'Make people happier . . . than they deserved to be.' We all thought about that for a minute. 'Would you two do me a favor?'

'You name it; anything for you,' Maya said.

'Go to East Hampton with your mother and Bryce.' Before she could say anything, he went on, 'I know you're worried about your father. I will personally visit him every day, even though he hated my guts.' That was news to me.

'He hates your guts – he's not dead.'

'I stand corrected.'

'Mom and Bryce don't need us there.'

'Maybe I think they do.' The Chief had spoken.

By the time I got home, Mrs Langley had already called to ask if it was OK for me to go to East Hampton with them. I could tell my mother had said yes, because she was ironing shirts for me when I walked into the house. She was so excited, you would have thought they were taking her to the beach. She gave me two crisp hundred-dollar bills, and instructed me that the first time we went out to dinner or lunch, I should insist on paying for everybody except if it was a private club. Tired of being the new boy, of having to have everything explained to me, I told my mother tartly, 'I think I know more about the way these people do things than you do.'

'How do figure that?' My mother stopped ironing.

'They're different around people who don't work for them.' My mother looked at me like she wanted to squirt me in the eyes with spray starch. I pocketed the hundreds, knowing the Langleys would never let me pay for anything. No matter what they said, I knew they felt guilty. I could smell it on them. It was a familiar odor.

The King Air was scheduled to take off at eleven the following morning. We were late due to last-minute packing. My mother was nervous I wouldn't have the 'right' clothes with me. I tried to explain to her that except for her birthday party, I never saw Maya in anything but a bathing suit or blue jeans, and all Bryce wore these days was a sarong. But she insisted I take her humongous, pink, fiberglass American Tourister suitcase. A dinner jacket, a blue suit, a blazer, six ironed pants, three pairs of shoes, and a pair of white tennis shorts – with a name tag that read Cottie Chubb – that we found in a drawer of the yellow house when we arrived.

I had the proper costume for every social event from a débutante party to a funeral. 'Better to have it and not need it than need it and not have it, lambie,' was how she explained the burden she insisted I carry that morning.

When we got to Osborne's airstrip, the Langleys were already there. Maya waved as she tried to untangle leashes that held two Jack Russells who were simultaneously trying to mount her three-legged Lab. Mrs Langley was nursing a Tab, while Bryce talked to the pilots. Jaded before the fact, even though I'd never seen a private plane, much less taken off in one, I was a little disappointed the King Air wasn't a jet. When my mother started to get out of the car, I quickly told her, 'Mom, please don't embarrass me – let's say goodbye here.' My mother was all dolled up for Mrs Langley. Tulip-pink sweater set, velvet headband, and the newest addition to her Vlyvalle look: these queer squishy loafers with little bows on them she called Belgian slippers.

'I don't know why I'm crying.' I hadn't even noticed my mother's tears. Now I really didn't want her to get out of the car.

'What's wrong, Mum?'

'I just realize this is the first trip you've ever taken without me.'

'I went to Nana's and Grandpa's in Maine last summer.'

'This is different.' It certainly was. Last summer I took the Greyhound from the Forty-Second Street terminal to Augusta. This summer, the King Air to the Hamptons.

'Everything's OK.'

'It is, isn't it . . . it's just, everything's happening so fast.' I quickly kissed her on the cheek, pulled the big pink suitcase from the back of the Peugeot, and hit the fender with the flat of my hand to remind her to leave.

The Langleys had three small overnight bags. When Bryce saw the size of the suitcase I was dragging behind me, he called out, 'How long are you planning to stay with us?' He helped me with the bag. 'What do you have in there?'

'Books . . . in case it rains.' I stole my mother's line. 'Better to have them and not need them than need them and not have them.' I could tell Mrs Langley was charmed. She obviously wasn't familiar with Eddie Haskell.

'Mother, what did I tell you? A gentleman and a scholar.'

Maya kissed me on the mouth, Mrs Langley kissed me on both cheeks, and Bryce cracked, 'Do you three know that dogs have cleaner mouths than humans?'

The pilots wore wire sunglasses and short-sleeved shirts with ties. Maya told me they used to work for the CIA. I wasn't at all nervous about flying in such a small plane, until the engine started up and I saw Bryce was sitting at the controls. The co-pilot was handing out cold drinks and cookies his wife had baked that morning.

'Bryce is going to fly the plane?'

'Mom thinks it's safer if Bryce gets his pilot's license, in case Pete and Tom both have heart attacks at the same time.'

'He doesn't have a license?'

'He has a license, just not for a plane with this many engines,' Maya explained. 'Don't worry, Pete's next to him in case he screws up.' Just then, Bryce left the controls to get something. As he passed me on the way back from the cockpit, he whispered, 'Want some of the acid I took this morning?' He had two pink tabs in his hand.

Maya heard him. 'That's not funny, Bryce.'

He laughed as he turned to Mrs Langley. 'Here are the anti-histamines you asked for, Mother.' When he told us under his breath, 'She'll be tripping all weekend,' it actually was pretty funny.

After that, Bryce put on mirrored sunglasses, and was all business as he went through the checklist and talked to the tower and did the stuff pilots do in movies. I was impressed, especially when we took off without crashing.

As the blue and white turbo-prop banked and climbed up into Osborne's airspace, I glanced down. Vlyvalle, with its neat fields, lavish rooftops – faux French chateaux, palatial slate-roof Colonials, Italianate villas – landscaped rivers and lakes, looked so small and disconnected from the state that surrounded it, it didn't seem real. It looked like a theme park in search of a theme.

At six thousand feet, one of the dogs farted. Maya blamed it on the Jack Russells, but the Lab looked guilty. While Bryce flew, the co-pilot played gin with Maya, her mother and me at a nickel a point. I was seventy-eight dollars in the black, when I heard Bryce suddenly call out in a nervous voice, 'Tom, can you take over here for a minute? We've got a problem.'

As bodies shifted in the plane, I fastened my seatbelt and looked out the window, expecting to see fire and smoke billowing out of one of the engines. Bryce was white-faced when he crouched next to his mother and said, 'That was the hospital – it's something about Dad. They couldn't find Dr Leffler, but Grandpa's doctor thinks we should come back.'

Maya started to cry. 'Is Daddy . . .'

'They didn't say.'

Gates was waiting at the airstrip when we landed. As they hurried to his car, Maya turned and gave me a half-hearted wave and shouted, 'Call me.' Pete offered to drive me home. On the ride back, I tried to get him to admit he used to work for the CIA. When I spotted Dr Leffler's BMW in the driveway, I lost interest in the pilot's secret history, and and asked to be dropped off at the head of the drive.

'You sure?'

'Positive.' I closed the car door softly, and waited until he was out of sight to stash the pink suitcase behind the lilacs.

A strange combination of discretion and curiosity kept me from barging right in on them. I felt stupid for thinking she'd got all dressed up in her Belgian slippers to make a good impression on Mrs Langley. After a couple of minutes of sulking on the edge of the lawn, I decided I was being a jerk. Why shouldn't my mom be friends with Dr Leffler? Just go in and say hello.

When I heard my mother shriek 'Oh, my God', I knew the toaster oven wasn't on fire even before she groaned 'Yes!' I tried telling myself he was a lot more appropriate choice than Mr Osborne or the rock 'n' roller. I halfway convinced myself her and Dr Leffler hooking up was a good thing. I mean, he was separated, and had a good job, and would keep my mother from meddling in my life. If they hadn't talked so loud, I wouldn't have crept closer to hear what they were saying.

'I feel so guilty.' It gave me some small satisfaction that those were the first words my mother said after they'd finished. They were in the living room. On the couch? The floor? One or both of them was having a cigarette. I could see a swirl of smoke from where I stood by the open window.

'Why do you feel guilty, darling?' *Darling?* It sounded awfully hokey, but I guess it was better than 'babe'.

'You know what they say when you start AA.' My mother sighed. 'Go to a meeting every day for ninety days, and don't get involved romantically with anyone in the program for six months.' I began to realize that I didn't figure in this equation.

'I'm your sponsor. If anyone should feel bad about this, it's me.' I wouldn't have pegged Dr Leffler for a born-again drunk, then again my mother didn't look like someone who'd been supplementing her diet with speedballs only a month ago.

'Do you feel bad . . . that this happened?' My mother posed the question with a teenage hesitancy. She knew the answer she was fishing for.

'I feel better than I've felt in years.' He'd been separated from his wife for how many months? I wondered if he was just saying what my mother wanted to hear. There was quiet after that, then a moan. I was more fascinated than jealous. Which isn't to say I liked the idea that an hour after I left town she's getting her ashes hauled in our living room in the middle of the goddamn day.

I didn't want to stand there imagining what they were doing, so I looked. My mother was on top of him. His clothes were scattered all over the room. Hers were neatly folded over the back of a chair. She

165

had time to think about what she was doing. From the way the cushions were crunched, it looked like they started on the couch and ended up on the floor. My mother looked younger naked than she did with her clothes on. They switched positions awkwardly. He had one sock on. It wasn't much different from the way Maya and I went at it, except I knew they'd done it from the torn-open condom wrapper on the coffee table.

'God, you're beautiful.' My mother's whole body blushed at the compliment. A hastily torn-off corner of the condom wrapper was stuck to his sweaty back.

'I bet you say that to all your girls.'

'There are no other girls.'

'Really?'

'Really.' It was all so corny and familiar out of their mouths. I stopped looking through the window, and felt immature and old at the same time. There's no such thing as a grown-up person. I made up my mind to leave them alone and go for a walk. Then I heard Dr Leffler say, 'God, I know it's selfish, but I'd just like to get on a plane with you and leave it all behind.'

'What about your daughters?' I hadn't met Boopie's older sister.

'They have their mother. During the year they're in boarding school and well, dammit, I have a right to a life, too.' Great dad.

'I know the feeling.' I felt like I'd just been slapped. My jealousy rose to the surface and took flight as anger. My mother went on, 'If you left them behind, you'd miss them so much it wouldn't be much of an escape. As much as I'd like to be free of Finn sometimes, I know in the end I'd miss him.' Thanks Mom.

I listened as she ran naked to the kitchen to get a fresh pack of Marlboro Lights. She walked back into the living room announcing, 'Finn's doing so well here, I'm really proud of him. When I took your advice and talked to him about the drinking, I was really impressed how he admitted he was wrong, looked me in the eye like a man, and promised he'd never do it again. I couldn't do that at his age. I couldn't do that two months ago.' It might have been my turn to feel guilty if Leffler had kept his mouth shut.

'I hate to get between you and your son, but when I was at the club the other day, I saw him holding a beer.'

166

'Are you sure?'

'Positive. I didn't think it was my place to say anything.'

'He swore to me . . .' Her tone of voice made it clear she had decided to get mad, rather than get sad.

He put on his doctor's voice. 'Kids lie.' And parents don't, asshole? I considered barging in on them naked. Give them something to explain. I was trying to decide how I should play it. Have a temper tantrum, or try to well up tears? I was too pissed off to cry. I would have snuck in the kitchen, tiptoed up the back stairs, and taken a picture of those two buck-naked hypocrites, if I hadn't wasted my last roll taking pictures of Maya and her stupid horse.

'What do you think I should do?'

'I'm not his father, but from what I've seen, Finn needs a healthy dose of reality.' What had I been getting? 'You have to draw the line with teenagers. Make it clear you're the adult, and they're the child.' Angry and bitter, I mouthed the words, 'Some fucking adults.'

'I can't believe he lied to me . . . What am I doing wrong?'

'You've made life too easy for him.'

'His life hasn't been that easy.'

'It's going to get harder if someone doesn't teach him there are rules.' His voice was so calm and soothing, he could have sold a comb to a bald man. 'Rules for adults, rules for children. He needs structure. And I'm telling you, he'll straighten up and fly right a lot faster if he doesn't just get the message from you, darling. He needs to hear it from the real world. He needs to learn his actions have repercussions. And for God's sake, you got to get him away from those Langley kids. Bryce and Maya are out of control. With all that money, they can get away with it, but he can't.'

'He's with them now in East Hampton.'

'If I were you, I'd call them up and tell him to get his butt home. He's broken his word – and the law. A fifteen-year-old drinking at the club . . .'

'You're right.' It was a good thing my mother didn't let her second-to-last boyfriend give me that BB gun, because I would have shot them both in the eyes.

'You know, there's this new kind of camp in Colorado called Outward Bound . . .' I knew about it because Paige's parents had sent her there last summer. It was one of those places where you have to get through Labor Day weekend with just a fish hook, a plastic garbage bag and three matches. She called it a gulag for rich kids. One of the counsellors gave her herpes. 'The discipline would do him good. It would give him the self-esteem he needs to resist peer pressure. And it would give you time . . . you can't forget about yourself in all this.'

'Is it expensive?'

'If you decide to send him, I'll pay for it.'

'I couldn't let you do that for me.'

'I'd be doing it for us.' I'd heard enough to know what I had to do.

I hid in the woods until Langley drove off in his BMW with a cat-that-fucked-the-canary grin on his face, waited five minutes, then I picked up the pink suitcase from behind the lilac bush and barged in the house like I was all excited and concerned.

'Mom, you're not going to believe what happened.'

'Why aren't you in East Hampton?' She had her clothes on, but I caught her with the condom wrapper in her hand. I pretended not to notice – tactical advantage.

'Just when we were about to land, the hospital called about Mr Langley. Something happened to him. They turned the plane around and flew straight back. Gates took them to the hospital. The pilot dropped me off . . . is there anything to eat, I'm starving?' I thought the last bit was a convincing touch. Hunger always seems like an innocent urge.

'Is it serious?'

'Must have been. Mrs Langley said they tried to call Dr Leffler but no one knew where he was.' That one rattled her cage.

'Well, right now I have something serious I have to talk to you about.' I poured myself a glass of milk and bit into a brownie.

'What's Dr Leffler like?'

'We'll talk about it later, what I have to say is . . .'

I interrupted her. 'Well, in case you run into him and he says something, I saw him at the club the other day and he gave me this weird look. I guess cause I was holding a beer for George Westover. He was trying to light a cigarette in the wind.'

'Who's George Westover?'

'That bald guy who's a big-shot at Morgan Stanley.'

'And Dr Leffler gave you a weird look?'

'He gave everybody at the snack bar a weird look, I guess because the grown-ups were all getting bombed and, you know, what with him having had a drinking problem, probably bothers him to see people getting loaded in the afternoon . . . bothers me, actually.'

'Dr Leffler doesn't have a drinking problem.'

'Oh, he doesn't now, but everybody knows he's in AA, I mean, like you said, it's nothing to be embarrassed of – it's a disease and . . . well, him being a doctor and all, it's good he was able to . . .' I almost said 'straighten up and fly right', but I caught myself. '. . . you know, stop drinking before he messed up his life.' My mother looked at me as if she were staring in a mirror. She saw what she wanted to see, and hugged me.

'You should call Maya and see how her father is.'

I had completely forgotten about the events that had brought me to this point with my mother.

'What if he's dead?'

'Then she'll need a friend.'

I certainly needed one.

I called Maya's house. It rang a long time before an answering service picked up. They didn't know anything about Maya's dad, but they took a message that I'd called. My mother called Mr Osborne, but all Herbert would tell her was that Osborne was at the hospital with the rest of the family. I couldn't resist suggesting, 'Why don't we call Dr Leffler – maybe he knows something.'

'What do you think of Dr Leffler?'

'He seems like a great guy.'

I was sure I'd won until she told me, 'He likes you, too.'

I read once (or more likely, I saw a cop say it in a movie) that with guys in jail, when they finally break down and tell the truth and confess, they sleep like babies. With me, it was just the opposite. Whenever I pulled off a really big lie, or disseminated a major piece of misinformation to save my own ass, I always slept like a log.

When I woke up the next morning, it was raining. Mr Osborne's butler called and said my mother wouldn't have to come to work. He wouldn't tell her anything about Mr Langley's condition, other than that the family spent the night at the hospital. My mother and I were suspiciously polite at breakfast. I wondered what she was up to when she offered to make me pancakes. She gave me a distrustful look when I volunteered to do the dishes.

It was too wet to go outside. We were two very different creatures sharing the same cage. When I finished the washing-up, I found her standing in the front hall adjusting her grip on a putter, a dozen golf balls lined up in front of her. I watched her make two putts into a plastic cup at the other end of the Oriental runner.

'What are you doing?'

'Learning how to play golf.' I should have seen that one coming. 'I hear Dr Leffler's a big golfer.'

'He gave me the putter and the balls.' She sunk another shot.

'You know, I was thinking about learning to play golf.'

'That's a good idea . . . maybe if you got a job, you could save up enough money to buy some clubs.'

'What sort of job?' I enquired cautiously.

'Well, I was thinking of letting Jilly go. You could do the chores, and I'd pay you whatever Jilly got.'

'Like *Cinderfella*.' It was an old Jerry Lewis movie we laughed at once when she first started to get high.

'I think you need to do something constructive with your summer.'

'You bring me here, to a place where everyone's rich, and you want me to be a maid?'

'I don't want you to be a maid . . . I just don't think it's good for you to suit yourself all day. You need structure.'

'But as Grandpa would say, it's telling that the job you came up with for me is being the maid.'

'Let's leave your grandfather out of this.'

'What about Jilly? She needs this job. She's saving up for college, for chrissake. She wants to be a doctor – like you.' It worried me she didn't rise to the bait.

'It's just that I think you should be doing something with your days besides running around and . . . having fun.'

'If you hadn't been having so much fun in New York, I'd be in South America with my father. And you're a liar if you try to tell me you came here for me.' I expected her to cry. She didn't.

'I don't want to talk about this anymore.'

'I have to write a letter to Dad, anyway.' She sunk two more putts in a row. We were both on our game.

I wasn't planning on writing my father a letter, but after saying it in an unsuccessful effort to get to my mother, it actually seemed like a good idea. I used an old manual typewriter that I'd found in my closet, so she could hear the clickety-clack of my poisoned pen.

Dear Dad,

Mom and I just had a long talk about you. She told me not to tell you, but she misses you, and thinks about you all the time. She told me lots of stories about the time you spent together before I was born. I'd love to hear your side of the story. (I don't mean that like it sounds.)

Your film was great. I showed it to my friends, Bryce and Maya Langley. Bryce read your book for his anthropology class at Harvard. (He'll be a Senior in the Fall.) They liked it so much, we watched it three times . . .

I left out the fact that we were high, and one of those times we watched it backwards. I was just typing out how impressed Bryce was that he was my dad when I heard a car honking, louder and louder. I looked out the window just in time to see Maya in a Land Rover, top down and soaking wet in the rain, swerve into the drive and slam on the brakes. The Land Rover skidded sideways across the lawn, leaving big muddy gouges in the grass.

'Finnnnn!' I was at the top of the stairs when she burst in the front door without knocking. I thought my mother was going to hit her with a putter.

171

'My dad's OK . . . he's out of the coma!'

I hugged Maya and told her, 'That's great.' Seeing an opportunity to suck up to the Langleys, my mother decided not to get pissed off about Maya tracking mud into the house, and started doing her June Allyson act again.

'That's wonderful, Maya. Let me get you a towel.' We went into the kitchen, my mother made hot chocolate, and we listened to how this local miracle had come to pass. Her father had gotten worse before he got better.

'When the hospital called the plane, Daddy had developed some sort of allergic reaction to the antiseizure medicine he'd been taking. It's called Johnsons–Stevens or Stevens–Johnsons syndrome, I can't remember which. But whichever, his skin turned bright red, began to peel all over his body . . . it was horrible. Then when Dr Leffler finally showed up . . .' My mother and I exchanged a look. '. . . they took Dad off all the medication he'd been on all this time, and this morning, he just woke up. It was unbelievable. He just opened his eyes, looked at Mom and me and said the sweetest and strangest thing. He said, "What has happened to us?"'

'What'd you tell him?' I could tell she didn't know what to make of her father's first words.

'Well, we all talked at once . . . I mean, a lot happens in three years. I think it was kind of overwhelming for him, because then he started to cry.'

The phone rang. It was Dr Leffler for my mom. She took it in the other room. Before I put down the receiver I asked Maya loud enough to make sure my mother and Dr Leffler heard, 'So, it was the medicine Dr Leffler gave him that kept him in the coma?'

'I hadn't even thought about that.'

I heard my mother yell, 'Hang up!'

'What'd your mom do?'

'First, she started to cry, then she started to laugh, then Dr Leffler gave her a tranquilizer.' Maya lit a cigarette, and exhaled. 'If you ask me, Bryce is the one who needed medication.'

'What happened?'

'It was weird. He didn't say a thing, he just walked out of the

172

hospital room. And when he came back an hour later, he'd dyed his hair.'

'What color is it now?'

'Baby-shit brown. My father was so out of it he didn't even notice Bryce's hair. But it was a big deal to Bryce. He's still at the hospital. He insisted they move in a cot so he could sleep right next to Dad. I guess he feels guilty.'

'For what?'

'For giving up hope. He never thought Dad would get well. I tried to tell him it doesn't matter now, but he didn't want to talk about it.'

Maya forgot to kiss me goodbye when she left. It bothered me until she slammed on the brakes and ran back into the house and kissed me full on the mouth and whispered, 'Everything's perfect now.'

My mother had just wiped up the puddle Maya had left when she'd first run in with the good news. As she watched Maya drive across the grass, she said, 'Look what she did to our lawn.'

'It's their lawn, not our lawn.'

'It's the principle.'

'Grass grows back.'

That night Maya called and told me in the morning they were flying her father up to some neurological institute at Harvard for some tests. She gave me his whole medical rundown. Me not being a doctor, it didn't make a lot of sense. I kept saying, 'Sounds good,' and 'That's great,' but that wasn't how I felt when I realized Maya and Bryce were going with their father to Boston.

'I'll only be gone a week.' She yawned as she said it. Was she being casual, or just sleepy?

'A week!' My voice broke with panic. Under the present post-Dr Leffler regime in my house, that was a long time to be left to my mother's new-found puritanical devices.

'I'll be back for the Fourth of July.'

'What happens then?' I asked sullenly.

'Vlyvalle Street Dance.' Silence on my part. She heard it. 'I know it sounds queer, but it's fun. Grandpa has the Girardi Brothers come out and put on a big fireworks display. Then there's a dance, and then . . . I'm going to give you a really, really big surprise.'

'What is it?' I knew what it was.

'Something you want.'

'What . . .' I wanted her to say it out loud.

'It's top secret.'

'So?'

'So if I tell you I'd have to kill you and then you'd miss out on your surprise . . . for a second time.'

After that, she told me she loved me, and we played the I'll-miss-you-more-than-you'll-miss-me game, which always cheered me up. But still, her leaving, her father waking up, Bryce dyeing his hair, my mother's post-coital talk of tough love – it all worried me. Just when I was getting a fix on the stars in my heaven, the constellations began to shift.

I went to sleep, feeling lonely, and woke up with a sense of loss that was so nonspecific and yet pervasive that halfway through slicing up a banana for my cold cereal, I bolted out of the house and began to run towards the airstrip. I knew that seeing her before she left was the only way I could shake the feeling that something was wrong.

I ran along a cornfield, cut through a meadow calf-high with clover, then a cramp in my side slowed me to a trot as I followed the old railroad tracks overgrown with thistles that Osborne used in the old days when he brought his guests out in private railroad cars, on a spur off the Erie–Lackawanna line.

Panting, drenched with sweat and covered with burrs, I got to the airstrip just in time to see the Ambu-Jet taking off. The King Air was already taxiing out onto the field. I thought I saw Maya wave and blow me a kiss from inside the plane, but at that distance I knew it was wishful thinking. I felt stupid for making the desperation of my need so obvious.

Gates, the ambulance drivers, the guys who took care of the field, all looked at me as if I were a stray dog who'd wandered into a yard he wasn't welcome in. Even the three-legged Lab in the back of the station wagon that had dropped the Langleys off barked at me.

'You missed her, Finn.' It was Osborne. From the way he looked at me, I could tell he was wondering what I was doing there, too.

'I didn't come to see Maya.'

'Really? . . . Not exactly dressed for jogging.'

'It was you I wanted to see, actually, Mr Osborne.'

'You couldn't call me on the phone?'

'If I asked you face to face, I thought it'd be harder for you to say no.' He thought that was funny.

'Pretty shrewd. What'd you want to ask me?'

'I need a job.'

18

My mother was out when I got home. After her morning session with Osborne, she met Leffler for lunch. They had an AA meeting for dessert, and nine holes of golf at the club for a *digestif*. When she got back to the house, I was in my room typing out the last of the letter to my father. I figured Osborne would have mentioned something to her about our conversation. But when she didn't come into my room, I knew he hadn't. I could tell she was in a good mood. She was singing a Joni Mitchell song off-key in the shower. 'And the seasons go round and round . . .'

When I went downstairs to get something to eat, I saw a new set of golf clubs in a cream and turquoise bag that had her initials on the side. I knew it was a gift from Leffler, because the card was sticking out of her purse. Naturally, I had to read it. Given my situation, I wasn't snooping – I was doing recon. 'To My Soulmate, xxo, Dick.' I hadn't known his first name. It was perfect.

When she came downstairs she was wearing a blue dress with a white collar, the pearls she had refused to give back to Nana when she got kicked out of college for getting pregnant, and yet another pair of those Belgian slippers. She was the kind of dressed up they called casual in Vlyvalle. Dr Dick showed up in a blue blazer, a tie that reminded anyone who might have forgotten that he went to Yale, and white flannel pants. We were a hundred miles from the ocean, and he looked like he'd stepped off a yacht. They were both nervous. Pleased, and thinking it was me, I made a point of hanging around. I was more than a little disappointed to discover I had nothing to do with their anxiety. They were making their first public appearance as a couple.

'You think this is all right?' My mother held up her arms and spun around like a ballerina on a cheap jewelry box.

'You look like a poem!' *A poem?* No question, Dick wanted to play doctor with my mom.

'What are you two all dressed up for?'

'The McCallums are having a party.' My mother said it like she'd been going to their soirées for years.

'Gee, I wonder if Dwayne will be there.' Leffler didn't think it was funny.

'Who's Dwayne?' my mother asked.

'I'll explain in the car.' If my mother didn't have any problem sucking up to the jug-eared asshole who made jokes she could overhear about her fucking Osborne, I doubted she'd be bothered by the Dwayne story.

'Now, Finn, I think it'd be a good idea if you stayed home tonight.'

'No problem.' Leffler was herding her out the door. 'I've got to get to bed early anyway.' That stopped her in her tracks.

'Why's that?'

'I start work tomorrow. I got a job today.' The best part of getting the job was seeing the expression on their faces.

'That's commendable, Finn. Congratulations.' Leffler shook my hand. He had sweaty palms.

'Wait a second. What sort of job?'

'I'm working for Mr Osborne. Four hours a day, fifteen dollars an hour, tax free.' We negotiated the deal as he drove me home in his Rolls. My mother didn't see that one coming.

'You have no right pestering Mr Osborne . . .'

You would have thought I'd sucker-punched her. I had. 'I didn't pester him, and it's better than being your maid.'

'We're already indebted enough to Mr Osborne.'

'You're indebted to him, not me.'

'That's not a tone of voice to use with your mother.'

I knew he couldn't resist getting into it. My mother grabbed my arm. 'You're going to call Mr Osborne right now and say you've changed your mind.'

'But that's not true. You want me to lie to someone who's done so much for us? If you want, what I will do is call and explain why I think you don't want me to work for him.'

'You don't tell your mother what you will and won't do.'

'She's the one that wanted me to get a job. You said I needed structure. I get the same guy you two work for to hire me, and that's not OK?'

'I don't work for Mr Osborne.'

'He built your hospital.' Leffler was about to get mad until I said, 'Mom, actions have repercussions.'

It was what Leffler said about me when they were naked. I could tell the line sounded familiar to him. 'Maybe it's not the worst thing, Liz.'

'It gets me out of the house.' They knew I knew.

'Just exactly what sort of job is this?'

'I'm helping Mr Osborne take inventory.' That was how Osborne put it.

'Of what?' My mother noted that Leffler was looking at his Rolex.

'I don't know. He didn't say. He just wants me to make a list of some of his stuff.'

Leffler looked at his watch. 'We're going to be late to the party.'

'What kind of party are the McCallums having?'

'Cocktail party.' My mother's voice was terse. 'You should have told me before you did this, Finn. In a family there's something called communication.'

'Cocktail party! Isn't that sort of a weird thing for people to go to who don't drink?' I was communicating.

I watched *Three's Company* on the one channel we got on our TV, and ate potato chips for dinner out of a blue and white Chinese bowl my mother said belonged in a museum along with the prayer rug. She knew a lot about stuff for an ex-hippie. Materialism was the most recent stage of her rebellion against Nana and Grandpa.

Maya called from Boston at about ten. I smoked a joint of homegrown, and drank the last of the beers from the basement, and we talked about whether her father coming out of the coma was a miracle, or just good luck.

Dr Leffler brought my mother home earlier than expected. I was glad they made out in the car before she came in. It gave me just enough time to throw open the windows, air the pot from the room, and run down to the kitchen to get some mints for my beer breath. Unable to find any mints, I ended up having to take a swig of garlic salad dressing. It wouldn't have been such a gross idea if there hadn't been a hairy glob of mold in it. When my mother walked in, I was eating ice cream out of the tub, trying to get the mold taste out of my mouth.

'Finn, I owe you an apology. I told you to get a summer job, and you got one.'

I said, 'Apology accepted,' and burped. Except for the fact that the ice cream on top of the moldy salad dressing on top of the beer was making me sick to my stomach, it felt good that she had finally apologized for something.

'When I mentioned Osborne mentoring you to some of the other parents at the party, they were green with envy.' *Mentoring?* I didn't know what the word meant, but I sensed my mother had turned my act of defiance into something she could use. 'I mean, everybody in Vlyvalle has tried to get Mr Osborne to give their kids a job, because it looks so good on their college applications. And he's never hired a single one of them. Not one, ever, until you. I'm proud of you.' My mother had a knack for making things better and then making them worse.

'I wish I could say the same about you.' The acorn doesn't fall far from the tree.

'At least I'm trying, Finn.'

'Why don't you just try being yourself?'

'Look who's talking.'

She got me good that time.

179

19

My mother passed me on her way home from work. We waved to one another, because it would have made us feel even worse if we hadn't. We weren't strangers. We just didn't appreciate the people we were growing up to become.

When I walked up to his house, Osborne was out in front, pitching pennies into his fountain.

'Making a wish?'

He was wearing a big straw hat, pleated khaki shorts that came up to the middle of his chest, and two different-colored espadrilles. His legs were so skinny, and his stomach so bloated, he looked like an egg on stilts.

'No. Just trying to remember why I liked to do this when I was a boy.' He borrowed a rake from the gardener and retrieved the change he'd just tossed into the water. Thrifty? Senile? Or both? It was hard to tell.

I followed him into the house and into an empty closet that turned out to be an elevator.

'You'll be working upstairs.' We got off at the third floor.

'What will I be taking inventory of?'

'The past.'

I didn't get it until he opened a mahogany door and we stepped into a billiard room. A huge felt-topped table was piled chest-high with old photo albums and envelopes and manila folders stuffed with snapshots, portraits, and pics of every shape, size and description. Sepia-toned, platinum prints, black-and-white, Kodachrome color, and eight-by-twelve glossies: there were literally thousands of them. It was the first mess I'd seen in Vlyvalle. I felt comfortable there. There were tiny snaps from the twenties, no bigger than a

Triscuit. Early-fifties pics where the colors weren't true, and the edges looked like they'd been cut with pinking shears. Photos of people that were young and beautiful and dying; posed in gaudy and understated oases of wealth and privilege in all four corners of the globe.

Osborne buried both his arms up to the elbows into the pile, and roughly pulled up a double handful like he was Scrooge McDuck washing his hands in money.

'I've been putting off sorting through these for the better part of the last century. I keep thinking I'll reach an age where it won't be so goddamned depressing . . . doesn't work that way. Ten years ago I put them in here. I thought I'd sort through them between games.' The legs of the pool table were carved to look like the hind legs of horses. 'That's when I gave up billiards.'

Osborne let the pictures fall through his fingers. 'I hear you think you're some kind of anthropologist. Let's see if you can make some sense out of all of this.' A couple of photos fluttered to the floor. I picked them up and handed them to him. He put on a different pair of glasses, peered at them, and began to fill me in. One was a picture at a nightclub of him and somebody named Bill Paley, who he told me owns CBS. I, like Osborne, was more interested in the redheaded woman with the girlish smile. Especially when Osborne told me, 'Can't remember her name, but she killed her husband and got away with it. He was a friend of mine. So was she, for that matter.' He discarded that one, and looked at the back of a photograph so old and brittle its edges stained his fingers with sepia dust. 'Christ, this one's older than me.' It was pretty clear Osborne wasn't crazy about getting old. On the back of the old photograph, a fancy hand had written, 'Columbian Exposition 1893.' Osborne turned over the photo, and held it at arm's length. It was a picture of a girl, about Maya's age, dressed up like the Statue of Liberty, licking an ice-cream cone on the Midway of the Chicago World's Fair.

'Who's that?'

'My mother, trying to look innocent.'

'Did you like your mother?'

'Loved her, until I was about your age.'

'What happened?'

181

'We got rich.' He flicked the picture back in with the rest of the pile.

There were stacks of cloth-covered archive boxes on the leather couch at the far end of the room. 'There's a box for every year there. Each year, a different box. Sort out and file the pictures that have dates on them, we'll go through the others later on and try to figure out when the hell they were taken.' It seemed like an easy job, until he pointed to an electric typewriter on the desk by the window. 'I want a chronological list and description, including size, of all the pictures. If you don't know who the picture's of, or where it's taken, put it in the "See Osborne" file. That's what the "C" stands for, in case you wondered.' He laughed at his bad joke.

I wanted to ask why he was doing all this. Instead I said, 'That's going to be a pretty big pile.'

'That's why they call it a job.'

His hand went back to the pile. He came up with a picture of himself and a woman, both young and golden, looking like they'd live for ever, taken amongst Roman ruins. 'God, I feel like a tourist in my own life when I look at these.' On the back was written, 'Honeymoon, Sicily.'

As he shuffled towards the door, he suddenly looked just like an old man. I wanted to say something to cheer him up, or at least get his mind off the past.

'Do you think Mr Langley coming out of the coma was a miracle?' He closed his eyes and considered the question for so long I thought he'd fallen asleep.

'A real miracle's a reminder and a warning that the line that separates the possible from the impossible isn't as firm as we like to think it is.' I didn't get it. 'Here's the latest.' He handed me a packet of pics fresh from one-hour-developing. Inside, was a photo of Maya sitting in my lap at the party. We're sharing the same smile. It was a moment one should never forget. I couldn't believe it. It happened only two weeks ago, and I had no memory of it.

20

When I showed up for work the next day, Osborne was talking to a photograph. 'What a bunch of fucking assholes.' He was staring at an eight-by-ten black-and-white glossy of a bunch of guys sitting around a table with FDR. Osborne was about thirty in the picture – pencil mustache, chalk-striped suit: he looked sharp. Without my even asking, he started pointing out the guys in the picture with a finger stained brown from one of the cigars he wasn't supposed to smoke.

'That one's Standard Oil, that's Ford – he was a Nazi, Walter Chrysler – nice guy, that AT & T prick, and what's-his-name, that fucked up the railroads . . . FDR brought us to the White House to figure a way out of the Depression.'

'What'd you tell him?'

'Sell ad space on the dollar bill.' I was still laughing at his joke when he said, 'You want to see something funny, look at this.'

It was the St Mark's JV football team, 1919. Osborne was the little guy whose socks wouldn't stay up. 'God, it's great to be young . . . except when you're young.' He looked at the picture with an ivory-handled magnifying glass.

You could see he had pimples. 'We were undefeated that year. Of course, we only played girls' schools.' Some of his jokes were better than others.

'You think I'm smart enough to get into St Mark's?'

'Can you snap your fingers and chew gum at the same time?'

He didn't notice that he'd made me feel stupid for asking.

'Why the hell would you want to go there? I hated it. Boarding school's like prison, except the food's better in prison. And in case you're thinking how the hell does he know, I had lunch at Sing Sing once, ex-partner of mine did a post-graduate course there in embezzlement. Trust me, St Mark's isn't for you.'

'Bryce went there.'

'Bryce didn't have a choice.'

I didn't have one either, but I didn't tell him that. A little alarm in his wristwatch went off.

'Christ, gotta go get my blood changed.' I wasn't sure if he was kidding. Osborne handed me a stack of leather-bound family photo albums and left the billiard room without bothering to say goodbye.

At first it was sort of fun, seeing pictures of what Bryce and especially Maya were like when they were younger. But after about the hundredth time I typed in 'Langleys having fun in Paris, London, Ceylon, Serengeti, East Hampton, Palm Beach, St Bart's, St Moritz, St Tropez' – it got a bit monotonous. At about the hundred and fifty mark, it began to piss me off. They always looked so pleased. And why not? If they weren't on vacation they were in Vlyvalle, which was like taking a vacation from a vacation.

It made the time go faster, studying those family pictures for cracks. After a while I noticed that Maya was usually hugging an animal; either a real dog, horse, cat, or a stuffed bear. Mrs Langley, Tab in hand, was invariably looking at her husband, not the camera. And always with the same wide-eyed, frightened smile. Like the guy was a saint, with stigmata in the palms of hands that always seemed to be holding a tennis racket, fly-rod, ski pole or golf club. Bryce was either showing off or posing, which, after a while, I began to realize wasn't the same as looking happy, even if you were smiling at the camera. Wealth and comfort of their lives was so glaring in those photos it made the reality of their lives harder to focus on. It was like looking into the sun.

By the end of the week, I'd filed so many images of them it was as if I'd been there with them all along. The photos made stories they'd shared; references that had been made in my presence, but I had not understood, seemed clearer and less second-hand.

By then, Osborne had started to get into it. He'd shift through the 'See Osborne' file, until he found one he felt like talking about, i.e., remembering. Most of the pictures he chose were of old girlfriends and guys he'd made money with who were dead. Hearing him reminisce about the old girlfriends was a lot more interesting than his late partners. When he came across a picture of this blonde on water skis, all he said was, 'Creamsicle.' I was at the typewriter.

'Her name was Creamsicle?'

'No, she smelled like a Creamsicle.'

'Creamsicles don't smell.'

'Oh yes they do.' The way he licked his lips and smiled, goat-like, you knew he knew what he was talking about. He called the butler and had a couple of Creamsicles brought up to give me a scent of what he was talking about. I took a bite and inhaled. Fruity, and vanilla, they reminded me of Maya, but I didn't tell him that.

When I finished my Popsicle, I held up a brown legal folder I'd found amongst the jumble on top of the billiard table. The folder contained a dozen undeveloped rolls of 35 mm film. With them was a letter from a lawyer in New York. All it said was:

As we discussed, await your decision.

'What are these?'

'Pics of me and my last fling.' He held one of the film canisters up to the light. There was nothing to see, but he looked proud of himself. 'She was an Australian and played the cello. Her name was Sue.' He pulled on his beard. Santa the satyr. He began to sing in an Australian accent. 'Tie me kangaroo down, sport' in an Australian accent. It was this really lame song from the sixties. I laughed, but I was sort of shocked.

'You mean you hired someone to take pictures of you and her . . . ?'

'No. About two years ago, maybe three, just after my son-in-law's accident. Sue and I grew . . . fond of one another. She'd come out and we'd rendezvous in the playhouse. Wife got wind of it, had a private detective install a hidden camera in the ceiling over the bed. It was rigged up to a motion detector. She got pictures of everything. She'd been wanting a divorce and with these, she had me by the balls.' I thought of the scar where his testicles had been.

'If she had the pictures, why didn't she divorce you?'

'I got the big C. And well, once she cut off my *cojones* she thought it'd be kind of fun to stick around and see me live without them.'

'Wow.' I didn't know what else to say.

'My wife's a funny woman. She gave me the film the following Christmas. Told me she never had it developed. Probably some pictures of Bryce on here. He had some good times of his own down in the playhouse, from what I hear.' I thought of Bryce and Jilly.

'How should I file them?'

'Tricky. Love to see what's on 'em, but . . . it's not exactly something I'd like to see floating around Fotomat.'

'I could develop them for you. All I'd need is an enlarger and some developing fluid and fixer. I was in the Camera Club.'

'Give Herbert a list of what you need.' He tossed me the rolls of film. 'Let's keep this our little secret, *amigo*. And for God's sake, keep these where no one's going to find them.' The phone was ringing.

'Yeah?' It was his way of saying 'Hello'. A smile cracked across his face. 'Who?' He shouted, playfully gruff, into the receiver. Given what he'd just told me, I was surprised he was so jolly. 'I don't know if he can come to the phone.' He pulled out a cigar and motioned for me to give him a light. 'Why . . . because he works for me now . . . well, I'm glad you approve. What are we doing?' He winked at me. 'We're talking about girls . . . ask me no questions, I'll tell you no lies.' He handed me the phone, and left the room singing a new verse of 'Tie Me Kangaroo Down'.

'Tan me hide when I'm dead, Finn, tan me hide when I'm dead.'

Maya wanted to know what was so funny. It was hard to explain.

21

Four days later, it was the Fourth of July. I was so excited about seeing Maya, I didn't mind going to the Street Dance with my mother and Dr Leffler. Maya was going to come straight from the airstrip.

Leffler showed up in jeans, cowboy boots, white cowboy hat, and a brand-new pickup truck, with 'Sawbones Farm' written on the doors. Like five acres made him a farmer. Like dressing like a cheesy country-western singer made him a cowboy. I was relieved my mother came downstairs costumed as a snob, as opposed to Annie Oakley.

'Where are the new cowboy boots I gave you?' was the first thing out of Dr Dick's mouth.

'The boots gave me blisters, and I know how you love to dance.' My mother wasn't a complete jerk yet.

The main and only street of Vlyvalle was closed off from the church to the post office. We got there early, and there were already three hundred people. Red white and blue bunting, American flags, free rides in a hot-air balloon bearing the *Forbes* magazine logo, hot dogs and hamburgers on barbecue grills made of fifty-gallon drums split lengthwise, and a bar that only served beer and wine that were kegged in New Jersey – it was as down home as Vlyvalle gets.

Everything was free, if you lived in Vlyvalle. If you didn't, it was cheap at ten bucks a head. They had a big milk can set up on a table that outsiders were supposed to drop their money into. By the time I ditched my mother and Leffler and had gotten Tommy Fowler to snag me a beer, the crowd had swelled to four hundred. At least a half of them were from the suburbs that surrounded Vlyvalle. They stood out, because they were too well dressed. Rich people dressing up like they lived in a trailer park made the suburbanites nervous. It's fun to wear an Agway hat and Sears Roebuck overalls when you drive a dusty old Ferrari. I kept hearing people from the 'burbs saying, 'Who's paying for this?' like they were complaining.

Doctors and lawyers and businessmen from Summit and Morristown and Short Hills who had woken up that morning feeling righteous in the belief that they'd gotten more than their fair share, got an eyeful of something in Vlyvalle that made them feel suddenly short-changed. You could see it in their faces – it pissed them off to see the Governor and the Secretary of the Treasury – both Vlyvalle residents, hobnobbing with a three-toothed old farmer named Walter Pickle, who chewed Red Man and raised endangered breeds of swine for Mr Osborne. The visitors had all their teeth. They had Volvos and Mercedes Benzes and BMWs. And their children were on basketball teams that would have won the state championship if it weren't for the Negroes in those high schools in Newark. Why didn't the big-shots go for a photo-op with them? You had to wonder why they kept coming back, year after year.

When I looked into the milk can to see how much the visitors had contributed, all I saw was a handful of change and a dollar bill ripped in half. Gates must have checked it out, too, because he sicced the Hunt Club's game wardens on the crowd, and they started asking strangers where they lived in Vlyvalle. It was funny, after people paid, the event seemed less offensive to their democratic sensibilities.

Osborne wore overalls just like Walter Pickle's, and a straw hat that looked as if a horse had taken out a mouthful of brim. I knew he'd probably deliberately stepped in cow manure to give his boots and himself an authentic shit-kicker look. But when you like somebody who's really, really rich, and they like you, there's a natural tendency to think they're eccentric, rather than phony. You're not making excuses for them, you're making excuses for yourself.

I was surprised how many people I knew, not just from shaking their hands at parties and pools, but from Osborne's photos. That's how I recognized Walter Pickle. Leffler tried to play the big-shot, and introduced my mother to people he was right to think she'd be impressed by. I took pleasure in being able to step forward first and shake their hands and say, 'Good to see you, Mrs Graham' like I was good buddies with the woman who owned the Mets and the guy with the magazine and the hot-air balloons. There was a righteousness to my sucking up. Or at least, that's what I told myself as I waited for Maya to show.

A bluegrass band started to play, and Walter Pickle climbed up onto the platform at Osborne's urging and began to call out a square dance. 'Do-si-do, and Star right, and Promenade.' Then everybody began to try to square dance. It was pretty funny, watching the rhythmically challenged of Vlyvalle try to get into it. Especially when I noticed each time Walter Pickle shouted 'Square around the left-hand lady,' he'd smile and spray the dancers near the bandstand with tobacco juice spittle from the wad of Red Man that bulged his sunburned cheek. That's when I spotted Maya and her mother. Maya pushed through the crowd, stepping on toes and knocking people's drinks from their hands to get to me. She was too happy to say 'Excuse me'.

Osborne smiled and gave me an 'OK' sign with trembling fingers as Maya whispered in my ear, 'Where have you been all my life?' Her mother, Tab in hand, kissed me on both cheeks and said 'Bonjour, Finn.' Even though it was the Fourth of July, I felt kind of French.

After I heard how great her dad was doing, and how the doctors thought he'd be able to come home in three, but maybe as early as two weeks, I asked 'Where's Bryce?'

'I'm right here, sir.' Maya had told me he had dyed his hair back to normal. But she'd failed to mention that his makeover included a whole new wardrobe. Instead of a sarong, he wore a seersucker suit and a bow tie. I guess he must have worn contacts before, because he now had horn-rimmed glasses. He looked like Clark Kent.

I knew it wasn't just a new look, but a whole new attitude when Maya said, 'I'm gonna get Tommy Fowler to get me some wine. Want some, Bryce?'

Bryce snapped, 'No, and you shouldn't have any, either.'

'Right, I forgot. Finn, meet the new Bryce. He looks a lot like my brother, only he's a lot less fun.'

'No new Bryce. With Dad back, we have a second chance – I'm not going to blow it.' As Maya went off to hit up Tommy Fowler for

189

a drink, Bryce told me solemnly, 'My father's recovery just made me realize I've got to get my priorities straight.' He acted like he'd done something wrong. Maya was back with two white wines.

'It's good to see you, Finn. I hear you and Grandpa are thick as thieves.'

'Look out, Bryce, Grandpa's told him family secrets even we don't know about. Did you know Grandma put a hidden camera in the playhouse? Grandma put it in to catch him in the act with the Australian. Finn has the film. He's developing it.' I had told Maya that was a secret. 'He won't even tell me where he's hidden the film.'

I was suddenly glad I'd refused to tell Maya that I'd stashed Osborne's x-rated rolls of film with my pot in the old hot-water bottle I found in the back of my bedroom closet.

'You better hope that camera wasn't running when you and Jilly were at it. Can you imagine if Dwayne saw those pictures?' Maya was needling her brother at my expense. That was the second secret I regretted telling her.

'Bryce, I'm sorry, I shouldn't have told her about Jilly.' Suddenly, somebody slapped me on the back so hard I dropped my beer. It was Dwayne.

'Hey. How's my fishin' buddy doing?' Jilly said hello to everybody. They were both loaded. As they headed back towards the bar, Dwayne yelled over his shoulder, 'I'm gonna come get you one of these days, and we're gonna have some fun.'

Bryce waited until they were out of earshot to speak. 'You don't have to apologize, Finn. It's just that I realize what went on in the playhouse is nothing I'm very proud of.'

When Walter Pickle finished calling his tobacco-spitting reel, Bryce handed me his jacket. 'Could you hold this for a minute?' As he climbed up on the bandstand, Bryce rolled up his shirtsleeves and took hold of the microphone. 'My family and I have two pieces of wonderful news: our father will be coming home in a few weeks.' The crowd applauded. They were as puzzled as I by his new look. But they liked it. 'And he told me he looks forward to telling each and every one of you how much your prayers and friendship have meant during his illness.' The decadent smirk that made him impossible to hate was now an earnest smile, so big and open and apologetic it made everyone think this new seersuckered Bryce was an omen of better things to come. 'And as way of acknowledging the good fortune that all of us have enjoyed in Vlyvalle, I want to announce that next year, on those fields right over there . . .' He pointed to the ten acres of feed corn that grew behind the Butler's Pantry. 'We will be opening the doors of the Langley Youth Facility. A year-round home for inner-city young people in our state who haven't had the opportunities and good fortune we all take for granted.' From the reaction of the crowd you would have thought he'd just announced construction of a leaky nuclear reactor. The only people that applauded after that were the out-of-towners.

Osborne smiled and nodded like everything was fine. But I could tell from the way he pulled out a cigar and began to smoke it unlit that this was all news to him. Walter spit Red Man and said out loud what everybody was thinking. 'Why the hell does he want to ruin this place? Those people shit in their own backyard, now they're going to shit in ours.'

The only person who thought it was funny was Marcus, as he and Slim drifted by, he wise-cracked, 'Now Vlyvalle really has everything.' Gates gave him a look that said 'Shut up.'

I asked Maya, 'How did Bryce come up with this idea?'

'Talking with my dad.'

'Looks like you're going to have to start giving back your Christmas presents again.'

'Just as long as I can keep you.'

When I first came to Vlyvalle, I would have loved the idea of a regiment of jive juveniles, armed with ghetto blasters and cans of spray paint lurking outside the Butler's Pantry. I would have said, 'Serves them right. It's about time they got tagged.' But now that Vlyvalle had become mine, I didn't want to see anything happen to endanger this world that had transformed me into somebody that wouldn't have given me the time of day two months ago.

Maya said it was the first year people left before the fireworks. I figured they'd already seen them. As the Girardi Brothers' rockets boomed and showered the night sky with gaudy starbursts of light, I watched Bryce try to explain himself and this good deed to the grim-faced farmers and millionaire farm owners. His smile and earnest charm turned wild-eyed and impassioned. He wasn't used to people turning a cold shoulder to the heat of his personality.

'You haven't even asked me about the surprise.' Maya nibbled my ear with a whisper. Goosebumps rose up the back of my short-sleeved arms.

'What is it?'

'I decided I don't want to wait. I want us to do it tonight.' Blood rushed to my crotch so fast I felt hard and dizzy.

'You're sure?' I wanted to hear her say it again.

'Positive.'

'Where?'

'In a bed.'

'Whose?'

'Mine, silly.'

'What if your mother . . .'

'We both know that my mother will have had so many Tabs by then she wouldn't hear a bomb go off in my bedroom.' We'd never discussed it. I wondered how she knew I knew.

'What about Bryce?'

'I told him you're coming. He's going to stay over at Grandpa's. Give us some privacy. I've covered for him so many times, it's the least he can do.'

'But . . .' I so wanted it to be right, I was thinking of everything that could go wrong.

'I'll put the dogs in the kitchen, the screen porch door will be unlocked. Go into the library. Right behind the desk, there's a door that looks like it's part of the paneling. Inside, there's a staircase that goes right up to the guest room next to my bedroom. There's a door that connects them. You won't even have to go out into the hall.'

Maya and I made a point of saying goodbye in front of my mother and Leffler. She asked me if I wanted to come over after work tomorrow and have dinner at her house. I laid it on thick and asked my mother if it was OK. She liked that. Dr Dick jumped on the opportunity to invite himself over for dinner. 'Since you'll be all alone, why don't you let me come over and make you some of my famous *coq au vin*?' That's one word for it.

Bryce was still pleading his case on the other side of the crowd. I held up his jacket. He waved me off. 'I'll get it from you later.' The temperature had dropped twenty degrees. I put it on for the ride home in the back of Leffler's pickup. The guy was such a poser he had a bale of hay put back there to make it seem like he grew something on that bogus farm of his.

I lay in bed for a full hour with my clothes on before I snuck down the back stairs and ran across the lawn into the night. I was still wearing Bryce's jacket. I couldn't believe how cold it was. Wishing I'd put on a sweater, I began to run. I wondered if Maya would be waiting for me naked, or would she be in a bra and underpants. I preferred the latter. The erection in my jeans and the furrows of the freshly plowed field I was shortcutting across made it hard to run very fast. Backlit by the waning moon, Bryce's sports jacket on, I remember I was thinking what a long and elegant shadow I cast across the upturned earth, when something hit me on the back of my head.

The blow was so sharp, so unexpected, I fell face first, into the dirt, before pain registered. I was in the middle of a field. It was like something had fallen on me from out of the sky. I put my hand to the back of my head. I was bleeding. Blood spurt between my fingers as my heart raced. I was pulling my hand back from the gash that was searing my skull when someone pulled a feed bag over my head. Then the kicking started. Once, twice, first one side of my body, then the other. When I screamed and tried to pull the sack off my face, a boot came down on the back of my neck. Inhaling dirt, I began to gag. The last thing I remember was someone kneeling on my back, pushing my face into the ground.

I woke up in a bedroom at Osborne's house. My eyes were almost swollen shut. My field of vision was narrowed and blurry, like I was looking out a dirty window through Venetian blinds. It hurt to breathe. An older doctor I'd seen taking Osborne's blood pressure was injecting a syringe into the vein on the inside of my left arm. Gates was talking to Osborne in the doorway. I'd learn later Gates had found me when he'd shone a spotlight across the fields, looking for poachers. When the doctor was finished with the syringe,

Osborne took his place at the side of my bed. He looked grim as he gripped my hand. The phone rang. Gates answered. I couldn't hear what he was saying.

'Do you know who did this?' Osborne gripped my hand so tightly his ring cut into my flesh. I never noticed he wore jewelry before.

I tried to say 'No.' Nothing came out. I shook my head. I reached for a glass of water. He held it to my lips. They were split in two places. My mouth still tasted like dirt.

'They didn't say anything, they just kept kicking me.'

Gates put down the receiver. 'We know it wasn't Dwayne. New Brunswick police arrested him for drunk-driving on the turnpike.'

'Do you remember what happened?' Osborne asked cautiously.

'I was going to see Maya.'

'I know . . .' I saw Bryce's jacket and my pants on the arm of a chair. The jacket was ripped. The seat of my jeans was caked with blood. Painkillers numbed me to the big hurt. But I felt the crinkling of a bandage underneath me.

'Am I cut?'

A look was passed from Osborne to the doctor to Gates and back to Osborne. The old man's hands shook slightly as he cleared his throat. 'I'm going to lay this out for you so you know everything. You want to ask questions, we'll answer. If you want to talk about it, we'll talk. If you don't, that's fine, too.'

'What happened to me?'

'You were beaten. You have a couple of cracked ribs and a concussion. There's no other way to say this: you were raped.' He went on before what he'd just said could fully register. 'The bastard wore a rubber, so we can't get a blood type. But I swear to God, I will take care of this.'

The three men stared at me. They weren't just frightened of how I would react. They were scared that something like that could happen to them. My imagination filled in the event I could not remember. I was fucked. Someone had drawn a line across my life. I was just getting used to the me that had cast such an elegant shadow. Now there was a whole new person inside of me to get to know. I wanted to cry, but couldn't.

194

'I don't want my mother or Leffler or Bryce or Maya or anybody to know.' Osborne wouldn't let go of my hand when I tried to jerk it away.

'I can take care of that,' Gates volunteered. 'You got my word. Police report will just say you were beaten.' There was a knock on the door. Gates opened it a crack. It was Bryce, wearing one of Osborne's bathrobes. He'd just woken up. His voice was full of sleep.

'What the hell's going on? What's Finn doing . . .'

Osborne cut him off. 'He was beaten up.'

'By who?'

I turned my face to the wall. I didn't want Bryce to see me like this.

'We don't know yet, Bryce.'

'When did this happen?'

'When you and I were talking about your goddamn youth center.'

Bryce looked like he'd just been slapped. Gates ushered Bryce out the door. 'Look, Bryce, your grandfather's upset. Right now, you know as much as we do.' I heard Gates and Bryce talking on the other side of the door. The doctor packed up his bag.

'Anything else you want?' Osborne asked softly.

There was, but he couldn't give it to me.

Osborne drove me home in a Rolls I'd never seen before. I was wearing one of his silk bathrobes. Gates kept my clothes for evidence. Blood seeped through the bandage and the bathrobe and stained the fawn leather interior of the car. Before I could say anything Osborne told me, 'Forget about it.'

Osborne had already called my mother. He'd kept his promise. He just told her I'd been assaulted. He left out the sexual part. She was standing on the lawn in the morning light, wearing her bathrobe and her pearls. She'd put on her makeup for the occasion. Leffler had his arm around her. I didn't need to imagine how he got her through the night. She was crying.

Gates and the old doctor helped me out of the car. Leffler, trying to play the big-shot, followed them and started asking questions. When Osborne barked, 'Dr Schiller is going to handle this case,' Leffler got the hint and let the screen door slam in his face.

When they got me up to my bedroom, Gates left and Dr Schiller rolled me over and checked my sutures. The old guy was trying to be gentle when he said, 'You might want to talk to somebody about this.'

'Like who?'

'Me, or a psychologist.'

'The deal is, no one knows.' As the doctor told me when to take my painkillers and stool softeners, I heard my mother's tears turn to rage on the front lawn.

'You don't have any idea who beat up my son?'

'No, ma'am, not at this moment.' Gates sounded awfully official for a cop who'd just filled out a false report.

'Well, why did they do it to him?'

'He doesn't know, and we don't know.'

'What's going to happen when you find the person who did this to my son?'

Osborne answered for Gates. 'I'll take care of that.'

I heard the cars drive off, then listened as my mother slowly climbed the stairs. When she looked at me, all she saw was two black eyes and some bruises. She'd started to cry again, then caught herself and lit a cigarette.

'You're lucky.'

'How do you figure that?' She made it easier not to cry.

'You could have been seriously hurt.'

'I'm hurt.'

'If you hadn't lied and snuck out this wouldn't have happened.'

'You don't know what you're talking about.' It was easy to forget her ignorance was my fault, not hers. My mother leaned over and looked at me, a focused squint on her face, like she was about to pull a splinter out of my eye.

'You're not telling me everything.' I looked away. 'Who are you protecting?' She sounded just like Nana.

'Me.'

I was raped. The fact that I was unconscious when it happened didn't change the fact that I was fucked by a man. Though I couldn't remember penetration, I had six stitches in my rectum to remind me to be ashamed. I had been trying to lose my virginity, but not like this.

The painkillers knocked me out for six hours. When I woke up, my room was full of flowers. Everybody in Vlyvalle knew I'd been beaten up. Crime had come to Paradise. There was talk of enlarging the police force. Lots of people called. The ones that wanted to suck up to Osborne sent flowers. Except for Maya. Hers were a pitcher stuffed with peonies she'd picked herself. They were on my bedside table. My mother told me she'd called twice and stopped by with Bryce once. When I smelled her flowers, I smiled and buried my face in their bouquet. It was a relief, until it occurred to me that was the sort of thing a fag would do.

Maya called again. When my mother brought the phone to my bedroom, I said I didn't want to talk to anybody. She told Maya I was in the bathroom and I'd call her back.

'Maya Langley is worried about you.'

'I'm worried about me.' The painkillers weren't the only thing making me feel numb.

'This isn't the end of the world, Finn, you got beaten up. It was a horrible thing to happen, but there's no permanent damage.' I wanted to say, 'That's what you think,' but I knew if she found out what happened, it would never go away. If I never told anyone about it, it would be easier for me to pretend it had never happened. Without realizing it, I had reconciled myself to the fact that life was a command performance a long time ago.

I took the phone from her and dialled Maya's number, 'You're right, Mom. I got beat up – I don't have cancer.'

'It may not seem it right now, but you've made a good start here, Finn.' My mother was proud of all the flowers and calls that she had received. 'I've made a list of all the people who sent you flowers. When you're feeling better next week, I'll get you some stationery to write thank-you notes. Did you know you're not the first person in Vlyvalle who's been attacked?'

'Who else?' Maya's line was busy.

'Mr McCallum was pulled out of his car in Newark and nearly beaten to death.' I remembered Marcus telling me about McCallum's retribution for dead-horsing Dwayne's mother. I thought of Marcus kissing Slim. I wondered where they were when I was deadhorsed. Could it have been them? One of the gay Japanese

197

gardeners? A flash-fire of homophobia was extinguished as I remembered the number of times my assailant had kicked me. He had already hurt me when I passed out. He hadn't stuck his dick up my ass because he liked me. He just wanted to hurt me more.

Was he waiting for me, or just a warm body? Was it just bad luck, or my bad luck? It wasn't much of a choice. Wanting to make some sense of it, I told myself it was me they were after. I remembered the laughter that had chased Maya and me off the island that night. I vowed to find out who did this to me. It felt good – well, not good, better – to get angry. But then I realized that if I tried to figure out who fucked me I'd never be able to pretend there was no permanent damage. Like I said, I was totally fucked.

I called Maya. She cried and said she was sure it was one of the poachers. When I didn't show up at her house, she went looking for me. She got to the field where I was jumped just as Gates sped away, cherry-top flashing with me laid out in the back seat. I wasn't totally unlucky. At least she wasn't the one to find me face down in the dirt with my pants around my ankles. I changed the subject, and asked her about her dad. That made her cry again.

'You're the most amazing person in the world.'

'How do you figure that?'

'You get beat up, and you're worried about my dad?' I didn't say anything. It's easy to play the strong, silent type over the phone.

She and Bryce showed up at the house about an hour later. I heard my mother say, 'I'll take you up to his bedroom, and then get us some iced tea.'

Bryce was trying to help me out when he said, 'Mrs Earl, let's give Maya and Finn some time alone. I'll help you with that iced tea.' The thing was, I didn't really feel like being alone with Maya.

She knocked as she opened the door. 'Can I come in?'

'You better.' I was trying to be manfully cheerful. She stepped into the room with a smile that was a guarantee of good times to come. I expected her to start crying at the sight of me. My face was swollen, purple-black. My lips were scabbed and my nose was broken.

'You look sort of handsome.'

'That's not funny.'

'Sexy-handsome, like a prize fighter.'

'What do you know about prize fighters?'

'Nothing, but when I got dragged by my pony, I looked like a smashed pumpkin for about six months.' Looking at me, she could tell this wasn't the response I wanted. She bit her lip, and thought for a moment. 'Want me to go back out into the hall and come back in and be all upset? Because I am upset. I mean, it's sort of my fault, but I just figured you'd want me to get your mind off what happened.' She knew my mind, she just didn't know the truth.

'What do you mean it's your fault?'

'It was my idea for you to sneak over last night.' She sat on the edge of my bed and kissed my left ear. It was the only part of my face that didn't hurt. 'I still want to give you that surprise.'

She giggled as she reached her hand under my sheet. 'It's been a long time.'

I pushed her hand away. 'My ribs are cracked.' It wasn't my ribs I was worried about.

'I could kill those fucking poachers.'

It was an unfortunate choice of words.

'It wasn't Dwayne.'

'He's not the only one who hates us.' I was one of them now. 'His father's the most twisted one in the bunch.' It hadn't occurred to me I'd been fucked by an old guy.

'Twisted how?'

'Well, it's pretty disgusting.'

'I'm interested.'

'There was a rumor he got fired from McCallum's Dairy because he got caught getting sucked off by a veal calf.'

Bryce carried in the tray with iced tea and cookies. With all that had happened, I'd forgotten that he'd dyed his hair back and changed his look.

'What are we talking about?' Mom passed the cookies.

'Who beat me up.' I gave her a look I thought made it clear I wanted to be alone with my friends. She answered by sitting down on the other side of my bed.

Bryce took the chair. 'Finn, I talked to Gates.' For a minute, I thought he knew. 'You're lucky to be alive.'

199

'I just got beat up.' My jaw ached when I bit into my cookie.

'Do you have any idea why someone would do this to you?'

'I'm a gentleman and a scholar?'

'You are indeed, sir,' Bryce laughed. 'And a most excellent liar.' For a moment he was his old self again.

'What's that mean, Bryce?'

'Private joke between Finn and myself.'

My mother stood up. 'Maya, could I talk to you downstairs?'

As Maya said 'Sure,' I demanded, 'What about?'

'Your birthday's week after next. I wanted to have a party for you and your friends.'

'Don't.' It wasn't just that I didn't feel in the party mood. The thought of my mother entertaining my friends with cake and punch was just too lame to bear.

'Come on, Finn, it's your birthday,' Maya announced. 'We're throwing you a party whether you like it or not.' My mother didn't like the way Maya said 'we'.

Maya bent over, kissed my good ear and whispered, 'I know what you're worried about; leave it to me.'

When they left the room and went downstairs, Bryce closed the bedroom door. 'You know, Finn, there's a good possibility they were after me. You had on my jacket. It was dark. You were heading to our house.'

'Who'd want to do this to you?'

'Announcing our plan to build a youth center hasn't exactly made me popular.'

'Maya thinks it was one of the poachers.'

'My sister blames the poachers for everything.'

'Somebody chased us off the island two weeks ago.'

'Why didn't you tell me?'

'Didn't seem like a big deal.'

'Well, you've got to be prepared, if they try to do this to you again.' I hadn't even considered that possibility. Bryce reached in his pocket and pulled out a pistol. It was a pearl-handled revolver, just like the one Osborne carried. 'Be careful – it's loaded.'

As soon as Bryce and Maya drove off, my mother stormed up the stairs. I was spinning the cylinder of the revolver, thinking about where I'd put the first bullet when I found out who fucked me. I hid the gun under the covers, my finger was on the trigger.

'That girl has a lot of nerve. If I were giving you a birthday party and wanted her help, I would have asked.'

'You did ask her.'

'All I wanted from her was a list of names.'

'What'd you get?'

'She called her grandfather, and before I could stop her, she asked him to have the party at the playhouse.' I still didn't want a party, but at least with Osborne throwing it, everyone could get loaded.

'I guess *we* are having a party.'

'The point is, I wanted to use this as an opportunity to reciprocate.'

'What does that mean?'

'I want to entertain all the people who've been so welcoming to us.'

'It's not our house.'

'For your information, I've leased this house for two years.'

'Thanks for asking me if I wanted to stay here.'

'Why in the world would we want to live anywhere else?'

I don't care how natural it looks in the movies, it's hard to fall asleep with a loaded gun under your pillow. I kept thinking it could go off in the middle of the night. Feeling like blowing your brains out and having it happen by accident are two very different things. When I took the bullets out of the gun, I rested easier. Until I thought of what Bryce said about the guy coming back to get me. I nervously reloaded and looked for a place to hide it where I could get to it in a hurry. I wedged it behind the headboard and practiced reaching up for it in a blind panic. It was too much of a reach. It made my stitches bleed. The drawer of my bedside table? If I didn't lock it, my mother would find it. And if I did, by the time I turned on the light, and got the key in the hole – he'd have me. Either way I'd be fucked. I finally settled on slipping the gun between my mattress and the boxspring. The same place I used to hide my beat-off magazines.

The next day, Herbert showed up with an enlarger and the photo-developing stuff I'd asked for. I had forgotten about the film I was supposed to develop for Osborne. I didn't feel like developing his dirty pictures. I had enough inside my head.

Jilly showed up at work that morning with a get-well present of an ounce of pot and a fifth of Jack Daniel's. She told me as soon as Dwayne got out of jail, he'd find out who jumped me. Osborne had posted a $50,000 reward for information leading to the arrest of my assailant. I told Jilly to tell Dwayne I appreciated his interest. I meant it.

22

Maya came by in the afternoons when my mother was at her AA meetings. Just before she'd arrive, I'd have a Jack and Coke, and half a joint or so. That, on top of my painkillers, made it easier to act like I was getting better. After Osborne's doctor took out the stitches, it was more comfortable to walk around. But I was still nervous enough around Maya to feel the need to fortify myself before her daily visit.

A week later, we were sitting on the lawn, sharing a joint, her first of the day, my third, when she suddenly asked me, 'Does it hurt to kiss me?'

'No.'

'Well, why don't you?' I kissed her. It hurt the scabbed split on my lip, but I didn't say anything. She pulled me on top of her, careful of my ribs, whispering, 'I miss you.'

'I miss you, too.' I did. If she had just lain there, it might have been OK. But when she started to move beneath me, it was too much. The world began to spin. I tried to fight through the nausea and excitement. For a second, I thought I was going to come in my pants. Instead, I rolled off her and vomited. I told her it was the Percodan. She got a cold dishtowel and wiped my face, and held my head in her lap beneath the sugar maple and told me, 'Everything's going to be good again.'

When my mother left for work the next morning, I did my daily routine of painkillers, a joint, a Jack and Coke. Deciding it was time to do something different, I read an article in *Cosmo* titled 'How to Tell if Your Lover has an Alcohol or Drug Problem'. Feeling strangely ambitious, I took the quiz that ran with the article, and checked off the boxes that applied to me.

'Does he Drink and/or Take Drugs by Himself?' – Yes. 'Does he Hide the Fact he Drinks and/or Takes Drugs from his Family and Friends?' – that one got half a Yes. 'Does he Drink and/or Take Drugs During the Day?' – I checked Yes and made a mental note of 'Whenever possible'. 'Does Alcohol and/or Drugs Affect his Sexual Performance?' – I thought about that one for a while. When I tallied up my score, I discovered I qualified for 'Dump him Unless he Seeks Professional Help Immediately'. I was pretty bummed until I got to the part of the article that said substance abusers were more often than not high achievers in school and at work. Having been a lifelong under-achiever, I figured if I kept getting fucked up on a regular basis, at least my grades might improve.

There were a few more days like that. Then one afternoon, without any warning, Osborne's Rolls pulled up to the house. I was getting high, watching *Speed Racer* (I had forgotten Speed Racer's brother's name was Racer x). The chauffeur was at the door before I'd had a chance to air out the pot.

'Mr Osborne wants you back at work.'

'When?'

'Now. I'll be driving you to and from the house from now on.'

Herbert answered the door. As he took me up to the billiard room, he asked me if I was feeling better, and I lied and said 'Sort of.' It was obvious Osborne had been rummaging through the photos since I'd been gone. The 'See Osborne' pile that I had so neatly stacked was now as much of a mess as the mound on top of the billiard table.

Osborne showed up about thirty minutes later. He was all dressed up, chalk-striped suit, with an old-fashioned double-breasted vest with piping around the edges.

'Sorry I'm late.' It was a relief to meet someone who didn't ask how I was feeling. 'Spent all goddamn morning at a board meeting. Believe you me, I was Chairman of the Bored.' He thought that was pretty funny. I looked at the cuff of his pants. I wondered if his business associates had noticed he had forgotten to take off his pajama bottoms before he put on his suit pants. When he took off his jacket, I saw the shirt he was wearing was a pajama top. It didn't look bad with a tie but you had to wonder whether it was affectation or early Alzheimer's. I suspected the latter when he got down on all fours, with a slow, joint-cracking snap, crackle and pop and began to crawl towards a corner of the room.

'You lose something?'

'I sure as hell hope not.' I saw what he was up to when he pulled back a corner of the Chinese rug and revealed a floor safe. Osborne took off the glasses he was wearing, put on another pair, and spun the dial to the left, the right, then paused. 'Fuck. Can't remember the goddamn combination. Get me my book.' I fished a worn crocodile agenda with a doubled rubber band around it out of his jacket pocket. The date the suit was made on Savile Row was written on a label inside the inside pocket. It was older than my mother. Osborne consulted his little black book and tried the combination again. His hands shook. Left, right, left – no click. He tried it again. His hands shook so bad, you would have thought he had his fingers in an electric socket. It would have been funny if it were a cartoon. 'Shit. You open it yourself.' He sat back on his ass, out of breath from the aggravation.

'What's the combination?'

'One . . . two . . . three.'

'That's pretty obvious.'

'All I can remember.' His safe opened with a twist of my wrist. Our heads bumped as we both peered into the sunken steel cylinder of the safe. I saw a half-dozen crisp bundles of hundred-dollar bills and a couple of jewelry boxes – blue from Tiffany's, red from Cartier. And a beat-up metal cash box that looked like it was bought at Woolworth's a hundred years ago.

'Hand me the box, partner.' It was so cheaply made you could have opened it with a bobby pin. He pulled on the gold chain that disappeared into his vest pocket, and produced a tiny stamped metal key. 'I want you to look at something I've never talked about or shown another person in my entire life.' He unlocked the box with a sigh. Inside was a codicil to his will, three marbles, and a dirty picture from about 1915. It was of a naked woman lying across a bed, stockings rolled down to her knees, legs up in the air. She was wearing a cross and a look of disbelief on her face. Her head was turned to a window. A fat man with a walrus mustache, naked except for garters and socks, is holding onto the bedpost, bracing himself while he fucks her standing up.

'Wow. She's got a lot of pubic hair.'

'Ladies didn't wax in my mother's day.' Osborne took the picture, looked at it closely, then handed it back to me. 'Good-looking woman, my mother.'

'That's your mother!'

'In the flesh.'

'Who's the guy?'

'That's the president of the telegraph company, who gave my father a very large contract when he saw that picture.'

'How'd your father get ahold of the picture?'

'He took it.' Osborne explained matter-of-factly that the guy who was doing his mom owned a bunch of other stuff, including a railroad. That dirty picture netted Osborne's father a couple of contracts every year. Osborne called them 'sweetheart' deals. He said it like a joke, but you could tell he didn't think it was funny. Then, with a shaky finger, Osborne pointed at the gap in the drapes. I looked closer. It was Osborne, about my age, staring blank-faced at the camera.

'Why are you showing this to me?'

'*Ex malo bonum* . . . Latin. "Out of bad comes good."'

The chauffeur showed up at five to drive me home. As Osborne walked me to the door, the sun was streaking through the big stained-glass window in the front hall. Now wearing a long dressing gown, washed in a spectrum of light, Osborne looked kind of like a priest. It was the first time I noticed his family crest was lettered out in colored glass at the top of the window. The heraldry was telling. A woman's head, with her arm across her eyes – beneath it the motto *Ex Malo Bonum* was written. I guessed it was a good thing to believe, if you were rich enough to make it true.

23

Bryce was on TV. Mrs Langley had everybody over to her house to watch it. The town, as Osborne put it, still had their tit in a wringer about Bryce bringing Negroes to Vlyvalle. But they still came. They knew if they didn't, they wouldn't be invited to Osborne's next party, or the party after that, or the party after that. As Osborne said, what's the point of holding a grudge if you can't hold it for ever?

The next party on the summer social schedule was my birthday. Maya had decided to make it a costume party, with a gods and goddesses theme. My mother was really pissed off about it at first. But once the golf-course crowd started sucking up to her to get invited, she rewrote history, and pretended it was her idea to make it costume. It was pretty disgusting, actually. Anyway, back to the social outing at hand.

The Langleys weren't big TV people. They only had one set, in the library, which was about the size of my bedroom. The room was full of paint cans, turpentine and drop cloths. An English guy was painting a family mural in honor of Mr Langley's homecoming.

So that everybody could get a clear picture of the new, improved Bryce, the Langleys bought four 36-inch TVs and stacked them up by the pool. Since it was a hot day, and there weren't enough chairs, Maya, me, Marcus, Slim and Paige put on our bathing suits and watched from the shallow end. Bryce times four was on the six o'clock news with the mayor of Newark. He bought a new seersucker suit for the press conference. He and the mayor were standing in front of a burnt-out building on Clinton Avenue, surrounded by guys in dashikis. Bryce handed the mayor a check for $200,000 from Osborne's Foundation. They announced the building was going to be renovated and turned into The Langley House, a halfway house for troubled youth. Bryce called it 'a sanctuary for children who'd had their childhood stolen from them'. It was surreal: us in the pool; the Langleys' black maids serving drinks and passing crab claws and mustard dip to rich white people, applauding and saying stuff like, 'Isn't it wonderful Bryce wants to do something,' all the while hoping the Langley House in Newark means they aren't building one in Vlyvalle. As Maya hung on me in the pool, she whispered 'Newark was Grandpa's idea. He's trying to distract Bryce.'

But most surreal of all was watching Bryce on TV. There was nothing phony about him on the big screen. The soul-shake he handed the major was sincere. His earnestness was totally telegenic. You would never have guessed that this was the same guy who had displayed his social conscience by dyeing his hair white, wearing a sarong, and taking a Nigerian princess named Coco to débutante parties and introducing her as his fiancée. The change in him was so complete, the follow-through so well orchestrated, you had to wonder if he had planned to grow up all at once all along.

Bryce stood apart from the crowd and watched himself. He smiled bashfully when the news segment was over and everybody clapped. It was hard to tell whether he was more pleased with his performance or what he had done. Somebody from the crowd said 'God, Bryce, it looks like you took acting lessons from Bobby Kennedy.'

'I'll take that as a compliment.'

It wasn't meant as one.

'You should run for office,' somebody said.

'I'm afraid I have too sordid a past for that.'

Mrs Llewellyn, the blue-haired lady that I met at Maya's birthday party who had five husbands and got kicked out of boarding school for having a diamond engagement ring in her school bag, stood up and announced, 'Bryce, while you're at it, why don't you do something about our Indians?' She was wearing lots of turquoise jewelry and, like I said, it was surreal.

'Well, I thought it made more sense to concentrate on the issues in our own state.'

'New Jersey has Indians. Lenni–Lenape in the south, and Algonquins lived right here. Isn't that right, Marcus?' Marcus was wrestling with Slim underwater in the deep end. When Marcus surfaced for air, everyone was staring at him. Mrs Llewellyn peered down at him. 'Marcus, your mother's part Algonquin. Don't you think there should be some compensation for the white man's inexcusably shabby treatment of the indigenous peoples of New Jersey?'

Marcus, relieved that no one saw him feeling up Slim underwater, smiled broadly. 'Mrs Llewellyn, you're an honorary member of our tribe already.'

A WASPY guy, who took a helicopter to work and who'd had too many Long Island iced teas, thought he was being funny when he said 'What about our tribe? Who's looking out for us? Christ, we're practically an endangered species.'

Osborne answered, 'We're already extinct. We just don't want to admit it.'

While the adults got quietly bombed and argued, the young climbed out of the water and snuck behind the poolhouse and shared a joint. I knew Marcus was stoned when he said, 'You know, if you guys gave me a Reservation, I could legalize pot and we'd make a fortune.'

I knew Paige was high when she announced, 'I think I'm just going to get some Quaaludes, sneak into Bryce's bed and jump your brother before he gets so conservative he won't want to fuck me.'

When the joint had been passed around, down to a nub, too small for the roach clip Paige was wearing around her neck, Slim ate it. Maya pulled me back as the three of them giggled their way back to the party in search of a tray or two of *hors d'oeuvres* to placate their munchies.

'What's wrong?'

'Nothing.'

'Have you, like, lost interest in me, or something?' She paused between each word, shocked by what she was saying and how much it made her want to cry.

'No . . . how can you say that?'

'Because you never want to be alone with me.'

'That's not true.' I didn't want it to be, but it was. 'Slim asked us if we wanted to get high. What was I going to do? Say "give me your pot and get lost"?'

'I don't mean right now.' Five times in the last week, without making a big deal about it, Maya had arranged things for us to be alone. A picnic on the island. An afternoon by the pool, when Bryce and her mother were at the hospital helping her dad with physical rehabilitation and the maids had the afternoon off. Each time, at the last minute, I invited somebody to come along, or drop some pot by. Once I even arranged for my mother to call, and pretended she was being an asshole and making me come home early.

I held her face in my hands, and kissed her. 'It has nothing to do with you.' I was trying to be honest.

'What is it, then?' She had her hand inside my bathing suit. My erection popped out of my waistband. Wanting to be happy, wanting to draw a new line across my life and start fresh, I pulled off her bathing suit and tried to see us as we were the first time we got naked. But when I closed my eyes, all I saw was myself getting fucked in the field by a faceless figure. I buried my face in the softness of her neck. Pressed my eyelids against her collarbone until blackness turned red. Desperate, I tried to think of something else. All I could conjure up to keep me hard was the image of the Yanomamö maiden I used to beat off to. I could have put it in. The mechanics were no mystery. Unable to bear the thought that life had reduced me to this, I stepped away from her and lied.

'I feel dizzy.'

'What should I do?'

'Nothing. It comes and goes.' I put my hand on the side of the poolhouse, like I was going to fall down. It was funny, faking I was dizzy actually made me dizzy.

'You want me to get you a drink of water?' If she hadn't been naked, I would have told her to get me one, just to avoid looking her in the eye.

'No, I'll be fine . . . the doctor thinks I'm having an adverse reaction to the concussion medicine.' I paraphrased a line from a soap opera I had watched while I was still in bed. I watched Maya pull up her bathing suit. One of her nipples stuck out of the top. I tucked it back in.

'This sucks.' The worst part was, I still found her sexy as hell.

'You'll be better in a few days.'

'Yeah.'

'Don't worry. It'll still be a surprise when we finally do it.' The trouble was, I didn't want any more surprises.

Maya wanted to drive me home. It was still light. I told her I wanted to walk. 'What if you run into the guy who jumped you?'

'He'll be sorry.' I seemed braver than I was. I had the pistol in the inside pocket of my jean jacket. Bryce was watching us.

'You don't have to act brave around me. Let me take you home – you can drive.'

'Maya, give Finn a break,' Bryce called out. 'He can take care of himself.' I preferred the old Bryce, but the new version wasn't a bad guy either.

As soon as I was out of sight of the Langleys', I pulled out the pistol. I cut through the woods, gun in hand, hammer cocked, looking over my shoulder every few steps. I figured if he was following me, he'd be more likely to try something there than out in the open. Part of me hoped he'd try to jump me. Part of me questioned, could I really shoot a human being? I thought of him putting the feed sack over my head. Remembering the way it felt to have stitches in my ass, I stopped wondering if I could shoot him and started thinking where I'd put the first bullet. In his stomach? In the balls? Maybe the knee. I'd like to see him crawling around, begging me to stop. But then again, if I shot him in the jaw, I could hear him gag on his own blood as he screamed for mercy. The pistol Bryce gave me had six shots. That's a lot of ways to hurt someone.

I entered the woods thinking that if I shot the guy, it'd be over. Before I'd gone very far, I realized: it wasn't that simple. If I shot the bastard and didn't kill him, there'd be questions asked I didn't want to have to answer. The fact that I used Bryce's gun would make it even more complicated. And if I shot him and killed him, chances were I'd have to stand trial for manslaughter, unless I admitted he raped me. If that came out, everyone would know I'd been permanently damaged by what had happened because I'd tried to hide it. Sure, they'd feel sorry for me. A lot of them would even be extra nice, and go out of their way to act normal. But for the rest of my life, I'd be: 'You know, Finn Earl, the guy who got beat up and fucked by some guy. He's OK, considering . . .'

Even if I did pull myself together, and stopped getting fucked up, and studied for my SATs, and got into Harvard, and made first contact with a tribe not even my father had been able to discover, people would say, 'After he took it up the ass, he really got his shit together.' And even Maya, if she found out the truth, she'd still give me her surprise. But no matter what, I'd know she did it mostly because she felt sorry for me. And even if she did it without a touch of pity, no matter how good it was, she'd know it would have been better if I hadn't gotten myself raped in her grandfather's field.

My mind needed a smooth combing. And my heart was like one of the Anjou pears that Mr Osborne grew inside glass bottles for his brandy. I could see them in the orchard to my right. They were ripe, untouchable, and green, inside glass that tinkled softly in the evening breeze.

I aimed my pistol at one, and fired. The gun was louder than I expected. Less than five feet away from my target, and I still missed. I felt stupid and scared, and looked around, relieved no one had seen me trying to kill fruit with a handgun.

The phone started to ring as I walked up our drive. I ran across the lawn and into the house. I made up my mind. If it was Maya, I was going to tell her to come right over. We'd go someplace and . . .

'Listen, Maya? I've been thinking . . .'

'Who's Maya.' The woman's voice sounded eerily familiar.

'Who are you?'

'You don't recognize your old Nana?'

'It's your grandparents!'

They were both on the line.

'Why are you calling us?' It was a relief to be honest for a change.

'Because we love you.' That was Nana.

'Right.'

'We love you and your mother, unconditionally.'

'Save it for your patients.'

'I don't think your grandfather deserves that sort of hostility.'

'No, Finn's entitled to his hostility, but it's only fair you also know

212

how happy we are that things have turned out so well for both of you.'

'If you bother us again, I'll tell Mr Osborne.' That shut them up for a moment.

'Is your mother there?'

'No.' There was a note – she was at Leffler's.

'Will you give her a message for us?'

'Sure.'

'Tell her we wouldn't miss your birthday party for the world.' You would have thought, after all the shit that had happened to me, that it would take more than a phone call from them to make me cry.

I dragged a kitchen chair out to the sugar maple, climbed up on tiptoe, and dropped the revolver down a hole in the trunk that had been home to a family of squirrels. I knew there was no danger of me shooting anybody other than myself.

I woke up tired of caring about how things turned out. I lay in bed with a piss-boner, and debated whether or not masturbating would make me feel better or worse. Two tugs later, I'm wondering if he touched me when he fucked me.

When I came downstairs and joined my mother for breakfast, I told her, as I sliced up my banana, 'Oh, yeah, I forgot to tell you. Nana and Grandpa called last night.' Before she could jump me for not writing down the message, I volunteered, 'I think it's great you invited them to the party.'

'Actually, I'm surprised you feel that way.'

'Forgive and forget.'

'I haven't forgotten what they did.'

'If you thought I didn't want you to invite them, and you haven't forgotten, why'd you invite them?'

'I wanted them to see how we're doing.'

'You mean, so they won't worry.' I knew she just wanted to impress them but, like I said, I was tired of caring. My mother smiled, reached across the breakfast table and took hold of my hand.

'It's so nice to be able to talk with you about this in an adult way.'

The phone rang. It was my grandmother. My mom took it in the other room. When she came back, she said, 'Nana says you were hostile on the phone.'

'They're projecting.'

'She said you threatened to call Mr Osborne.'

'Mom, I was the one that came in and said I was glad you invited them. You know how manipulative they are. They'll say anything to come between us.'

'Nothing could come between us, Finn, could it?'

'You're the only mom I've got.' I couldn't even be bothered to say something mean.

24

Osborne called and said I didn't have to go to work. He was hosting a lunch for Bryce in Washington. He had invited senators and newspaper publishers and CEOs of *Fortune 500* companies who owed him favors. I hoped he remembered to take off his pajama bottoms before he put on his suit. Osborne told me the idea was to get Bryce so busy building Langley halfway houses around the country he'd forget about opening one in Vlyvalle.

'Why don't you just tell him you don't want him to build it?'

'Christ, I want him to build the thing, in fact, the only thing I'd like to see more of downtown is a low-income housing project.' It was weird to think of the Butler's Pantry as 'downtown'. 'Wouldn't that be a beautiful thing, Finn? Little brown and yellow babies running around?' Even though we were talking on the phone, I could see him smile at the idea. 'I'd give 'em all scholarships to Vlyvalle Country Day.' That was the local private school. It only went up to eighth grade. After that, everybody went away to boarding school.

'What's the problem, then?'

'I just want the boy to wait until Walter Pickle dies or retires, and my Tuckernucks are safe.' Tuckernucks were a breed of pig.

'Safe from what?'

'The American consumer. They stopped breeding them because there wasn't enough meat on them to turn a profit. Walter and I brought the breed back from extinction. That's the same line of pig the Pilgrims brought over. Pioneers took those swine west. Christ, their bacon made this country. Walter'll quit me over this thing, and if he quits, my pigs'll be lost. And . . . I just don't want it all to go to hell in a handbasket on my watch.' I didn't know what to say.

Osborne filled the silence. 'Why don't you come on down to Washington with us? Maya's coming.'

'Thanks, but I've got to write my father a letter.' It was just an excuse. My father had dropped off my radar screen.

'I'd like to meet your father.'

'So would I.' Osborne thought that funny. He laughed so hard he started to wheeze.

'Gotta hang up. I wanna die laughing, but not now.'

My mother was at the playhouse to talk to the florist about centerpieces for the tables at my birthday party. Osborne had hired Slim's band. A hundred people were coming. The whole town was talking about which gods and goddesses they were going to be. Maya was coming as Diana, goddess of the hunt. She had spray-painted her crossbow gold. My mother was all set to be Athena, until Osborne pointed out she had six breasts. Mrs Langley was going as Shiva. She didn't know that was the goddess of destruction, but she'd been to India for Christmas, and had bought a lot of uncut rubies she was looking for an excuse to wear. Everybody wanted to know what god I was impersonating. I hadn't decided for sure. But I had narrowed it down to either Jesus Christ or Ogden Osborne. I was still trying to figure out which one was in worse taste.

It was Jilly's day to clean. It seemed like years, not weeks, had passed since I'd first mistaken her for a bird in the chimney. I was reading a magazine article about DNA and genetics when her mother dropped her off. Beehive hairdo dyed the color of a Cheez Doodle, and an ass as wide as a Frigidaire, I wondered if Jilly worried about ending up like that. Her mother's goodbye was, 'Screw you, too, young lady.'

Tube-top, cutoffs, and uniform unbuttoned to the waist, Jilly was sniffling and red-eyed. I could tell she was upset. But I had too many problems of my own to be entertained by hers.

'Hi, Jilly.' I pretended to be too interested in the double helix to say more.

She started to put together the vacuum, then shouted, 'Shit!' I tried to escape into the kitchen. She followed me. 'Thanks for asking what's wrong.'

'If your wool allergy's bothering you, don't wear the uniform.'

'Fuck you!'

'Fuck you, too.'

'You think you're the only one with problems?'

'I'll trade mine for yours.'

'OK, you tell me what's wrong with you first.'

'All right . . .' I thought about whether I should just tell her outright, or work up to the subject slowly. 'But you've got to promise not to tell anyone.'

'I promise.'

'Swear it.'

'OK, I swear it. What's wrong?'

'I'm out of pot.'

'You're an asshole.' She tossed me a joint. I lit it and inhaled.

'All right. I'll tell you the truth. The guy who beat me up fucked me.' I held my breath.

I felt better until she said, 'Very funny.'

'Not really.' I looked at my feet.

'Don't be a jerk, Finn.'

'OK, what's wrong with you?'

'My mother won't let me take my college money out of my savings account.'

'What do you need it for?'

'That's my business.'

'Can't Dwayne give it to you?'

'Dwayne says it's not his.' She could tell I didn't get it. 'I'm pregnant.'

Suddenly, I was looking at my mother, as she must have been when I was first inside her. 'Have you told Bryce?' I remembered what I saw through the playhouse window.

'Why would Bryce care?' She was mad I even mentioned his name.

'I don't know, I just thought . . . you want to have an abortion?'

'No, but I . . .' She was crying too hard to speak.

'I'll be right back.'

'You're not going to tell anyone?'

'I know how to keep a secret.'

She was blowing her nose on a kitchen towel when I came back

217

downstairs. 'Is that enough?' I handed her the six hundred and forty-five dollars I'd made working for Osborne. She handed me back a hundred. I was thinking the last thing the world needs is another fucked-up kid when I told her, 'Keep it. You might need it.'

Jilly hugged me and gave me an unhappy smile. 'I'll always owe you for this, Finn.' She squeezed me tight, then pulled away. Laughing, and sniffling, and clutching her tube-top. 'God, my tits are so big they hurt.'

We smiled at each other. We weren't happy. It was just nice to be close to somebody who didn't expect anything. And the next thing I knew, we were kissing each other on the mouth. If somebody told me they'd done the same, I would have said, 'That's weird,' but it wasn't.

When she stepped away from me, I expected her to make a joke. I was about to apologize when she took hold of my hand and led me up to my bedroom. We undressed ourselves without saying a word. There was a kindness in our silence.

When I was naked, and on top of her, I put her breast in my mouth and imagined I tasted milk. The thought did not bother me. I was hard and inside her, and I was happy. It was a relief not to think. Just to be a body. We used each other to soothe ourselves. Sex is a far more reliable drug than love.

It was funny. The first thing I thought of when I was finished was Maya. Now that I'd done it for myself with Jilly, I was sure I could do it with her. Everything was going to be OK now. I felt like I had fixed things, until the front door opened with a squeak and I heard Maya shout, 'Hey, Finn, guess who decided not to go to Washington?'

Jilly was halfway to the bathroom and I was pulling on my pants shouting, 'Be right down,' when she walked in on us. Pathetic, but true, when she looked at me, I began to cry. It would have been easier if she'd yelled, or screamed, or hit me. Anything would have been better than the way she said, 'Goodbye, Finn.'

I called Maya's house a dozen times. The maids took turns telling me she couldn't come to the phone. Finally Mrs Langley picked up. She spoke slowly and deliberately, so there could be no misunderstanding. I could just see her, spiked Tab in one hand, cigarette in the other, looking off into the distance as she said, 'I cannot speak for Bryce, but please tell your mother neither Maya nor myself will be attending your party.' She wasn't just cold, she was arctic. 'And please, at least have the good manners not to call my daughter again. This is something she is asking you, and, more importantly, I'm telling you to do.'

'Mrs Langley, I'm sorry.'

' "Sorry" won't do you any good.' I sat by the phone for three hours straight, watching my shadow lengthen, then disappear in the darkness of the room.

My mother got back to the house at eight. 'Sorry, lambie. Dr Leffler and I were working on my eighth step.'

'What's the eighth step?' She put down her golf clubs and turned on the lights. I knew it was AA-speak for something.

'You make a list of everyone you've ever harmed, and become willing to make amends to them.' She kissed the top of my head and went into the kitchen. 'I thought I'd make spaghetti.'

'Do you have a long list?'

'Well . . . everybody does.'

The joint Jilly and I smoked was in the ashtray on the kitchen table. I couldn't even be bothered to get up and hide it.

'I invited Dr Leffler over for dinner. He's alone. His daughters are with his wife in Nantucket. You don't mind, do you?' My mother put the water on to boil and started setting the dining-room table.

'Whatever.'

'The playhouse is going to look absolutely fantastic for your birthday. I mean, it's a pretty fantastic place to begin with. But I've got Casablanca lilies, white tablecloths with gold tassels, purple overlays, lots of laurel – very Roman.' My mother's voice was slightly manic with self-satisfaction. 'So many people have house guests, we're going to have to add two more tables. We won't know a lot of the guests, but what better way to meet people?'

'I don't want to have a party.'

'Oh, Finn, we've been through all that. Maya and I have gone to a lot of work . . .'

'Maya and I had a fight . . . not exactly fight. We broke up. Her mother called. They're not coming.'

It wasn't what my mother wanted to hear.

'Well, you're going to get on the phone and make up with her.'

'You don't understand . . . it was my fault.' I didn't know how much to tell her.

'Well, call up and apologize. Say whatever she wants to hear.' My mother was getting impatient.

'She won't talk to me.'

'It's your birthday. If little Maya wants to act like a spoiled brat, we'll have the party without her. I've always thought she was rude.' Determined to stay positive, she wasn't listening.

'Don't you get it, Mom? I'm the one who fucked up.'

'Where do you get off using that language with me?'

Dr Dick's headlights flashed across the room as he pulled into the driveway.

'Me saying "fuck" wasn't half as offensive as seeing you do it with that asshole on the living-room floor.' I had my mother's attention now.

'What the hell have you done?'

'I was with Jilly . . . and Maya walked in.'

'What were you doing?'

'What do you think? We were in my bed.'

'You and Jilly have been . . .'

'It was the first time.'

'You threw away Maya Langley to screw the maid?'

'It wasn't like that. And what the hell difference does it make that Jilly's the maid?'

'Because little Maya is Osborne's granddaughter. Jesus Christ, Finn, the only reason we had a chance to make it here was because Osborne liked us.'

'You saved his life.'

'And you, to use your charming expression, fucked over his granddaughter and fucked over your mother while you were at it.'

I used to think it was funny when my mother cursed.

'You don't have to tell me that.' I was wailing.

'Oh, but I do. Because it affects me. If I lose my job, what do we do? I invited your grandparents to your fucking birthday party.'

'I told you I didn't want a party.'

220

'Shut up. You've ruined everything we've worked for.'

'I wasn't working for anything.' That was a lie.

'Well, I was!' My mother slammed the plate she was holding down on the table. It shattered. A shard of china flew up and cut her cheek. She didn't even flinch. It looked like she was crying blood when she told me, 'You don't get second chances twice.'

'Don't you think I know that?' I was shouting when Leffler walked into the kitchen.

'Have you seen this, Liz?' Leffler walked into the dining room, holding the joint. My mother looked at me as if I were a mistake.

'You little idiot.'

'What do you have to say for yourself, young man?' He held the joint in my face.

'Got a light?'

My mother hit me so hard across the face I fell off the chair. My mouth tasted of blood. She pulled her hand back to hit me again, then caught herself.

'You finally got the mother you deserved.'

Leffler put his arm around her shoulder. 'Liz, don't do this to yourself. Call Gates. Put him through the system. It's the only way he's gonna learn his lesson.'

'What system?'

'Drop the innocent act. Your mother told me all about you getting busted for buying cocaine in New York.'

'No she didn't.'

Leffler started to dial Gates' number.

'Put the phone down.'

'Liz, you're not doing him any favor . . .'

'I think I need to have a private conversation with my son.'

I stayed. The doctor left. She was finished with both of us.

25

Osborne's driver showed up the next day to take me to work like nothing had changed. Herbert opened the front door and escorted me to the elevator, same as always. It was a relief to fall back into the routine of sorting through pictures until I came across one of Maya and me.

'What do you think?' I turned round and Osborne was standing in the billiard-room doorway, wearing horns, hooves, and fur chaps . . .

'The horns are good. The hooves are a little cheesy.'

'Jesus Christ, a cheesy satyr. This rig cost me a thousand bucks.'

'Mr Osborne, I don't want a birthday party.' My mother had informed me at breakfast that with the exception of my birthday and working for Mr Osborne, I was grounded for the rest of the summer.

'But your mother does.' They had obviously talked.

'But I don't.'

'Finn, I know how these things work. It'll all blow over a hell of a lot faster if we just go on with the party like nothing has happened.'

'My mother said you'd be mad at me.' He was amused.

'I'm a son of a bitch, not a hypocrite.' Suddenly, it seemed that this was all just entertainment to him. 'These things happen. At least, they happen to me . . . more than once.'

The old satyr took off his horns and lit a cigar. 'Trust me. In twenty years, you both will think it's funny . . . least, Maya will pretend she does.'

I shook my head no. It took Osborne three matches to get his cigar to draw right.

'After you've both had a lousy marriage or two under your belts, it will give you something to laugh about when you bump into each other.' It was not something a lovesick boy on the verge of sixteen wanted to hear. 'You'll laugh, you'll flirt, if you're lucky you'll be foolish and drink too much and find yourselves lying in a strange bed together, and it'll all seem so foreign and yet familiar . . . you'll be glad you lost something you never had so you can pretend you've found it.'

'You're wrong.'

Osborne realized he was talking to himself. 'Finn, if you hadn't disappointed her, she would have disappointed you.'

'Maya's different from you and me.'

'You mean, she's a woman.' Osborne was looking at the photo of his mother dressed up like the Statue of Liberty.

'She's not afraid to believe in people.' Suddenly, I didn't want to be around Osborne.

'Well, then you've done her a service.'

'Screw you and your party.'

As I stormed out of the room, I heard him call out after me, 'You're setting yourself up for a lot of heartache, but I like your style.'

I wanted to go home. But clearly, that was no longer the yellow clapboard I lived in with my mother. Nor was it the loft on Great Jones Street. At breakfast, after informing me that I was grounded, my mother told me she had sublet the loft at double the rent to somebody at the Hunt Club who had a daughter who wanted to go to New York and become an artist. My mother had turned into the kind of person we didn't like a long time ago. It was just official now.

One of Osborne's cars appeared behind me as I walked down the dirt lane. I figured Osborne had sent his driver after me. The Rolls honked twice. I waved it on without looking back. When it honked again, I shouted, 'Shut the fuck up and leave me alone.' The car pulled up in front of me. It was Bryce and Dr Schiller. Bryce started to get out of the car. I didn't want to talk to him. 'Leave me alone.'

I ran into the field. I didn't know where I was going, I just wanted to get away. He yelled for me to stop. I didn't know he was chasing me until he tackled me. The sensation of being struck from behind, pushed down face first in the very same field where I had been fucked was such an ugly flashback I screamed, kicking and twisting beneath him, all elbows and fists, 'Get the fuck off me!'

'It's OK, Finn.' He let me up slowly. As soon I scrambled to my feet, I swung wildly at him. He caught my wrists in mid-air. I was surprised how strong he was. 'Finn, I'm your friend.'

Dr Schiller started to get out of the car. Bryce called out to him, 'We're OK.' Then he looked at me and smiled. 'Finn, I'm going to let go of your wrists.' I was still struggling to get free. 'If you've got to hit someone, you can hit me . . . But just once.' He made me feel ridiculous in the nicest possible way. Bryce closed one eye and grimaced for the punch he knew I'd never throw. At that moment, it seemed as if he was the only friend I had left.

'Bryce, what happened with Jilly wasn't like what it seems.'

'I'm no one to judge you.'

'I never wanted to hurt Maya, I just . . .'

'Finn, you should be telling Maya this, not me.'

'It's too late.'

'I know my sister. If she saw how torn up you are about what you did, I know she'd give you another chance.'

'But she won't talk to me, she won't even pick up the phone. Your mother told me not to call.' Thinking about the hopelessness of my situation made me even more frantic.

'Just come over.'

'I couldn't.'

'All she does is sit in her room and cry.' It was an encouraging sign but still, I wasn't sure. 'Come by tonight. My mother and I will be at the hospital visiting Dad. I'll take her to dinner after. The maids leave the house at nine. We won't be back until midnight. I'll leave the front door unlocked. Sneak in and surprise her.'

'What if she tells me she hates me?'

Bryce had to think about that one for a minute. 'I can't say for sure that won't happen. If she does, you'll just have to turn around and walk home. But at least you will have tried.'

'I don't know . . .'

He could tell I was thinking about what happened the last time I tried to sneak over to his house. 'If you're scared about walking over after dark by yourself, I'll pick you up.'

'You don't have to do that.' I didn't want to seem as pathetic as I felt.

'Bring the gun I gave you, just in case.'

I didn't want to tell him I'd hidden it in a hollow tree. 'Which one is Maya's bedroom again?'

26

My mother gave me the full treatment that night. A can of Spaghetti-Os and a can opener by the stove was my dinner. And she was singing along with Barbra Streisand and the cast album of *Funny Girl*. Ignoring me completely, she sat over the dining-room table, bent over a yellow pad and an adding machine, *The Beginner's Guide to the Stock Market* and a bunch of How-to-Get-Rich-Quick books were stacked around her. Pencil in hand, biting her lip as she wrote down figures, she looked like me cheating on my math homework.

'What are you doing?'

'I decided I want money.'

'You've turned into a real go-getter, Mom.'

'One of us has to be.'

'Maybe I'm a late bloomer.'

'Let's hope.'

I went up to my room and waited for my mother to go to bed so I could sneak off to Maya's. It was ten-thirty now, and she still hadn't come upstairs. I couldn't wait any longer. Shoes in hand, I eased myself down the kitchen stairs. I avoided the steps that creaked. When her tea kettle whistled, I paused and waited for her to pour a cup and walk back into the dining room. As she settled into her chair with a squeak, I tiptoed across the kitchen. I opened the screen door without a creak. I had one foot out into the night.

'What do you think you're doing?'

'I have to talk to Maya.'

'You're grounded.' My mother pulled the screen door closed and locked it. 'Call her.'

'Her mother won't let me talk to her.'

My mother looked at me hard and long, then unlocked the screen door. 'Good luck.'

I was amazed. My mother was letting me go. As the door slammed behind me, I wondered if I had misjudged her.

'Finn, remember to tell Maya I need to go over the place settings with her tomorrow.'

As I ran out into the moonlight I called back to her, 'I'm a go-getter, too, Mom!'

I stayed off the road. I didn't want to run into Gates. I couldn't be sure Mrs Langley hadn't told him to keep me away. The woods were full of noises. Weather rustled in the tree tops and branches fell around me. It occurred to me that whoever had jumped me was out there waiting to do it again. But I was too busy thinking about Maya to be scared of my bogeyman. I had to see her. In my mind, it had become simple: if she forgave me, I could forgive myself.

The Langley house was long and pink and quiet. There was only one room lit on the second floor. I had never been in Maya's bedroom before. I imagined her sprawled out on her bed sad because I had not come to explain my shortcomings. I didn't know how I was going to say it, but I had made up my mind to tell her everything about how we came to Vlyvalle, about getting raped, about Jilly's abortion – my life was my apology. I was desperate enough to believe the truth would set me free.

The Langleys' dogs barked in their pens behind the barn as I climbed the garden fence. Needing all the good karma I could get, I stopped long enough to help a drowning toad out of the swimming pool. The front door was unlocked, just as Bryce had promised. The foyer was jammed with furniture that had been moved for the painting of the family mural. My plan was to sneak up the library stairs that led directly to the bedroom that adjoined Maya's. But there was a sign taped to the library door that said 'Wet paint. Will kill anyone who walks on these floors.'

I peered inside. The library floor, painted to look like an old-fashioned quilt, glistened under a fresh coat of polyurethane. The mural was finished. Mr and Mrs Langley in a carriage, Maya and Bryce on horseback, Osborne at the wheel of his Bentley with a pig in the front seat, and the King Air flying overhead, with the tiny face of

Mrs Osborne peering out a window. On the hills in the background were flattened renderings of all the house and barns on the farm. There were little caricatures of everybody who lived and worked on Osborne's place: the Japanese gardeners; the chauffeur; Herbert the butler; Walter Pickle by the pig pens; and Jilly's dad, the dairyman, by the cow barn with Jilly and her mom and the brother I'd never met lined up according to height. In the corner was our yellow house. I wasn't sure if it was the paint fumes or paranoia, but from where I stood, it looked like my mother and I had been painted out of their picture. The guy had done a pretty good job of turning us into a bush and a birdbath.

I knocked over a can of turpentine as I turned back to the front staircase. Mopping it up with a drop cloth, careful to make sure my sneakers didn't track, I made my way upstairs. The carpets silenced my footsteps. On the second-floor landing, there was a big arched window that looked out to the east. The lights of the real world twinkled in the distance. I had forgotten how close it was.

I opened the hall door, and closed it carefully behind me. Bryce had said Maya was the only one home, but I didn't want to risk it. It was the oldest wing of the house. The narrow hallway was dark and long. I had never been upstairs before. Light fanned out from a doorway at the end of a hall. As I crept closer, I heard the sound of sobbing. I wanted to call out, 'Maya, it's me, I'm here,' but I was afraid she'd lock the door and tell me to go away. I had to see her face to face to tell her the truth. As I reached for the doorknob, the light went out.

The door opened with a groan, the room was all shadows. She was lying on top of a made bed with her back to me.

'It's me.'

'I knew you'd come.' Her face was buried in the pillows. Her voice muffled. As she rolled over, her kimono fell open. She reached for the light.

'Maya, I . . .' The light came on. I saw the can of Tab on the bedside table and an open prescription bottle.

'Mrs Langley, I'm sorry . . .' She was looking right at me, eyes wide open and pharmaceutically blind.

'I missed you.' The words were slurred. She reached out and

grabbed for my hand, her nails scratched me as I pulled away and backed towards the door. She stumbled as she tried to get off the bed. She wasn't wearing any underwear.

She was on the floor now, legs spread. The white of her tan line made her crotch look radioactive. 'Don't go.' She still didn't recognize me.

I ran down the hall, hoping she was so fucked up that when she woke up, she'd think I was a bad dream. Bryce would cover for me. I'd come back and see Maya in the morning. I'd still have time to . . .

I threw open the door at the end of the hall and looked out in disbelief. The furniture in the downstairs foyer was on fire. Flames skittered up the staircase, bubbling the Chinese-silk wallpaper. Smoke billowed up to the ceiling. Spellbound by the disaster, I stood transfixed by the heat and the fire. I inhaled. Panic and smoke filled my lungs. Coughing, I slammed the door and ran back down the hall as smoke swirled in after me.

I didn't shout 'Fire!' I just ran. Halfway down the hallway, Mrs Langley lurched out of the doorway and grabbed me.

'What the hell are you doing in my house?' Tab in hand, she suddenly recognized me but was oblivious to my words and the smoke that was making us both cough.

'You don't belong here!' she screamed at me. She was as frightening as the heat that was coming up after us. I pushed her out of the way.

'She doesn't want to see you!' she screamed after me. I wasn't thinking about rescuing Maya as I threw open doors to bedrooms and linen closets. I was just looking for a way out. Mrs Langley staggered after me, coughing and shrieking, 'Leave us alone.' I was at the second-to-last door in the hall. When I opened it, Mrs Langley pushed me from behind. I tripped over a chair. When I looked up, a wave of black smoke poured into the room. Mrs Langley was screaming 'Get out!' When she threw open the door to the back staircase to show me the way out, a huge tongue of fire burst up and licked her. She reeled back and fell on me, her kimono in flames.

I could smell her hair burning. Flames from her kimono scorched my hands. There was less air than I needed. The ceiling was a black rectangle of toxic smoke coming down on us. I tried to get to my knees. Mrs Langley shrieked, 'Help me!' and grabbed at me. Her arms were around my neck. I tried to push her away. When she wouldn't let go, I punched her. As I crawled towards the window, she clung to my leg. I kicked her with all my might.

My mouth to the floor, I gulped down what seemed to be the last breath in the world, and pulled myself to my feet. My eyes burned, I couldn't see. Feeling my way – first to the wall, then to the window – I tried to pull it open. Mrs Langley came at me out of the furnace, hair on fire. We fell backwards through the window. Glass shattered. The fire seemed to follow us out as we fell. It didn't want to let go. Neither did she. We twisted in mid-air. She was still clawing at me. The rhododendrons broke our fall. Were those bones or branches snapping? I landed on top of her. There was a sickening crunch beneath me.

Her arms were tight around my neck. Her embrace so unforgiving, she was choking me. Bryce and Gates ran to us. I could hear the sirens in the distance. As they lifted me off her, she looked me in the eye and smiled.

I was still coughing up soot when the ambulance and the fire trucks arrived. Somebody put a blanket over my shoulders. The house was engulfed in flames. People from the neighboring farms were pouring out of pickup trucks. A section of roof collapsed with a crash that sent sparks and embers the size of charcoal briquettes raining down on us. Gates was yelling for everybody to get back. I heard a fireman say, 'It's too late to save her.'

I suddenly remembered what I had lost, and what I had snuck into that house hoping to find. I staggered towards the blaze, screaming her name. 'Maaayaaa!' Bryce pulled me back.

'She's not there.'

'Where is she?'

Gates answered for him. 'We don't know. Her car's gone.'

27

I was back in the same examination room where Maya took me when I'd stepped in her trap. It was after midnight. Leffler was putting ointment on my burns. As the nurse handed him squares of gauze, she told me, 'You're a lucky boy.'

'How do you figure that?'

'You won't have any permanent scars. Poor Mrs Langley . . . well.' Leffler told the nurse, 'I'll finish up here by myself.' The phone rang. It was Gates.

When Leffler hung up, I asked him, 'Have they found Maya?'

'Her cousin Paige hasn't come home, either. They think they might be together.' He was bandaging my hands. It looked like I was wearing white mittens. He was being gentle, considering the fact he hated my guts.

'I was wrong about you.'

'No you weren't.'

'You didn't have to save Mrs Langley.'

I knew that's what they thought. But I knew what I had done. I hadn't even had the courage to shout 'Fire!' I just ran. For all I knew, Maya could have been in that house. I didn't know where she was when I ran. And as for saving Mrs Langley, I had pushed her and punched her, kicked her away, trying to save myself. Wondering what would happen when Mrs Langley told them the truth about me, I look at my feet and mumbled, 'I didn't do anything.'

'What is it with you? Are you trying to be cool? You finally do something you can be proud of and you act like . . .' Leffler was exasperated with what he perceived to be my false modesty.

There was a knock on the door. Leffler said, 'I'm busy.' It opened anyway. Osborne and Bryce stood there staring at me.

'My mother told me what you did.' Bryce's voice was flat. I was sure he was going to hit me.

I lowered my head and waited for the axe to fall. 'I'm sorry . . .' Tears streamed down my face. I began to sob. The weird part was, it was a relief to know I was finally going to be found out. 'When I saw the fire, I didn't know what to do.'

Leffler knew I was no hero. 'What really happened?'

The muscles of Bryce's jaw tightened. 'Because of this kid's . . .' His voice cracked. He was trembling. Osborne put his arm around his grandson's shoulder to calm him and looked at the floor. I was falling from grace and looking forward to touching bottom when Bryce cleared his throat and started again. 'Because of this kid's total disregard for his own safety, my mother's alive.' I couldn't believe what I was hearing. Leffler could barely hide his disappointment.

'You both talked to her?'

'Just Bryce.' Osborne looked at me with tears in his eyes. 'She was sedated by the time I got there.'

Leffler grudgingly gave me a Tylenol with codeine and a Dixie cup full of water. He started to hand me the bottle of painkillers, then changed his mind. 'I think it's best if your mother hangs on to these – the directions are on the label.' It was his way of telling Osborne he didn't trust me. 'Did your mother say how the fire started?'

'All she remembers is Finn waking her up and helping her down the hall. When the smoke got to be too much for her, she collapsed. He picked her up and carried her the to the window. When she panicked, he made her jump with him.' My mind reeled. Why would Mrs Langley make me out to be a hero? Bryce hugged me and whispered in my ear, 'We'll never forget what you've done for the family.'

Osborne made me feel even worse when he smiled and patted my cheek with his trembling hand. 'Hell, he *is* family.'

I had to tell someone the truth. 'Is Maya here?'

'She hasn't come home yet.' Osborne tried to sound casual.

Bryce did a better job of acting like it was no big deal. 'Paige probably talked her into driving to New York.' Paige had lost her driver's license for DWI. 'I already called all the bars they usually go to.'

I didn't know Paige and Maya went to bars in New York. To add to all the other shit that was going on in my head, now I had to worry about college guys hitting on her over Long Island iced teas. Paige had said her brother who got kicked out of Princeton's room-mate had the hots for Maya. He had a nickname I couldn't remember. I'd done it with Jilly to make myself feel better – why shouldn't Maya?

Bryce said, 'I'm going to go back to the house and wait for Maya. She'll freak if she comes home and finds it like that.'

When I heard my mother coming down the hall, I knew the weirdness had just begun.

28

As my mother turned out of the hospital parking lot that night, she told me, 'It's a wonderful thing you did.'

'That's what they say.'

'People will remember you.' She exhaled thoughtfully.

'Your blinker's still on.' My mother drove like her father now. She had her eye on everybody.

'A lot of doors will be opened to you because of this.' She smiled into the lights of the oncoming traffic.

'Christ, you act like the fire was a career opportunity.'

'I never said that, Finn. It's tragic what happened to Pilar.' So tragic that Mrs Langley was now 'Pilar' to my mom. 'But how you responded says a lot about you, lambie.' She took her eyes off the road just long enough to blow a kiss at me. 'I may not have been a great mother, but I have a great son.' My mother was so choked up with pride, she missed the turn-off to Vlyvalle. I stared out the window at the summer's darkness and wondered if there was any way my life could get more fucked up.

When we got to the old metal bridge on Osborne's place, we had to pull over to let the fire trucks pass. My mother rolled down the window and waved for them to stop.

'Don't, Mom.'

She ignored me. 'Hello, I'm Elizabeth Earl, and I just want to thank you all for doing such a wonderful job.' Her voice was so casually pretentious, she sounded like she had lived in Vlyvalle her whole life.

When one of the firemen saw me, he told her, 'That's a brave boy you got there.'

Another one shouted, 'You did good, kid!' It would have felt good if it were true. I waved a bandaged hand to them and smiled like it was the closing scene in a feel-good movie. If I thought my mother was a phony, what was I?

As we crossed the bridge, my mother asked, 'Do you have any idea what Maya was arguing with her mother about?' She even used the la-di-da accent with me.

'What are you talking about?'

'Dick told me the Langleys' maid heard Maya and her mother shouting at each other just before Maya drove off.'

I liked the idea they were arguing about me, but what if they were fighting because Mrs Langley didn't want Maya to run into New York and grudge-fuck The Trunk. I wished I hadn't remembered Paige's brother's room-mate's nickname. 'Maybe she told her mother she should go to AA.' I wanted my mother to shut up.

'Does Mrs Langley have a problem?'

'Jesus Christ, Mom.'

When I woke up the next morning, it was official. I was a hero. Mrs Langley's version of the fire was on the front page of the *Newark Star Ledger*. TEEN SAVES HEIRESS FROM FIRE was sub-headed across page three of the *New York Post*. My mother showed me the papers before I got out of bed. She bought extra copies so she could send clippings to Nana and my grandfather. She finally had proof she'd been a good mother. I just wanted the story to go away.

The phone rang while she was making me pancakes. It hurt my hand to pick up the receiver. I was sure it was going to be Maya. It was a reporter asking for a statement and a photograph. I hung up and told my mother it was a wrong number. When the phone rang twenty seconds later, she made a point of answering it. She covered the mouthpiece of the phone and handed it to me. 'It's a reporter. Be careful what you say.'

'I'm not going to say anything.'

'You've got to tell them something.'

'No I don't.'

My mother cleared her throat and put the phone to her ear. 'My son says he just did what anyone would have done.' She was always good at putting words in my mouth.

When she hung up, I told her, 'It's time for me to take a painkiller.' She looked at the label on the prescription bottle to make sure I wasn't hustling a buzz. I was a hero in her eyes, but that didn't change the fact that I still had a 'problem'. I popped one in my mouth and palmed four while she looked for a photograph to give the papers.

I could not comprehend why Mrs Langley had told Bryce I'd saved her, but I knew she hadn't done me a favor. The lie had mushroomed into reality. My mind was so busy trying to claw a way out of this miasma of fact and fiction, I didn't notice my mother had started to count the painkillers in the bottle I'd just handed back to her. She would have busted me for sure if we hadn't been interrupted by a sharp knock on the kitchen door. It was Bryce. Hollow-eyed and unshaven, he was wearing the same clothes he'd had on last night. He still smelled of the fire. My mother stopped counting the pills when he said, 'Maya never came home last night.'

In my mind, there was no doubt about it. She had done it with Paige's brother's ex-room-mate. I felt like I'd been kicked in the stomach. I didn't know what the bastard looked like, but I knew why they called him The Trunk. He was hung like Mothra. I could see him doing it to her again and again and again. Punching the wall with my bandaged fist didn't stop the porno loop from playing inside my head.

'Finn, what are you doing?'

My knuckles slowly bled through the gauze. 'She did it to get back at me.' As always, I thought it was all about me. My statement stopped Bryce in his tracks. His head pivoted like a surveillance camera in a convenience store. He was looking for someone to blame.

'You think my sister set the house on fire?'

'Nobody set your house on fire.'

'Yes they did. Grandpa had Gates and the fire inspectors up there at dawn. The only thing we're sure of is it was arson.'

'What did you mean, Finn, when you said she did it to get back at you?' My mother sounded just like Nana at Juvenile.

'Since Maya and Paige went to New York, I figured Paige was fixing her up with her brother's room-mate, and I thought . . . I mean, I didn't want to think, but I figured, it served me right if she spent the night with a guy to get back at me for Jilly.' It was embarrassing to give them a glimpse of how my brain worked.

'Trunk is in Europe.'

'Why do they call him The Trunk?'

Bryce gave my mother a look. When she figured it out, she pretended she was shocked. Maybe she was. My mother blushed and tried to redirect the conversation. 'How's your mother, Bryce?'

'She has third-degree burns over most of her body. She's going to live, but . . .' He bit his lip and looked away. 'Even with skin grafts and plastic surgery . . . she's going to be scarred.'

'Oh my God.' My mother put her hand to her mouth.

'Luckily, her face wasn't burned. She's beautiful, you know.'

She was.

'How can they be so sure it was arson? I mean, there was all that turpentine and stuff. I knocked over a can of it getting to the stairs.'

'The fire started in two places at the same time. Front hall, and by the back stairs in the library.'

'I didn't even go in the library.'

My mother was relieved to hear that.

'Nobody thinks you started the fire, Finn.'

'I should hope not.' My mother jumped back into the conversation. 'Finn was nearly killed by that fire.' She lit a cigarette and opened a fresh can of Diet Coke.

'I wasn't nearly killed, Mom.' I shrugged her off when she tried to hug me.

Bryce lit a cigarette off my mother's match and exhaled slowly. 'Whoever did it must have seen you go into the house. Waited until you were upstairs, and then set the fires.'

'I was only upstairs a couple of minutes before I saw the fire and ran and . . .' I almost told the truth right there.

'It doesn't take long to splash some paint thinner around and light a match.'

'You're making it sound like whatever crazy person did this wanted whoever was upstairs to be trapped in the fire.'

'That's how it looks to Gates, Mrs Earl. Anyway, he and Grandpa are up at the house. He sent me to get you.' My mother picked up her purse. 'My grandfather wants to talk to us by himself.'

'What are you going to do about Maya?'

'She has to be gone forty-eight hours before we can officially file a missing-person's report. But Grandpa has already pulled every string. Believe me, the police are looking for her everywhere. And unless she has a very good excuse for taking off, I, for one, am going to be very pissed off at her for being so fucking irresponsible.'

I was surprised he used the F-word in front of my mother. Bryce was usually so Eddie Haskell-polite in front of grown-ups. 'Excuse my language, Mrs Earl, but she knew how important today was to the family.'

'That's all right, Bryce, we're all terribly upset about this.'

'What's so special about today?' I asked.

'My father's coming home.'

My mother gave Bryce a hug. 'We understand.'

I didn't.

Bryce got into a green old-fashioned sports car I hadn't seen before. It was all fenders and running boards, and had two spare tires on the back. 'When did you get this?'

'It's my father's Morgan. It's been in storage since the accident.' The Langleys weren't as fortunate as they had once seemed to me. Even though I knew it was silly to think Osborne could have used up their luck making all that money, the idea that they were cursed, that all the headiness of their lives exacted a price, made them all the more tragic and attractive to me. I guess I finally felt we had something in common.

The Morgan had a starter button instead of a key. The second time Bryce pushed it, the engine caught. 'I had it completely over-hauled when Dad came out of the coma.' The car backfired. He had tears in his eyes when he told me, 'Jesus Christ, all I wanted was for things to be like they were when Dad came home.'

I told him, 'The car looks great.' I felt sorrier for them than I did for myself. It was a novel experience.

Once we were out of my mother's sight, Bryce pulled over. 'You want to drive it?' He was trying to cheer us both up. I shook my head no, and swallowed two codeine Tylenols dry. My head ached with questions I was too chicken to ask.

We drove in the back way. It was strange. The sky was picture-postcard blue, and the gardens were in full bloom, but there was so much soot from the fire, all the flowers were dusted charcoal gray.

All that was left of the house was a couple of blackened chimneys and a kitchen wall. The morning's dew hadn't yet burned off. The air had a sodden, burnt smell. Like a beach bonfire the morning after. The scene of the crime wasn't just in your face – you breathed it in, tasted it on your tongue. There was no escaping it. The copper roof that spanned the main part of the house had fallen in one piece. A backhoe and a bulldozer were lifting it up when we arrived. They got it about four feet off the ground when one end slipped off the claw of the backhoe. The whole thing fell back on the charred rubble with a thud that sent up a nasty cloud of ash that made the small crowd of workers turn away and pull dust masks up over their faces.

Bryce pointed to a corner of the copper roof. 'My bedroom used to be under there.'

As we got out of the Morgan, he told me the two guys wearing orange coveralls were fire investigators who used to work for the FBI. One of them talked into a little tape recorder as he shifted through a mound of burnt kindling that used to be a desk that had belonged to Thomas Jefferson. The other one methodically marked off where the different rooms used to be with stakes and strings.

Osborne had them flown in on his helicopter in the middle of the night. The old man had a white silk scarf wrapped around his face to keep the ash out. Old-fashioned sunglasses and a gray fedora on his head, Osborne looked like the Invisible Man.

The fire investigator with the tape recorder told a workman he could start shoveling the charred remains of the library into the dumpster. I didn't realize it was Dwayne until he pulled off his dust mask and held up a half-melted silver bowl that used to be a trophy. 'You want to save any of this?'

Bryce spit on the prize and rubbed the engraving with the heel of his hand. You could just make out the inscription, 'Maya Langley, Best in Show'.

I was surprised when Bryce told him, 'Throw it all away.' I felt guilty for not rescuing it when Dwayne said he was going to keep it for the silver.

Now that the dust had settled, I recognized Marcus working the backhoe. Jilly's dad was on the bulldozer. Gates was shouting directions, and Osborne was chewing an unlit cigar when we walked up.

Marcus waved and shouted, 'My man, the hero!'

Gates growled at his son, 'This isn't a party, Marcus.'

Jilly's dad offered me a drink from his Thermos. 'When that hand heals up, I want to shake it. Took guts, what you did here last night.'

The ex-FBI guy stopped stringing out the rooms and watched me as I shrugged and said, 'I just did what anybody would have done.' I stole my mother's line. I had no idea how a local hero was supposed to behave, but there was no question in my mind now – I was too deep in this lie to think about telling the truth to anyone, even to Maya.

I told myself it wasn't my fault it had gone this far. Mrs Langley had started it. If everybody didn't keep making such a big deal about it, I would have admitted what really happened by now. But I was my mother's son. The reptile lobe in my brain knew this fire was the opportunity of a lifetime. I liked how Jilly's father's eyes softened when he said I had guts. Better yet, Osborne put his arm around my shoulder, gave me a hug that smelled of medicine and Bay Rum, and asked, 'How are we doing today, son?' I wanted to be somebody's son.

When Dwayne volunteered, 'I think the same son of a bitch who beat up on Finn torched the place,' it hit me. This was the first morning I had woken up without thinking about being dead-horsed. It suddenly seemed like the fire was my deliverance; a second chance I didn't deserve or merit, but would be a fool not to make the most of.

By the time the backhoe and the bulldozer went back to work on the roof, it was all clear to me. When Maya came home from wherever she was and heard that I had risked my life searching for her in the fire and saving her mother, I would be forgiven and I could start fresh. Sure, I would know the truth, but with everyone telling me what a great guy I was, that didn't seem like much of a cross to bear.

I didn't know why Mrs Langley had lied. But if she came out of the hospital and changed her story, it'd be easy to make her seem crazy. I just had to remind them she drank vodka from a can of Tab all day. That reptile in my head had it all figured out, until they dragged the roof away and one of the ex-FBI guys shouted, 'Get the camera!'

Bryce's brass bed was melted. Where the mattress had been was just enough flesh on bone to smell like burnt meat. While one fire inspector shouldered the video camera, the other gently probed what was left of the pelvis with an aluminum wand and talked into his tape recorder in an unexpectedly high-pitched voice.

'Female Caucasian . . . looks to be young . . .' I vomited as Bryce wailed, 'Maya . . . no!'

Osborne teetered for a moment like he was about to fall over, then slowly sat down in the cinders, closed his eyes and looked up.

Gates called an ambulance, even though she was dead. As they shifted what was left of her onto a stretcher, a charred bit of lip crumbled off what was left of her face. None of us could watch until Dwayne said, 'That's not Maya.' The diamond Paige had inlaid into her left incisor glistened in death's grin.

Gates helped Osborne to his feet. His prayers had been answered, but not as he would have wished. 'What the hell is that girl doing in your bed, Bryce?'

Bryce was speechless. It was the first time I had ever seen him at a loss for words. He didn't know what happened, but I did. I wiped a gob of vomit from my chin. 'She said she was going to do it.'

'Do what?' Gates demanded.

'She told me she wanted to sneak into Bryce's bedroom some night and wait for him. Marcus was there – he heard her.' Gates glared at his son.

'She said it like a joke, Dad.'

'We thought she was just kidding. We never even mentioned it to Bryce . . . but she liked Bryce,' I added idiotically. The fire inspector turned the video camera on us.

'Was she under the influence of alcohol or drugs when she made this statement?' Marcus and I looked at each other and shook our heads no.

I wondered if Paige had passed out or just taken too many 'ludes to get out of bed when the smoke hit her lungs. I told myself it wouldn't have made any difference if I had shouted 'fire.'

They took Paige's body to the hospital in Griggstown. A morgue was one of the few things Vlyvalle didn't have. Gates tried to call Paige's parents, but the maid said they were out playing golf. Gates decided to get our statements first, then drive over to the club and give them the bad news. The Vlyvalle police station was an eight-by-ten room behind the post office. Since there were so many of us, Osborne suggested everybody make their statements at his house. Gates looked at him like he was crazy. 'Everybody?'

'Let's do it right.'

Osborne started to take everybody into the library. Gates looked at Dwayne and said, 'The kitchen will do.' Gates was a snob, too. It was contagious.

From the way they eyeballed everything, I could tell Marcus, Jilly's dad and Dwayne had never been in the big house before. Dwayne was clearly disappointed, and more than a little pissed off about being sent to the kitchen. He made a point of sitting on a silk, creweled wing chair with gold feet, just to see how it felt. I'd never been in a hotel kitchen, but that's what Osborne's must have been like. Refrigerators with double-glass doors, a quartet of ovens, copper pots of every size and description hanging from the ceiling, like instruments in a pawnshop. Osborne told his chef to take the afternoon off, and made everybody really bad coffee.

It was almost funny when Dwayne announced, 'I don't believe it, Mr Osborne – you and me got the same Mr Coffee machine.'

One by one, Gates took statements, first from Jilly's dad, then Marcus, and finally Dwayne in the servants' dining room with the door closed. When they were finished, Gates told them to go back to work. Since they all rode up with Gates, Osborne's driver had to chauffeur them back to the dumpster in his Bentley. Dwayne said, 'I could get used to this.'

242

As soon as they left, the fire inspector with the high voice put his hand on my shoulder and said, 'Why don't you just tell us why you started the fire, Finn.' I was so startled, I dropped my coffee cup.

The other fire guy stepped in, face close to mine. 'Were you mad at Maya and her mother for not wanting to have you around anymore?'

Osborne was as surprised as I was by the ambush. I couldn't be sure about Gates. The one with the high voice was about to hit me with another question, when Bryce stepped between them and me. 'This is bullshit. Finn's no more guilty than I am. I told him to come over to the house and talk to my sister. It was my idea. Christ, if it wasn't for him my mother would be dead.'

The fire guys weren't buying it. 'He could have started the fire and had a change of heart. This is what we do for a job, Finn. We're going to find out what happened in there sooner or later.'

I shook my head no. I hadn't started the fire, but I was a long way from innocent.

'You did it, and then you chickened out. Maybe you knew Maya wasn't home and you just wanted to teach them a lesson.'

Bryce was shouting now. 'If that's what he was trying to do, he wouldn't have started the fire in two places.'

'Maybe he's just dumb.'

'Finn's not dumb.' Osborne was watching me.

Gates stepped forward. 'I hate to admit it, but I don't think Dwayne was far off when he said the same person who assaulted Finn two weeks ago set the fire. We've got to consider the possibility it was Finn this person or persons were after.'

'What sort of assault was that?' The taller of the ex-FBI guys was interested. Gates calmly lied.

'Physical assault – concussion, two broken ribs.' Osborne slowly swept the pieces of the broken coffee cup at my feet into a dustpan. 'Finn. I want you to know I didn't know these gentlemen were going to make aspersions on your character. And since they're not offering you an apology, I am.'

'That's OK.' My voice was a whisper.

'We're just doing our job.'

'You brought us in here because you didn't want a state fire inspector asking questions. But we were under the impression you still wanted us to find out the truth.'

'I did. And I do, goddammit.' Osborne sat down on the cook's stool.

Bryce flicked the stove on and off. 'I think the person we've got to talk to is Maya.'

'You think Maya saw somebody?' It suddenly occurred to me that she was staying away because she was scared.

'Finn, your loyalty to my sister is admirable. But Paige died and my mother's in hell because of that goddamn fire.' He looked at Gates and Osborne. 'We're standing around letting these two grill Finn when we all know Maya got kicked out of boarding school for setting her dorm on fire.'

'She didn't do it on purpose. She was stoned, she told us about the hot-plate . . .' It wasn't the best way to stick up for her.

'Look, she's my sister, and I'll stand by her whatever, but she's been out of control for years. Riding around with a crossbow, talking about shooting hunters, setting traps for poachers – that's crazy stuff.'

I could tell everything Bryce said made sense to Gates and the fire investigators. Even I could see the logic of it. But I refused to believe it. If Maya was crazy, what was I? I was terrified to think my heart could have been so wrong about someone I was so sure of. 'How can you say that about Maya?'

'I don't want to say it. I don't even want to think it. But why'd she run away?'

'Because of me.'

Bryce gave me a look that was equal parts awe and contempt.

'Maybe it's that simple . . .' Osborne thought about it. 'Maybe it isn't.' A knock on the door brought in the butler with Osborne's medication on a silver tray. As I watched him pop his pills, I asked if it was OK for me to go to the bathroom. I wanted to feel better, too. On the way to the john, I slipped into the library and washed down my last two codeine pills with a slug of Stolichnaya that made me gag. By the time I finished in the bathroom, I was starting to feel something. Not better, just different. I thought another hit of vodka might help. Desperate was too hopeful a word for how I felt. I was

244

on my way back to the library when the front door opened. It was Maya's father, and a nurse I recognized from the hospital. Shuffling across the marble floor, both hands on a walker, he looked lost and confused. He wasn't the only one. Mr Langley squinted at me.

'Should I know you?'

'I'm not sure.'

29

The next day, a photograph of Paige taken at Maya's birthday party was on the front page of the *Post*. It was crowned by the headline, 'DEBUTANTE DIES IN MYSTERY FIRE'. There were pictures in the *New York Times* and local papers, too, but Paige would have liked the one in the *Post* the best. It was taken from an angle that made her look like she'd finally shed those ten pounds she was always trying to lose. The article made a big deal about the diamond in her smile and how she went to Studio 54; they made her out to be so wild and worldly and hip, you would have thought Bianca and Mick were coming to the funeral. Even though most of it wasn't true, Paige would have loved it.

Maya still hadn't come home. It had been forty-eight hours. She was officially a missing person now. The police, the FBI, everybody was looking for her. Not even Osborne had enough money to keep it out of the papers. I didn't know why she'd run away. But I knew Maya wasn't going to come home of her own free will when my mother woke me up with a headline that screamed 'BILLIONAIRE'S GRANDDAUGHTER WANTED FOR QUESTIONING IN ARSON DEATH'. There was a photograph of the smoke-scorched boarding school dormitory. 'One of Maya Langley's classmates at the exclusive girls' school, who requested that her name not be mentioned in this article, stated: "Maya took a leave of absence, but it was a joke. Everybody knew she got high and set the place on fire. Her parents were really nice about it. They bought us all new stuff. Maya thought it was funny."'

My mother was furious. Not because the paper made Maya out to be a pyromaniac, but because Osborne might think she'd aided and abetted the reporter by supplying a picture of me in the thrift-store

246

tux she'd bought me a lifetime ago. I was beyond getting mad at my mother about things like that.

I think it was the day after that the New York police found her zebra-striped Land Rover in a chop shop in the Bronx. They arrested a Puerto Rican named Jesus who was cutting it up to sell for parts. We were at Osborne's for dinner when it came out Jesus had been to prison for auto theft and assault with a deadly weapon. Bryce got so hysterical Dr Leffler had to give him a sedative. Bryce was convinced Maya was lying in some vacant lot, dead or unconscious. For Bryce, the downer wasn't as much of a relief as finally having a reason for her disappearance.

I took the news with uncharacteristic calm. Usually, I'm the first to panic. I believed Jesus's story, about a loco girl with a scar on her face selling him the Land Rover for two thousand bucks, only because I had received a birthday card in the mail from Maya that morning. It read:

Dear Finn, Hope you like being sixteen more than I do. The less you know, the better it is for everybody. None of this has anything to do with you, anyway. Still love you, Maya.

It was a relief to know she was OK enough to write. I couldn't blame her for not trusting me with a phone number or return address. But I would rather have heard she'd run off with Trunk than be told it had nothing to do with me. I told my mother it was a card from Nana, and burned it.

The only part of this mess that I'm remotely proud of is that I never told Gates or the FBI guys Maya sent me a card.

Bryce and Osborne found out she wasn't dead when Maya made a phone call to the New York Police Department to say that Jesus had bought, not stolen, her Land Rover and should be let out of jail immediately. She hung up before they could trace the call. The newspapers made a big deal when they found out about that. She was still a firebug, but she had a social conscience. It freaked Bryce out that his sister was more worried about a 'fucking Puerto Rican car thief' than her own family. His social conscience had limits. I could tell he would never forgive her for running away, from the way he kept saying, 'She needs help.'

Leffler recommended Oak Knoll, the same mental hospital my grandparents wanted to send my mother to when she got pregnant with me. My mother told Osborne and Bryce that, when they found Maya, her father would be happy to help them get her admitted discreetly. Christ, they made it seem like getting her into boarding school. Osborne sort of stuck up for her. 'I want to hear what she has to say before I make any decisions.' But you can see why I never wanted Maya to come home.

30

July burned through to August. Four weeks without rain and temperatures in the nineties turned the green farm towns around us a combustible brown. The Governor declared a water emergency. It was against the law to water your lawn in every township except Vlyvalle. Naturally, they had their own water. Osborne's big farm sprinklers hissed day and night. I heard Walter Pickle tell Jilly's dad through a mouthful of Red Man, 'Hairspray's put holes in the goddamn ozone, price a pork down to twenty-two cents a pound on the hoof, and Elvis is dead. Jesus H Christ, if that ain't the end of the world as we know it, I don't know what is.'

I went back to working afternoons at Osborne's, sorting pictures. But things had changed. When he came across a photo that made him think of the good times, he'd still fill me in on the back story of who was who, where it was taken, and what was happening just outside of the viewfinder. Sometimes he'd even make a bad joke but when he was finished remembering the fun, instead of handing the photograph to me to catalogue, he'd slowly crumple it up into a ball and toss it towards a garbage can brought up for that purpose. He'd say 'Two points', even when he missed. Sometimes he'd shout, 'Goal!' My point is, his heart wasn't the only part of him that was in a different place.

My mother dumped Dr Leffler, and was dating a partner at Lazard Freres. He had hairplugs planted across his bald spot as neat, straight and natural as rows of corn and drove a chocolate-brown Mercedes convertible. He'd just left his wife and four kids in Millbrook and had bought a horse farm next to the McCallums'. He was teaching her how to play the market. He said she had a nose for investments. One night, from my bedroom window, I watched her

249

kiss him goodnight after she gave him a blowjob. Shocked? Only that I wasn't. Like I said, things had changed.

Jilly and I took over tending Maya and Bryce's pot garden. Digging a ditch with Jilly to bring water to the parched pot was the closest thing to fun I remember about that time. In the evenings, when my mother was out, I'd smoke homegrown and answer the phone. After my picture was in the paper friends of Maya's, mostly girls but guys too, began to call. Since I didn't have the vaguest idea who they were, and I was stoned, it was easy to make small talk. They'd always start off by saying how worried they were about Maya. But mostly, they were just fishing for some ugly bit of gossip they could use to impress their friends at Bailey's Beach or Maidstone, or Hobe Sound or one of the other WASP watering holes I acted like I'd been to. Sometimes I'd tell them they were fucking ghouls and hang up. Other nights, I'd feel chatty and go into graphic detail about the way Paige's charred flesh hung from her bones. It pretty much depended on my mood, and the amount of insecticide on the pot.

Occasionally, I was pleasantly surprised. Trunk turned out to be an OK guy – no question I would have been a lot less jealous if Maya had told me he had a lisp. When the room-mate from boarding school who talked to the *New York Post* called, I felt proud for telling her I hoped she got reincarnated as a dung beetle because she sure as hell deserved to spend her next life pushing around a ball of shit. When she started to cry and told me she felt terrible, I said 'Good,' and hung up. She responded by sending me an invitation to her sister's débutante party in East Hampton. My mother thought it was wonderful I was becoming so popular and made me go. I don't remember much about the party, except I got loaded and let her give me a hand job. I was too numb to feel guilty.

The day I got back from the jerk-off weekend in East Hampton, Bryce called to invite us over for supper. We had dinner with him and Osborne three or four times a week now. We weren't part of the family, but we were linked by blood. Our special status with Osborne's clan had netted my mother membership in the Garden Club and gotten her appointed to the Ladies Golf Committee. But this dinner was special. Mr Langley was going to eat with us.

250

I didn't mind the fact that Mr Langley's still-limited motor skills landed more food in his lap than in his mouth, it was the way he'd stop the conversation dead cold by suddenly asking, 'Where's Maya?'

Each time, Bryce would say, 'You remember, Dad. I told you. Maya's showing her horse in Europe.'

'Where in Europe?' Mr Langley demanded, childlike, at one point in the meal.

'She was in Holland last week. She's starting a four-day event tomorrow outside of Bruges. She told me she thinks of you, Dad, every time she asks for ketchup with her *pommes frites*.'

Bryce lied with such gentleness and grace I almost believed she was eating French fries in Belgium. I could tell Osborne didn't like the lies. He left the table four times before dessert. First to get his pills, then a cigar, then a match. Finally, to make a phone call. 'All this talk about Maya makes me miss her. I'm gonna go see if I can track her down.'

After Mr Langley's nurse took him upstairs to go to bed, Bryce sent me to get Osborne. I found him in the billiard room, smoking an unlit cigar, crumpling up pictures of his family and tossing them into the garbage can. He didn't even have it in him to shout 'Goal!'

When we came back to the dining room, he told his butler he'd like a dish of pistachio ice cream and some Oreos. My mother gracefully segued into asking whether or not he thought one of his companies was going to buy some other company that had the dopey idea of making machines that could show old movies on your TV set. She was getting pushier about hitting him up for stock tips since she started doing the Lazar Freres guy.

Osborne split an Oreo and scraped off the vanilla with his yellow teeth. 'Liz, if you don't mind, I don't feel very much in the mood for insider trading tonight.' The way my mother blushed, you would have thought he'd slapped her. I smiled, not so much because my mother had made a fool of herself, but because Osborne wasn't as out of it as he seemed.

The old man popped the cookie part of the Oreo whole into his mouth and ordered a brandy. He was suddenly in a good mood. 'If I'm not mistaken, I think I still owe Finn a birthday present.'

I lowered my eyes, stopped eating my dessert, and hoped for a motorcycle. 'You don't owe me anything. I owe you.'

'In that case, you can't say no.'

'Just as long as it's not a stock tip.' My mother pretended she thought that was funny.

Osborne chugged his brandy. 'I've arranged for you to have a free ride at St Mark's.' It wasn't a motorcycle, but it was a way out of Vlyvalle. I was the first, and only, recipient of the Ogden C Osborne Scholarship. I could tell he hadn't run it by my mother. She was so happy and surprised, she knocked over her water glass hugging Osborne.

I shook the old man's hand and said, 'Thank you.'

'No big deal, Finn. Just cost me a library.'

As Bryce patted me on the back and told me I'd be staying in his old dorm, Osborne made it clear there was one hitch. 'Liz, I hope you don't think I'm overstepping my bounds, but I'd like to take Finn up to St Mark's and get him settled by myself. Just the two of us.'

My arrival was hers. She wanted to witness it, but she wasn't about to let the deal get taken off the table. 'Of course you can take him. I'd be in the way anyway. But you have to promise to take pictures.'

As my mother kissed Osborne's cheek goodnight, I heard him whisper, 'Buy as much as you can when the market opens tomorrow morning. Sell when it hits thirty-seven on Friday. Then re-invest when it drops to seventeen.'

31

On September 1, Osborne's G3 touched down at Framingham airport in Massachusetts. As the plane taxied towards the terminal, I saw another new boy getting out of a Lear Jet. Osborne told me the kid's father was a Saudi prince who got kicked out of the Ritz in Paris for sacrificing a sheep in the bathtub to mark the end of Ramadan.

Osborne got pissed off that the limo he ordered to drive us the twenty-eight miles to St Mark's wasn't waiting. While he went into the office to raise hell, I helped the pilots unload my stuff. I had two suits, a tux and three sports coats custom-made by Osborne's tailor in a set of Hermès luggage Bryce gave me as a going-away present. When you arrive by jet, rich people aren't suspicious of new.

Osborne waved me into the snack bar that adjoined the terminal to wait for the limo. He ordered us two pieces of blueberry pie à la mode. There was a TV blaring behind the counter. People were staring at us. I figured they recognized Osborne, or were impressed by the jet, or maybe my new luggage. They looked at me the way I used to look at rich people. I thought of the afternoon Bryce announced it all comes down to fuck/kill.

I no longer felt like an impostor, I was one. The pie wasn't very good, but the ice cream was OK. Osborne picked a bit of blueberry from his teeth with a gold toothpick as he opened his briefcase.

'I've got a going-away present for you.'

'You've done enough.'

'I'll be the judge of that.' Osborne pulled out a bundle wrapped in a Caracas newspaper. It smelled like it was alive. He unwrapped it for me. There were stares and snickers as Osborne placed a Yano-mamö shaman's headdress made out of a monkey tail and parrot feathers on my head. I had to laugh when I checked myself out in the mirror. When I looked back at him, a tear trickled down the old man's face. I thought he was sad to see me go, until I noticed his watery eyes were fixed on the TV screen behind the counter. The moment derealized as the six o'clock news showed Maya flanked by two men in FBI windbreakers being taken into custody in Philadelphia.

Osborne gave the limo driver a hundred bucks to help get me settled in my room. As he hurried across the tarmac to his jet, he turned and waved and shouted, 'I'll call you when I know what the hell's going on.'

I called after him, 'Tell Maya . . .' I was still trying to figure out how to put it into words as he climbed into his jet.

32

When we got to St Mark's, it took us about a half-hour to find my dorm. I told the limo driver I didn't need anybody's help and lugged my suitcases towards the old, red-brick building that had been donated by the son of the guy who figured out how to make rubbers out of rubber. The plaque bolted to the front of the dorm didn't say how he made his money. Osborne had once shown me a picture of the condom king at a six-day bicycle race in the old Madison Square Garden, when we were sorting though photos. Believe it or not, the guy named his kid Ramses. I was thinking about stuff like that partly because I had washed down that Vicodin I had been saving for an emergency with three swigs of vodka in the back of the limo on the way from the airport. But mostly, I was afraid that if I let myself think about Maya, I'd begin to weep.

I had been assigned a room on the fourth floor. With each step I took schlepping up the stairs, I deliberately swung my two-thousand-dollar luggage into the metal banister. It felt good and distracting to fuck up something valuable.

'*Bongiorno, Finnito.*' I looked up the stairwell. I had forgotten Giacomo had to repeat his senior year at St Mark's. He was dribbling a soccer ball back between the toes of his Gucci loafers, one of which was cobbled with adhesive tape. A plume of shaving cream spewed out into the hall, just missing Giacomo's head. '*Porco Dio!*' Giacomo kicked the soccer ball into the room where a shaving-cream fight was going on. 'Blow me, you peasants.'

Someone kicked the soccer ball back out into the hall and yelled, 'Eat me, Guido,' as Giacomo turned back to me.

'We are room-mates. End of the hall. Not the Ritz, but we have two windows.' Giacomo took one of my suitcases and passed me the soccer ball. I wasn't in the mood for games.

A peasant named Rory grabbed hold of my shoulder. 'You're Maya Langley's boyfriend, aren't you?' Before I could admit to it, he added, 'So, was it hot or what, boning a pyro?'

'Shut the fuck up.'

'Word to the wise, you're going to have a hard time here if you can't take a joke.'

I turned to kick him in the balls. My foot connected with the soccer ball on the way. It hit him square in the middle of the face. He doubled over, clutching his nose. Anger poured gasoline on my hurt. A moment ago it had taken all my strength to lug the steel-reinforced Hermès two-suiter up the stairs. Now I was effortlessly swinging it up over my head, intent on bringing it down somewhere in the vicinity of the base of his skull. Rory looked up, blood spurting out of his nose like a broken spigot. 'Jesus Christ, are you crazy?'

The eleven other boys on the floor all had their heads out in the hall, watching. No question, I would have smashed the rest of his face in if the dorm master hadn't intervened. 'We got to get you on the soccer team.'

It's strange, there are only two places on the planet where that kind of violence makes you popular – boarding school, and the land of the Yanomamö.

Our room would have been considered spacious if it had been a prison cell. Two beds, two desks, and an Italian who beat off with the lights on, all in an eight-by-fourteen rectangle. I would have asked for a new room-mate if Giacomo hadn't suggested right after lights-out that first night, 'Hey, Finn, maybe if we telephone Bryce he can tell you about what is happening with Maya.' I was waiting for him to go to sleep so I could cry.

'Brilliant idea, Giacomo, except for the fact that we don't have a phone.' There was a payphone students could use outside the cafeteria, but it was locked at night. The housemaster said I could use his phone if I wanted to call my mother. I passed. I had already considered and discarded the idea of running away. If Maya hadn't made it, what chance did I have?

'But I am a ham-operator.' I thought he said he was a ham-dodger, until he opened the trunk at the foot of his bed and revealed a short-wave radio. He used the radiator for an antenna.

'Hello, this is the SS *Minnow*. Could you patch me in to a telefono operator.' He convinced a ship-to-shore operator we were a pleasure craft, and they patched us through to Bryce's apartment in Boston.

The phone rang six times and no one picked up. As I thought about who I should try to call next, Giacomo put a lighter to a chunk of black hash that had the look and consistency of toe jam. 'Put it out,' I hissed. The last thing I needed was to get busted my first day of school.

Feeling adrift, I was about to ask the ship-to-shore operator to call Osborne's number in Vlyvalle when a woman with a pissed-off English accent picked up. 'Bryce isn't here,' she snapped. Giacomo had opened the windows and was spraying deodorant to cover the stink of the hash.

'Well . . . uh . . . can you tell him Finn called?'

'Oh, sorry I was so frosty.' The voice relaxed into familiarity. 'The fucking reporters have been ringing up all night. Bryce told me not to take the phone off the hook in case you called about your sister.'

'She's not my sister.'

'Sorry. Freudian slip. The way Bryce is always going on about you, I forget you're not part of the family.'

I liked hearing that so much, I accepted a hit off Giacomo's hash pipe. 'Who are you?'

'Coco.' The legend lived.

When Giacomo heard the name of the Nigerian princess, he whispered, 'Does she sound naked?'

Coco heard him. 'Tell Giacomo I'm wearing a thong.' At first, it seemed indecent of her not to be taking the conversation more seriously. Then Giacomo fell back into his bed, and began to rub his crotch, and pant about Coco being his beautiful fig in Italian. He was so exotically gross, I had to laugh. Then I thought of Maya taken into custody on the TV screen, and felt guilty for having fun.

'What's happening with Maya?'

'Bryce flew down to Philadelphia with the lawyers.'

'Lawyers?' I don't know why I was surprised. The newspaper said they were going to press charges against her.

'They're all there with Mr Osborne. Bryce said for me to tell you he'll call as soon as he knows anything.'

'Is she OK?'

'I don't know, but from the bit on the telly I saw, whoever gave her that haircut ought to be arrested. It looks horrible short like that. I'm surprised they caught her, I didn't recognize her.'

'Jesus Christ, Coco, I'm not worried about her fucking hair.'

'Right, sorry, stupid thing to say. Bryce told me they flew a shrink down. Bryce called your mother to get his name.'

I hung up without saying goodbye. If they brought my grandfather in, the alternatives were grotesquely clear: Oak Knoll or jail. I wondered which had better visiting privileges.

Three days later, the dean was marching me into the headmaster's office. His hand was around my neck, and he was squeezing. Bryce said he was an asshole. I wish he'd warned me the guy had a Vulcan death grip. I was sure Rory had turned us in for smoking hash, until the dean asked me, 'So, I understand your mother is Mr Osborne's physician?'

When I told him, 'She's his masseuse,' the dean stopped squeezing my neck and looked at me like I was trying to be a wiseass. It seemed hopeless, trying to tell the truth.

The headmaster had his feet up on his desk, and was talking on the phone. An old oil painting of the minister who founded the school looked down disapprovingly as the headmaster played with a model for the library Osborne had promised to donate to get me in. I knew I wasn't in trouble when the headmaster said, 'Mr Osborne, thank you again for all your help with the building fund . . . he's right here.'

I couldn't hear what Osborne was saying, what with the headmaster telling me, 'Take as long as you want, Mr Earl.' They were being so nice, I could tell they were really excited about the library.

As they closed the door behind them, I shouted, 'Maya's what?'

'I said . . .' Osborne was drowned out by a buzzing sound. 'Jesus Christ, get this hearing aid off me.' He sounded older and crankier than he did three days ago. The hearing aid was new, too. 'I said, Maya's doing as well as can be expected, considering.'

258

'Considering what?'

'That the District Attorney is an ambitious son of a bitch. The pissant thought he was going to make a name for himself taking my granddaughter to trial.'

'But if Maya didn't start the fire, how can they arrest her for . . .' My voice cracked in panic.

'Fortunately, the District Attorney came to see the wisdom of that conclusion. I'll get the bastard elected to Congress, but I'm sure as hell not going to vote for him.'

I heard the deferential voice of a lawyer interrupt. 'Mr Osborne, it's not a good idea to discuss this over the phone.' Weirder than Osborne admitting he had bribed him was how much it bothered me.

'But you know she didn't do it.'

'Maya says she didn't do it, and I choose to believe her.' It wasn't the answer I wanted. I didn't trust any of them.

'What's my grandfather doing there? You're not going to let that asshole talk you into sending her to Oak Knoll?'

'Finn, relax – no one's putting Maya into a loony bin. No question your grandfather's an asshole. But for your information, it was his psychiatric evaluation of Maya that convinced the DA she wasn't capable of setting the goddamn fire.' I wondered what my grandfather had gotten in return. A grant, a consulting job at one of Osborne's companies, a clear conscience for what he did to my mother?

'Let me talk to Maya.' That's all I really wanted.

'Maya's on her way to Switzerland.'

'If you believe her, why are you punishing her?'

'If I wanted to punish her, I'd . . .' Osborne caught himself. 'Finn, she has to finish school somewhere. And since I'm the one who's paying to clean up this mess, we're all going to do it my way. She'll be better off someplace where everybody and their cousin doesn't know about the fire and her running away and all the rest of it. It's not going to be easy being Maya for a while.'

'Did she ask about me?' I had to pause after each word to keep from sobbing out loud.

'She said if you write her, she'll write you back.'

I tried to tell myself, considering all that had happened, things could have turned out a hell of a lot worse.

'What's the address?'

'That's the attitude. And listen, tell you what, you make Honor Roll – something, I might add, I never came close to doing – and come Christmas time we'll fly over to Switzerland together and see Maya. You two can have the pleasure of watching me die on skis.' He was trying to cheer us both up. He handed Bryce the phone to give me the address.

'Finn, write her care of Monsieur Bouret, Le Rosey, 26 Rue de Ruen, Geneva, Switzerland.' I figured Le Rosey was the name of the school in Switzerland. I wondered how much Osborne had to bribe them to accept her. Like it or not, I was learning how the world really works.

'Who's Monsieur Bouret?'

'Her housemaster. How's Giacomo as a room-mate? He still beat his meat with the lights on?'

'Yeah.'

'Well, tell him it looks just like a penis, only smaller.' It was good to hear the old Bryce. I felt better, until he added, 'Listen, Maya has a second chance at her life. You and I have to make sure she makes the most of it.' The new Bryce was talking now. He sounded suspiciously like my mother. 'We've got to take care of each other, Finn.'

'Right.' So what if it was a pep talk? It made me feel better.

'So you're going to write my sister?'

'I can't call her?'

'School's really strict. No phone calls. It's for the best. We don't want reporters calling up hassling her. Or, worse, Paige's parents.'

I hadn't thought about them in weeks. Now they were just one more thing standing between me and Maya.

'I'd just like to speak to her once.'

'You heard Grandpa. Make the grade, and you'll see her at Christmas. You know how to ski, Finn?'

'No.'

'You're a fast learner. Maya and I will teach you.'

'OK . . . Bye.' I wanted to get off the phone before I started to get bummed again.

'Finn . . . never forget I love you.'

It wasn't like when my mother or my grandparents said it. When Bryce told me he loved me, it was like the way Maya said it. You believed it.

I wrote to Maya every day that first week. The second week, I cut back to a letter every other day. I had run out of ways to apologize for Jilly. The routine of boarding school was so inane I didn't want to repeat most of what I had to say and do to fit in for fear I'd come across as an even bigger jerk than I was. When I found out my algebra teacher was coach of JV soccer, I joined the team – Giacomo told me he always gave players a break at exam time. I knew I was going to need all the help I could get if I was going to make Honor Roll and get that ticket to Switzerland. No question, I became a full-time suck-up. I fell asleep over my textbooks, looked up the words I didn't know in the leather-bound dictionary my mother sent me, and sought extra help when Giacomo and my dorm mates were in town buying cigarettes and trying to pick up townies. Unbelievable but true – I became known as a grind.

There was just one problem: Maya wasn't answering my letters. Bryce and Osborne called to check in on me every other week or so. Sometimes together via conference call, sometimes separately. When they asked what I'd heard from Maya, I'd lie and say she was doing great and everything was good. Part of me was embarrassed of the truth, part of me thought if I said it enough, it'd be true.

It wasn't so hard getting through the days. When I felt nauseous with the reality of my predicament – I'd written her forty-seven letters and she hadn't thought me worthy of a postcard of the Alps – I'd tell myself that Maya was teaching me a lesson. Or, if something had happened to bolster my confidence – acing a bio exam, scoring a goal (accidentally, when the ball ricocheted off my back), or successfully pretending to be gagging on the cap of my Bic pen to distract the housemaster just as he was about to open the hollowed-out bible where Giacomo hid his bong – I'd kick through the fallen leaves that carpeted the campus, convincing myself that her not writing had nothing to do with me. I'd tell myself she was still embarrassed about running away. On good days, I'd actually be on the verge of believing Maya was at her desk at that Swiss boarding school, trying to figure out how to put how much she missed me into words.

It was harder to kid myself after lights-out. After the room was filled with darkness, and Giacomo was just a snore, and I'd touch myself, pretending it was her hand, not mine, making me hard, my fantasies would ambush me. When I tried to remember the things she did to me, in my mind her hands and mouth would be on someone else. Sometimes she was doing it with a student (I'd discovered, much to my dismay, Le Rosey was co-ed). Sometimes a teacher. Once, she was going down on this guy who looked exactly like Bryce. Trust me, jerking off with thoughts like that isn't very satisfying.

When I was awake, I could pull my hand away, turn on my light, and start memorizing the periodic table, or take a cold shower. But you've got real problems when stuff like that happens inside your head after you're asleep. When my dreams betrayed me, and I'd wake up with a gasp and a load of cum in my jockey shorts, there was nothing left for me to do but wait for dawn.

By the time there was frost on my windowpane, sleep had become my enemy, dreams my undoing. When soccer season ended, I went out for winter track, hoping if I ran in circles long enough, I'd exhaust myself and I'd finally be able to get some rest. Unfortunately, they pegged me for a hurdler, and all I ended up with was scabs up and down my shins. When exercise didn't work, I traded my Hermès luggage and my Bernard Weatherill wardrobe to a sartorial sixth former for a Ziploc bag full of Rohypnols. Medicating myself with roofies was a tricky proposition. One hit made me horny. Two hits, I didn't wake up, even when Giacomo poured bong water on my face. But once I got the dosage right my dreams would fade to black on command.

33

The trees were leafless and the grass was frozen. Five o'clock, and the sun had already set. When I came out of my last class, Bryce and his glistening new black 7-Series BMW were parked in a No Parking zone. The whole dorm was crowded around him. It was like he was going to start signing autographs any second.

He smiled at me as if happiness were a foregone conclusion – he had a college girl on either arm. I recognized Coco from photographs. He turned to the blonde who wore leather pants. 'Didn't I tell you he was cute?'

The dorm was impressed. No way would he have brought girls along if he had bad news to give me. Bryce walked towards me with open arms, mouthing the words, 'She's crazy about you.' I didn't get it.

'What's happening with Maya?' I asked.

As he walked me away from the crowd, he said, 'To love the game beyond the prize.'

'What's that mean?'

'Maya didn't tell you?'

'No, what?'

'Jesus Christ, I'm sorry, I thought you knew . . . that's why I brought Phoebe along.' Phoebe was the blonde's name.

'What's Phoebe got to do with Maya?'

'Look, Finn, there's no good way to say it. And it's not fair or right Maya hasn't had the decency to tell you herself . . . she has a new boyfriend.'

I felt like I was being flushed down a giant toilet. 'Thanks for telling me.' I was getting what I deserved.

'Finn, I'm sorry she did this to you.'

'I did it to myself.'

'Come to dinner with us. Phoebe likes younger guys.'

'What?'

'I don't mean to be crude, but it's like Grandpa says: after you get dumped, the best thing to do is get back in the saddle.'

'Another time, OK Bryce?'

'You can count on it, Finn.'

It started to snow as I walked away. There was nothing gradual about the storm. One minute the sky was cold and clear, and the next, flakes were swirling down so fast you couldn't see more than a few feet in front of you. When I looked back, everything seemed to disappear in the white-out. The snow filled my footprints; there was no trace of me. I found my way to the dorm, but people get lost in storms like that.

When I got to my room, Giacomo was on the edge of tears, and all my stuff was moved around.

'Finn, I am so sorry.'

'It doesn't matter.' The room was actually neater than I had left it that morning.

'The fuck it doesn't. The housemaster did a drug search.'

'Are we kicked out?'

'No.' It was weird, but I was almost disappointed. 'But I had to flush everything. *Porco Dio*. My hash, my prescription cough medicine, your roofies, even the NoDoz. My bong is stuck in the drainpipe.' He was trying to fish it out of the rain gutter with a straightened coat hanger.

Considering I hadn't been able to function without these substances for more than a month, I was strangely calm. 'Maybe it's all for the best.'

'Please, do not tell me you are going straight on me.'

'Nothing like that, Giacomo.'

By midnight Giacomo was snoring, and I'd typed the last of a thousand words on corruption and redemption in *The Scarlet Letter*. It wasn't particularly original, but I wanted to leave something finished behind. I had my escape all figured out by then. Wanting to make sure I wasn't caught, I lay on my bed fully clothed for an hour, listening to the plow rumbling back and forth, the snow piling up as fast as they pushed it aside. I thought about leaving a note, but there's no good way to say goodbye. Would I have embarked on this same plan if Giacomo hadn't been forced to flush my roofies? Who knows? But not wanting to risk any more dreams, I silently got up off my bed, opened the window and put the shaman headdress Osborne had given me on my head. I guess I wanted him to know I was thinking about him. I waited a long minute for the plow to pass just below me. Giacomo opened one eye and shouted, '*Porco Dio!*' just as I jumped out the window.

Four floors up, macadam below: as the family therapist would have said, I looked forward to closure. It felt good to have finally done something right. I closed my eyes and screamed as the ground flew up to greet me. It wasn't like I expected. No bone-cracking crunch, no artful flashback of my life: just a dull, cold thud. I could not breathe, I could not move, I did not feel. But I was alive. It was when the word *paralyzed* flashed through what was left of my brain I screamed, 'Fuck me!'

My voice echoed through the snowfall. Giacomo squatting in the window, chattering like a monkey in the cold, looked down at me and shouted, 'Fucking fantastico!' I had landed in the snow-filled basement window-well piled high by the passing plow. My feet had never touched ground.

As I pulled myself up out of the snow, lights went on in the rooms above me. Windows were thrown open. One after another, I watched in dumb wonder as my classmates began to leap from their windows. Pajamas billowing, bathrobes fluttering, shouts of fear, boredom, and ecstasy echoing in the storm – I looked on as the brightest and the best of my generation rained down around me into the snowdrifts piled high around the building. I decided right then and there if I wanted to live, something was going to have to change. I just wasn't quite sure what, or where to begin.

34

I called my mother the night before I was supposed to come home to Vlyvalle for Thanksgiving break, and asked if I could spend the holiday with a friend from school who lived in New York City.

'No, lambie, absolutely not.' She'd called me lambie, but I could tell it pissed her off that I'd even asked.

'Mom, it's not like I don't want to see you.' She was just a small part of the puzzle I didn't want to face.

'Mr Osborne invited us to his home and we're expected. Bryce and his parents will be there. I know his mother wants to see you. That poor woman, I don't think her last skin graft took. Mrs Langley told me herself she's looking forward to having a long talk with you.'

You can see why I dreaded going home. 'I just don't want to go.' I hadn't told her about jumping out the window, or Maya having a boyfriend.

'Finn, I've gone through a lot of effort to make this a nice holiday for us. I made cranberry relish, and baked three pies.' The thought of her, back on Great Jones Street, just starting to get high, singing along to Van Morrison, rolling out pastry dough with the wine bottle she'd just finished because she didn't have a rolling pin softened me to the idea of home for the holidays.

'What kind of pie?'

'Pumpkin, apple, and mince.'

I was about to give in. 'Why are you making all this stuff if we're having Thanksgiving at Osborne's?'

'Well, I wanted to bring something, since Mr Osborne was nice enough to include Gerald and his daughters.' Gerald was the Lazard Freres boyfriend.

'I get the picture.'

'I don't think you do. Gerry and I have a project Mr Osborne's investing in.'

'So what do you need me for?' I was about to say I had run out of quarters, but I remembered I'd called collect.

'We're a family.'

'Then why aren't Grandpa and Nana coming?'

'As a matter of fact, they are.'

'What are they going to do, stuff the turkey with Valium so everyone's in a good mood?'

'Why can't you enjoy the life we made for ourselves here?'

'I don't want to fight, I just want to have Thanksgiving with my friend in New York.'

'What's so special about Thanksgiving in New York? There'll be lots of young people home from boarding school in Vlyvalle. It's important for you to maintain your contacts out here.'

'Mom, please don't make me.'

'I am absolutely under no circumstances going to permit you not to come home for Thanksgiving.'

I could see I was going to have to take another tack. 'I thought you wanted me to make the most of St Mark's.'

'You can visit your school friends in New York another weekend.'

'That'd be great, except Thanksgiving is when Jackie Kennedy invited this kid's family over.' There was a long pause. I knew that'd give a Jackie-freak like my mother something to think about.

'Jackie Onassis knows you're coming for Thanksgiving?' My mother's voice was shrill with possibilities.

'I think she goes by Kennedy now, but yeah, my friend's parents asked if they could bring me, and Jackie asked who I was and they told her and she said "Great."' There wasn't a word of truth in it, but telling the truth to my mother would have been cruel and unusual punishment. Even she didn't deserve that. I figured one person in the family jumping out the window is enough. Besides, she was really getting a kick out of the idea.

'Are John-John and Caroline going to be there?' I could almost hear her whistling the theme song of 'Camelot'.

'He doesn't like being called John-John. But yeah, we're all going

267

to be at the kids' table.'

'Well that's just wonderful, Finn.'

'That's what I thought you'd think.'

'Why didn't you just tell me you were invited to the Kennedys' at the start of this conversation instead of making me pry the truth out of you?'

'I didn't want to hurt your feelings.'

'Lambie, you're a complicated boy. What's the name of the people taking you to the Kennedys'?'

The truth was, Giacomo had invited me to have Thanksgiving with his Italian mother and his third stepfather, who was German, and a bunch of foreigners in NYC. I wasn't crazy about the idea, but it beat having to go back to Vlyvalle and to pretend nothing had happened. I mean, I knew I'd have to act like everything was great at Giacomo's, too, but I figured it'd be easier to pretend I hadn't just tried to jump out a window around strangers. I would have said Giacomo's family was taking me to the Kennedys' but one of his ex-dads lived in Vlyvalle. I could just see my mother running into his old man and her going on about how great it was they took me to Jackie O's.

'Their last name's . . . Mars.' I was eating a Mars bar.

'You mean Mrs Mars who has the candy fortune?' I suddenly wished I'd bought an O'Henry bar.

'You know her?'

'I'd love to meet her. She has a horse farm in Far Hills.' That was twenty minutes from Vlyvalle. 'I hear she's fascinating. She has over a billion dollars.'

'Yeah, they're really rich: look, Mom, someone's waiting to use the phone.'

'Finn, don't hang up, this is important.'

'Yeah?' I figured she was going to make me feel guilty by telling me how much she loved me.

'You still have that hundred dollars I gave you for emergencies?'

I'd spent it on pot before I had traded for the roofies. 'Yeah.'

'When you get to New York, go to Balducci's and buy a pot of caviar for Jackie. Make sure it's Beluga.'

'Good idea, Mom.' I started to hang up the phone.

'Oh, and Finn – one more thing.'

'Yeah, Mom?' I thought for sure she was going to remember to tell me she loved me.

'Don't forget to take the price tag off.'

35

The train to New York was packed with boarding-school kids going home for Thanksgiving. When Giacomo and I boarded the train, the last three cars were a party in full swing. Boom boxes blared, beers and quarts of cheap vodka – flavored Gatorade green – were passed around in communion. The air was thick with hormones and cigarette smoke, and a couple of kids had already vomited before they had time to make it to the toilet. When the conductor threatened to call the police, everybody cheered like storm troopers on leave from the Russian front. It felt good to remember that being young could be fun.

Giacomo called it the 'Trim Train'. And, sure enough, within thirty minutes, he had us out in the cold and noise of the platform between cars with two sophomores from Concorde Academy who had punked up their school uniforms with motorcycle jackets and combat boots, and used the word 'fuck' in conversation more often than all four of the Sex Pistols combined. Their schoolgirl kilts hiked up an inch from their crotches, and the wind showing me the color of their panties, life was definitely looking up.

At first, it was hard to tell which of the two girls Giacomo liked more. I listened as he told the one to his right, 'You have hair like the Madonna.' Which was funny, because her hair was gelled into spikes and dyed blue. Funnier still was him in the next breath ogling the other's legs as the wind flashed red-pantied beaver and announcing, 'In my country, a woman does not show a man the menu unless she is going to give him the dinner.' On account of his Italian accent, really queer stuff like that went over big. I couldn't do it myself, but it was inspiring. When the girls went back inside to pee, Giacomo high-fived me and shouted, 'Orgy!' I began to get nervous.

When the girls came back and agreed to a double-date tomorrow night with us and four hits of this new love amphetamine that made you super-horny called MDMA, I told myself, 'Why not?'

I was high and laughing, and every time one of them said 'fuck', it seemed like the funniest thing in the world. And as the train bounced down the track towards New York, I realized that one of the girls was no longer stepping away from me when the train jostled her into my arms. Forgetting about Giacomo and the other girl and every-thing else, I made up my mind to kiss her the next time we passed through a tunnel. Would she kiss me back? What would her spiked hair feel like to my fingers? It looked greasy, compared to Maya's braid, but I didn't care. I was reassured that a stray thought of Maya didn't put me off my game. No question, I was feeling pretty goddamn good about my place in the universe until Giacomo mentioned the fact his mother was serving sushi instead of turkey and mashed potatoes for Thanksgiving. I don't know why it made me so sad, but when I found out sushi was raw fish, I went up to the car at the front of the train and sat next to the conductor and wished I really had been invited to Jackie Kennedy's for Thanksgiving.

Giacomo's mother was an elegantly disheveled Milanese whose New York *pied-à-terre* was a four-bedroom penthouse on Central Park West with black enameled walls, gilt molding and poison-green banquettes. If I'd ever been to Studio 54, it would have seemed less exotic. She told me to call her Donata and called me 'beautiful boy'. Her arms were bangled with jewelry she'd picked up on Third World holidays and her hair had that bleached blonde, slightly snarled look of someone who'd ridden through life at high speeds with the top down. Giacomo said she was a trip. The German stepfather's name was Dieter. He was a baron. When I made the mistake of asking him what he did he answered with pride, 'As little as possible.'

There were thirty-odd people for Thanksgiving brunch. I passed on the sushi, but not wanting to seem provincial, I explained a great bullshit excuse about how I was so allergic to fish that if it just touched my tongue, my throat would close, and Donata would have to perform a tracheotomy. She felt so sorry for me she went into the kitchen and made a bowl of pasta for me with her own bejeweled fingers. She was the first rich person I'd ever met who could cook.

There was a lot of talk about the Red Brigades and the Baader-Meinhof Gang, and the friends of theirs who had had ears cut off and been buried alive and held for ransom by terrorists. It was funny, sort of, listening to a couple argue about how much they'd be willing to pay kidnappers to get each other back. As the husband put it, 'If you have a hundred million, it is nothing to pay a million dollars' ransom for someone you love – a wife, a child. But if you only have two million, you have to think.'

'Think what?' I asked.

'Perhaps it is cheaper to remarry or adopt?'

Like I said, it was funny – sort of.

I was wondering if I would have felt less like a refugee if I'd been at Mrs Kennedy's, or Mrs Mars's, when I looked out the window and saw a huge set of antlers floating by. For a moment, I thought Donata had dosed the spaghetti sauce with acid. It wasn't impossible – they passed around joints between courses. Then I remembered the Macy's Day Parade, and reidentified the antlers as belonging to the inflatable Bullwinkle my mother could never get it together to take me uptown to see when I was a kid.

The next float was just coming into view when the German stepfather leaned forward and told me conspiratorially, 'The brilliance of the American aristocracy is they've convinced the world they don't exist.' The more he drank, the more he sounded like Colonel Klink. 'It's safer that way. Unlike us, you're invisible targets.' Him assuming I was rich made me feel like I was part of a gigantic plot. I looked out the window and waved to Casper the friendly ghost.

'Doesn't anybody want to watch the parade?'

Everybody ran to the window and clapped as the cartoon characters drifted by. Donata ordered more champagne and, pointing to the little people that crowded the avenue, she raised her glass and announced, 'We are up here and they are down there: for this, I am thankful.' It was then I noticed she was wearing dark sunglasses indoors, just like the ones Jackie O wore.

Dieter lit a cigar and looked down. 'It's very clever – you teach them in America anyone can become rich, so that when they hate the rich, they hate themselves. It paralyzes them. All they can do is eat.'

Then they all started to make jokes about the size of American portions and how fat everyone was who lived between New York and LA. I was thinking about taking offense when the guy who mixed the drinks came in and whispered in Donata's ear, and she told me, 'It is a phone call for you.'

I took the call in an octagonal mirrored hall. I was everywhere and nowhere as I picked up the phone. Figuring my mother had tracked me down, I was rehearsing excuses about why I wasn't at Mrs Mars Bars', getting ready to go have turkey with the Kennedy clan as I put the receiver to my ear.

'What's wrong with you, Finn?' It was a simple enough question. The last person I expected to ask it was Maya.

All my reflections stared back at me, slack-jawed and wild-eyed, as I took in the sound of her voice – soft, and familiarly hoarse. As she waited for my answer, I imagined her exhaling a halo of smoke and poking her finger through it. Unable to stop there, I conjured up the boyfriend sitting next to her. I heard noise in the background.

'You know what's wrong.' I was mad and glad at the same time.

'That's true. I do.' I heard her suck softly on a cigarette.

'How's everything in Switzerland?' Except for the fact that my voice cracked and I was choking on the lump in my throat, I was doing a pretty good job of playing it cool.

'I'm in New York.'

I wasn't expecting that. I thought about what I should say next. I picked the most belligerent possibility.

'Where's your boyfriend?' I regretted the question as soon as it was out of my mouth.

'You tell me.'

I didn't get it. 'Why are you playing games? Bryce told me you met a guy. You could have at least written me one letter.'

'I didn't get your letters. And there's no boyfriend . . . except for you.' It was so exactly what I wanted to hear, I had trouble believing it.

'But why did Bryce –'

She cut me off. 'Finn, I don't want to talk about Bryce, or what happened in Vlyvalle.'

'But we have to talk about it.'

'If you want to see me, you've got to promise not to ask me any questions.'

'But I have to know.'

'I'll tell you everything tomorrow.'

'But why?'

'Promise me.'

'OK, I promise.'

'Swear it.'

'All right, I swear I won't ask any questions.' In the next breath, I broke my promise. 'But what difference is a day going to make?'

'I'll be stronger after I spend the night with you.'

'When's that going to be?'

'Look out the window.' As the parade rolled by, a hand waved from the crowd that swarmed the payphone on the corner of Sixty-Seventh Street and Central Park West.

Giacomo was standing in the doorway smiling when I hung up. 'You think I invited you to have Thanksgiving for my mother's cooking? Maya called me three days ago. I told her about you going out the window.' Giacomo had given no hint that he perceived my swan dive as anything but a prank. To say the least, he was a better room-mate than I deserved. 'I told her you were a mess. You're not mad?'

'No.' My emotions were having trouble switching gears.

'You happy?'

I didn't like the part about not being able to ask her any questions.

'Yeah. I guess that's what you call it.'

'*Benissimo.* Then you don't mind I already took your hit of ecstasy?'

I left without saying goodbye, thank you, or bothering to take my suitcase.

When I hit the street, there were bagpipes playing, firemen marching, and a helium turkey floating overhead. The crowd lined up ten-deep behind the police barricades along the parade route swallowed me up. I couldn't move, much less see Maya. I jumped up and down, hoping to get a glimpse of her. It was hopeless. And then . . . I felt her lips whisper, hoarse and slow and surer than anything

274

I'd ever tried to grasp, 'I – missed – you.' Like I said before, her whisper always killed me. I forgot I was ever mad at her, or anyone else in the world as she kissed me.

Her tongue still tasted of Gummi Bears and Marlboro Lights. Then I remembered. I'd forgotten she'd cut off her braid. Her hair was shorter than mine now. Without a tan, the scar on the left side of her face stood out. A beret, a long leather coat, and a knapsack slung over her shoulders, she looked like she was still on the run.

We both knew it was too weird, trying to talk in the crowd. She grabbed my hand. Jumping the barricade, dodging a float carrying a band of Polish pilgrims playing polka music, we cut into the park.

I pulled her off the path and pinned her up against the trunk of a leafless tree. One of her buttons popped off and fell to the ground as I pushed my hands inside her coat. She was wearing this sweater thing and leggings, like cashmere long johns. Without even bothering to kiss her, I shoved my cold, dirty hands inside her underwear, and began to squeeze and finger the parts of her body that had kept me awake all fall. I was angry and lonely and she knew it. I didn't know if I wanted to fuck her or hurt her or both.

The ground was littered with condoms. My pants were down around my ankles. A few feet away, a rat stole stale bread from some pigeons. Maya turned her face up to the winter sun and closed her eyes to the ugliness of our circumstance. Trembling, wincing ever so slightly, she was like a kid in a doctor's office waiting for an injection. She knew things were going to have to get worse before they got better. She would have let me do anything I wanted to her, except ask 'What do you mean you didn't get my letters? I wrote you every fucking day.' I stopped feeling her up and started shouting questions. 'What the hell are you doing here? Did you run away again?' She didn't give me any answers but when she began to cry, I felt better.

Finally, she sobbed, 'This was a mistake,' and pulled up her underwear and buttoned her coat. I still had a hard-on. 'I should have waited to see you. It's my fault. I just don't want to be alone tonight.'

'Tomorrow you'll tell me everything?'

She nodded and wiped her nose on the sleeve of her coat. 'Trust me. I'm going to fix things.' Holding hands, like we were both lost, we walked along Central Park South without saying a word. I followed her through the revolving brass doors of the Plaza Hotel. Even after she unlocked the door to her sixth-floor suite and drew the curtains and made it night, I still didn't know where she was taking me.

'Want to fuck the minibar?' She was nervous and trying to sound cool. Without waiting for me to answer, she started to make us drinks. She tossed her purse on the chair nearest the veneered fridge. A gold American Express card, a Concorde ticket, and a pink plastic wheel of birth-control pills fell out onto the floor. Maya saw me staring at the contents of her bag as she handed me a rum and Coke.

'I started taking them when I met you.'

I wasn't reassured. 'Wow, that's romantic.'

'It was for me.' She popped three in her mouth and finished her drink in two gulps. 'I keep forgetting to take them.' She burped. 'You think I'm going to grow a mustache?' I laughed at her joke, but only half-believed she was taking the Pill for me. I mean, if I was the only person she wanted to sleep with, why did she keep taking them when she ran away, and after they caught her and sent her to Switzerland?

When she came over with the bourbons and Coke, and sat next to me on the bed, and took my hands in hers and held them in her lap, as much as I wanted to take advantage of the x-rated possibilities of being alone with her in a hotel room with a minibar and a king-sized bed, all I could think of was how many Swiss dicks had those child-like fingers gripped while she was away.

She asked me, 'What are you thinking?'

Naturally, I answered, 'How great it is to see you.'

'Come on, it's weird and we both know it.' Getting up and taking two more mini-bourbons from the minibar, she poured them over the melting ice in our glasses and flopped down on the couch.

'I thought maybe if I said it, I'd feel it.'

'Is that why you always tell people what they want to hear?' She frowned as she picked up her Concorde ticket off the floor. Jetlag and disappointment made it easy to see how her laugh lines would turn to crow's feet when she got older. She was already older.

276

'Maybe if I were rich I could afford to give people more of the truth.' The thought didn't begin as meanly as it ended.

'When you're grown-up and you're rich, you'll realize money doesn't make it any easier to be honest.'

'What makes you think I'll ever be rich?'

'Grandpa says you will.'

'Bullshit.'

'You like hearing that, don't you?' When I didn't say anything, she rummaged a joint out of her purse and added, 'He thinks you're like him.' She lit the joint, blew a smoke ring, and poked her finger through it. The gesture didn't seem as cute as it did in my memory. 'Grandpa says you've got what it takes to end up with the most toys.'

'What's that supposed to mean?' I didn't feel like getting high, but I smoked it anyway.

'You don't trust happiness.'

After we drank everything that mixed with Coke, I cracked open the Tanqueray. I was too loaded to remember my mother's warning that gin makes people mean. By then, Maya was so bombed, she tried to put on her lipstick without taking off the cap. Clumsily trying to fill a gap in the conversation, I started blabbing about the goal I scored in JV soccer. I left out the fact the ball ricocheted off my back and into the goal, and was doing a pretty good job of turning dumb luck into a World Cup moment when she interrupted, 'Did you miss me?'

'I worked my ass off for you.'

'For me?'

'You grandfather said if I made Honor Roll he'd take me to see you in Switzerland at Christmas break.'

'You made Honor Roll?'

'Does that surprise you?'

'Everybody said you're ambitious.'

'What the fuck does that mean?' We weren't trading paper cuts anymore.

'I didn't say it. People said it.'

'Said what?'

'That you didn't waste any time worming your way into all the right people's hearts – mine, Grandpa's, Bryce's. My mother thinks you and your mother had it all planned when you came to Vlyvalle.'

'Fuck you.'

'I wish you would.' She didn't say it like a joke. When she saw the expression on my face, she threw her head back and laughed. A can of Tab in her right hand, it was freaky how much she looked like her mother.

Reeling on alcohol, guilt, and shame, I backed away from her like a kid who's broken something that belonged to somebody else. Something precious and valuable that you knew you didn't have permission to play with and could never replace.

'I better go home.'

'Don't you want to see my tattoo?' I was almost to the door. I wouldn't have stopped to look if she hadn't added, 'I made it myself.'

Getting to her feet with a stagger, Maya pushed up her sleeve. There, across the veined whiteness of her left wrist, was a series of dirty slashes that spelled out my name. 'I did it with a razor blade and charcoal.' It was the way the Yanomamö tattooed themselves. 'Sorry I left off the second N. I passed out before I finished . . . *Fin.*' She said it with a French accent, like it meant 'The End'. 'At least you know I was thinking of you when I tried to . . .' I imagined her leaving me behind in every ugly way but this.

Suddenly, I was leaping out of my dorm window all over again. The ground below swirled up at me. Certain in the knowledge that we were both broken and falling, I was finally able to let go of everything but her.

Drunk, but sober, we pulled off each other's clothes and fell onto the bed. That we were alive and naked seemed like some kind of miracle.

278

36

When I woke up, the shades were still drawn. I didn't realize it was already tomorrow, until I turned on the bedside lamp and saw the digital clock slowly click into the moment: 11.43 a.m. Clothes, and underwear, and mini-bottles of bourbon and gin (when did we open the rum?) littered the hotel room. A hangover inside my head, rumpled sheets that smelled of sex, the sound of Maya in the bathroom turning on the shower – it all seemed grown-up and glamorously similar to something I had seen in an R-rated movie, until I realized my fingers and cock were stained with dried blood.

Maya called out from under the shower, 'If you're awake, please don't look under the sheets.' Naturally, that was the first thing I did. But I surprised myself when I reached out and touched the dark, wet, red mark in the middle of the bed. The bloodstain, blotted and strangely symmetrical, reminded me of the Rorschach test my grandfather had given me in the eighth grade to see if I was going to turn out crazy as my mom. Of course, he didn't put it that way when he pulled out his inkblots. I could still hear him inquiring, neutral and creepy as Mr Rogers in Switzerland, 'What do you see in this, Finn?'

A red bat, that's what it looked like. A Yanomamö blood sacrifice, that's what it made be think of. Proof Maya was a virgin. Either that, or something was seriously wrong. I stopped free-associating long enough to check my bloodstained penis for damage. There was no wound that I could see.

From then on, there was no stopping my mind from connecting the dots between darker thoughts. Was I remembering or imagining the way the blood-smeared dick of my attacker shined limp and dark as an eel in the moonlight as he got up off me that night in the field?

Did he really drop a lighter and enjoy a smoke after he had me, or was my head just fucking with me?

Reaching for a cigarette, trying to wash the image from my brain with nicotine, I struck a match. Fire was the next dot I connected. I didn't want to think about that either, but Maya's house was still smoldering inside my head. And there, beneath the rubble and ash, was Paige – a cinder with a diamond in her tooth.

When Maya called out to me from the shower the second time, 'Why aren't you in here with me?' I blew out the match that was just beginning to burn my fingers and pulled up the sheets to hide the evidence. As cool as it was to be able to take a shower with her and not have to worry about a grown-up bursting in on us, I couldn't shake the thought that we were connected by blood.

We did it twice more that day, once standing up in the shower, and again quickly on the couch while we waited for room service to bring us breakfast. I was thinking about trying our hands at sexual positions preferred by the Yanomamö and the readers who wrote letters into *Penthouse* when, a piece of bacon in my mouth, eggs on my fork, Maya leaned across the tray, kissed my bulging cheek, and asked, 'You want to ask me your questions now?'

'Right now?' It seemed safer to just keep having sex.

'I thought that's what you wanted.'

Suddenly, I was pissed off at her again. Why'd she have to make things complicated? 'Why didn't you answer my letters?'

'I didn't get them until last week.' She walked over to her suitcase and took out a stack of opened envelopes tied into a bundle with a shoelace.

'But Bryce gave me the address. I know I got it right. Monsieur Bouret, 26 Rue de Ruen, Geneva.'

'Monsieur Bouret is Billy Bouret who was a year ahead of Bryce at Harvard. After he graduated he took a year off to teach geometry and screw rich girls at Le Rosey.'

'Why didn't the asshole give them to you?'

Her look told me I wasn't going to like her answer. 'Bryce told him not to.'

I had that same sick-to-my-stomach feeling I used to get when I'd lay awake at night, imagining Maya fucking other guys. But mixed in with the seasickness of betrayal was overwhelming confusion. After walking in on me and Jilly, Maya had a reason to turn on me. But what had I done to make Bryce want to keep my letters from ever reaching his sister? If he'd decided I was a jerk, or wasn't cool enough, why did he keep calling me up and come to school with Coco, and try to hook me up with what's-her-name, and tell me Maya had a new boyfriend?

'What do you mean?' I demanded. 'I thought Bryce liked me. I thought he wanted us to get together. He told me to go up to your house the night of the fire. He was my friend. Why would he want to split us up now?'

'He knew if we ever got together like this, I'd tell you the truth about the fire.' Maya nervously pulled up the shades and looked out at the frozen park. It was like I was a passenger in a car that was skidding into a brick wall. Maya was doing the driving. Any second, I was going to be hit head-on with the how and why she had torched her home. The only thing in doubt was how I was going to rationalize not doing the right thing. Paige was dead. Punishing Maya wouldn't change that. Maybe it was an accident. And maybe, just maybe, my silence would keep Maya safe and show Bryce I was one of them.

These were the thoughts in my head as Maya began to explain: 'When they caught up with me in Philadelphia, Bryce tried to get Grandpa to make me sign something that said if I ever told anybody I'd be disinherited. But Grandpa said, besides the fact it wouldn't hold up in court, I was old enough to know . . . how did he put it?' Her hands shook as she lit a cigarette and mimicked Osborne. ' "Washing your dirty linen in public doesn't make it any cleaner." '

'Bryce thought I'd tell?'

'He said sooner or later, you'd think you had a good reason to make us pay.' Pay how? I wondered. Did he really think a sixteen-year-old was going to try to get money out of them? My own thoughts kept getting in the way of what I was hearing. 'I promised him I wouldn't tell you, but he knew I was lying. So he fixed it so I wouldn't get your letters. I guess he figured if I thought you didn't care enough to write, and you thought I was having too much fun to answer your letters, we'd write each other off as assholes. And he wouldn't have to worry about me sitting here and telling you . . . my mother set the fire.'

'I was there – that's impossible. Your mother couldn't have started the fire.' Tired of being lied to, I shouted, 'I thought you were going to tell me the fucking truth!'

'You think I did it?'

I didn't say anything.

'So all that stuff in your letters about knowing I was innocent, and always loving me, was just bullshit? You're just like everybody else.'

'No I'm not.'

Maya kicked over the breakfast tray as she began to pack her suitcase. 'For your information, Finn, my mother admitted it, to Bryce and me and Grandpa in the hospital when she came out of intensive care.'

Wanting to believe her, I frantically retraced the events of that night in my mind. Sneaking into the house, going into Mrs Langley's room by mistake, then running back to the landing, opening the door and seeing the fire and . . . but there was no way Maya's version of that night made sense. The fire was set while I was upstairs with her mother.

'Your mother said all sorts of crazy stuff after the fire.'

'Like what?' Maya stopped packing her bag.

'Like I was a hero and saved her life. I didn't look for you or try to help her.' 'I was a total chicken. I pushed your mother down, I kicked her, all I cared about was saving myself.'

'I know that.' She reached out to hug me. I was too ashamed to accept comfort. 'It was my brother's idea to make you out to be a hero.'

'Why?'

'Bryce thought if he told everyone you rescued my mother, it'd keep anyone from suspecting she tried to kill herself.' It was strange, I could forgive Bryce everything, except turning me into a hero.

'Osborne knew?'

'Not at first.'

'What'd he say when he found out?'

'There're all kinds of heroes.'

'Great.'

'Grandpa's still mad at Bryce for doing it. He feels sorry for you.'

'You can tell everybody in your family to relax. I got a scholarship to St Mark's. My mother's a masseuse who Osborne calls a doctor. I'm not stupid. I'm not going to tell anybody. But that doesn't change the fact your mother didn't start the fucking fire. And she wasn't trying to kill herself.'

'She was, and it's my fault!' Maya's wail shut me up. No longer sixteen going on thirty-six, she suddenly sounded like a guilty child. Looking at her feet, pausing between words, her upper lip quivering as she licked away the tears, she slowly and deliberately recounted the events of the day of the fire. I listened carefully, opening my ears to every pause and fluctuation in her voice. Not because I wanted to understand, I was listening for another lie. I listened for another betrayal, hoping it would give me the courage to turn my back on their tribe and free myself from the aching, humiliating need I had in me to be loved by them.

'I was mad at you for Jilly. She came by that morning and told me it only happened because something bad had happened to you, and she thought you were kidding when you told her but afterwards she realized you must have been serious. And when she wouldn't tell me what it was, I went ballistic. I told her to get out, and said I was going to get her father fired, which I wasn't going to do, but I couldn't believe you trusted her more than me.'

'I wanted to tell you, but . . .'

She put her hands to my face the way a little kid does to silence their mother. 'You can tell me later. I just want to get this out. So, I was driving around the farm, looking for my mother. I wanted to tell her Paige and I were going to go to New York and stay at her brother's apartment. I saw the Peugeot parked at the playhouse. The door was locked. And when I looked in the window, my mother was . . . naked on top of some guy.'

'What guy?'

'All I could see were his legs, and when she got off, she started to . . .' Maya gagged on her tears, 'I mean, she waits all those years while my father's in the hospital, and when he finally gets well, she has to . . . and I waited around, and when she comes out, she pretends she's sweaty from her fucking tennis match.'

The glimpse of two people fucking, the locked door, Mrs Langley in the tennis dress: my mind seized on a moment that changed my life that was eerily similar to the one Maya had just described. I remembered a day earlier that summer when I, too, had been looking for my mother. Like Maya, I had stumbled upon a blue Peugeot parked outside the playhouse. I thought it was my mother's car, but it was Mrs Langley's. The door was locked that day, too. I had peered in that same window as Maya. But what had I really seen? A faceless woman's body, a white-blond head between her wide spread legs. When Bryce appeared in the window naked, I was talking to his mother. He motioned for my silence. After Mrs Langley left, Bryce turned and said something to Jilly. But I never saw Jilly. And later, when I asked Jilly about Dwayne being jealous of Bryce, the way she laughed . . . 'You're the only one Dwayne's got to be jealous of.' She wasn't bullshitting me. She was telling me the truth. And if it wasn't Bryce and Jilly . . . could it have been Bryce and . . .

I would have blurted out what I was thinking right there, if Maya hadn't started talking. 'And then when I go to see who my mother's doing it with, the guy bolts the door from inside, and I'm screaming for the creep to let me in, and my mother starts yelling, "You don't understand, it's not like you think."'

I braced myself for the conversation to go nuclear. I knew it was Bryce behind that locked door. He had been with his mother, not Jilly, that first day at the playhouse. He pretended to be screwing the maid so I wouldn't suspect. 'Do you know who your mother was with?'

'Ben Nicholson.'

'Who?'

'The fucking tennis pro. You saw them flirting at my birthday party.' I didn't, but even if I had, there was absolutely no doubt in my mind it was Bryce, but I nodded like I saw it her way. In my own defense, it wouldn't have exactly been easy, telling Maya that her mother was screwing her brother. But that wasn't the reason I didn't tell her.

'What happened then?' I felt vaguely superior knowing such an ugly secret about them. It was like dissecting some exotic species and discovering it's more human than you.

'I went back to the house and started to pack. I just wanted to get away. And then Bryce came home.'

'Did you tell Bryce about seeing your mom and the tennis guy?' She nodded yes. 'What'd your brother do then?'

'It was sweet, really. He started to cry, like he did at Christmas when he had to give away his presents. And then he went into my mother's room, and when he came out, he said she'd made a mistake, and it would never happen again, and I had to promise not to tell Grandpa or my father. Like that's what I was going to do. But then my mother came out holding a fucking can of Tab in her hand, and when she saw my suitcase she slapped me and said I wasn't allowed to leave the house, and who was I to judge her, sneaking off and screwing you. If only I hadn't told her I was going to tell Grandpa . . .' Her body shook as she sobbed into the soft part of my neck.

'Did you tell Osborne?' There were more dots to connect than I ever imagined.

'No. I drove into the city and walked around the Village. Slept in my car. I was going to come home, then I saw Paige's picture in the newspaper. She and I were going to go to New York together. She had bought these 'ludes. I guess when I wasn't there, she took a bunch and went into Bryce's bedroom and waited. She always had a thing for him.' We all had a thing for Bryce.

I told her I understood, but I didn't. I got her to stop crying by telling her about waking up and hearing my mother screwing strangers on the other side of the wall on Great Jones Street. I don't remember what I said exactly. The whole time I was talking, all I was really thinking about was Bryce chanting 'fuck/kill' as we watched the Fierce People feast.

37

We never set foot out of out hotel room that day, but we were never alone. Even when we stopped talking about Bryce, he was with us. Eating room service, watching TV, having sex (especially when we had sex), he was there. He had always been crowding us. I just didn't begin to hate him for it until now.

The last thing Maya said before she fell asleep in my arms was, 'I feel better now that I told you everything.'

Staring wide-eyed at the ceiling, I pretended to be sleepy and murmured sweetly, 'Me too.' The truth was, I felt poisoned. Bryce's secrets were so toxic, having them inside my head made me feel like I'd snorted radioactive waste. My thoughts glowed inside the darkness of my mind, luminously lethal, too cancerous to share with someone you want to love you.

I was ashamed I wasn't more shocked to discover Bryce was having sex with his mother. Every time I tried to work up moral indignation, I'd remember that tingly feeling I got between my legs when the shower curtain fell and a blast of hot water scalded my naked mother into my arms.

Stranger still was recalling all the details of the first time I met Bryce at the playhouse. Remembering how, when I saw the Peugeot station wagon, and a glimpse of his head between a set of female legs, I jumped to the conclusion it was my mother he was devouring. In a twisted way, I almost admired Bryce for how deftly he tricked me into thinking it was Jilly. Now, when I conjured up what I saw through that window, I could see those weren't the legs of a seventeen-year-old. There was cellulite on the backs of those thighs, and the calves were shorter. Why didn't any of us wonder why we never saw Bryce, the consummate ladies man, the legendary stud, the

White Snake of Harvard, ever doing it with any of the chicks that mooned after him in Vlyvalle? Paige was begging for it. And if I was so oblivious to what now seemed so obvious in retrospect, what else had I been blind to?

No question, I would have been more disconcerted to find out about Bryce screwing his mother if I hadn't realized about six hours earlier that Bryce had tried to kill me when he set fire to the house. Bryce knew Maya was going to be in New York when he told me to go up to the house that night and sneak into her room. There was some sense to the sick logic that Bryce wanted to get rid of his mother because he was afraid she'd have one too many cans of Tab and vodka and let their secret slur out. But why did Bryce want me inside when he lit the match? Was he going to blame the fire on me? Or did he think I knew something I didn't? Bryce was always giving me credit for being smarter than I was.

It was clear now why Bryce never wanted me to see Maya again. He knew if his sister and I talked about the events of leading up to the fire, I'd realize he'd started it. Maya was right. Bryce didn't hate me, he just couldn't keep on being Bryce if I was around. And if he tried to kill me once, why wouldn't he try to kill me again? Scarier still, maybe he had tried and failed without me ever realizing.

Fear – and steam heat – had me sweating paranoia. Shortly after four a.m. it occurred to me that Bryce had been the one who pulled the feed bag over my head and raped me in the dirt. As the image of him on top of me ripped into my imagination, I opened my mouth to scream. And then I remembered: Osborne said he and Bryce had been talking about the fucking youth center when I had been jumped. Bryce had slept over at his grandfather's that night. Osborne was still in his library when Gates brought me in. I remembered Bryce coming to the door in his bathrobe. Osborne wouldn't have lied to me about that. That much I was sure of. It's strange, but I was relieved to acquit Bryce of rape.

I jumped when Maya rolled closer to me. Bryce was between us in the bed now. There was no escaping him. I was no longer tempted to shake Maya from her dreams and tell her all I knew about her brother. I couldn't prove any of what I was thinking, and even if I did convince Maya, the reality of her good life was far uglier than she

287

feared. Who would believe us? She was just a spoiled rich girl who set fire to dorms, put out steel traps for poachers, and was taken into custody by the FBI on TV. And I was the boy who got busted buying blow, and jumped out of windows, and made up stories about candy-bar billionairesses taking him to Jackie Kennedy's for Thanksgiving dinner. She was a menace and I was a joke.

And who would we go to with this sordid tale? Gates? Paige's parents? My mother? Maybe Osborne would believe us. But what would he do? How could he wash this clean? In public or private? He wasn't going to turn in his grandson, and he wasn't God.

And then, of course, there was Bryce. The new improved Bryce that suddenly decided when his father was coming home, he'd wear suits and horn-rimmed glasses and bring Negroes to Vlyvalle. Was it all an act? Did he do it to distract everybody? To make himself seem better than the rest of them? Or was he just like me – trying to be the person he wished he was.

How I figured it didn't matter. He would deny everything. And his convenient change of heart would make it all the more impossible for people to believe my accusations. They'd say I was jealous, crazy, ambitious, that I wanted to be him. All true but the last.

Bryce would use the fact that Maya had snuck back to the States to hole up in the Plaza with me as proof that she was nuts and I was a horny opportunist. It would be our word against his. No, in the end it wouldn't even be that. Bryce would remind her about me and Jilly. He'd catch me on a thousand lies. He'd find out I said I was going to Jackie O's. Blood and money gave them kinship I could not compete with. In the end, Maya would side with her own, and they would stand together. I could feel the poison spreading to my heart.

38

Maya slept on her stomach beside me, her naked leg hooked over mine, her flattened breast pinning my right arm to the bed, the tickle and tease of her pubic hair against my hip, distracting my central nervous system – even though I managed to untangle my leg and free my arm and slip out of bed without waking her, I knew I was trapped.

There are telephones next to the toilets in the suites at the Plaza. As I emptied my bladder, I looked at the phone and remembered when I was a little kid, my mother dropping me off at kindergarten and telling me, 'If you don't like it, you can always come home and watch cartoons with me.'

It was a dopey idea, but at that moment, all I wanted was to be back on Great Jones Street, watching *Speed Racer* with my mom. My nostalgia for a simpler past was so strong I found myself reaching out for the phone, convinced that if I dialed her number she would call me 'lambie' and pack up her old pink suitcase, lock the door on Vlyvalle and we could run off to a new town. Hide out in someplace that had sidewalks and American cars, where there were no King Airs, or Hunt Clubs, or billionaires, or sixteen-year-old girls who trapped poachers, and we could have a second second chance. My hand was just ready to lift the receiver when the phone rang.

'You're a hard man to track down.'

I pissed on my foot when I realized it was Bryce. 'How did you . . .'

'Ran into Giacomo at Studio 54. How's my little sister?'

'Great.'

'What did she say when you told her you knew about her new boyfriend?' Bryce was testing me.

'I didn't say anything.'

'That doesn't sound like you.'

'If I made a big thing about being jealous and all, I wouldn't be with her at the Plaza now, would I?'

Bryce laughed. 'You're learning.'

'You want to talk to her? She's asleep, but I can wake her up.' I was testing him now.

'No. I don't want Maya to think I'm checking up on her. She's such a prude she'd get embarrassed if she thought I knew she spent the night with you.'

'I spent two nights with her, actually.'

'Making up for lost time?'

'Sort of.'

'Enjoy it while it lasts. Listen, the only reason I called was your mother lost her power in the big snowstorm we had yesterday.'

'It didn't snow here.' I looked out the window, the sun was just coming up over the east side of the park.

'Well, we got dumped on. Anyway, your mom's spent the night at my grandfather's. And she told me all about Mrs Mars taking you to the Kennedys' for Thanksgiving.'

'That was a good one, wasn't it?'

'Like I always said, Finn, you're a gentleman and a scholar. And a most excellent liar.' I used to laugh when he said that. 'Hey, buddy, relax, your secret's safe with me. But if you want to head her off at the pass, I'd give her a jingle before she calls Mrs Mars. She's dying to hear what Jackie was like.'

'Thanks for the warning, Bryce.'

'Hey, I'm counting on you to get Maya back to school on time. We don't want to get her in trouble again.'

'I'll get her back. She's leaving today.'

'Really?' He said it like he didn't believe me. 'Well, in that case, why don't you take the train out to the country? I can tell you everything about Jackie's apartment. I see Caroline and John all the time up in Boston . . . love to watch you feed it back to her. You'd have cracked up if you heard your mother going on at Thanksgiving about your social conquest.'

It pissed me off to hear Bryce make fun of my mother's social climbing. At least when I did it, I was criticizing her style, not her ambition. I almost said something, but caught myself. I didn't know what I was going to do, but I knew I couldn't let him know I was angry. I tried changing the subject. 'How much snow did you get?'

'Over a foot. It started out as rain, then it froze.' The way he talked about the weather, you never would have guessed he had tried to kill me. I had no idea how to stop him until he told me, 'It split that big maple in front of your house right in half.'

'Which tree?'

'The one closest to the house. Branches punched a hole right through the roof. It'll be a week before your mother's back in.'

'Thanks for letting her stay.'

'Come on. Take the train. We'll go ice skating on the lake.'

'I don't know how to skate.'

'Like my mother says, you're a fast learner.' By the time I hung up, I had made a decision that would change the rest of my life.

Maya finally woke up an hour later with a one-eye-open stretch. She smiled at the sight of me chain-smoking, naked, in the corner of the room, watching her. 'You know, I always used to think men's things were ugly.'

I was thinking about the lake where Bryce wanted to give me a skating lesson. 'What things?'

'You have a beautiful penis.'

Until that instant, I did not know I had been waiting my whole life to hear a girl say that. But instead of being able to enjoy the compliment, I was only able to envy the gossamer wrap of innocence, ignorance, and security that allowed her to relax and enjoy the present. It wasn't that there weren't cares in her world, she simply believed her world would always take care of them.

I wondered if that's what made her such a natural at fly-fishing and sex.

Maya sat on my lap, kissed me, and told me she loved me in a whisper. I could tell she was wondering why I wasn't getting hard. For my plan to work, I had to tell her just enough of the truth so she would always think I had been completely honest with her.

'Bryce called while you were asleep.' I couldn't risk it coming out later that I had lied about that. 'He found out we were here from Giacomo.'

'What did he say when you yelled at him for trying to break us up?'

'I didn't yell at him.' It wasn't what she wanted to hear. She got off my lap and put on a robe. Even if it made me look like a wimp, I had to convince her I bore her brother no ill will. 'I didn't say anything about the letters, or your mother, or the fire, or anything else.'

'I can't believe you're not mad.'

'I just don't want any more trouble for us, or your family. I want everything to be like it was.' In a way, that was true.

'Well, I'm going to call him right now and tell him I think he's a shit.' She walked toward the phone. I couldn't let her call Bryce. He had to think I trusted him. Harder still, I had to seem calm. My heart raced and my hands shook as I tried to nonchalantly light another cigarette. I was so nervous I had to remind myself to breathe.

'You know, if Bryce tells your school you flew to New York and shacked up at the Plaza with me, they'll kick you out.' I could tell she hadn't considered that possibility, but it didn't scare her off. 'Maya, why risk it? We know the truth. If you're on the next plane to Geneva, no one will know, and Osborne will take us skiing at Christmas.'

'It's the fucking principle, Finn. Bryce has got to stop. Someone's got to tell him he's gone too far.'

She was dialing the number. She was going to ruin everything. When she said, 'You may be scared of my brother, but I'm not,' I played my lowest card.

'I'm not scared of him, I feel sorry for him.' When she put down the phone, I saw an opening.

'Why would you feel sorry for Bryce?'

Knowing that what she really meant was that he had everything and I had nothing didn't make me love her any less. It just made it easier to sound like the forgiving person I wasn't.

'Your brother was trying to protect your mother. Paige died in the fire. Your mother could go to jail. Once Bryce started lying, he was trapped. The poor guy must have been on the edge of a nervous breakdown, covering up for his mom.' Was I talking about Bryce or myself?

'You think Bryce already knew about Ben Nicholson?'

It took me a moment to remember she thought her mom was in the playhouse with the tennis pro. I had always been operating in two realities – hers and mine – it was just clearer now.

'Probably . . . think about what it must have been like for Bryce. He had no one to turn to. There wasn't time for him to ask your grandfather or his lawyers what to do after the fire. Once he realized what your mother did, what was he gonna do? Turn her in? What would you do? He didn't know Paige was in there. He knew I was OK. He just thought the house burned down. He didn't just lie to us; he had to lie to Osborne, Gates, and the fire inspectors. You should be worried about your brother, not mad at him.'

It isn't easy, sticking up for a guy who had lied and betrayed you and set a house on fire with you inside. I knew I had Maya when she started to cry. If I felt guilty about anything, it was that poor Paige, even with that diamond in her tooth, didn't figure in any way into the equation of my revenge.

Maya sat back down on my lap and put her arms around me and wept. 'My brother doesn't deserve a friend like you.'

39

There is no direct route to Vlyvalle. At least, not by public transportation. While Maya took a limo to Kennedy for a first-class seat
on the 14.30 flight to Geneva, I made my way to the Jersey side of the
Hudson, on a subway called the PATH. I had to wait for more than an
hour in Hoboken's Erie–Lackawanna station for a local train west.
The storm must have just missed New York. Twenty-seven stops
later, there was a foot and a half of snow on the ground, and I was at
the end of the line, a town called Gladstone, where Maya had once
taken me to buy barbless nymphs.

Three black ladies in church clothes and a Portuguese couple
who shivered in jogging suits got off at the snowbound station
with me. Out of uniform, I didn't recognize them as the servants
who had passed my lamb chops, and opened doors, and mixed
drinks for me during the glory days of my summer, until Bryce
drove up in an old pickup truck from the farm with chains on the
back wheels.

He called out to each of them by name, asked the Portuguese
couple about their child, and offered the oldest of the black ladies a
ride, before he got out of the truck. Then he turned his charm on me.
'It's been too long, brother.'

His boots crunched on the packed snow as he walked towards me.
His calm was so dominant, it was as if he was willing the moment
into slo-mo. Bulked up in a red down parka, a smile that was all
teeth, breath steaming out of his nostrils, reindeer dancing across his
sweater – he looked like a movie star. Or Satan, *après-ski*. When I
caught sight of my reflection in his mirrored sunglasses, all I saw was
fear. My panic was visible – when he reached out to hug me, I
jumped back and slipped on a patch of ice. The servants in civilian

dress laughed when he caught me mid-fall and announced, 'You can't break your leg before we go skating.'

As Bryce accelerated out of the parking lot he said, 'Got a present for you.' He tossed me a small box, wrapped up with a little bow like Christmas had come early. 'I'll give you five hundred bucks if you tell your mother it's from Jackie O.' I thanked him for the Dead Kennedys tape, but didn't take him up on his bet. 'How's Maya doing?' he asked innocently.

'Great.' I was trying not to think about what he'd do to me if he caught me before I was ready.

'I'm really happy you guys could work it out. What's Giacomo up to?'

'He's great.' It was snowing again. Flakes so big they looked fake. I felt like I was in one of those glass paperweights, and Bryce was turning it upside down.

'Hey, anytime you need help with papers or anything, just give me a call. Feels good to make Honor Roll, doesn't it?' His questions were so innocent, his interest so genuine, I began to wonder if I had imagined this whole thing. What if I was wrong?

'It's all great.' Hope is the last temptation.

After about the fifth or sixth time I lamely assured Bryce everything was great, he popped the Dead Kennedys into the tape deck, slammed on the brakes and spun the wheel. We were just starting down the steep hill in front of the Hunt Club. As the truck swerved into a 360, I looked over at Bryce. Smiling he began to sing along to the Dead Kennedys.

As the truck continued its skid, the landscape blurred and the snow whipped around us.

Halfway through the second 360, I caught sight of the metal blade of the snowplow on the front of the jeep that was plowing out the McCallum's drive. When I screamed at Bryce to stop, he shrugged his shoulders and let go of the wheel. As we skidded towards the snowplow sideways, the only question was whether we were going to roll before we hit. Bryce kept singing 'Holiday in Cambodia'.

Closing my eyes, I braced for the crash. The car jerked as it suddenly hit a patch of snowless pavement. I knew we'd just missed getting broadsided by the plow when Bryce said, 'It's time to open your eyes.'

'What the fuck did you do that for?'

'If everything's so good, I figured I'd shake things up.'

I had no more doubts. Willing to do anything to stay alive long enough to make good my escape, I kept Bryce happy and distracted by chanting the Dead Kennedys chorus along with him as we drove into Vlyvalle.

' "Pol Pot Pol Pot Pol Pot Pol Pot Pol Pot Pol Pot Pol Pot Pol Pot." '

The worst part was, I hated the song even before I had to sing it with Bryce.

Driving in the back gate of Osborne's estate, following the same route I took with Gates and my mother that first day, everything seemed different – and it wasn't just the snow. Our yellow house, with its roof thick with snow, and icicles hanging from the eaves, looked smaller and cozier than I remembered. I could see my mother's old, pink suitcase in the attic through the hole the branches of the sugar maple had torn in the roof.

'You mind if we stop and I get out to take a look?'

'Insurance will fix it.'

'I want to see the damage.'

'If it's that important to you . . .'

It was more important than he knew. But him getting out of the truck with me wasn't part of the plan. I pretended to be interested in the hole in the roof. The big sugar maple by the kitchen door was split in half lengthwise from top to bottom, right down to the base of the trunk. You could see it was hollow and rotten inside. If Bryce hadn't gone back to the truck to get cigarettes, I never would have been able to grope beneath the bed of dead leaves and cracked nuts where the squirrels had nested. For an instant, I thought it wasn't there. Frantic, I reached deeper. Finally my fingers closed around the pistol Bryce had given me for protection and I had dropped into the hollow trunk, when the only solution seemed to be a bullet in my own brain. It was heavier than I remembered. Hoping it still worked, I slipped it into my pocket just as Bryce reappeared with the smokes.

'Let's get out of here and go skating.'

'One more stop.' It hadn't been part of the plan, but I suddenly wanted to see my mom before I pulled the trigger.

As we drove up to Osborne's mansion, in the last light of day, I saw a speck moving across a distant hillside. It wasn't until we came closer, and turned into the Belgian block drive up to the pillared entrance and the frozen fountain in front, that I realized it was a one-horse sleigh, with Osborne holding the reins. Wearing a fur coat and a red stocking cap, cracking a whip and waving a mittened hand, he looked just like Santa Claus.

Bryce had told my mother I was coming. She beat the butler to the front door.

'Oh, my God, lambie, you look so grown up!' Was she being nice, or just not wearing her contacts? I hadn't changed my clothes for three days.

She hugged me and kissed Bryce on the cheek. I didn't like it when he casually put his arm around her shoulder and chimed in, 'Our lambie's a man now, Liz.'

'Stop it, Bryce.' My mother laughed nervously. I could tell she wasn't crazy about Bryce being so touchy-feely.

Bryce wasn't stopping. 'Finn, I don't know how else to tell you this, I have a major crush on your mother.' Was he trying to get under my skin, or did it just come naturally?

'Bryce, stop trying to get all the attention.' She sounded like Maya. It was all getting mixed up inside my head. I was sure Bryce was on to me. And if that was true, there was no beating him. Would he wait for spring to invite my mother down to the playhouse? Or would he cop a feel when he comforted her at my funeral? The idea of him hitting on her after I was dead was so distracting I almost let Herbert take my coat. No way I wanted him to notice I had a pistol in my pocket.

'Come on.' My mother pulled me toward the couch. 'Sit down and tell me how it was.'

'I can only stay a minute. Bryce is going to teach me how to skate.'

'There's no rush. The ice isn't going to melt tonight.' No question, Bryce was toying with me. 'Herbert can make us some coffee. I want to hear about the Kennedys, too.'

My mother was all for it. 'You don't mind, Herbert?' The butler was paid not to mind. After spending one night at Osborne's my mother was acting like she'd had a butler her whole life. It was funny, knowing it was all going to be over soon, it didn't piss me off.

'You know Bryce, if you don't mind, I'd like to talk to my mother alone for a minute.'

'Take as long as you want. I'm not going anywhere.' As my mother and I waked across the marble foyer, he added, 'I understand. Secrets between a mother and son are a beautiful thing.'

My mother closed the library door behind us. 'That was rude, Finn. We're guests.'

I was tired of being a guest. 'I have to tell you something you're not going to want to hear.'

My mother sat down in a gilded chair and stared at me. 'You got kicked out of school.'

'It's got nothing to do with school.'

My mother was so relieved she jumped up out of the chair and hugged me. 'Oh, my God, you scared me. That's all I've been hearing all fall. Gigi Meyer's son got kicked out of Deerfield for smoking pot. The McCallum boy got thrown out of Rollins. I've heard so many horror stories at the club, I just assumed the worst.' Her idea of the worst would have been almost funny if I didn't have that pistol in my pocket.

'So what is it I'm not going to like hearing?' My mother checked her makeup in the mirror and waited for me to disappoint her. I had plugged so many holes in our life with lies, I just wanted to know how it felt to be honest with her about something.

'I lied to you about Mrs Mars taking me to the Kennedys' for Thanksgiving. I never met the lady, her kid doesn't go to St Mark's, I made the whole thing up.'

'Why would you . . .' My mother shook her head in disbelief. She fumbled through her purse for a cigarette like she was searching for a lost gram.

'Because I didn't want to come here. Because I knew you'd think sucking up to a candy-bar billionaire and ass-licking my way into

298

Jackie Kennedy's was like winning the Nobel Prize. I told you what you wanted to hear. You love this shit.' I was waiting for her to get mad.

'I love you, Finn.'

'Please, don't give me "I did this all for you".'

'I did it for me, Finn. Not for you. It's easier for me to pretend here.'

'Pretend what?'

'That I'm safe.'

'From what?'

'From myself.' She lit a cigarette and looked away. For a second, I thought she was crying. If she'd had tears in her eyes, it would have spoiled it. But she wasn't embarrassed, or feeling sorry for herself, or making excuses. 'Where did you end up going for Thanksgiving?'

'Giacomo's. Then Maya called. We spent two nights at the Plaza.'

I expected her to ask me all sorts of questions. All she did was kiss me on the cheek and walk towards the door.

'You don't want to know how it was?'

My mother shook her head. 'It's yours.'

But it wasn't mine. Bryce had been there the whole time and I knew if I started telling her that, I'd have to tell her what I was planning. Even though I couldn't tell her everything, my mother and I had never been as close as we were at that moment. I didn't want to lose the feeling. I didn't want her to open the door, and let Bryce and his world come between us. And as weird and corny as it sounds, suddenly there was no one else I would rather have had for a mother. And at the heart of the uneasy warmth I felt for her, there was a certainty that she alone could help me understand why I felt so defeated.

It wasn't so much a question as a feeling I wanted her to help me with when I blurted out, 'It was wonderful, but sad.'

My mother put both her hands on my shoulders the way dads do in the movies and looked me in the eye. 'That is life.' We stood there like that for what seemed like a long time. She sensed I wanted more. She was about to say something when Bryce knocked on the door. It opened before either one of us were ready to say 'Come in'.

'Look who wanted to see you.' Bryce pushed his mother's wheelchair into the room. The fall from the burning window had broken most of the bones in the right side of her body. They said she'd walk . . . eventually. I was remembering the crunching sound I heard when I landed on top of her when I looked at her face. Blood-blister red and pasty white, it was marbled with skin grafts and scars. The tips of a handful of fingers were missing. And the white of one of her eyes was angry, red, and inflamed with blood – like the fire inside her wasn't out yet.

Bryce massaged her shoulders. 'The plastic surgery's not finished, but Mom looks great, doesn't she?'

'Great.' It was like in the car. I couldn't think of anything else to say.

My mother turned the wheelchair so Mrs Langley didn't have to look at herself in the mirror and tried to change the subject. 'How's the hip, Pilar?'

Mrs Langley ignored her. 'Dear Finn . . .' Her voice sounded like she'd smoked a million cigarettes before breakfast. 'How's my hero doing?'

Bryce answered for me, 'He's doing great – just look at him.' Bryce threw his arm around my shoulder.

'We've missed you, Finn.' Mrs Langley held out what was left of her hands for a hug. My mother could tell I didn't want to touch her.

'Bryce and Finn were just going skating.' She knew I wanted out of the room.

'Just one kiss to say thank you.' Bryce gently pushed me towards his mother. There was no escape. She smelled of ointment and lavender. Her red eye opened wide as she kissed me on the lips. 'I told Bryce to look out for you.'

'I'd be lost without him,' I said. We were all putting on a show, but it wasn't over yet. On cue, Bryce's father made his entrance. The shuffle was gone, but he still wasn't all there. I figured that's why he looked so happy.

'Bryce told me I've met you before, but I still have trouble remembering names.'

'I'm Finn. Nice to see you again, Mr Langley.'

Grinning like an idiot, he shook my hand.

'Finn can give us the update on Maya, Dad.'

'You've seen her?' Mrs Langley rasped. I wasn't expecting the question. Her husband was still shaking my hand. I didn't want to get her in trouble.

'We write to each other a lot.'

'Care of Monsieur Bouret.' Bryce knew I knew.

'Yeah.' I just wanted to get it over with. 'Time to skate, huh?'

'Looks that way.' Bryce had his arm around me again.

My mother stopped me as I started to leave. 'Are you going to be warm enough? Maybe you should borrow a parka.'

I told her I was fine as I was. The last thing she said to me was, 'It was good talking to you, Finn.' It was better than that.

'Come on, let's go.' Bryce was getting impatient.

'I have to go to the bathroom first.'

'Go in the woods.'

'I want to wash my hands.'

Bryce leaned forward and whispered in my ear. 'Do you do it before or after you touch your dick?'

I locked the powder room behind me and turned on the faucet. A framed photo of Osborne and Albert Schweitzer watched me as I pulled out the silver-plated revolver. Tarnished, and pitted with rust, it looked like the squirrels or mice had tried to make a meal of the ivory grips. I flipped open the cylinder and ejected the bullets. I had five shots left. It didn't matter that I hadn't been able to hit a glass bottle with a pear in it from five feet away. I had something more intimate in mind. I dry-fired at my reflection in the mirror. The action was stiff, but it seemed to work. It was weird, but I never once thought about chickening out. Courage had nothing to do with it. My desperation had peaked into calm fatalism.

When I looked at the cartridges in my hand, I didn't think about the impact they would have on flesh and bone. I only worried about them not going off. What if water had leaked inside the brass casings? What if the powder was wet? What if I pulled the trigger and nothing changed. I wiped the bullets with toilet paper, like that was going to do any good.

'What are you doing in there?' Bryce's voice shattered my calm. I dropped one of the bullets. It rolled behind the toilet. I had to get down on my hands and knees to reach it. My hands were shaking again.

'Be out in a second.' I flushed the toilet to make it seem more realistic. As I watched the water swirl down I tried to vomit, but nothing came up. I was cold-sweat green, the color of the frogs we dissected in bio class. Bloodless, I was just a heartbeat. I gave the room a blast of air freshener to cover the stench of myself.

Bryce looked at me when I came out. 'If you don't feel up to it, we can do this tomorrow.' He was courteous to the last.

'I'm good to go.' It was something I heard someone say in a war movie.

'That's the attitude.'

There were two sets of skates, and a couple of hockey sticks in the back of the truck. Bryce put the truck in low and we were on our way. It had stopped snowing, and the moon was up. New Jersey looked like a frozen planet. We got stuck in a drift on the farm road that leads to the lake. When I got out to push, I was careful not to give him the opportunity to back over me. I was right to think Bryce had something planned for me, but it was nothing as pedestrian as hit and run.

A sleepy herd of deer bolted as we turned into the pine forest that curtained the lake. The trees were so close together there was barely room for the truck to get through. Branches smacked and scraped at the sides of the pickup as Bryce accelerated through the trees. There was no point telling him to slow down. I gasped when he drove right out onto the ice. For an instant, I thought he was trying to drown us both.

'Relax. The ice is a foot thick here.' He killed the engine. As we glided to a stop he added, 'That's the place you have to worry about.' He pointed to a dark hole in the ice at the far end of the lake that was guarded by four long sawhorses. 'That's where the spring comes up, feeds the lake. Summer, winter, the temperature never changes. Constant thirty-seven degrees. Fall in there, and it's like going down on the *Titanic*.' I remembered feeling its chill in the heat of summer as I swam back to shore with Maya that night laughter chased us off the island.

Bryce had a regulation hockey rink all laid out, goals and everything. Maya told me her brother had been the first kid in the history of Harvard hockey to start on the varsity team as a freshman. The pros scouted him. It was funny, remembering Maya telling me he had quit because hockey was too violent. There was an inch of snow on the ice. We started walking towards a little John Deere tractor with a plow on it that was parked under a tarp. 'As soon as I Zamboni the ice, the lessons will begin.'

I knew I had to do it now. People would wonder why he bothered to clean the ice if he was going to kill himself. That was going to be my story. I had it all rehearsed. I was prepared for any question Gates, or Osborne, or Maya, or even my mother would ask after the tragedy.

I'd say he confessed to starting the fire, that he told me he couldn't live with himself, knowing he'd killed Paige and crippled his mother. Osborne and Gates would stop the questions after I took them aside and mentioned Bryce saying something crazy about having slept with his mom.

'Bryce, come here, I've got to talk to you about something.' Gloves off, he breathed into his cupped hands as he walked towards me. I needed him close to me when I pulled out the gun. His hands had to be on it. There would be blood and powder burns on both our hands. I'd blame myself for not being able to stop him. If the first bullet didn't kill him, I'd fire again, and say there was a struggle. Like I said, I had it all planned.

'What's the problem now?' Bryce had a cigarette in his mouth and was digging in his pocket for a light. I measured the distance between us. I wanted him just out of reach – close enough to grab for the pistol, but not close enough to get it away from me. It was my last chance. The moment had arrived. My finger was on the trigger. The gun had cleared my pocket. I leveled it to his heart just as he pulled out a Zippo lighter. A flame illuminated his face just at the moment he saw the gun. My finger closed on the trigger. Dropping the lighter, and lunging for the gun, his hands closed around mine. It was all perfect until I pulled the trigger.

Stunned that it didn't go off, I looked down. The hammer of the revolver had slammed home on Bryce's thumb. He hit me twice in the stomach then headbutted me hard enough to break my nose, then twisted the pistol free.

It was in Bryce's hands now. Exhilarated by the rush of fear, he looked at me, and the gun, and threw his head back and laughed. And as his laughter echoed across the frozen lake, I realized it was his cackle that had chased us from the island.

'You tried to kill me.'

He liked the idea. He smiled and cocked his head, pausing to relish a new sensation. 'Wow. This is a first time for me. Have you ever tried this before?'

'I know what you did.'

'I did a shitload of things.' Bryce picked up his lighter and lit a cigarette. 'You mean my boundary issues with my mother? For the record, she came on to me. Or do you mean me setting fire to the house with you inside? That was a hot one, wasn't it? Or, dear Finn, are you talking about . . .'

'Fuck you!' I screamed.

'No, I fucked you.' Bryce snapped open the cylinder of the revolver. 'Amazing. It's even loaded.'

Lunging at him, I just managed to get my hands around his neck before his knee slammed into my balls with enough force to lift me off the ground. Crumpling at his feet, clutching my crotch, I gagged on my hurt. When the pain subsided it was replaced by fear. He pressed the barrel of the pistol to my temple and pulled back the hammer. 'Now put on the skates.' I was finished, but he wasn't.

The padding was stiff and cold, and my socks were too thin. My fingers shook as I pulled them on. I remember they were made by a company called Bauer. As I laced them up he cautioned, 'Make sure they're tight, lambie. Don't want you breaking an ankle.'

Laced and knotted, he ordered me to stand up. Like I said, I'd never skated before. My ankles buckled, my arms windmilled. Just when I got my balance, he pushed me back down. He got his skates, two sticks and a hockey puck out of the truck. As he walked past, I tried to grab hold of his ankle. All I got for it was a boot to the side of the head. Bryce was lacing up now. When he began to whistle 'Holiday in Cambodia', I started to cry.

'Don't you want to know why I did it?' His voice was serious and soft.

'You're crazy.' I shouted.

'And you're normal? Your mother gives backrubs and you tell everybody she's a doctor who studied in Paris? And everybody believes you? Come on, Finn. They're crazy, not us.'

'I told Maya everything.' I was trying to scare him.

'No you didn't. Maya called me from the airport. She told me how you explained to her how hard it was for me to cover up for my mother starting the fire. Clever, though, pretending you were worried about me. Establishing the psychological strain, setting my sister up to think I killed myself. That was it, wasn't it?'

Maya had promised me she wouldn't call Bryce.

'Fuck you.'

'We've been through all that. Look, it's important to me that you know how we got here. It's not like I'm happy about this. I liked you. I still like you. But when I found out Grandpa gave you those rolls of film to develop, I mean, my mother and I didn't know about the motion detector by the bed in the playhouse. You can see I had to do something.'

'I never developed it. It's in the hot-water bottle in my closet. Bryce, you can have the film.'

'Have? It wasn't your film in the first place. But thanks for telling me where it is.' He put the muzzle of the pistol to my forehead and smiled down at me. 'You did this to yourself, Finn, sucking up to Grandpa the way you did, volunteering to develop his fuck pictures. In the old days, he never would have fallen for a pair of hustlers like you and your mother. Grandpa's getting old and soft. He swallows whatever people feed him. That's how I tricked him the night I nailed you. I slipped a sleeping pill in with all the rest of his meds that night. Chased it with Oreos and milk. The old bastard never knew I was gone. And while he dozed . . . you and I made – what's that expression? "First Contact."'

Bryce took the gun away from my head and scratched his chin thoughtfully with the end of the barrel. 'You know, Finn, none of this had to happen. You and your mother just wouldn't leave. I wasn't counting on you being able to keep it a secret. I tried to give you the hint. I mean, you've got to admit, Finn, your average kid who gets the shit beat out of them and cornholed tells his mother, or at least has a nervous breakdown. At first, I thought you must have liked it. But when I saw how you and your yummy mummy worked it for a free ride at St Mark's, and a dollar-a-year lease . . . and then coming here with a gun? It's a cliché, but true: what doesn't kill you makes you stronger.' My mind couldn't get past the reminder I'd been cornholed.

'Why did you have to . . .'

'Come on, say it out loud, Finn. You'll feel better. Why did I fuck you?' Bryce waited for me to give him the satisfaction of saying it, not realizing my humiliation was already complete. He pressed on. 'Initially, my plan was just to beat you up, hurt you enough to scare you off. But when I looked down at you, unconscious, the feed bag over your head, you were so helpless, more helpless than you are now, you were so utterly at my mercy, I just had to see what it would feel like. I mean, everybody wonders what it would be like to do whatever you wanted. But how many follow the urge to the end of the street? To take whatever you want, not have to ask for it, or pay for it, or write thank-you notes. To own your own hunger is . . .'

He realized he was talking to himself. 'Let's leave it at enlightening.' Bryce put the pistol in his belt and skated towards me, and tossed me a hockey stick. 'Pick it up. It'll help you keep your balance.'

I stayed on my knees and picked up the stick. When he came close, I swung it at him and missed. As he skated around me, knees bent, body limber, stick in hand, his inhuman ease was visible. Gliding first backwards, then forwards, just the sound of his blades on the ice, he came closer and closer. 'It's game time, Finn.' When he did a little pirouette just to show off, I threw the hockey stick at him. He caught it with his left hand and braked in front of me, his skates showered me with an icy spray, then spun around behind me and

jerked me to my feet. 'Just relax,' he whispered. 'I won't let you fall.'
Each time I twisted around to grab him, he pushed me further out on
the ice. I caught hold of his hair for a second, but he just twisted free
and skated off. Ankles wobbling, I tried to skate away. But before I'd
gone three feet, he was back. Arms around me, strangely gentle,
making sure I didn't fall, he pushed me further and further from
shore. I knew he was taking me to the black hole where the water
never freezes.

There was no dignity to my desperation in those last minutes. I
screamed, I pleaded, I cried. Begging 'til my throat was raw,
I promised if he stopped pushing me towards the hole in the ice,
I'd drop out of St Mark's, I'd make my mother leave Vlyvalle,
and he'd never hear from us again. Bryce just smiled and pushed
me down so he could move the sawhorse away from the hole in
the ice.

'Finn, we both know you'd come back.'

'Jesus Christ, Bryce, there's nothing for me here. I know that
now.'

'What about Maya?'

'I don't care about your sister. I just want to get out of here.'
Nothing I said surprised him but that. He looked at me with
real disappointment. My willingness to betray Maya caught him
so off-guard, he grabbed hold of the sawhorse to steady
himself. He was about to say something when I lunged at
the other end of the barricade. The board he was holding onto
hit him just below the belt. He slipped backwards and tried to
catch himself.

Scrambling on all fours, I pushed on my end with all my might.
His skate caught, the sawhorse toppled, and he was free. Standing
there, catching his breath, he hacked up a mouthful of gob. Just as
his spit hit my face, we heard the ice beneath him crack. He plunged
straight down into the water. He disappeared completely, then
surfaced, clawing at the ice and shaking his head like a bear.
Grabbing hold of the barricade with one hand, he'd half pulled
himself out of the water when I slammed the hockey stick across his
wrist.

'I'm going to fucking kill you.'

'No, Bryce, I'm going to kill you.' I pulled the sawhorse away from the edge of the hole. Each time he got his chest up onto the ice, I pushed him back, checking the hockey stick against his throat. His hair was starting to freeze. 'Don't you want to tell me?' I mimicked him without thinking.

'Tell you what, motherfucker?' His lips were turning blue.

'Actually, Bryce, you're the motherfucker.' He smiled and stopped clawing at the ice.

'What do you want to know?' His teeth chattered.

'Why did you start the fire with your mother in the house?'

He looked at me like I'd asked the stupidest question in the world. 'My dad was coming home.'

I nodded like it made sense, and pushed him out into the middle of the spring hole with the hockey stick. I wasn't killing a person, I was drowning a monster. It was amazing how long he could tread water with skates on. He inhaled a mouthful of water, gagged, coughed, gasped for breath, and began to flail wildly. When I saw his eyes brightening with panic, I felt a rush of adrenalin. The exhilaration warmed me. I didn't want to miss a second of his suffering. He was drowning and I wasn't. I felt stronger as he grew more desperate. And when I heard him gag on the word 'Help', I got to my feet.

Balancing myself with the hockey stick, careful to keep my ankles stiff, I started to skate. 'Thanks for the lesson, Bryce.' It was almost all over for both of us.

When he sputtered out the words, 'I was right about you, you're just like me,' I looked back at him.

'No, I'm not, Bryce.'

'Your mother even said it.'

If he hadn't mentioned her, it all would have been different. 'Shut the fuck up about my mother,' I shouted. Lifting the hockey stick up over my head, I wanted to silence him once and for all. As I brought the stick down, he let go of the ice. The face I wanted to smash smiled up to me as he slipped below the water. He'd had the last word after all. Now I was like him, and my mother . . . every word I spoke to her for the rest of my life would be part of the lie I would have to tell her when I got back to Osborne's and told them Bryce had drowned. Once again, I was helpless. He had beaten me.

It wasn't a change of conscience or an attack of guilt that made me drop to my knees and scramble to the ice and reach into the numbing darkness of the hole. It was rage at being fucked one last time. I heard the ice crack beneath me as I ducked my head into the water. The cold hammered my temples. I could see him in the sepia murk of the lake below, floating just out of reach, eyes wide open but seeing nothing, his white silk scarf billowed up above him. The cold paralyzed my fingers. I felt its silky smoothness, but could not grab hold. I reached into the hole with my other hand, caught hold of the scarf and tried to pull him up. Determined to bring me down with him, Bryce went limp. The ice gave way beneath my chest. I felt the lake embrace me. In the end there would be no difference between us. We would both be dead. I felt the cold tighten around my heart and still I held on. Then I felt something else. A hand clamped around first one ankle, then the other. Slowly we were being pulled up onto the ice. Someone was shouting. My ears were too cold to hear what. I was gasping for breath. When I looked back, I saw Osborne. The heels of his hobnailed boots dug into the ice, inch by inch he pulled me back onto the frozen surface of the lake. The veins bulged purple under his yellow skin. Tears streamed down his face, and snot ran from his nose. I could hear him clearly now.

'Let go, I can't save you both.' He was weak and old, and he looked like a cadaver, but the way he said it, I knew Osborne wanted me to let Bryce drown. I had Bryce's head out of the water now. I could have let him go, I could have blamed it on Osborne. It would have been easy.

I'm still not sure how or why I was able to pull Bryce up out of the water and onto the ice. I guess it was my only way to show myself I wasn't like him.

Bryce lay wide-eyed and motionless between us. His lips frozen in a childish smirk, his gaze focused on a wild darkness that was beyond our appreciation. Osborne's sleigh was only twenty feet away. How much had he heard? How much had he seen? As the old man gasped for breath, all he said to me was, 'We're going to pay for this.' Then he raised his hands up over his head, balled them up into a fist, and slammed them down on Bryce's chest again and again and again. He kept hitting Bryce, even after lake water gurgled up out of his mouth like a clogged drain and his focus returned to earth.

40

When I woke up the next morning, it was two o'clock in the afternoon and I was in the hospital. My mother was sitting on the edge of the bed, watching *Speed Racer* with the sound off on the TV that hung from the ceiling. She was crying. Osborne slept with his glasses on in a chair in the corner of the room.

'Mom . . . I'm all right.'

They had treated me for hypothermia and frostbite the night before. Walter Pickle had driven all three of us to the hospital.

'I know, lambie,' my mother whispered, careful not to wake Osborne. 'I was just thinking about how we used to watch cartoons together. It's silly, but it made me sad that I couldn't remember the name of Speed Racer's brother.'

'Racer X.'

'It's good I have you to remember for me.'

I pulled the Saran Wrap off a plate of chocolate-chip cookies she had brought me, ate two, and started to chug a carton of milk when she asked, 'What was Bryce doing so close to the hole in the ice?'

'You know Bryce.' It's hard to make people safe without lying.

'Osborne said you saved him.'

'We both fell. I was just trying to save myself.'

'Well, you're all lucky to be alive. Especially Bryce.'

'How is he?'

'Osborne had his helicopter fly him to a New York hospital for tests. He was underwater for so long, they weren't sure if there was any permanent damage. But he sounds fine. He called here an hour ago.'

'What did he say?' The sharpness of my voice woke Osborne up.

'Oh, you know Bryce. Everything's a joke.'

311

'What did he say, though?'

'Something about, he still owes you a skating lesson. But you listen to me, young man. If you ever go skating on that lake again . . .'

'There won't be any more skating lessons.'

Osborne sneezed twice and blew his nose. My mother told Osborne, 'You should be in bed.'

'Haven't you heard? I've decided to live for-ever. Want to see how it all turns out.' My mother laughed. Osborne bit into a chocolate chip cookie. 'Liz, if it's not too much bother, could you get us some more milk?' There was an unopened carton on the table. My mother was getting good at taking hints.

As soon as she left the room, Osborne lit a cigar. 'I bet you think I made a mess of things.'

'Not exactly.'

'Well, we'll see how you do.' Osborne blew a smoke ring and looked at the age spots that ticked his hands. 'Christ, I've got skin like a crocodile.' As if he were imagining what that would be like, he pulled back his gums and snapped his teeth together a few times. I was waiting for him to tell me something that would make me feel safe.

'What the hell do you suppose that was about, him wanting to "own his own hunger?"' Osborne had watched us. I should have been shocked, but I wasn't.

'I don't know.'

'Well, neither do I, that's why I'm talking to you. Jesus, a dog owns its own hunger.'

'I guess he was just trying to face up to what was in him. He once told me it all boiled down to fuck/kill. That's why he liked the Fierce People.'

Osborne stunned me when he recited from one of my father's books. '"A small, primitive tribe in a remote corner of Amazonia who offer us a unique glimpse into what it means to be human."'

Osborne blew his nose again and chuckled. 'Vlyvalle without money.' We both thought about that for a moment. Then he asked, 'You think he would have been different if he'd been someone else's grandson?'

'Well, he wouldn't have had a free ride to the end of the street.'

'What happens when you get there?'

'You still want more.'

'Between my daughter and Bryce, I fathered quite a tribe.'

'You can't always buy people what they need.'

'Lord, I knew Bryce was off . . . I lost him a long time ago, years before I found you. If he was a company, I would have sold him for a loss. Not that easy with people.' When Osborne's cigar went out, he realized he was talking to himself. 'You don't think money makes people happy, do you?'

'Not now I don't.'

'That's too bad.' Osborne looked at his watch. 'Christ. I gotta see a bunch of lawyers who're going to tell me I'm crazy.' He put a handful of chocolate-chip cookies in his pocket as he opened the door. The last thing he said to me was, 'You'll do fine, Finn. Just stay away from the Fierce People.'

41

Knowing I wasn't ever going to be safe made it less scary . . . sort of. I tried to think of it like I was a smoker, and Bryce, like cancer, was out there somewhere. That doesn't mean I stopped worrying. A kid in my Spanish class, whose older brother went to Harvard, told me Bryce hadn't gone back to Boston. When I asked my mother about it, she said Osborne fixed it so Bryce could finish his fall semester by mail.

Osborne called me my second day back in school from his jet. It was a bad connection. When I asked him about Bryce all he said was, 'Can't hear you. Static.' Funny, I heard him perfectly clear. Then he shouted, 'We leave for Switzerland on the 26th.' It was like it never happened.

'What if I flunk all my exams?'

'I'll make you fly tourist.'

It was funny, but I didn't laugh. 'I'm worried about Bryce.'

'So am I. I'm handling it. I'll get back to you on everything when I touch down.'

Maya called that same day. Osborne had told her we'd fallen through the ice. But from the way she said, 'Serves Bryce right,' I could tell he hadn't made a big deal out of it. When she asked me why I wasn't more excited about the ski trip, all I could think to say was, 'Can't hear you. Static.' When she repeated the question in a shout I whispered, 'I still love you,' and hung up and waited for Osborne to call back.

Osborne didn't get back to me that day or the next or the day after that. I left messages for him at Vlyvalle and at the office he never went to in New York – still no word. My mother thought he'd flown south to clear his cold, only because she'd heard him tell the butler to pack his Madras shorts.

While everyone else at St Mark's crammed for exams, I stared blankly at my textbooks and outlines and silently raged at Osborne for abandoning me. The more I thought about everything he'd said since I pulled Bryce onto the ice, the more pissed off I was. 'Stay away from the Fierce People'? 'I'm handling it'? How? Was he fucking senile, or did he just not give a shit? The Cliff Notes I bought went uncracked. Even Giacomo, armed with a prescription for Ritalin – which he chose to snort rather than swallow – studied more than I did.

Exams started December 15. The tests were two hours long, and they counted for half your grade. They made a big deal of it, and it was a big deal – if you didn't want to flunk out. It occurred to me that's what I was trying to do, but that's beside the point.

They filled the gyms up with tables and chairs, and made you write your answers in these little blue pamphlets they called Blue Books. And even though they were always going on about the honor system and the importance of trust, the whole set-up was based on the assumption that if they gave a kid half a chance, he'd cheat his ass off. Everybody had to take the same test at the same time to prevent the more enterprising students from selling the questions. And an empty chair was placed between each kid, making it impossible to copy off your neighbor without binoculars.

My first exam was algebra:

1. What is the sum of all the numbers between one and a million?

I knew there was some formula some French guy had come up with a couple hundred years ago when his teacher had made him stay after school and add up all the numbers between one and a hundred. I could have done one to a hundred the slow way: 1+1=2, 2+3=5, 5+4=9 . . . but up to a million? I had two hours, not two weeks.

2. What is the sum of the following infinite series:
$1 + (1/2 \times 1) = (1/2 \times 1\frac{1}{2} > \times 1) + \ldots$

Even if I hadn't been too pissed off at Osborne to study, I couldn't have figured out that one. Not wanting to waste time on what I didn't know, I moved on.

3. Simplify and solve:
   $sin(17)cos(13)+cos(17)sin(13)$

By the time my algebra teacher announced, 'Gentlemen, you have one hour left,' I'd given up trying to add the numbers between one and a million, and was concentrating on what I was going to tell Osborne when I finally saw him. I was so busy composing my big 'Fuck You', I didn't notice the dean walk over to our table until I heard Giacomo scrambling to get his loafers back on. I was sure he was going to get busted for the crib sheets he had hidden inside his shoes, when the dean suddenly clamped his Vulcan death grip onto my neck and whispered, 'Take your exam and follow me.'

Since I hadn't even bothered to cheat, I knew it had to be Osborne. As pathetic as it sounds, in a millisecond I forgot all about the rant I'd been rehearsing. The old man hadn't forgotten me. I knew all I had to do was whisper in his ear and he'd save my ass. I could work it so the dean would leave us alone. Osborne didn't give a shit about exams. He'd think it was funny. Christ, if he fixed it so Bryce could take his exams by mail, he could do the same for me. I'd be able to study now. Everything was going to be OK. I was smiling as the door closed behind us and the dean said, 'Mr Osborne is dead.'

Instead of crying or asking how it happened, or shouting 'No!' the old reptile inside my head mumbled: 'I think . . . I need to go to the bathroom.' The dean thought I was going to get sick, and pushed me towards the men's room. I went straight to a stall, locked the door, and flushed my exam and my empty blue book down the toilet. I was neither ashamed nor proud of my deceit. All I knew was, with Osborne gone, I had no one to break the rules for me.

When I came out of the bathroom, the headmaster was there, too. 'What am I supposed to do now?'

The headmaster told me, 'There's a plane waiting for you at the airport.'

316

That wasn't what I meant. 'Who sent it?' I knew it wasn't Mrs Langley, or Bryce. Maya?

'Mr Osborne's attorney.'

The dean volunteered to drive me to the airport. The headmaster said he'd do it. I could tell they weren't sure whether they still had to be nice to me. As the two of them watched me pack a suitcase, I wondered if Osborne had already given them the money for the library he had promised in return for accepting me.

We were just getting in to the headmaster's Volvo when the dean said, 'Your exam.'

'What?'

'Your blue book. I told you to take it with you.'

'I gave it to you, sir, before I went to the bathroom. Don't you remember?' The dean looked at me like I was trying to sneak out of the country without a passport as he patted down his pockets. 'You gotta have it!' My story was bullshit, but the panic in my voice was genuine. 'I wasn't finished, but I was doing well.' I didn't give a shit about the exam. It was just a way to keep me from thinking about what I was going home to. 'Let's go back and look for it.' I didn't want to go back to Vlyvalle.

When I started to run back to the gym, the headmaster grabbed me. 'We'll sort this out after Mr Osborne's funeral.' Bryce would be there. And without Osborne . . .

I was surprised they'd sent a plane for me. When I saw Osborne's black Gulf Stream jet warmed up and waiting for me on the tarmac, I was stunned. It all seemed like a bad joke. It cost, like, five thousand dollars an hour to run the G3. Osborne's attorney hadn't sent the plane. Osborne had wanted me to have one last ride. But why? Did he think it would be funny to give me a final taste of the high life before it all vanished? Or did he do it just to piss off some big-shot who'd think the Langleys would send the big bird to take them to Osborne's final send-off? The Vice-President? No, he had his own plane. His wife? Making the woman who cut his balls off fly commercial would have appealed to Osborne's sense of humor. My mind explored every oblique angle of the situation, except the one that cut the deepest. My friend was dead.

The cabin was close with his aroma: Cuban cigars, medication, and Bay Rum. His weight indented the swiveling captain's chair he sat in. The leather headrest was dark and pomaded with the oil he used to slick back what was left of his hair. I buckled my seatbelt and started to cry as we took off.

When I looked down, the school grew even smaller than it was below me. Smaller still was that part of me that wondered between sobs at eight thousand feet 'I wonder if he left me anything?'

Forty-two minutes later, we were circling Vlyvalle. Everything had melted. The co-pilot said it was seventy degrees on the ground. The runway was pooled with water, and spotted with geese. The snow was all gone, the ice was out of the lake, but the black hole was still there.

As I got out of the plane I braced myself for the sight of my mother, and the 'Oh-lambie-it's-so-sad' sob I knew she'd greet me with. But she surprised me; she wasn't there. And when I called from the hangar, all I got was her Audrey Hepburn imitation on the answering machine.

The pilot dropped me off at the yellow house. The front door was open. The pink suitcase that used to embarrass me was packed and waiting in the front hall. All the rest of our stuff was crammed into cardboard boxes. I knew she'd thrown the golf bag Dr Leffler had given her from the second-floor landing from the way the clubs lay scattered on the floor. My mother sat frozen at the kitchen table, an uncorked wine bottle and a full glass at her fingertips. It had been there long enough for a moth to drown. 'Sorry I couldn't pick you up at the plane.' Her voice was flat, and her makeup was streaked with tears. She hadn't had a sip, but she looked like she'd been on a three-day bender. Before I could say something smart she explained, 'They took the car back this morning.'

My mother handed me a letter from Mrs Langley's secretary.

Dear Miss Earl,

This letter is to inform you that your services will no longer be required. Since your lease was contingent upon your employment, we would appreciate it if you could have the house vacated by January 1. Someone will be by to pick up the Peugeot on Monday morning. Your son's tuition at St Mark's has already been paid for the entire year. Whether or not you keep him in school is entirely your decision. But we have instructed the school that any additional school costs, transportation, extracurricular activities, etc., will be billed to you. I have included two weeks' severance pay.

Thank you for your cooperation.

Betsy Dunne

I looked at the paycheck that was paperclipped to the letter. I never knew Osborne paid her two thousand dollars a week. What would have seemed like a lot suddenly seemed like a very little.

'They didn't waste any time.'

'What do you mean "they"?'

'Mrs Langley, Bryce . . .'

'You pulled Bryce out of the lake, you saved Mrs Langley from the fire, why would they want to . . .'

I took the glass and the wine bottle to the kitchen sink. As I poured them down the drain, I began to explain.

The sun had set by the time I finished. The ashtray was full – we'd smoked a pack and a half of cigarettes between us. You're supposed to feel better when you finally tell the truth. I just felt empty. My mother lit the last cigarette in the pack, then passed it to me. We held hands as we smoked it down to the filter.

42

There are no taxis in Vlyvalle. Gates drove us to the funeral in his green and white patrol car. Me, scared in front, watching him split pumpkin seeds with his gold tooth and gob them into a Styrofoam cup; my mother, cold sober and fucked up in the back seat behind the wire grille; both of us wishing we were going somewhere else – everything, and nothing, had changed since Chief Gates first drove us into Vlyvalle.

Gates took the long way through the farm. Across the metal bridge and up through the woods where Maya had first pegged me as a poacher. Stripped of its green, winter had rendered the forest transparent. The red barns and their silos, Osborne's pillared mansion with its fountain, the charred skeleton that had been Maya's pink palace, the playhouse by the falls – nothing in this universe was more than a quarter-mile from the road. How could I still feel so lost?

I tried to shake the feeling by focusing on Osborne. It was his funeral, not mine. I wanted to remember him how he really was when he was alive, not just replay the sound of his Foghorn Leghorn voice, or wax nostalgic about the first time I laid eyes on him stepping out of his black Bentley convertible in his bathrobe and unlaced hiking boots to taste the feed corn. But as hard as I tried to concentrate on the man I was going to say goodbye to, I found myself thinking only of how I would say hello to Maya when we got to the church where the service was being held. Should I hug her first, or kiss her on the lips? Would I be able to get her alone? Would it be like it was at the Plaza? Would I feel less cheated once we were naked?

As I tried to conjure up what I needed to hear her whisper in my ear, I was interrupted yet again. This time it was Bryce who pushed Osborne into the back of my brain. Bryce would be at the funeral, too. How would I greet him? I knew he wouldn't say or do anything there, but he would let me know it was just a matter of time. I hadn't even seen him, and already I could feel him pushing me back towards the black hole.

But before I could work myself into a genuine panic about Bryce, my mind moved on again. And for no reason that made any fucking sense, suddenly all I could think about was Walter Pickle and his pigs. What would happen to the Pilgrim swine he and Osborne had tried so hard to save from extinction? Why did it seem so sad I'd never bothered to go see them when I had the chance?

We were on the paved county road now. The church was still more than a mile away, but the traffic was already bumper to bumper with mourners. I expected the stretch limousines and black town cars from the city filled with the children and the grandchildren of the men Osborne had made rich. And I was as unimpressed when the cop radio in Gates' dashboard crackled that the Vice-President's helicopter was *en route* as I was by the cortège of bogus country squires in their mud-spattered BMWs and Mercedes. What startled me was the parade of farmers and dairymen and grooms and gardeners in pickup trucks and four-by-fours, and a Plymouth with mismatched fenders I recognized from the help's parking lot at the Hunt Club.

Gates turned on the flashing light of his cherry-top and we passed them all on the shoulder of the road. When a GTO with racing slicks tried to do the same, Gates picked up his microphone and announced over the loudspeaker, 'Get back in line, Dwayne.' Jilly sat so close to him she had to be straddling his stick shift.

'Who invited everybody?'

'Funerals are open to the public.' Gates took off his hat and rubbed his freshly shaved head. 'There's a reception up at the house afterwards that's invitation only. Mrs Langley's list.' I could tell by the way he said it he wasn't invited either.

'He told us he was going to live for ever. Remember, Finn?' My mother still hadn't forgiven Osborne for dying.

'I guess he changed his mind about wanting to see how it all turned out.'

Gates spit a husk out the window. 'Maybe he already knew.'

*　　*　　*

321

Out of the patrol car and in the shadow of the steeple, I watched couples and families hurry into the church to get a good seat. Organ music wafting out from inside the church provided a princely soundtrack to the moment. I didn't know the names of all the faces my mother had called 'friends' when she played golf at the club. But I recognized them now. They looked away when they saw us, and pretended to be too sad to make small talk. Those who had kissed my mother's cheeks, and more, now gave her the snub. Dr Leffler practically broke into a run to avoid eye contact. The Lazard Freres partner with his neatly planted hairplugs – who I'd once watched my mother go down on from my bedroom window – walked across a grave to get out of having to greet us. Word was out – we weren't just moving away: we didn't exist. As far as Vlyvalle was concerned, Pharaoh was dead, and we were being buried with him.

We sat in the last pew, with Gates and his wife. Marcus was away at college. My mother had taken one of the engraved programs they handed out at the door. Bryce was scheduled to speak right after the hymn 'All Things Bright and Beautiful'. I made room so Walter Pickle could sit down next to me. He wore a plaid jacket and a tie as wide and soiled as a napkin. The church was packed, and flowers cascaded from every surface that could hold a silver urn. A choir was singing, and I heard somebody say the minister was a bishop. Secret Service men stood at the exits. The Vice-President sat alone in the first pew, looking solemnly sad. Was he missing Osborne? Or the good times that rolled when they both had their prostates? Or was he just missing the checkbook?

Every time the door in the back of the chapel opened, I and everybody else in the church looked back in unison to see if it was the Langleys. Between Maya and Bryce – I so dreaded and longed for their arrival – it took longer than you'd think for me to notice that instead of a coffin, there was a large TV set in front of the altar.

'Where is he?' I whispered to Gates.

'Cremated him last night.' From the way Gates' wife squeezed her husband's hand, I could tell he was pissed off.

Walter Pickle parked the wad of Red Man he had in his cheek into a bandanna and forgot to whisper. 'I saw Mrs Langley toss the ashes down into the trout pool in front of the playhouse this morning.'

Osborne's wife was the first of the clan to step into the church. She paused in the doorway and waited for everybody to get a glimpse of her in black cashmere trimmed in mink. She looked less like Cruella de Vil and more like an old lady than I remembered. Then she turned her back to tease the crowd and reached out to someone just out of my view. Bryce? No, it was Maya she had chosen to accessorize her entrance.

Maya wore a velvet hat that looked like a turban and a double strand of pearls I'd seen draped around her mother in photographs. Her hair was wet, and her black dress was midnight blue and rumpled. Its couture label stuck up against the nape of her neck, and there was a run in one of her stockings. She was even paler and thinner than she had been at the Plaza; her red lipstick just missed the outline of her lips – she looked like an expensive doll someone had dressed in a hurry.

I leaned forward to catch her eye. She never looked in my direction. Staring straight ahead, as if she saw something in the distance that I missed, she passed right by me. The whispers were deafening as she walked her grandmother down the aisle. Mrs Osborne stopped at every other pew to reach out a multi-carated hand to somebody important. It was like she was taking a victory lap. All that was missing was a high-five. She was the last one standing. After the fourth or fifth time Osborne's wife paused to accept her condolences with triumph, Maya's lower lip began to tremble. She put her hands to her face to hide her tears and walked the rest of the way down the aisle by herself. Slumping in the corner of the family pew, Maya sobbed out loud. The crowd liked it when the Vice-President leaned over and patted her on the back like a stray dog.

Mr Langley walked down the aisle by himself. Elegantly funereal in an impeccably tailored black suit, his smile flickered on and off his face like a broken light. He didn't know whether he was at a wedding or a funeral, but he was having fun.

I wasn't. My mouth was dry, and I had begun to hyperventilate in anticipation of Bryce pushing his mother's wheelchair into the church. What was taking them so long? Were they having trouble getting the wheelchair out of the limousine, or up the steps? The congregation went suddenly silent when Mrs Langley finally came

323

through the door. No wheelchair, not even a cane, she stood on her own two feet. Her skirt was above her knees. Dark stockings hid the burns on her legs. She walked so slowly, she seemed to float. The broad brim of her silk hat was tilted to one side, its veil curtained the scars and skin grafts that made one half of her face look like it belonged on a butcher's block. The half of her smile you saw was still flawless.

I was still looking for Bryce when the minister who was a bishop climbed into the pulpit and said, 'Let us pray . . .' I got down on my knees but I kept my eyes open for Bryce.

As we stood to sing the first hymn an oak door behind the choir opened and someone ducked into the church. I couldn't see for sure, but Bryce was with us, I could feel it. My mother put her arm around me, and sang hoarsely in my ear. The Vice-President read from the New Testament. Every time he said the word 'Jesus' it sounded like he'd just hit his thumb with a hammer. The pews groaned, and feet shuffled and someone dropped a hymnal as we stood up again and started singing 'All Things Bright and Beautiful'. Bryce was up next in the program.

No one was more stunned than I when the pulpit remained empty, and Bryce flickered to life on the TV screen in front of the altar.

'I'm sorry I can't be there with all of you in person on this sad day. I hope you understand; I know Grandpa would.' Bryce's voice seemed to be coming from everywhere, and nowhere. I strained with the others to get a better look at this apparition. From the whispers that passed from pew to pew, it was clear I wasn't the only one who expected a personal appearance. Bryce's face was in sharp focus, but the background was a rippling blur of brown and green. You couldn't tell where he was. All you saw was that he was sunburned and wasn't wearing a jacket, or even a tie. 'Ogden C Osborne believed in helping people. He took pleasure in leveling the field and tipping the scales. And in this, there is a lesson it is important for all of us to remember as we mourn his passing.' Sweat trickled down Bryce's forehead. His white, short-sleeved shirt was soaked through. It seemed as if he was broadcasting live from hell, even after my eye followed the cables from the TV screen to the one-inch video machine by the organist.

'My grandfather believed in changing people's lives.' Wherever the hell he was, Bryce was still running for office. 'He taught me the thrill of giving.' Bryce paused to look sad as he squinted into the sun. 'The satisfaction that comes of giving of one's self to those less fortunate.' The camera still loved him. 'Last summer I had the privilege of working with my grandfather, creating the first Langley halfway house. We built it in Newark, just down the road and in another world from where you are all sitting right now.' It was unbelievable. He was actually making them feel guilty. 'A few weeks before his death, my grandfather gave me the chance to make a difference to a world and a people who aren't simply under-privileged, but who are in danger of extinction.'

The camera pulled back. The strip of brown was a river. The green was a jungle. My heart stopped when I saw the pointed quills that pierced the cheeks of the naked children playing in the shallows behind him. The river was the Orinoco. Bryce was with the Yanomamö.

Bryce's words after that were drowned out by the memory of the last time I saw Osborne when he left me in the hospital, his pockets full of chocolate-chip cookies, cautioning me. 'You'll do fine, Finn. Just stay away from the Fierce People.' I knew Osborne had engineered this ultimate adventure for Bryce, to protect me. But what power was keeping Bryce there now? Neither Bryce's words nor his expression gave me any clue.

Bryce sniffed sadly on the TV screen. Seemingly overcome with emotion, he bowed his head and blew his nose on a clean hand-kerchief. I could see he'd been snorting *enebbe*. But his humility was so superior, the look in his eyes so glazed with inspiration, the fear and hatred I felt for him were spiked with a strange admiration. He was saying something now about tens of thousands of acres of land the 'Osborne Family of Companies' held the mineral rights and oil leases to being turned into a Rhode Island-sized preserve for the Fierce People. Slack-jawed and nauseous with the ways of the world, I watched Bryce smile into the camera as he casually draped his arm around the shoulder of a naked twelve-year-old Yanomamö madonna who nursed her baby on her breast as she played with a shiny new axe. 'Thank you, Grandpa, for everything.' Bryce did everything but wink.

When the screen went black, the congregation sang one last hymn and gossiped between verses about Bryce. None of them understood what he was doing, but they all agreed it was a wonderful thing, just as long as Bryce didn't do anything crazy and decide to bring the little brown people to Vlyvalle. I always knew deep down inside I was never going to get to see the Yanomamö. In one last burst of panic, I wondered if I should call my father, warn him of a shaman called Bryce. No, my father could take care of himself better than me. After all, he was an expert on fierce people.

My mother and Gates walked ahead to the patrol car while I waited outside the church for Maya. The maroon stretch Mercedes pushed me out of the way as it pulled up to the family. The driver told me to step back as he opened the door for them. Maya's back was to me as she came out of the church. I reached and grabbed for her hand, but there were too many people in the way. When I called out her name, everyone turned to look at me but her.

Mr Langley was the only who seemed glad to see me. As he reached out to shake my hand, he said. 'I'm sorry, I can't remember your name, but I know I've met you.' Mrs Langley pushed Maya into the back of the big Mercedes. The driver took Mr Langley's elbow and turned him to the car. The door slammed, and someone inside clicked the electric locks. Were they locking her in, or locking me out? As the limo pulled away from the church, I ran alongside of it, pounding on the smoked rear window, shouting, 'Maya, stop! We've got to talk.' The limousine jerked to a halt. Slowly, Maya turned her head to face me. The tint of the two-inch thick bulletproof glass made her look as perfect and beautiful and lifeless and untouchable as a wildflower trapped in amber.

When Mrs Langley barked to the driver 'What the hell are you waiting for?' the limousine lurched into gear and I was left panting and frantic on the roadside, like an abandoned pet.

Gates pulled up. My mother slid over so I could sit in the front with them. After a few miles, my mother decided to break the silence. I had no idea what I was going to do until she asked, 'What did they have to say?'

'They want me to come to the reception up at the house.'

43

The wrought-iron gates in front of Osborne's mansion were closed. A uniformed guard with a guestlist was checking names.

'Is there a problem, Chief?'

'Not yet.' The chief spit a husk at the guard's feet, and the bars opened. Gates knew I wasn't invited, and my mother understood why I had to go. As we turned into the Belgian block circle, I saw the guard step back into the gatehouse and pick up the phone. As we pulled up under the pillared portico in front of the empty fountain, Gates warned me, 'This is as far as I can take you.'

My mother grabbed my hand as I started to get out. 'Be careful.' We all knew it was too late for that.

I didn't know what they had done to Maya, but I was certain we were both in need of rescue. I told myself if Mrs Langley hadn't been there, if they'd just let Maya out of the goddamn limousine, if I could just steal a moment alone with her, I was sure we could magically stumble on a word or a kiss that would somehow give us a chance to make it feel right again.

An old-fashioned wooden wagon-wheel with a broken spoke, festooned with lilies and a black bow, hung on the front door. I didn't know what it meant, but I saw the stained-glass window above it, and the words *Ex Malo Bonum*. I hoped Osborne was right.

The door opened before I knocked. Mrs Langley greeted me with 'You're not welcome in this house.'

'Where is she?' The front hall was crowded with the top end of the food chain; millionaires sucking up to billionaires. Nobody looked very sad.

'If you don't leave now . . .' She stepped out onto the welcome mat and closed the door behind her. '. . . I'll have to call the police – and I don't mean Gates.'

'Fine. Let's call them. Probably be good for both of us to get this out in the open.' I thought I had nothing left to lose.

Mrs Langley put her face so close to mine, I thought she was going to bite me. Trembling with rage, she lifted her veil and glared at me with her watery red eye. 'You really think it's wise to have me as an enemy?'

'I know I don't want to have you as a friend.' I looked down at the ground, half expecting her to hit me. The toe of one of her black, velvet Belgian slippers was smudged gray with Osborne's ashes.

'You know, Finn, if you had come to me, instead of my father with your . . .' She licked her lips as she searched for the right expression. '. . . sad story, you could have had anything you asked for . . . within reason.'

'You don't have anything I want.'

'Oh yes I do.' She smiled as she rolled down her veil and opened the door for me – the picture of hospitality. 'You'll find her in the billiard room on the third floor.'

The billiard table was still a jumbled mound of old photographs, but the chaos had spread. The thousands of family pics I had catalogued with envy and neatly filed away in curatorial boxes over the summer now lay scattered across the floor. Whether Osborne had made the mess or just not lived long enough to clean it up was not important to me anymore. All I cared about was the fact that Maya was on her hands and knees, crawling and softly weeping as she foraged through snapshots, glossies, studio portraits and Polaroids of a past she could neither reclaim nor make sense of.

'What are you looking for?' She didn't look up when I stepped into the room.

'Did I call you?' Was she pretending, or was she really more interested in looking at that eight-by-twelve of her and Bryce in a hot-air balloon over the Serengeti than in meeting my gaze?

'No, but I thought . . .' As I stood there awkwardly, Maya slowly raised her head and stared. Even though she was on her knees and I was standing, it was like she was looking down at me.

'Then get the fuck out of here, asshole.' I never heard her talk like that to anyone, not even Dwayne. My head snapped back and my cheeks flushed. It wasn't just a slap in the face. My heart was being mugged.

'Maya, what did I do? Please tell me.' I dropped to my knees and reached out to her.

'Get out!' she screamed, and pushed me away.

'Not until you tell me what I did.' I closed my eyes and tried not to hate her. I was waiting for her to calm down, when her hands flew up at my face like barn owls. It felt like her right hand was taloned into a fist, her left was five freshly manicured nails, two of which drew blood as she clawed the right side of my face. When she got tired of hitting me, she sat back on her haunches and began to sob.

I sat there, paralyzed with anger and astonishment. Maya picked up two halves of a photo that had been ripped in half by our struggle. It was a picture of us taken at her sixteenth birthday party that Osborne had never shown me. Maya and I are about to blow out the candles of her cake. You can see what she is wishing by the way she looks up at me. Our faces glow in the flickering candlelight. Everyone is crowded around. Bryce has his arm around his mother's naked shoulder. I could see Giacomo and Paige and Slim and Marcus and Jilly sneaking a butt while she collects dirty glasses. Dr Leffler's whispering in my mother's ear. And there, behind it all, Osborne stands alone on a gilded party chair. His gaze is not directed at us, but at the night sky. It was his birthday, too. He's looking up, like he just bought a new galaxy for himself.

'You ruined everything.' Maya leaned over and dropped the two halves of the picture into the wastebasket that had once been an elephant's foot. 'When you told Grandpa those lies about Bryce, and my mother, and the fire.'

'They weren't lies.'

'Bryce told me you'd say that.'

'Bryce beat me unconscious and fucked me. Did he tell you I'd say that, too?'

It was as if she hadn't heard what I said.

'I didn't turn him in to the police. I could have, but I didn't. I did that for you.'

'You told Grandpa. That's worse. He has to stay down there for ever now. You think he wants to spend the rest of his life in some goddamn jungle?'

'Osborne's dead. Nothing's keeping Bryce there.'

'How can he come home? If he sets foot in America, he loses everything.'

'What?'

'His whole trust fund gets given to charity if Bryce ever comes home again.'

'Give him half of yours. You'll both still be rich.' I started to get to my feet. She pulled me back to her.

'Jesus Christ,' she sobbed. 'Don't you see, Finn? Money can't make this right.' Taking my face in her hand, she was Maya again. Rescue was within our reach, as she began to slowly eat me with her kisses. 'Oh, God, Finn, just say it's not true.'

'What?'

'Tell me you made it up. I don't care why you did it, I'll forgive you, just tell me you lied to Grandpa about us.' I felt dismembered by her gaze. She was pulling me down with her. Her dress was hiked up to her hips. Her mouth was all over me. 'I'll do anything, Finn, just tell me it's not true.' Mrs Langley was wrong, Maya didn't hate me, she just wanted the impossible.

'No.'

It was a word Maya wasn't used to hearing. She looked at me with wonder and disappointment and told me, 'I knew you'd say that.'

I closed the door behind me and hurried down the hall. Maya had no idea how close I'd come to saying 'Yes'. I left by the servants' entrance.

*   *   *

Osborne's moon and stars weren't out that night. The temperature dropped twenty degrees. It was winter again. The mud was frozen in ruts, the puddles glazed with ice. I fell more than once as I struggled to find my way home in the darkness. It's weird when you're sixteen years old and want to feel young again.

44

The next morning, my mother and I hurriedly packed up what was left of our life in Vlyvalle into cardboard boxes, and paid Walter Pickle fifty dollars to drive us back to New York in his pickup truck. My mother said we were lucky that the rich girl who had sub-let our place in the city to become an artist had decided the space wasn't conducive to creativity. When we climbed the five flights of stairs at Great Jones Street, and my mother opened the door, Walter took a slow look around our apartment and muttered, 'I pictured it kind of different.'

The roof had leaked through and the walls were streaked yellow-brown, like we'd been pissed on from a great height. The phone was disconnected, and there was a dead mouse in the toilet, which Walter discovered when he asked if he could use the bathroom. Later we found the fifty we'd given Walter on top of the toilet after he left.

To come back to this wasn't just a setback, it was a fall from grace, a humiliation so acute it made me want to rip off my own skin and crawl under a rock and hide.

'I'm going to paint it all white. Floor, ceiling, walls – everything.' My mother was trying.

'That's great, Mom.'

'And white slipcovers for the foldout. I'll make them myself out of dropcloths.' I had reduced her to this; it was my fault we had landed here.

'I think I'll go down to the diner and get some French fries.' I wasn't hungry, I just wanted to get the hell out of there before I said something mean, like the truth.

The firemen who used to call out to me on the street didn't recognize me, and a new waitress at the diner told me Slurpee had become a born-again Christian. It didn't seem like a bad idea, but I didn't think it would work for me. I came back upstairs just in time to help my mother move the bookcase. She said it would make the room look bigger. Anything to make it feel less like the end of the line. Before we got to see if it helped, the bookcase tipped and our library scattered across the floor. It didn't land on top of her this time, but I knew she was crushed when she lay down on the musty foldout, turned her back to me and silently began to weep. As I picked up the books, the gram of coke she'd lost that morning our journey'd begun fell out of the M–N volume of the *Encyclopedia Britannica*. I filed it away in my pocket for future reference.

We went to bed early that night. As I lay down, I heard my old beat-off magazines crinkling under the mattress but I didn't have the heart to look at them. The leak had buckled the plywood wall my mother had built between us. Now all that separated us were our dreams.

I woke up in the middle of the night and didn't know where I was. And then it came to me: the Yanomamö call it *heitä bebi*, the place that was created when the sky fell. Like ours, it is a world where souls are stolen and eaten by ghosts.

45

I didn't get out of bed when I heard my mother flush the toilet and walk to the kitchen sink to make coffee. When she called out, 'Want some breakfast, lambie?' I remained silent and pretended to be asleep. It was pathetic, but I didn't want anyone who knew me in Vlyvalle, not even my mother, to see me like this. I was ashamed of the shame I couldn't help but feel. I had failed, but I wasn't sure at what.

When I heard her leave the apartment, I finally got out of bed. There was a note on the kitchen table. 'Went to hardware store. Won't be long.' She signed it with a happy face. Yanking on my jeans, not bothering to brush my teeth, I wanted out of there. I didn't know where I was going, but I couldn't bear to watch my mother come home and try to fix things up.

I was heading towards the door when I heard footsteps coming up the stairs. They weren't my mother's. I looked through the peephole as an owlish-looking man whose last strands of hair were carefully coiled around his bald spot like a snake knocked on the door.

He wore a pinstripe suit and carried an Hermès briefcase. Since he didn't look like a robber, and there was nothing left to take, I opened up.

'Good to finally meet you, Finn.' He shook my hand and smiled as he stepped into the apartment uninvited. 'Sorry to chase you down like this, but you caught us off-guard when you and your mother left Vlyvalle so quickly. Since the phone number we had for you here was disconnected, I thought it might expediate things if I . . .' He sat on the foldout and opened his briefcase.

'Who are you?'

'I'm Jack Haskell.' He handed me a card. He was an attorney at

Sloan, Peabody, and a half-dozen other guys I hadn't heard of. 'And I'm here to talk to you about something very serious.' I wasn't surprised they tracked me down.

'Tell Mrs Langley just to leave us the hell alone. I'm not going to go to the police about her or Bryce, or . . .' I looked at the clock. I wanted to get him and me out of there before my mother got back with the goddamn white paint.

'I don't represent Mrs Langley. I represent you. But of course, if you have your own attorney . . .' He smiled at me. '. . . I'll be glad to turn this matter over to him.' I didn't like the way he was smiling at me. He made me feel stupider than I already felt.

'Perhaps you should read this first.' The lawyer handed me an envelope. My name was scrawled across the back in blue ink. The only person I knew who had handwriting worse than me was Osborne.

Dear Finn,
    Let's see if you can do it any better. Ever the optimist, I'll sign off with,
    See you later,
    Ogden Clementine Osborne

I always wondered what the C stood for. 'Do what better?'

'Though one can't be sure, I would assume it would have something to do with the fact that Mr Osborne has left you a number of assets . . .' He began to read from a three-page, single-spaced list. I didn't hear most of what he said. The roar of the money was too deafening. It didn't solve my problems, it flattened them, like a tidal wave or a nuclear explosion. The shantytown I lived in inside my head was being washed away as I sat there. There was no shelter from the storm I'd inherited.

335

A NOTE ON THE AUTHOR

Dirk Wittenborn was born in New Haven, Connecticut. He spent his teenage years in a community not unlike the fictional village of Vlyvalle. He's the author of two previous novels, *Eclipse* and *Zoë* and has written for television and film. He lives in New York City with his wife and daughter.

A NOTE ON THE TYPE

The text of this book is set in Linotype Sabon, named after the type founder, Jacques Sabon. It was designed by Jan Tschichold and jointly developed by Linotype, Monotype and Stempel, in response to a need for a typeface to be available in identical form for mechanical hot metal composition and hand composition using foundry type.

Tschichold based his design for Sabon roman on a fount engraved by Garamond, and Sabon italic on a fount by Granjon. It was first used in 1966 and has proved an enduring modern classic.